STUDY GUIDES
General Editors: John Peck and Martin Coyle

Palgrave Study Skills

Authoring a PhD
Business Degree Success
Career Skills
Critical Thinking Skills (2nd edn)
Cite them Right (8th edn)
e-Learning Skills (2nd edn)
Effective Communication for
 Arts and Humanities Students
Effective Communication for
 Science and Technology
The Exam Skills Handbook
The Foundations of Research (2nd edn)
The Good Supervisor
Great Ways to Learn Anatomy and
 Physiology
How to Manage your Arts, Humanities and
 Social Science Degree
How to Manage your Distance and
 Open Learning Course
How to Manage your Postgraduate Course
How to Manage your Science and
 Technology Degree
How to Study Foreign Languages
How to Study Linguistics (2nd edn)
How to Use your Reading in your Essays
How to Write Better Essays (2nd edn)
How to Write your Undergraduate
 Dissertation
Information Skills
IT Skills for Successful Study
Making Sense of Statistics
The International Student Handbook
The Mature Student's Guide to Writing (2nd edn)
The Mature Student's Handbook
The Palgrave Student Planner
The Personal Tutor's Handbook

The Postgraduate Research Handbook (2nd edn)
Presentation Skills for Students (2nd edn)
The Principles of Writing in Psychology
Professional Writing (2nd edn)
Researching Online
Research Using IT
Skills for Success (2nd edn)
The Study Abroad Handbook
The Student's Guide to Writing (2nd edn)
The Student Life Handbook
The Study Skills Handbook (3rd edn)
Study Skills for Speakers of English as
 a Second Language
Studying Arts and Humanities
Studying the Built Environment
Studying Business at MBA and Masters Level
Studying Economics
Studying History (3rd edn)
Studying Law (2nd edn)
Studying Mathematics and its Applications
Studying Modern Drama (2nd edn)
Studying Physics
Studying Programming
Studying Psychology (2nd edn)
Teaching Study Skills and Supporting Learning
The Undergraduate Research Handbook
The Work-Based Learning Student Handbook
Work Placements – A Survival Guide for Students
Writing for Law
Writing for Nursing and Midwifery Students (2nd edn)
Write it Right
Writing for Engineers (3rd edn)

Pocket Study Skills
Series Editor: Kate Williams

14 Days to Exam Success
Blogs, Wikis, Podcasts and More
Brilliant Writing Tips for Students
Getting Critical
Planning Your Essay

Planning Your PhD
Reading and Making Notes
Referencing and Understanding Plagiarism
Science Study Skills
Success in Groupwork

Further titles in preparation

HOW TO STUDY
CHAUCER
SECOND EDITION

ROB POPE

palgrave
macmillan

Published by
PALGRAVE
Houndmills, Basingstoke, Hampshire RG21 6XS and
175 Fifth Avenue, New York, N.Y. 10010
Companies and representatives throughout the world

PALGRAVE is the new global academic imprint of St. Martin's Press
LLCScholarly and Reference Division and Palgrave Publishers Ltd (formerly
Macmillan Press Ltd).

ISBN-10: 0–333–76283–5
ISBN-13: 978-0-333-76283-7

This book is printed on paper suitable for recycling and made from fully
managed and sustained forest sources. Logging, pulping and manufacturing
processes are expected to conform to the environmental regulations of the
country of origin.

A catalogue record for this book is available from the British Library.

Cataloging-in-Publication data is available from the Library of Congress

Printed in Great Britain by the
MPG Books Group, Bodmin and King's Lynn

FOR MY BROTHERS
ALAN AND STEVE

CONTENTS

GENERAL EDITORS' PREFACE

EVERYBODY who studies literature, either for an examination or simply for pleasure, experiences the same problem: how to understand and respond to the text. As every student of literature knows, it is perfectly possible to read a book over and over again and yet still feel baffled and at a loss as to what to say about it. One answer to this problem, of course, is to accept someone else's view of the text, but how much more rewarding it would be if you could work out your own critical response to any book you choose or are required to study.

The aim of this series is to help you develop your critical skills by offering practical advice about how to read, understand and analyse literature. Each volume provides you with a clear method of study so that you can see how to set about tackling texts on your own. While the authors of each volume approach the problem in a different way, every book in the series attempts to provide you with some broad ideas about the kind of texts you are likely to be studying and some broad ideas about how to think about literature; each volume then shows you how to apply these ideas in a way which should help you construct your own analysis and interpretation. Unlike most critical books, therefore, the books in this series do not simply convey someone else's thinking about a text, but encourage you and show you how to think about a text for yourself.

Each book is written with an awareness that you are likely to be preparing for an examination, and therefore practical advice is given not only on how to understand and analyse literature, but also on how to organize a written response. Our hope is that although these books are intended to serve a practical purpose, they may also enrich your enjoyment of literature by making you a more confident reader, alert to the interest and pleasure to be derived from literary texts.

John Peck
Martin Coyle

ACKNOWLEDGEMENTS AND NOTE ON REFERENCES

It's now more than ten years since the first edition of this book and some thirty years since I began studying Chaucer. My debts in this area have steadily increased and are acknowledged with pleasure. Above all, I should like to thank students at Oxford Brookes University (formerly Oxford Polytechnic), the University of Wales and the University of Otago for sharing, challenging or simply putting up with my approaches to Chaucer – particularly those who have so generously and ingeniously conspired in 'retelling' his tales. I am also glad of this opportunity to record my gratitude to a whole host of former teachers, colleagues and examiners, namely Derek Pearsall, the late Elizabeth Salter, Alcuin Blamires, Douglas Gray, Susan Bassnett, Lisa Jardine, Bernard O'Donoghue, Colin Gibson, Ian Jamieson, Dorothy MacCarthy and Archie Burnett. None of these people has anything directly to do with the writing of the present book – so they have nothing, even indirectly, to do with its faults. But all have at some stage influenced my thinking, either about Chaucer in particular or the teaching and learning of early literature at large. I trust they will accept this (slightly bigger) 'litel bok' in the spirit and for the purposes it is intended.

Martin Coyle and John Peck, the series editors, gave invaluable advice and assistance on the first edition and were remarkably patient with an awkwardly novice author. They also saw the book through proofs and press at a time when I was unable to. Thanks to them for that then and for their continuing assistance with this now. Meanwhile, Margaret Bartley at the publishers has managed to keep the project on the boil with great tact and skill – even when I shifted it to the back-burner or appeared to have removed it from the cooker completely!

In fact, like cook-books, text-books are the result of many people's experience and expertise. Their ingredients and recipes need to be tried and tested over time and with a variety of people. I am therefore deeply grateful to all, early and late, who have in some way contributed to the 'proving' of the present offering. (That includes my family, who can justly complain about how little actual cooking I've been doing while revising this.)

All quotations from *The Canterbury Tales* are from the Everyman edition: *Geoffrey Chaucer: Canterbury Tales*, ed. A. C. Cawley, 2nd edn, Malcolm Andrew (London: Dent, 1996). Quotations from Chaucer's other works are from *The Riverside Chaucer*, ed. Larry Benson et al. (New York: Houghton Mifflin Company, 1987; Oxford: Oxford University Press, 1988). (In fact, the text and line references for *The Canterbury Tales* agree in most essential respects in all these editions, so the reader may use any.) The author and publishers wish to thank Dent, Houghton and Mifflin, and Oxford University Press for kind permission to use the above copyright materials.

I

Getting Started

The aims of this book are simple and practical: to help you understand Chaucer in the original language, and to help you form a critical judgement of your own as to what his poetry is about and how it works. We start together from scratch. I assume no prior knowledge of Chaucer, his language, the subjects he wrote about or the society he wrote in. You are shown how to read a few lines and taken on to the point where you should be able to build up a critical sense of the meaning and shape of a whole poem. At the same time, you are shown how to use literary and historical 'background' material so that it really works as part of a full and informed analysis. Towards the close of the book you are shown how to frame critical responses to a number of Chaucer texts simultaneously; also how to organize your approach in terms of topics such as 'author', 'comedy', 'narrative' and 'sex'.

Use this book as a companion to whichever Chaucer text you are studying. It will not solve every problem of detail, but it will show you how to solve the most common ones, and without the mind-sapping necessity of resorting to notes and a glossary all the time. You can then get on with understanding and enjoying Chaucer for yourself – but not on your own.

Who (or what) is 'Chaucer'?

If you are just starting a Chaucer text, a quick answer to this question may help. Otherwise, you may see only the details in front of you and never see the whole picture. In fact, 'Chaucer' is a handy way of referring to a number of rather different things. It is convenient to distinguish four. First, there is *Chaucer the man*, who lived and died in late-fourteenth-century England: the courtier, soldier, diplomat, administrator, Knight of the Shire and, of course, poet. Secondly, there is *Chaucer the works*, the Chaucer we know from the things he wrote, the texts rather than the man. A third Chaucer is *Chaucer the narrator*, the image of himself that Chaucer chose to project in his poetry – a kind of amiable and artful mask 'Chaucer the man' put on when he appeared in his own works. And finally (alas!) there is *Chaucer the exam*. This last Chaucer may well be your main reason for studying him at all. The point is that all these many and varied things go to make up what we mean by 'Chaucer'. We have distinguished four: the man, the works, the narrator and the exam. Each of them has its part to play in arriving at a full understanding of who and what Chaucer is, and we shall pay attention to them all.

We go on to look at the four Chaucers later in this chapter. However, this book is not planned so that you have to read through it all from beginning to end to extract what you need. To begin with, if you are reading Chaucer in the original for the first time, you should work through the next section, 'How to read five lines of Chaucer', before attempting a whole text. Chaucer is one of the most musical and stylistically versatile poets, but his language is not difficult once you have had a little practice. If you rely on someone else's translation, the trouble is that you will, quite literally, not know what you are missing. Next, to obtain some historical bearings, consult the 'Chaucer the man' subsection. You will then probably find it best to turn straight to the section dealing with your particular text. There you will find a framework and a method relating to your specific needs, as well as some detailed guidance on when and where to draw on further material in the 'Four Chaucers' section. As you will see, this book is basically a guide, and the sections you should read and the order in which you should read them will depend on your own particular needs.

How to read five lines of Chaucer

To help you start reading Chaucer's poetry in the original language, here are just five lines of it. They may not be from the text you are studying, but that is not important. The principles are the same whichever bit of his poetry you look at. Read these lines through now, trying to make some general sense of what is going on:

Now have I toold you soothly, in a clause,
Th'estaat, th'array, the nombre, and eek the cause
Why that assembled was this compaignye
In Southwerk at this gentil hostelrye
That highte the Tabard, faste by the Belle.
                (*Canterbury Tales, General Prologue*, II. 715–19)

Even after just one reading, you have probably got the general idea: this is about some people being assembled somewhere. You have probably understood that the somewhere is 'in Southwerk' and that you are being told all this directly by the 'I' of the opening words: 'Now have I toold you'. However, other than that, much of the detail may have escaped you. What is it about the word order which is initially so confusing? What – or who – are 'the Tabard' and 'the Belle'? And so on. You have a fair general impression, but are not clear about the details. In fact, this is about as far as most people get without resorting to a translation or rooting around in the glossary. And yet, with just a little more educated guesswork, they could get much further on their own.

Here are four simple tips on how to turn Chaucer's English into reasonable Modern English. They will not solve every problem of detail, but they will solve most:

1. Go for the general sense first.
2. When words look familiar but are oddly spelt, keep the consonants, tinker with the vowels and drop the final 'e'.
3. When the word order feels odd, simply invert it and look for the subject.
4. Get to know the 'top 100' most commonly misunderstood words and phrases used by Chaucer (you will find them at the back of this book).

If we now return to our passage, you will see how simple these four tips are to apply. We have already established *the general sense* (tip 1): some people are assembled somewhere. But who, when, where? Well, 'compaignye' and 'hostelrye' certainly look like familiar words but they are oddly spelt, so we should try tip 2: *keep the consonants, tinker with the vowels and drop the final 'e'*. That done, it is not difficult to recognize the modern equivalents of these two words: 'company' and 'hostelry'. Even if you did not know that 'hostelry' is an old-fashioned word for 'inn', you could have guessed its meaning from its similarity to the modern words 'hostel' and 'hotel' and the immediate context.

So now we know that the passage is about a company assembled at an inn. And to know more about them we simply carry on applying tip 2. From the second line we know we are being told about their 'estaat' and 'nombre'. In context the former obviously has to be something like modern 'estate' or 'status', while 'nombre' – at first so perplexing – just has to be 'number'. Note how constant consonants are, and how changeable the vowels. Likewise, when we drop the final 'e' of 'Belle' we produce a plausible-enough name for an inn, and 'Southwerk' is only a vowel different from the modern 'Southwark', the name of a district of London.

Initial problems with word order can be solved as easily. The first and third lines feel odd till you realize that subject and verb are coming at you back-to-front. All you need to do is to apply tip 3: *invert the word order and look for the subject*. This gives you 'Now I have told you' from Chaucer's 'Now have I toold you', and 'Why this company was assembled' from Chaucer's 'Why that assembled was this compaignye'.

I hope you can see how easy it is to make sense of the text when you know what to look for and go about changing things systematically. In all these cases notice that all we are really doing is fastening on odd-looking but somehow familiar words, tinkering with the spelling and word order, and then seeing if the results fit in with the general sense. As for 'eek' (meaning 'also'), 'soothly' (meaning 'truly') and 'gentil' (which means 'fine' or 'noble' rather than 'gentle'), they all feature in the 'top 100' most commonly misunderstood words (tip 4). These words present no problems if you take the trouble to learn them from the list at the back.

Admittedly, there will be times when you have used all four tips above and are still stuck for a word, but this will not happen often. In fact, in our passage of 39 words there is just one ('highte') that you could not work out by tinkering with it and that is not common enough to make the 'top 100'. In such a case you need to turn to a glossary. There you would find that 'highte' means 'called'; hence 'this gentil hostelrye / That highte the Tabard' means 'this fine inn that was called the Tabard'. However, by the time you had made 'educated guesses' at the other 38 words, even a wild guess would have probably given you that last one!

FOUR CHAUCERS: THE MAN, THE WORKS, THE NARRATOR AND THE EXAM

I Chaucer the man

Here, we concentrate on the most critically useful aspects of Chaucer's life, and the most relevant features of the historical 'background'. The keynotes of Chaucer's life are its *variety* and comparative *comfort*. Born around 1343 into a well-to-do merchant family with court connections, Geoffrey Chaucer learnt the manners and expectations of upper-class life early on. He was first a page, then a squire, and then (at about 25) one of King Edward III's own personal attendants. During this period Chaucer also learnt the meaning of 'chivalry' first-hand, as a soldier fighting in the Hundred Years' War with France. In fact, he was captured and finally ransomed, the King himself making a personal contribution to the ransom. Between 1360 and 1381 he was often abroad on diplomatic and trade missions: negotiating peace with France (1360), trade with Italy (1372–3), and the terms of a proposed marriage between King Richard II and the daughter of the French king (1381). From 1374 to 1386 he was Controller of the Custom on wool and later wine in the Port of London – a kind of high-powered tax-collector. And that was followed by a two-year stint as Clerk of the King's Works, with senior responsibility for administering accounts and organizing a wide range of craftsmen. These were employed to build and furnish royal palaces and to organize royal tournaments. Chaucer was also appointed Justice of the Peace and Knight of the Shire for Kent (1385–6).

Chaucer thus held a wide range of diplomatic and business posts linking the royal court and the commercial city, and his responsibilities brought him prosperity and security. Around 1366 he married a prominent lady-in-waiting called Philippa Roet. She was the sister of Duke John of Gaunt's third wife, and by the 1380s the joint incomes of Geoffrey and Philippa Chaucer averaged £60 000 a year by current standards (about £100 then). Certainly, in an economic and social sense, late-medieval England was 'merrie' (meaning 'pleasant') for the Chaucers.

You might now ask what all this has got to do with Chaucer's poetry? The answer is: a lot. However, this will not become clear to you until you actually need to link such information with a specific poem. All I shall do at this stage is tease out some inferences and invite you to return this way when you have a better idea what you are looking for. The significance of 'Chaucer the man' can be summarized under four headings:

1. *Chaucer was a man of the world as well as a man of letters.* Chaucer moved freely between the court and the city, between England and the continent, and between business and writing. All this activity brought him into regular contact with a wide range of English, French and Italian diplomats and courtiers like himself, as well as the increasing numbers of merchants, lawyers and administrators who flourished in late-fourteenth-century England. In short, Chaucer moved in a world of teeming life as well as ideas and literature. As usual, 'variety' is the keynote.

2. *Chaucer kept a high personal profile – and a low political one.* This can be readily inferred from the generally stable pattern of Chaucer's fortunes at court. For the ambitious or contentious, life at court was like a rollercoaster: it could suddenly lift you to dizzy heights, or equally suddenly plunge you down into the depths. The heights were being given vast estates and privileges; the depths were imprisonment, exile and beheading. Both these extremes marked the careers of people whom we know were Chaucer's close associates, and yet he himself seems to have kept to the flat and smooth bits of the track. Apart from a brief dip in 1386 (when the Duke of Gloucester took over during the minority of the young King Richard), Chaucer seems to have negotiated the ups and downs of court life quite well. This is particularly remarkable considering the fact that during his lifetime he served under a total of three monarchs, and in unusually trying circumstances. Many of the problems arose because King Edward III (d. 1377) had a lot of sons, and this in turn meant a lot of wrangling over power. Chaucer, however, seems not to have become too embroiled. He ended his days out of the mainstream of court life, but still comfortably supported by it. His final job was the lucrative, and largely honorary, post of Deputy Forester for the King in Somerset. For the rest, grants and payments continued to flow from Henry IV as they had from Richard II, even though Henry had arranged for Richard to be deposed and murdered a year before! Putting it bluntly, Chaucer 'hedged his bets' and 'kept his nose clean'. It seems that he was liked and trusted at court. That qualification 'at court' is important, for it brings us to a third, usually neglected aspect of Chaucer and his times.

3. *'Chaucer's England' is not the whole story.* The commonly held view that 'Chaucer's England' is somehow a fair and comprehensive image of late-medieval England as a whole is inaccurate. The Peasants' Revolt, for instance, gets just one, disparaging mention in the whole of Chaucer's work. This is so despite the fact that what happened in *1381*, when Chaucer was in his late thirties, was the greatest popular upheaval in England before the seventeenth-century revolution. The London Palace of John of Gaunt, one of Chaucer's patrons, was burnt down; Simon Sudbury, the Archbishop of Canterbury and first minister of the King's government, had his head cut off; and King Richard himself was besieged in the Tower by large numbers of his own people. There is, however, hardly a word about this from Chaucer. In other words (and it is a point which is often overlooked), Chaucer's view of life may have been varied and capacious, but it certainly did not extend to all the 'lower orders' – to the radical preachers, the aggrieved tradesmen and the repressed peasants who made up the rank and file pressing for an end to serfdom. None of these have a voice in 'Chaucer's England'. And that brings us to our final inference on 'Chaucer the man', again obvious and again often overlooked.

4. *Chaucer was a man in 'a man's world '.* Women had little direct power in the public sphere. They had no place in Parliament, as Justices of the Peace or as Knights of the Shire. Their property rights, in general (except in the case of widows), were heavily dependent on men. Their opportunities for careers in law, medicine, education, the Church and business were nonexistent or severely limited. So, all in all, it is necessary to underscore the fact that Chaucer was born a man and that this automatically gave him powers and privileges which many women could only dream of. You will see that Chaucer's reaction to this situation in his poetry was both complex and flexible. However, the situation itself, while certainly complex, was all too often harshly inflexible as far as women were concerned.

This subsection has set out some major terms of reference to help you see Chaucer in the context of his times. The sheer variety of his experience of life, the world of books mingling with the world of affairs, the tactful subservience of the diplomat, the elegant refinement of the courtier, the more straightforward practicality of the businessman, the expectations of a sensitive yet privileged medieval male – all these must figure in any full estimation of who

'Chaucer the man' was. Later sections suggest how to make use of this material when exploring individual texts.

II Chaucer the works

Read this subsection through if you want an overview of Chaucer's writings as a whole. Otherwise, the material is best used in conjunction with later sections, when studying individual works.

As with his life, the keynote of Chaucer's works is their sheer variety. There are racy tales and stately tales, treatises on love and on philosophy, and the settings of these works are as varied as Fairyland, ancient Rome and contemporary fourteenth-century England. Yet, despite such a wealth and range of material, it is still possible to categorize Chaucer's total output according to just *six* story types. (The unfamiliarity of some of their names should not put you off. They made sense in Chaucer's day and, as you will see, can be understood easily enough now.) The six types are: *court romance, fabliau, sermon, holy life, confession* and *moral tract.* Sometimes, Chaucer uses one of these in a more or less pure form *(The Prioress's Tale*, for instance, is a straight 'holy life'). But more often he mixes one story type with another, and the result is a particularly rich and interesting hybrid. However, whether 'pure' or 'mixed', you will find that one or more of these story types forms the basis of any Chaucer text you are studying.

1.   *Court romance.* Court romances are tales which explore refined notions of love and war in a court setting. The plot usually revolves around the competition between two noble men for one noble woman. Court romances are characterized by elaborate, highly idealized forms of courtship (sometimes called 'courtly love') and elaborately ritualistic behaviour in general. This means that, when they are not agonizing over whether they should love one another, the lovers are engaged in other upper-class pursuits. For the men that means hunting, feasting, tournaments and war, with the odd distraught love poem thrown in for good measure. For the women it means walking in gardens, reading and visiting one another. You might say, then, that court romances are all about sex and violence, but in a peculiarly sublime form. *The Knight's Tale* is a good example. Two noble cousins fall in love with the same noble woman and finish up fighting a tournament for her. One of them gets her and the

other does not. In outline it is as simple as that! Of course, the actual treatment is more complicated and problematic, but it helps hugely if you establish the underlying story type and its basic shape from the start.

All the following poems use the court romance as their main base: *The Knight's Tale, The Squire's Tale, Sir Thopas, The Wife of Bath's Tale, The Merchant's Tale, The Franklin's Tale, The Book of the Duchess, Anelida and Arcite, The Parliament of Fowls, Troilus and Criseyde* and *The Prologue to the Legend of Good Women.* Most of Chaucer's shorter poems (such as *To Rosemounde* and *The Complaint of Mars*) are built round notions of refined love too.

All of the following use the court-romance type part of the time, as a subordinate, but still important aspect of their construction: *The Miller's Tale, Melibee, The Nun's Priest's Tale* and The *House of Fame.*

2.   *Fabliau.* The fabliau (plural 'fabliaux') is a kind of story dealing with an extended joke or trick, usually set amongst the lower orders of society. The trick invariably involves some unlikely, but uproarious combinations of raw sex and knockabout violence, and by the end everyone has received a kind of justice. *The Reeve's Tale* is characteristic of the basic shape and concerns of fabliau. In it, two students are cheated of some corn by a miller, so they get their own back by sleeping with the miller's wife and daughter. At the end there is a chaotic and very funny fight in the dark. A similar thing happens in *The Miller's Tale.* There, a carpenter's wife is being wooed secretly by two men, only one of whom she likes. As a joke she gets the unwanted suitor, who is expecting a kiss in the dark, to kiss her backside instead. The wife's lover then tries to repeat the trick, but the rejected lover has meanwhile got a red-hot ploughshare from the blacksmith's. The result, not surprisingly, is a lot of pain and a lot of laughs – and both are increased by the sudden arrival of the carpenter himself, crashing through the ceiling! Such a chaotic and farcical ending is wholly characteristic of the fabliau. In fact, you might say that fabliaux are the comic, cartoon equivalents of court romances. Where court romances are sublimely abstract and idealized, fabliaux are grotesquely concrete and physical. The former take place in a never-never world of solemn knights and ladies, while the latter (in line with traditional comedy) draw their figures of fun from amongst tradespeople, minor clerics and the peasantry. The two story types are exaggerated inversions of one another.

All the following use fabliau as their main base: *The Miller's Tale*, *The Reeve's Tale*, *The Cook's Tale* (fragment), *The Friar's Tale*, *The Summoner's Tale*, *The Shipman's Tale* and *The Canon's Yeoman's Tale*. And these others use fabliau elements for a significant part of the time: *The Wife of Bath's Prologue*, *The Merchant's Tale* and *The Nun's Priest's Tale* (an animal fable with much of the knockabout fun and trickery of fabliau).

Apart from court romance and fabliau, we have one other large area of Chaucer's output to consider, his *religious* writings. This is not to say that any of Chaucer's work is particularly irreligious or utterly opposed to Christianity. It is just that *The Knight's Tale* and *The Miller's Tale*, for example, are not primarily concerned with Christian instruction or piety, so they are broadly secular in appeal. For the rest, therefore, we can talk about an overtly religious cluster of story types. Chaucer used most of the major forms of religious writing available at that time, and together they make up the remaining four types: *sermon, holy life, confession* and *moral tract*.

3.   *Sermon.* Medieval sermons, like modern ones, were basically exhortations to embrace virtues and shun vices. Essentially oral and often highly rhetorical, they were the main way in which Christian doctrine was communicated. The preacher was, for the many people who could not read (more than 95 per cent of the population), the *only* bridge between the Latin of the Vulgate Bible and common English. Sermons, along with songs and stories, were as central to the communication system of medieval society as TV and radio are now.

The medieval preacher, who was usually a man, built his sermon around four types of material:

(i)   *an abstract 'theme'* (such as 'gluttony', 'avarice' or 'charity');
(ii) *a biblical story or quotation* (perhaps the story of the Good Samaritan, or a text such as 'render unto Caesar the things that are Caesar's, and unto God the things that are God's');
(iii) *popular stories and proverbs,* or *classical stories and maxims* for a more learned congregation (such moralized stories were called 'exempla');
(iv) *a contemporary event* (perhaps a recent storm or a bout of plague, or a local riot).

Chaucer steers clear of this last, most ephemeral and potentially most sensitive topic. References to contemporary events are not at all common in his work. However, he freely uses the other three methods of sermon-building 'theme', biblical material and popular (or classical) exempla – and often, like professional preachers, Chaucer uses all three in the course of a single sermon. In that case, much of the skill is in deciding precisely where and how to move from one strategy to another.

There are three full sermons in *The Canterbury Tales*: *The Pardoner's Prologue and Tale*, *The Nun's Priest's Prologue and Tale* and *The Parson's Tale*. In each case we carry with us a strong image of the preacher, as well as the sermon he delivers. We see him both as a human individual and as a divine authority figure. If you study any of these tales, you will become aware of how important this dual aspect is in forming your attitude to the sermons. Sermons play a conspicuous supporting role in the following tales: *The Friar's Tale*, *The Summoner's Tale*, *The Clerk's Tale*, *The Man of Law's Tale*, *The Wife of Bath's Prologue and Tale*, *The Physician's Tale*, *The Manciple's Tale* and *Melibee*. There is quite a lot of 'sermonizing' in the next type of religious writing too.

4. *Holy lives*. Holy lives are very like court romances, except that their heroes and heroines are holy people rather than knights and ladies. Like knights, they have adventures, often involving long journeys through exotic places, and they too meet and overcome enemies and obstacles, usually winning through to some kind of triumph at the end. However, in the case of the holy life, the driving force behind the action is not love between man and woman, but love of God. And the final triumph is not a knight winning a fight or the hand of his lady, but a holy person – often a woman – defeating the devil and his supporters. Significantly, this usually means martyrdom for the heroine, being stoned or boiled in oil, and there is often at least the threat of rape. It will therefore be clear that holy lives are full of sex and violence too – only in sublimely religious forms. For all their apparent piety, they often strike the modern reader as sensationally sadistic.

Chaucer uses the holy life as his main base in the following tales: *The Clerk's Tale*, *The Man of Law's Tale*, *The Physician's Tale*, *The Prioress's Tale* (here with a child as the holy martyr) and *The Second Nun's Tale*. These others all use elements of the holy life, usually to reinforce closely related elements from court romance: *The Knight's Tale*, *The Franklin's Tale*, *Troilus and Criseyde* and *The Legend of Wood Women*.

A note on prayers and 'complaints' will help clarify the connection between holy life and court romance. As you might expect, with so much suffering and injustice around, holy lives are full of prayers. These are the religious counterparts of the formal 'complaints' in court romance. The only essential difference is that Christian prayers are addressed to God, Christ and the Virgin Mary, while 'complaints' are addressed to secular concepts such as Fortune, or 'the God of Love' or pagan deities. The Prioress, for instance, prefaces her holy life with a hymn and a prayer to the Virgin Mary, while Emily in *The Knight's Tale* delivers a prayer and complaint to Diana. Dorigen in *The Franklin's Tale* complains to Fortune, and Chaucer, as narrator in *Troilus and Criseyde*, invokes the Muses of History and Poetry, the God of Love, and just about any assistance he can get. Many of Chaucer's shorter poems are 'complaints' in their own right.

5.   *Confession.* This story type is used in a strict religious sense in *The Parson's Tale*. There it is tied in with a sermon on 'penitence', in which the Parson goes through the Seven Deadly Sins (Pride, Envy, Anger, and so on). He instructs the other pilgrims how to recognize, confess and renounce each of them in turn. In this respect *The Parson's Tale is* a confession manual, concluding with a prayer from Chaucer himself. This prayer is sometimes called the 'retraction' and is itself a kind of confession. In it the author (presumably towards the end of his life) looks back over all his writings, recognizing that some may help him to heaven, whereas others certainly will not! He concludes with a prayer to 'Lord Jesus Christ and his blessed Mother, and all the Saints of heaven, beseeching them that they from henceforth to the end of my life may send me grace to be sorry for my sins and to look to my salvation'.

Confessions are used in a less formal, but still very important way in other works by Chaucer. Several of *The Canterbury Tales* show their tellers looking back over their lives and confessing openly to past loves, the tricks of their trade and sin in general. The joy is that sometimes the vices are so energetically flaunted they almost seem virtues. This is what happens with the Wife of Bath and the Pardoner, so that what would normally be a private confession is made flagrantly public. In fact, their open confessions are as exhilarating as they are shameless.

Texts which use confession as their main base are *The Wife of Bath's Prologue and Tale*, *The Pardoner's Prologue and Tale* and *The Canon's Yeoman's Prologue and Tale* (the confessions of an alchemist's apprentice – less well known, but well worth a read). However, in a sense nearly all *The Canterbury Tales* are 'confessional'. The individual prologues and epilogues, especially when read in conjunction with the descriptions of the pilgrims in *The General Prologue,* show us the tellers of the tales. The tales themselves then become a kind of indirect confession of the tellers' hopes and fears, aspirations and regrets. This is what happens in the cases of the Merchant and the Franklin. Taking *The Merchant's Prologue* together with his tale, we get an image of a man who wishes he had not got married. Reading *The Franklin's Tale* with his *Prologue* in mind, we sense a gentleman who has pretensions to be a knight. In this connection it is worth noting that a much earlier poem, *The Book of the Duchess,* also includes a long confession. In that case, a mysterious 'knight in black' delivers a long and sorrowful monologue, and so goes through a kind of therapy whereby he finally achieves consolation. Confession was a central religious practice of Chaucer's time, as well as a standard strategy of much secular and religious writing. Its presence in Chaucer's work is so pervasive as to seem natural. So is the presence of the sixth and final type of material habitually used by Chaucer.

6.   *The moral tract.* The moral tract is not the most attractive type to finish with, nor are some of the examples of it particularly attractive to read now. However, it is a common type of writing used by Chaucer, and both he and his audience obviously had a taste for detailed and systematic moralizing. So, if you are to understand Chaucer, you should at least recognize that taste, even if you do not acquire it yourself. The moral tract is in many ways like a sermon, except that it was written to be read rather than delivered orally. Like the sermon, it tends to be concerned with virtues and vices, the trials and tribulations of the world, heaven and hell, and so forth. *Unlike* the sermon it is not particularly diversified by incidental stories or direct address to the reader/audience. In short, moral tracts are high on analytical distinctions and low on dramatic impact. They often have the broken-up, schematized and labelled look of reference books (which they often were) rather than works you would sit down and read all the way through.

The following Chaucer texts use the moral tract as their main base: *The Monk's Tale, Melibee* and *The Parson's Tale* (notice that *The Parson's Tale* straddles three of the four religious types: sermon, confession and moral tract). These others make substantial use of the moral tract as a supporting element: *The Knight's Tale, The*

Merchant's Tale, The Nun's Priest's Tale, The Parliament of Fowls and *Troilus and Criseyde*. To these should be added Chaucer's *Boece* (a translation of Boethius's *Consolation of Philosophy)* and Chaucer's translation of *The Romance of the Rose*. Both are essentially moral tracts, but with very different moralities and for very different readerships. Both heavily influenced Chaucer's work as a whole, so it is worth knowing a little more about them.

Boece is Chaucer's translation of the philosophical autobiography of a sixth-century Roman noble. Boethius tells how he was thrown into prison and visited in a vision by a woman called 'Lady Philosophy', who eventually manages to console him even in the face of death. That is why Chaucer's source is called *The Consolation of Philosophy*. Like most other moral tracts, the book is broken down into sections, and each section shows a clear and systematic progression from the one before. There is, therefore, a gradual unfolding of the prisoner's understanding of the relationship between 'predestination' and 'free will'. This problem is what we might call 'the limitations and freedoms of human action', and Chaucer was evidently both fascinated and vexed by it. The 'free will' versus 'predestination' debate crops up in texts otherwise as different as *The Nun's Priest's Tale* and *Troilus and Criseyde*, and it is a sure sign that when Chaucer's verse takes a philosophical turn it does so on Boethian lines.

The Romance of the Rose is another and very different moral tract translated by Chaucer early in his literary career. His source is a composite work written by two very different French authors who were born 40 years apart and never actually met. The young poet and courtier Guillaume de Lorris began *Le Roman de la Rose* round 1237 but left it unfinished. None the less, it provided an encyclopaedia of court behaviour relating to refined love and courtship, and became one of the 'bibles' of courtly love. Guillaume's work was particularly influential because it used the fictional framework of a young lover dreaming about a spiritual journey towards his lady. She is symbolized by an unopened rose, and the quest takes place in a walled garden full of obstacles and temptations designed to delay and distract the lover. For instance, there is a woman called Leisure at the garden gate, and later the dreamer meets figures such as Jealousy and Flattery. Because it is peopled by such personifications and uses a consistent symbolism, *Le Roman de la Rose* is also called an 'allegory'. In our terms, however, it is best described as a combination of court romance and moral tract, a systematically idealized and fictionalized display of court morals. All this was utterly transformed by the person who picked up Guillaume's unfinished poem, Jean de Meun. Jean produced what Hollywood might call 'The Romance of the Rose II' and, in that he was both a scholar and a satirist, he did something which the courtly author of 'The Romance of the Rose I' would probably have loathed. He turned it into a racy satire on court manners and massively extended the range of knowledge covered. In fact, his continuation is a vast and fascinating encyclopaedia of late-thirteenth-century science, theology and social philosophy. Where Guillaume is spiritual and elegant, Jean is learned and irreverent. The one has a narrowly court-based experience, the other walks in a wider world, both of learning and of life in general.

Chaucer's debts to Boethius's *Consolation of Philosophy* and the two parts of *The Romance of the Rose* were immense. The former affected his powers of philosophizing, while the latter provided a model which embraced not only the court and book learning, but also the larger teeming world beyond. If Chaucer needed some guidance on how to combine his roles as courtier, scholar and practical man of affairs, then he certainly found it in *The Romance of the Rose*. And that, presumably, is why he went to all the loving trouble of translating it.

A Treatise on the Astrolabe is not a *moral* tract, but a tract it certainly is and, for the sake of completeness, it should be mentioned here. The *Treatise* is a step-by-step introduction to the use of the astrolabe, an ancient instrument for calculating the positions of the stars and planets. Chaucer prepared this manual for a little boy called Louis, who may have been his son, and the whole thing is very clearly and practically put together. *A Treatise on the Astrolabe* is also interesting because it points up the serious technical interest Chaucer had in astronomy. In the Middle Ages astronomy (the study of the nature and positions of heavenly bodies) was closely linked with astrology (the study of the supposed influence of those bodies on human affairs). Chaucer's works are full of precise astronomical and astrological details, and the *Treatise* is important because it confirms Chaucer's active fascination with the subject.

This subsection has provided a way of seeing Chaucer's output in terms of just six story types: court romance, fabliau, sermon, holy life, confession and moral tract. Occasionally, he used one of these in pure form, but more often we come across them mixed, with one type grafted onto another. This mixing of different materials and perspectives is one of the chief features of Chaucer's art and, as so often noted in this book, the overall result is one of sheer variety.

Here is a final suggestion for looking at Chaucer's works as a whole. (If you are studying just one text – and most of you will be – then skip the next bit if you wish.) It used to be common to talk of Chaucer's literary development in terms of influences from different national literatures. Traditionally, there were reckoned to be *three* major stages in this development: French, Italian and English. The last, 'English' phase was reckoned to be the most mature and was usually greeted with nationalistic satisfaction by English critics. There was also reckoned to be a corresponding change in Chaucer's literary style and subject matter, again in three stages. So, he started with poems such as *The Book of the Duchess*, which was based on French sources and dealt with delicately spiritualized courtly love in the French manner. He then wrote poems such as *The Knight's Tale* and *Troilus and Criseyde*, which also dealt with courtly love but in a more realistically textured, more heavily moralistic and more decorative manner. The influences now were Italian writers such as Boccaccio, Dante and Petrarch. Finally, there was the fully 'realistic', more consciously 'English' Chaucer who wrote *The General Prologue* and some of the other *Canterbury Tales*. The hallmark of this last stage was supposedly an 'English' reliance on personal observation rather than foreign ideas and literary sources.

In fact, if you discard the nationalistic claptrap, this notion of 'Chaucer-in-three-stages' still has some value. You can then describe his total output in terms of a progression from abstract and idealized romance to more heavily decorated and more deeply realistic (though still essentially 'literary') work and, finally, the stage where he leaves books behind and relies more on personal observation of the people around him. However, be careful! 'Chaucer-in-three-stages' may be handy, but it does not fit all the facts; nor does it do justice to the cumulative complexity of his works. *The Canterbury Tales*, for instance, is an awkward patchwork of early and late work. It was pulled together in the last dozen years of Chaucer's life, and yet it is clear that many individual tales were started well before and only fitted into the overall framework later. The notion of some continuous 'progress' or 'growing maturity' should also be avoided. At its crudest this can come out as: early French period equals 'immaturity'; middle Italian period equals 'growing maturity'; late English period equals 'maturity achieved'! Again this is too neat to fit the facts. It would also place *Troilus and Criseyde* (a poem which many people, including myself, would see as Chaucer's greatest work) in the Italian period of merely 'growing maturity'. In short, seeing Chaucer's development in three phases is generally helpful but often untenable in detail. He did start from French romance styles and subjects, but he changed and diversified them early on. Their presence, like that of all his major literary influences, faded or was transformed, but never disappeared completely. For all his ceaseless innovation, Chaucer was basically a conservative writer, transforming earlier materials but rarely rejecting them outright.

III *Chaucer the narrator*

There is a persistent presence in Chaucer's works: sometimes it is just a matter of distinctive tone and attitude, but often it crystallizes into an actual character. This tone and this character are what we can call 'Chaucer the narrator'. 'Chaucer the narrator' is the image of himself the poet chose to project, and it also goes under the name of the poet's 'persona'. This 'persona' is a mask Chaucer found both convenient and amusing when addressing his friends and superiors at court, particularly on delicate matters. We might therefore say that 'Chaucer the narrator' is those aspects of 'Chaucer the man' the poet chose to make public in 'Chaucer the works'. But whatever we call it (whether 'persona', 'mask' or 'the narrator'), it is clear that we need some such term to describe Chaucer's linkman between the real and fictional worlds.

'Chaucer the narrator' is already there in embryo in one of his earliest poems, *The Book of the Duchess* (1369). It is worth detailing his appearance there because the main features are constant throughout Chaucer's work. In fact, the first 400 lines of *The Book of the Duchess* are wholly devoted to building up a full and persuasive image of the poet. Gradually, as he eases himself into the main story, we get to know him quite well. He is having trouble sleeping, he tells us. He does not know exactly why, but he has had this trouble for the past eight years. There is someone who could perhaps help him, but, oh well, let that go – 'I don't want to burden you with my problems', he says. Then he remembers why he is telling us all this. He came across an old story a couple of nights ago when he could not sleep and was having a read in bed. (He could have played chess, he thought, but no, on the whole he preferred reading.) And so he goes on. At first the effect of all this on most students is mystifying. However, the more Chaucer you read, the more familiar this amiable but rather bumbling figure becomes.

So what is Chaucer up to? Why does he choose to present himself like this? The answer is simple, and closely tied up with the manner in which Chaucer's poems first made their way into the world. The simple fact is that *Chaucer performed his poems live*. Although they circulated later in manuscript, it appears that in the first instance most of them were written with personal delivery in mind. This would be to a small, well-to-do audience at court, some of whom would be his friends and some of whom would be his social superiors. And that, in a nutshell, is why there is such a strong sense of the speaking voice in Chaucer's poetry, why its tone is familiar and yet respectful. In such a court context it also made sense to appear bumbling and unassuming. Unless you were really powerful, it was a mistake to appear either too prominent or too clever. Courts were delightful but dangerous places, and Chaucer clearly opted for a safely amusing self-image.

One further piece of information will help confirm the subtle, but necessary role of 'Chaucer the narrator'. *The Book of the Duchess* was written for one of King Edward III's sons, John of Gaunt, Duke of Lancaster. He was just a few years older than Chaucer and probably his friend as well as his patron. Duke John had recently lost his first wife, the Duchess Blanche of Castile. Chaucer clearly wrote this poem as a memorial to her and as a piece of consolation for her bereaved husband. Now, imagine a situation in which Chaucer read this poem in person to John and other members of his court. Think how important it was for Chaucer to adopt a particularly discreet and tactful stance. To tackle his patron's grief openly and directly would be insensitive. However, by working round to it slowly and indirectly, and above all by presenting himself as a sad, confused and yet well-meaning figure, Chaucer was able to broach a sensitive subject sympathetically. In this way 'Chaucer the narrator' can act not only as a link between the real and fictional worlds, but also as a kind of buffer. He stops the worst shocks of reality getting through.

The Book of the Duchess set the stamp on Chaucer's projection of himself remarkably early in his literary career. In later work he modified and extended this self-image but never abandoned it completely. In fact, the main features of 'Chaucer the narrator' are so consistent that you can build up a kind of identikit. Here is one based on common or similar features in *The Book of the Duchess, The*

Parliament of Fowls, *The House of Fame*, *Troilus and Criseyde*, *The Prologue to the Legend of Good Women* and *The General Prologue to the Canterbury Tales*.

Do you recognize this man?

1. He has a tendency to ramble on about almost anything.
2. He seems a bit stupid or naive, but
3. in fact he is rather clever, and
4. knows more than he pretends.
5. He need not be approached cautiously as
6. he has a basically warm and open nature.

If you recognize this man, and if you have read any of Chaucer's poetry you can hardly have missed him, then you have met 'Chaucer the narrator'. He is what most people remember when they think of 'Chaucer'.

IV Chaucer the exam

More detailed guidance on how to write essays on Chaucer is supplied in Chapter 7. However, from the very beginning 'Chaucer the exam' may bulk large in your mind, so a few words here will be helpful, if only to allay anxieties and get you pointing in the right direction straightaway.

All experienced exam-setters know that there are just *three or four basic questions* on any author. There only seem to be more because of the many different ways of putting what is essentially the same question: long or short, using big words or small ones, with quotations from critics or Chaucer attached – or even with totally bogus quotations made up for the purpose by the examiner. But whatever their shape or size, there are still only three or four basic questions on Chaucer. So, without further ado, here they are.

1. *How does Chaucer produce a sense of variety and complexity in his work?* This is the first question because, in effect, it covers all the others. In that sense there is really only *one* question on Chaucer. Chaucer produces 'a sense of variety and complexity' by mixing his materials. On a larger scale this means that he often plays the world of books and stories against the observed world of reality, or the world of dreams against the waking world. The result is a mixture of

fact and fiction, a variety of ways of looking at reality. On a smaller scale the 'variety and complexity' may be a matter of characterization. We might see the same characters from different points of view: how they are dressed, what their job is, what they think, how they act, and so on. The 'complexity' of characterization arises simply because all these elements may not quite fit together. The characters may act differently from how they think; they may not do their job as they ought to; their dress may betray some minor but significant aspect of their character, and so on. In all these larger and smaller ways the main – almost only – question on Chaucer is 'How does he produce a sense of variety and complexity?' All the other questions follow on naturally from this.

2.   *How do narrators complicate their stories?* In other words, how do the narrators add 'variety' to the tales they tell? Nearly all Chaucer's poems have a narrator, and at the very least this is 'Chaucer the narrator' in his role of performer. But often, as in *The Canterbury Tales*, there are other fictional narrators as well. In all these cases the fact that we see or imagine the person telling the tale is obviously important. It complicates our view of the tale, so that we read the tale with the teller in mind, and vice versa. What could be a straightforward response therefore becomes more complex – in short, more 'varied'.

3.   *How does Chaucer produce his humour and what purpose does it serve?* Chaucer's sense of the variety of life is often playful and results in a humorous view of things. What makes us laugh or smile is usually some kind of incongruity, the way in which things do not quite fit together. The result can be anything between a belly laugh at something outrageously incongruous (such as a would-be lover being tricked into kissing his love's backside), or the effect can be more subtle, the sense that something is not being treated with complete seriousness. Such effects are termed *ironic,* and you will find that irony is very common in Chaucer (though not quite as obsessively pervasive as some modern critics suggest). Either way, whether he is being openly comic or discreetly ironic, you should be prepared for a writer whose sense of variety is closely tied up with his sense of humour.

4.   *How does Chaucer produce a sense of variety in his style?* This rarely comes up as an essay question in its own right, but it is important to

be able to relate Chaucer's style to the other aspects of his poetry, especially as this may be required in a commentary. All you do, in effect, is look for evidence of the varied yet ordered way in which the poet organizes his language. On the one hand there is the flexibility and variety of the speaking voice; on the other there is the underlying order of the verse form. Sometimes Chaucer opts for an essentially formal style, and sometimes he opts for a more familiar, colloquial one. And often he mixes formal and informal styles to produce an even more complex texture. Again, the key to an understanding of the smaller as well as the larger effects of Chaucer's verse is its sheer 'variety'.

These four questions will help you focus all the major critical aspects of Chaucer's work, and basically, they can all be reduced to the first: 'How does Chaucer produce a sense of variety and complexity in his work?' You can be sure that the question you will be asked in 'Chaucer the exam' will be one of these. The next step in this book, however, is to show you how to apply these questions to particular texts and how to go about forming a 'varied and complex' response of your own.

2

STUDYING *THE GENERAL PROLOGUE TO THE CANTERBURY TALES*

Everybody who studies *The General Prologue* experiences the same problems. The first problem is reading a work in a strange and unfamiliar version of English. However, I hope the previous chapter has shown that Chaucer's language is not that much of a barrier. You simply need to approach it systematically. In fact, most people really enjoy the poem, and usually for the same reason. *The General Prologue* is an astonishingly lively view of a group of pilgrims in fourteenth-century England. Six hundred years later we can still recognize familiar types in Chaucer's collection of characters, and Chaucer has a wonderful way of picking on people's revealing, and often amusing, idiosyncrasies. The language, which at first is such an obstacle, soon becomes a source of fascination and delight in its own right.

It is at this point, however, that most students become unsure how to tackle the poem as a whole. They can see that criticism must somehow amount to more than saying, 'The General Prologue is full of memorable characters', but they cannot see what. Consequently, there is a temptation to write about the poem as if it is only a portrait gallery, as if it is a mere introduction to the pilgrims who tell *The Canterbury Tales,* as if there is no larger meaning or purpose. The first thing I do in this chapter, therefore, is encourage you to see the poem as a whole, to get a sense of the overall shape and main ideas. Only then, when you have got a grasp of the whole, are you invited to look at the characters. First, we look at just a couple of them in detail, and then we see how to sort them into various groups. That way you will avoid the most common faults in students' accounts of *The General Prologue:* a remorseless trudge past all the characters with a brief critical comment dutifully attached to each. Close discussion of one or two characters means that you get a detailed acquaintance with Chaucer's way of constructing characters, his techniques of characterization. Sorting them into groups avoids the trudge and provides you with scheduled stopping places, as well as an overall sense of direction. At that stage you will be in a position to refine and extend your analysis. Such matters as 'Chaucer the narrator' and the relation of the text to actual life in fourteenth-century England can then be built into the critical framework you have already established. So can the matter of the poem's style and how to go about analysing an extract in detail. Let's begin, however, by trying to see the work as a whole, the first step in any analysis.

STEP I WHAT KIND OF WORK AM I STUDYING?

It always helps if you know roughly what to expect before reading a text, and this is especially so with a work written over 600 years ago. In the case of *The General Prologue,* the first thing to expect is a poem which is essentially descriptive rather than narrative. There is a story or situation, but really the bulk of the poem is taken up with the description of some 30 people: rich and poor, secular and religious, good and bad. In medieval terms this sort of thing was called an 'estates satire'. It is a survey of the various 'classes' or 'estates' of late medieval society, and each 'estate' is represented by a single figure or group of figures. We therefore have a knight and a squire representing the nobility, a monk, a prioress and a friar representing the religious orders, and so on. The 'satire' aspect comes from the fact that these are often figures of fun. They are there to be ridiculed or censured, and occasionally admired. 'Estates satire' crops up in all sorts of medieval literature, in sermons and moral tracts as well as poems and plays, and it is the main core of *The General Prologue.*

In modern terms you will find that *The General Prologue is* often called a 'portrait gallery' or 'pageant' of medieval life. These are useful terms, too, though slightly less precise than 'estates satire'. Certainly, they catch the sheer number, variety and colourfulness of the descriptions, but 'portrait gallery' perhaps suggests something too static and undramatic, and of the two, 'pageant' is better.

One last tip on what to expect: Chaucer never left a literary form or convention as he found it. He always transformed or mixed his basic materials, and this happens in *The General Prologue* too. In fact, he gives us not just an 'estates satire', but a dramatic situation to go with it. Quite simply, he put the whole lot in the context of an evening at an inn, and then further linked everyone by making them all pilgrims bound for Canterbury the following day. This part of *The General Prologue* is often called the 'frame story'. It is worth mentioning in advance because this 'frame' dramatically affects the way we approach and understand the poem as a whole. It is also the first thing you come across when reading it.

STEP 2   WHAT IS IT ABOUT?

So far we have not moved much beyond the idea that Chaucer is presenting a 'portrait gallery' or 'pageant' or 'estates satire'. What we have begun to see, however, is that there is some principle underlying the way in which he selects his cast of characters. This should encourage us to look at the shape of the text and its principles of organization. In order to do so, however, we need to establish a very brief summary of what happens.

We start with a grand vision of spring. This swiftly narrows down to one particular spring evening at a London inn called the Tabard. There, the poet tells us, he and some 30 other people were assembled before setting off on a pilgrimage to the shrine of St Thomas à Becket at Canterbury. Then the poet breaks off to describe each of the pilgrims in turn, all the way through from the noble Knight to the roguish Pardoner. This takes up the bulk of the poem (ll. 35–714) and includes observations made on the road later, as well as at the inn. When we are finally returned to the inn it is later that same evening. The innkeeper, whose name is Harry Bailley, is seeing to it that everyone is filled with wine and good humour. At the end of the evening he even proposes a game to be played on the pilgrimage. Each of the pilgrims is to tell four tales: two on the way to Canterbury and two on the way back. Harry himself will come along as 'master of ceremonies', and there will be a prize for the best story as well as a penalty for anyone who steps out of line. Everyone agrees and off they go to bed. The following morning the innkeeper gets them all up and on the road, lots are drawn and it falls to the Knight to tell the first tale. And that, as far as the story is concerned, is all that happens in *The General Prologue.*

In itself a story is potentially just a string of events. What makes it memorable as well as interesting is the fact that it has a basic shape, and perhaps some simple purpose behind it. In fact, once you have stripped away its detail, the underlying structure of *The General Prologue* is both simple and memorable. We start and finish at the inn, in the 'frame' part of the story, while the great middle section is devoted to the descriptions of the pilgrims, the 'estates satire' part of the story. Clearly, for all the rich and profuse detail, the whole thing is quite tidy and balanced. Another, more general way of putting this is to say that there is a great sense of vitality and of variety in the poem, but also a great sense of order and harmony. The opening celebrates natural and heavenly harmony with the coming of spring, and the close celebrates social harmony with everyone amicably agreeing to the storytelling game. At the centre of the poem, however, there is a highly varied and in many ways 'disorderly' vision of humanity. *Variety within unity, disorder within order:* these are handy and open-ended ways of talking about the poem's shape. They are also good ways of talking about its meaning, and that is what you need to do next.

So what are the main ideas in *The General Prologue,* the larger issues it explores? The characters start at an inn and are bound for a shrine. Their point of departure is a very human and worldly place, where they can enjoy wine and one another's company, and yet their ultimate destination and the very reason they are assembled at the inn is holy and other worldly. On the one hand, therefore, there are claims of humanity; on the other, the claims of God. These are clear and simple terms of reference and they span the entire range of experience in the poem. Another way of putting this is to say that the whole thing is built round a huge contrast or tension: 'love of the world' versus 'love of God'. But, however you put it, some such opposition is essential for any overview of the poem's meaning. And notice that, really, all we are doing is expressing that tension between variety and unity, disorder and order, in other terms. On the one hand, there is the teeming variety of the world and humanity; on the other, the unity and order of the divine scheme. These are the big ideas in *The General Prologue,* so hold on to them.

STEP 3   LOOKING AT CHARACTERIZATION

What we have established so far is that there is a tension at the heart of the work. This tension can be expressed in various ways, and to a large extent you need to describe it in your own words. The terms I have suggested are 'variety within unity', 'disorder within order', 'love of the world' versus 'love of God'. Now, to see how Chaucer breathes life into these ideas, you need to look closely at the characters. However, the big danger in discussing characters is simply to say 'This one's interesting' or 'Here's a colourful rogue' and leave it at that. You have said something but *explained* nothing. Clearly, to make a critical observation rather than a casual comment, you need some purpose or principle informing your analysis. And that is where the main ideas behind the poem come in. With each character, what you need to do is go through a simple set of questions. How does he or she contribute to the sense of variety within the poem? How orderly or disorderly is the character's behaviour? Is he/she motivated by 'love of the world' or by 'love of God'? Or, if there is a mixture of tendencies, then to what extent do they tend one way or the other? By repeatedly asking such simple but significant questions you are really engaging with the characters critically; you are seeing them as natural extensions of a larger argument.

The beauty of this method is that it can be applied to all the characters, regardless of their many differences. Chaucer himself says as much towards the beginning and end of the poem. He tells us that he is looking at each of the pilgrims in terms of *rank, clothing, physical and moral state* and *the person's actual reason for being on the pilgrimage* ('estaat', 'array', 'condicioun' and 'cause' respectively (ll. 35–41; 715–17). It obviously makes sense if we look at the same things too. The example I give here is the Knight, but you can apply exactly the same method to all the other characters. Read the passage a couple of times, and then see how we go about making sense of it.

> A Knyght ther was, and that a worthy man
> That fro the tyme that he first bigan
> To riden out, he loved chivalrie,
> Trouthe and honour, fredom and curteisie.
> Ful worthy was he in his lordes werre,
> And thereto hadde he riden, no man ferre,
> As wel in cristendom as in hethenesse,
> And evere honoured for his worthynesse.

At Alisaundre he was whan it was wonne.
Ful ofte tyme he hadde the bord bigonne
Aboven alle nacions in Pruce;
In Lettow hadde he reysed and in Ruce,
No Cristen man so ofte of his degree.
In Gernade at the seege eek hadde he be
Of Algezir, and riden in Belmarye.
At Lyeys was he and at Satalye,
Whan they were wonne; and in the Grete See
At many a noble armee hadde he be.
At mortal batailles hadde he been fiftene,
And foughten for oure feith at Tramyssene
In lystes thries, and ay slayn his foo.
This ilke worthy knyght hadde been also
Somtyme with the lord of Palatye
Agayn another hethen in Turkye.
And everemoore he hadde a sovereyn prys;
And though that he were worthy, he was wys,
And of his port as meeke as is a mayde.
He nevere yet no vileynye ne sayde
In all his lyf unto no maner wight.
He was a verray, parfit gentil knyght.
But, for to tellen yow of his array,
His hors were goode, but he was nat gay.
Of fustian he wered a gypon
Al bismotered with his habergeon,
For he was late ycome from his viage,
And wente for to doon his pilgrymage.

(ll. 43–78)

The first thing that might strike you here is the sheer weight of detail in this portrait. It is the same with all the characters. There is a lot of information to take in, but what you have to do is try to see through the detail to the few underlying ideas. Here, for example, there is a whole host of terms such as 'sworthy', 'trouthe' and 'honour'. And there is also a great list of names relating to the battles and tournaments the Knight fought ('Alisaundre', 'Pruce', 'Lettow', and so on). After that we are given more personal and perhaps surprising traits to consider. His speech is 'as meeke as is a mayde', he never spoke rudely ('no vileynye ne sayde'), his horse is fine but not flashy, and, most particularly, we are told that he has come straight from his sea voyage to be on this pilgrimage (that is why his surcoat is still spotted with rust). In fact, all these things can be summed up as the *variety* side of the Knight's presentation. To a certain extent they make him an *individual* and, coupled with the fact that all the places mentioned were real and historical, they even suggest that the Knight may be modelled on a real figure. Now, whether this last possibility is true is not immediately important. The point is that some aspects of him *seem* to be real, for there is just enough variety and complexity in the surface detail to suggest that he could have existed – even if in fact he did not.

Now simply go through the same material looking for ways in which it is unified. You will see that all this variety, in fact, comes down to a few simple ideas. For instance, notice that all those terms used to introduce the Knight are really of one sort: 'worthy', 'trouthe' and 'honour' are all highly abstract terms and all express grandly chivalric ideals. 'Worthy' and 'worthynesse' alone are used a total of five times. So whatever else he turns out to be, this character certainly starts off as a highly *idealized* knight. A single, essentially simple meaning also underlies all those battles and tournaments. All of them were in far-flung foreign places and most of them were against the heathen. Therefore, for all their number and unfamiliarity, they all give out just one message: not only is he an idealized knight; he is an idealized *crusading* knight too. See how we are building a simple cluster of ideas out of an apparently scattered range of materials. The final, more personal traits go together in a similar way. Meek in bearing, restrained in speech, so eager to go on the pilgrimage that he did not change his clothes – they too add up to a single quality. The Knight is 'modest', or you might say, with a more specifically religious tinge, that he is 'pious'. The point is that all the major aspects of this figure can be summed up in a single phrase. He is an *ideally modest and pious crusading knight.* And that in turn means that, seen as a whole, he is as much a 'type' of knight as an individual, a simplified 'caricature' as much as a complex character. Even if he was based on a real character, as Chaucer develops him he is also an ideal figure: 'a verray, parfit gentil knyght' ('a true, perfect and noble knight'). He is both 'real' and 'ideal'.

Clearly, Chaucer has it both ways with his characterization. As you read, the variety and detail contribute to a sense of individuality, and yet, when you take a second look, the underlying unity and patterning stand out. You know you are also dealing with a carefully constructed fiction, in some sense a 'type' of character. This applies in varying degrees to all the pilgrims. They are not all equally 'individual' or equally 'typical', and you will need to judge for yourself the contribution of these elements to their characterization. Notice that 'individuality within typicality' is simply the counterpart of 'variety within unity'. You will find that terms such as these are particularly durable because they can always be refined, but they never need to be completely replaced.

Let's take stock of what has been established in the discussion of the Knight. We have looked for a tension in the way he is presented. Essentially, it is a very simple tension to get hold of: that the Knight is a representative figure in a larger social and divine scheme of things, but that he is also an individual and a human being in his own right. Look for the same tension when you consider other characters. What you will discover is that with quite a few of them there is a conflict between their official role and the reality of how they actually live. The conflict can be presented in all sorts of ways, but there is always a sense of jumbling apparently miscellaneous observations together. Sometimes Chaucer will start with the character's appearance and then move on to the moral qualities, whereas sometimes (as with the Knight) he starts with the moral qualities and then moves on to past exploits, with perhaps only a brief mention of physical appearance. Occasionally you will feel that all these different aspects support one another and build up into an essentially simple and unified impression. But often the effect is more complex and teasing: the different aspects do not square with one another, and you are left wondering whether the character's clothing is partly a sham or the motives are to some extent suspect, and so on. If you keep Chaucer's own criteria in mind, they will help too. 'Rank', 'clothing' 'physical and moral state' and 'motive' come at you in different ways, so it is your job to notice how, and whether, they all fit together to produce a harmonious or conflicting view of the character.

In this section I have concentrated on the Knight and shown how he expresses the larger tensions within the poem. I have also, I hope, indicated how all the other characters can be approached in the same way. 'Variety within unity' and 'individuality within typicality' have never been far away as principles guiding our reading. Another very simple way of understanding the Knight or any other character is to place him or her on a scale running from 'love of the world' to 'love of God'. Remember, that is the range of experience offered in the poem as a whole. In the case of the Knight you might feel he can be placed very easily: he is an idealized crusading knight fighting for the 'love of God'. However, you might also argue (as some historians do) that he only *appears* to be fighting for pious motives, that in reality he is fighting for money and booty as well.

This is a vexed point and we pick it up later when looking at the poem's relation to contemporary history. Whatever your conclusions, however, the important thing to remember is that *all* the characters can be placed against the poem's main theme in this way. Every one of them will be 'worldly' or 'other worldly', and often they are a fascinating mixture of both.

STEP 4   DEVELOPING THE ARGUMENT

An understanding of the way in which individual characters are put together provides you with a strong critical base. The next step is to see how the various characters relate to one another, and the kind of groups they fall into. That way you can develop a fuller sense of the poem's argument in action. Starting with individual characterization and then 'comparing and contrasting' the characters is a standard critical strategy. In this instance our task is made easier because Chaucer has to some extent done it for us. He presents the pilgrims in a number of loose yet plausible groupings, so you should start with these. The pilgrims fall naturally into five groups. The first is the noble Knight, his son the Squire, and the Yeoman, a servant. The second comprises the Prioress, the Monk, the Friar, a nun and three priests, and they are nearly all members of fixed religious communities. The third and largest group are nearly all 'middle class': the Merchant, the Clerk, the Lawyer, the Franklin, the five guildsmen and their cook, the Shipman, the Doctor, and the Wife of Bath. The fourth are two brothers from the 'lower orders': the Parson and the Ploughman. And the fifth and last is a more or less motley collection of rogues: 'a Reve and a Millere, / A Somnour and a Pardoner also, / A Maunciple, and myself – ther were namo' (ll. 542–4).

A couple of things stand out about this arrangement. For one thing, a rough social hierarchy is observed, and yet not so rigidly as to become tedious and predictable. You might therefore say that this is another instance of 'variety within unity' and 'disorder within order'. We start with the noble Knight and his entourage, move on to the senior Church figures (the Prioress and others), and then through the 'middle' and 'lower' classes. Notice too how there is a rough moral dimension to all this. The out-and-out rogues are tagged on at the end, as if they are not fit to be mixed with more respectable society, while the exceptions to this rule are simply there as a welcome break and for the sake of contrast. So, the poor student ('Clerk') is included with the affluent Merchant, Lawyer and Doctor, while Chaucer, with a wry modesty, puts himself at the end in the company of rogues.

Let's look in detail at one of the groups of pilgrims and see how a sophisticated argument can be built up from an essentially simple set of contrasts. We'll start with the second group, concentrating on the three principal figures: the Prioress, the Monk and the Friar (the Nun and the three priests are merely mentioned). What links these characters is obvious. They are all members of religious communities and are all therefore supposed to be governed by strict rules of conduct. However, given what you already know about the main ideas of the poem, you might well suspect that they will all reveal failings and fall short of their ideals in one way or other. The passage describing these characters is lengthy (ll. 118–269), so you will need to read it through a couple of times. Just remember that you are on the look-out for a few basic things: the various ways in which these characters show their weaknesses and, more particularly, the different ways in which they mix up their 'love of the world' with their 'love of God'.

So, what judgements have you come to on these characters? How do they compare with one another in their basic attitudes? What you might have noticed about the Prioress, for instance, is that she is far more concerned with dainty eating for herself and her dogs than with charity for the starving poor. Comparison with the Monk helps point up this 'food issue' even more. He is much keener on hunting and feasting than he is on the rigours of the monastic life. Meanwhile, turning to the Friar, you will notice that he may be a stylish father confessor for the rich and pretty, but he has precious little to do with the genuinely needy. He, too, flouts the religious rule. In fact, you can say that all three have at least a tinge of worldliness in the way they carry out their religious duties. Measured against one another as well as against the larger scale of values in the poem, their various failings stand out all the more clearly. Once you have established the basis of your comparison in this way, all you need to do is clarify the differences. For instance, you might notice that all three characters are on a kind of sliding scale. In the case of the Prioress there is criticism, but it is gently affectionate and ironic. With the Monk the criticism is more openly satirical, even though there is also some admiration for his outdoor vigour. However, when we get to the Friar, the criticism becomes obvious moral censure: he is a smooth, sly and selfish rogue. The same sliding scale can be applied to these characters' attitudes to human and divine love. With all of them the two get awkwardly mixed up, but to different degrees. The Prioress obviously fancies herself as a demure romance heroine, and yet you may want to pass this off as mere affectation and in some way charming. The Monk is far more obviously lusty. There is the strong suggestion that he is active sexually as well as an active huntsman. The point would be clinched if you referred to the 'love-knotte' (l. 197) which the Monk uses to fasten his hood. Like the Prioress's brooch (which carries the ambiguous inscription *Amor vincit omnia*' ['Love conquers all'] –l. 162), this is exactly the kind of telling detail that is worth highlighting. You can then demonstrate – rather than just assert – that both these religious figures may have a sexual as well as a spiritual side. And again you could go on to show how the Friar's sexual tendencies are even more blatantly exposed, pointing to the fact that he seems to be an out-and-out womanizer (ll. 210–14).

The important thing to realize with this or any other group of pilgrims is that they are 'variations on a theme'. The 'theme' is what holds them together as a group – in this case, the ways in which all three fall short of their religious roles. The 'variations' are what distinguish the pilgrims within each group, what makes them in some way particular and individual. In principle it is as simple as that: 'variations on a theme'. So, now all you do is apply this principle to the other four groups of pilgrims. Follow through some of the contrasts in the first group, for instance. The Knight and the Squire are obviously variations on the theme of 'chivalry'. The Knight expresses the older, more traditional crusading ideals, while his son is younger and attracted by more fashionably romantic ideals. Take a closer look at the way they are presented and you will see that the one is not really bothered about how he looks, while the other is very fashion-conscious. And so you can go on with the smaller and larger aspects of the comparison. If you take a wider view, some other important differences stand out. For example, it seems that the Knight really loves fighting – it is his particular 'love of the world', if you like. However, it also seems that much of this is for a supposedly religious motive. In ideal terms he is a crusading knight and that means he should be inspired by the 'love of God'. The Squire, on the other hand, seems to like fighting for a quite different reason. He views it as one of many courtly accomplishments and does it above all to show off to his lady ('to stonden in his lady grace' – l. 88). Perhaps the Squire therefore expresses more of the 'love of the world' side of chivalry. All these things are obvious, as they say, when pointed out. It is your job to do the pointing out and to pick on significant details which will illustrate and support your argument. It is all a matter of 'comparison and contrast' and 'variations on a theme'. If you also keep the main ideas of the poem in mind, you will have no trouble in developing a convincing argument.

Now you are in a position to make your own way through the other groups. Money, status and personal pleasure are obviously the controlling ideas in the third, 'middle-class' group. Piety, hard work and duty are the idealized virtues which link the Parson and the Ploughman in the fourth group. And, of course, the rogues, in the final group, are linked by their roguishness. They, too, like the 'middle-class' group, are preoccupied in various ways with money, status and personal pleasure. Naturally, you need not limit yourself to Chaucer's groupings, though that is probably the best place to start. You can then go on to identify and explore criteria of your own. Contrasts and comparisons *between* groups, as well as within them, might focus on such matters as the presentation of *rich and poor,* or *women and men,* as well as a whole range of related contrasts between *the learned and the ignorant* (Chaucer's terms were the 'lered' and the 'lewed'). Once you get the hang of it the possibilities are huge and fascinating. And all the time you can bring these clusters of characters and ideas back into the poem's central orbit simply by seeing them in terms of the underlying tension between human and divine love.

STEP 5   RELATING THE TALE TO ITS TELLER

In this poem, as in most poems by Chaucer, there is a strong sense of a specific storyteller. In *The General Prologue* this storyteller is particularly obvious because he is actually one of the pilgrims, and we can therefore call him 'Chaucer the pilgrim' or 'Chaucer the narrator'. Either way, we need to add him to our analysis at this point for he is such a pervasive presence that he is bound to enrich our reading of the poem as a whole. You will find 'Chaucer the pilgrim/narrator' talking about himself in ll. 715–46. The first few lines deal with the rank, appearance and motives of the other pilgrims so, as we have discussed them already (see pp. 3–5, 26), we will not

dwell on them again here. However, you should read over the rest
of the passage a couple of times and try to pick out the main features
of his role as the narrator sees them.

> Now have I toold you soothly, in a clause,
> Th'estaat, th'array, the nombre, and eek the cause
> Why that assembled was this compaignye
> In Southwerk at this gentil hostelrye
> That highte the Tabard, faste by the Belle.
> But now is tyme to yow for to telle
> How that we baren us that ilke nyght,
> Whan we were in that hostelrie alyght;
> And after wol I telle of our viage
> And al the remenaunt of oure pilgrimage.
> But first I pray yow, of youre curteisye,
> That ye n'arette it nat my vileynye,
> Thogh that I pleynly speke in this mateere,
> To telle yow hir wordes and hir cheere,
> Ne thogh I speke hir wordes proprely.
> For this ye knowen al so wel as I,
> Whoso shal telle a tale after a man,
> He moot reherce as ny as evere he kan
> Everich a word, if it be in his charge,
> Al speke he never so rudeliche and large,
> Or ellis he moot telle his tale untrewe,
> Or feyne thyng, or fynde wordes newe.
> He may nat spare, althogh he were his brother;
> He moot as wel seye o word as another.
> Crist spak hymself ful brode in hooly writ,
> And wel ye woot no vileynye is it.
> Eek Plato seith, whos that kan hym rede,
> The wordes moote be cosyn to the dede.
> Also I prey yow to foryeve it me,
> Al have I nat set folk in hir degree
> Heere in this tale, as that they sholde stonde.
> My wit is short, ye may wel understonde.
>   (ll. 715–46)

As usual, there are many words and details, but only a few underlying
ideas. So what are they? Well, you are likely to have picked up the fact
that Chaucer was keen to record what everyone said and looked like,
and to do so as accurately as possible ('hir wordes and hir cheere ... as
ny as evere he kan'). The other big idea in the passage is fairly obvious
too: Chaucer is not too sure of himself and keeps apologizing in
case he offends anybody or says something stupid ('But first I pray
yow, of your curteisye ... . Also I prey yow to foryeve it me ... .

My wit is short, ye may wel understonde'). Again what we are dealing with is a *tension,* and in this case the tension is in the narrator himself. On the one hand, there is his claim that he is just observing and being objective; on the other, there is his admission that he may have missed or misjudged some things because his 'wit is short'. In other words, he offers himself as a kind of naïve reporter. He tries to record everything, but admits he may have done so in an easily impressed, ingenuous manner. Chaucer often cultivates this stance elsewhere, for the role of inquisitive simpleton was obviously an essential ingredient in his act as a performer.

The thing now is to gauge the effect of such a 'naive reporter' or 'inquisitive simpleton' on the whole poem. After all, everything that we see or hear in *The General Prologue* comes through him, so it must make a big difference to how we respond. For instance, take another look at the description of the Knight. Previously we concentrated on his character, but now you should look for signs of the narrator's presence as well. In fact, signs of inquisitiveness and highly tuned powers of observation abound. The entire description is packed with detailed information ranging from lists of past battles to the spots of rust on the Knight's tunic. So what about evidence of the narrator's 'naivete' or 'simplicity'? Well, once you know what you are looking for, that is not too hard to spot either. Notice how everything about the Knight is so enthusiastically and admiringly put: all those 'worthy' qualities and the final extravagance of 'He was a verray, parfit gentil knight' (l. 72). And just see how many words such as 'ful' (very), 'evere', 'nevere' and 'no ... no' (not at all) are applied to him and his activities. To put it mildly, the Knight clearly made a big and apparently favourable impression on the narrator.

Now look at another description and you will see that it was not only the Knight who made a big impression on the narrator. To Chaucer the pilgrim *everybody* appears 'very' this, or 'not at all that', or 'always' or 'never' the other. For instance, here are Chaucer's conclusions on the Pardoner:

> But trewely to tellen atte laste,
> He was in chirche a noble ecclesiaste.
> Wel koude he rede a lessoun or a storie,
> But alderbest he song an offertorie;
> For wel he wiste, whan that song was songe,
> He moste preche and wel affile his tonge
> To wynne silver, as he ful wel koude;

Therefore he song the murierly and loude.
(ll. 707–14)

Reading over this passage, you can hardly have missed all those 'wels'. And see how many other words there are which give a kind of exaggerated, superlative quality to the description ('trewely', 'noble' and 'alderbest' [the very best]). Obviously, yet again, the narrator seems to be highly impressed. And to be as impressed as this by everyone and everything is, quite simply, to be impressionable. In other words, to return to the terms with which we started this section, there is more than enough evidence of a *naïve* reporter, an inquisitive *simpleton*. We have found signs of him in descriptions at both ends of the social and moral scale, when presenting the Pardoner no less than when presenting the Knight. If you now look for similar signs in all the intervening descriptions, you will quickly find that they are the rule rather than the exception.

Having gauged the effect of the other pilgrims on Chaucer the narrator, the next step is to gauge the effect on us, the readers. They are not quite the same thing. For instance, all those extreme and emphatic words clearly contribute to the high 'colour' and generally exhilarating tone of the poem, but perhaps there is more to them than that. When you get to morally dubious characters such as the Prioress, or downright depraved ones such as the Pardoner, you may begin to wonder what Chaucer is up to. Is the Prioress so 'very unaffected and modest' ('ful symple and coy' – l. 119)? And is the Pardoner really such a 'fine churchman' ('noble ecclesiaste' – l. 708)? By then the answer is obvious: Chaucer is being *ironic*. That is, he is urging us not to take things at face value but to be critical, both of the extravagance of his words and the extravagance of people's appearances and actions. In fact, the ironic message is quite simple – beware! So, whenever you come across a whole host of overused terms, just ask yourself if they are being used in a deliberately indiscriminate manner, to make you critical. Among the common ones are 'fair', 'swete', 'pleasaunt', 'merye' (also meaning 'pleasant'), 'fetis' (meaning 'cute'), 'noble' and 'gentil'; 'good', 'bettre' and 'best'; 'evere', 'alway' and 'oft'; 'al', 'non' and 'many'; 'ful' and 'wel'. All of these words crop up so frequently and in such different contexts that they are bound to make you think – so do! Finally, in the same vein, do not take all of the narrator's asides at face value. When he says 'it seemed to me' ('me thoghte') or 'I think' and 'I believe' ('I gesse' and 'I trowe'), you should remind yourself that he may be being deliberately naïve. *He* may 'think' or 'believe' something, but it does not mean *you* should.

Now think again about the main ideas around which we have built our analysis. Try to see how this particular narrator creates a sense of 'variety within unity' and 'disorder within order'. From one point of view, his great powers of observation make him sensitive to the varied detail and apparent disorder of life, and yet his essential naïvety also makes him capable of reducing everything to a few simplistic impressions. He may *see* particular, individual people, but he often *thinks* in crude stereotypes. The final perception we are given is therefore a mixture of both, and that is why we in turn can also respond to these characters both as 'individuals' and as 'types'. It is the same when we recall the main theme in *The General Prologue*, the tension between 'love of the world' and 'love of God'. This, too, relates directly to the tension we have noticed within the narrator. On the one hand, his powers of observation and inquisitiveness show an intense engagement with the world around him – a real delight in it; on the other, he also needs a fundamental generosity and optimism – a real faith in the 'love of God' – to see that everything is ultimately for the best. However you put it, the narrator's contribution to the overall vision of the poem is fundamental. He sees a larger unity embracing the variety of life and a larger order embracing its disorder. There is also, he implies, a larger divine love embracing the earthly love between man and woman.

Once you have reached this stage of your analysis, the bulk of the work has been done. You know the kind of work you are dealing with, its overall shape and its main ideas. You also know how to tackle characters both as individuals and groups, and just now you have learnt how to understand the narrator by relating him to the strategies and issues of the whole poem. From a narrowly 'literary' point of view your analysis is more or less complete. You have a framework in which to develop responses. The next step is to develop them in a properly informed and historical way.

STEP 6   SEEING THE TEXT IN CONTEXT

Chaucer's poems cannot be fully understood unless you place them within the context in which they were written. This is especially so with *The General Prologue* because it draws so obviously on contemporary fourteenth-century life. And yet, equally obviously, *The General Prologue* cannot be a completely accurate and representative account of life at the time. Any account will depend upon the author's position and point of view, as well as any literary designs he may have. Chaucer is no exception. We have already seen over and over again how he draws on the substantial details of people's dress and occupations, and shapes them in line with his own very specific aims and expectations. Consequently, in order to see his vision of life more clearly, you need to connect Chaucer's writings to his life and times. Of course, you are likely to do this casually anyway, for while they are studying a Chaucer poem people tend to pick up all sorts of stray and fascinating information. The trick, however, is to coordinate this information and make it really work for you critically.

Here are some common scraps of 'background' information on *The General Prologue*. For instance, you might find out that Chaucer wrote it while living on the pilgrimage route to Canterbury from 1385 onwards (hence the idea for the pilgrimage framework); that there actually was a landlord of the Tabard inn called Harry Bailley (hence perhaps the jovial realism of this figure in the poem); and that millers actually did cheat when counting out the corn they milled (hence the reference to this in Chaucer's description of the Miller). You will also almost certainly be told – though remarkably few students remember – that a reeve was a type of manor foreman, while a franklin was a comparatively new and wealthy type of non-noble landowner, and so on. Clearly, all this is fascinating stuff. And yet, for all its obvious relevance, surprisingly little of it turns up in critical readings of the poem. More often it is relegated to the position of 'background material' – and then forgotten completely. This need not be the case. In fact, for a proper *study* of the poem (rather than just a *reading* of it) this should not be the case. Here are some tips on how to make full use of contextual and historical information in *The General Prologue*. They should be accompanied by an attentive reading of the subsections on 'Chaucer the man' and 'Chaucer the narrator' in Chapter 1 (see pp. 5–8, 17–19).

First of all, notice that all the critical terms we have used can be applied to actual people and periods of history as well as to literary texts. 'Variety', 'unity', 'order', 'disorder', 'individuals', 'types', 'love of the world' and 'love of God' are all words we might use to describe life in general and not just literature. The trick, therefore, is to take a wider view and apply them to Chaucer and the real world in which he moved. You can then more clearly see what particular vision of reality he favoured and maybe also suggest why he wrote as he did. The text alone cannot tell you the answer to either of these questions.

Take the term 'variety', for example. How does the variety of life represented in *The General Prologue* compare with the variety of Chaucer's own life, as well as the overall variety of life in England at the time? From reading the 'Chaucer the man' subsection you will know that Chaucer had a very varied life as courtier, soldier, diplomat, customs collector, royal clerk and Knight of the Shire – as well as, of course, poet. All these posts were well-to-do and connected with the court. Now simply turn to *The General Prologue* and look for signs of that 'variety' as well as that 'court emphasis' there. The sheer variety is obvious enough, as there are representatives of many – though not all – sections of late medieval society in the poem. There is everyone between a cook and a knight, a prioress and a pardoner. However, you will now have noticed that there are no representatives of the very rich and the very poor. The higher aristocracy and clergy went on pilgrimages with their own private retinues, while the great mass of the population could not afford to go on pilgrimages at all. The result is therefore that *The General Prologue* covers a much narrower range of late medieval society than most readers first think. Its variety is great, but far from comprehensive when compared with actual life.

Now consider the 'court emphasis' of Chaucer's life. Are there any signs of that in the poem? Well, the descriptions start with the Knight and it is the Knight who 'by chance' tells the first tale. So, from a court point of view, social propriety is upheld. The Knight is also, of course, extravagantly and admiringly idealized. Now look at the other end of the social scale, at the Parson and the Ploughman. These, too, are idealized types, but in this case they are shining examples of the pious, hard-working and dutiful lower orders. So again, from a court point of view, social propriety is upheld. The strong implication is that both 'high' and 'low' know their respective places in the divinely ordained scheme of things. Everything is as it should be – *from a court point of view.* Now, at this point you have a choice. A naïve response would be to say that actual knights, parsons and ploughmen were really like this. However, a more sophisticated and historically informed response would run something like this:

I know from the notes in my edition that there were many knights who fought for personal profit and pleasure, not for pious reasons at all. I also know that there were plenty of priests and ploughmen involved in the 'Peasant's Revolt' of 1381. So, all in all, I know that Chaucer is presenting a flattering image of two extremes of medieval society here. Maybe he is being ironic or maybe he is just being cautious and presenting things as they 'ought to be', rather than, more dangerously, as they often are. Either way, they are definitely 'idealized types'. In political terms, Chaucer was obviously no *radical*.

Naturally, this sounds contrived and you might not come to quite the same conclusions. However, it should give you the idea. See how the argument moves from the text into history, and then returns to the text with a stronger critical argument. You make the same kind of points as came up in the analysis, but in a much more subtle and convincing way. You can also suggest *why* things are written, even while you are commenting on *what is* written and *how*.

Exactly the same approach can be adopted to Chaucer's view of the other classes. Take his representatives of the merchant and professional classes, for example, or figures such as the Monk and the Friar. In all these cases you are faced with a tension between ideal and actual behaviour; however, the exact degree of tension can be gauged only if you know what actual merchants and friars got up to. For instance, you might think you can detect 'irony' in a character description, but you cannot be sure that Chaucer is indeed being ironic unless you have some notion of what was normal against which to measure it. It is one thing to be told, as students often are, that there was a deep crisis in late medieval society and that traditional landed wealth was being challenged by wealth based on trade and commerce. But it is usually quite another thing to be told that the pilgrims in *The General Prologue* are torn between 'love of God' and 'love of the world'. The trick is to bring these two kinds of information together. You can then show that Chaucer's pilgrims are so morally elusive, so superficially proper and yet so fundamentally dubious, precisely *because* society was undergoing such fundamental and often unclear changes at this time. Chaucer was particularly sensitive to this reshuffling of the traditional 'estates', and the result is an unusually rich and teasing 'estates satire'.

As a final example of the explanatory power of a contextual approach, consider the narrator in *The General Prologue*. Why does Chaucer present himself as naïve and rather simple? From a reading of the 'Chaucer the narrator' section you would already know about the kind of diverse and tricky pressures on a court poet: that he would deliver his poem in person, that he had to entertain and be interesting, but that he also had to avoid giving offence. Clearly it was wise to appear a little simple, just as it was wise to tinge everything with 'myrthe', the sense that everything is basically 'fair' and 'wel'. Reading the text you can see this rose-tinted realism, but reading the text in context you can also explain it. It is as simple as that. Literature and life, text and context have to be seen in terms of one another.

STEP 7   ANALYSING THE STYLE

So far we have talked about the story, the characters, the narrator and the social and historical context in which the work was written. The last of these approaches took a broader view of the text, from the 'outside'. Another, complementary way of looking at the poem is to focus even more closely than we have done so far on the actual words of the poem, on the details of the 'inside'. We are now going to take a look at Chaucer's style. In fact, most students dread having to write about style and usually do it badly. This is because they are not at all sure what is meant by 'style' and what the point is in talking about it.

What I shall do in this last section, therefore, is suggest some basic guidelines which will help you feel confident when it comes to discussing style. There are just two things to get hold of. One is that there are only a few features to look for: namely, *choice of words, rhyme* and *line length, rhythm* and *general sentence structure.* The other thing to get hold of is that your sense of a big tension in the poem (the pull between unity and variety, order and disorder) will also provide you with a framework for discussing the stylistic choices Chaucer makes. I shall illustrate this by looking at the opening lines of the poem:

Whan that Aprill with his shoures soote
The droghte of March hath perced to the roote,
And bathed every veyne in swich licour
Of which vertu engendred is the flour;
Whan Zephirus eek with his sweete breeth
Inspired hath in every holt and heeth
The tendre croppes, and the yonge sonne
Hath in the Ram his halve cours yronne,
And smale foweles maken melodye ... .

(ll. 1–9)

Start by establishing an idea of what the passage is basically about, and particularly look for the kind of tension around which it is built. For instance, what stands out about this passage is the strong sense of purpose as the year continues its cycle, as spring comes again, and as people's thoughts turn to making a pilgrimage to Canterbury. These things give a reassuring sense of pattern and routine to life – in a word, 'order'. What also stands out, however, is the ceaselessly teeming life in these opening lines, how Chaucer conveys a sense of growth and a great explosion of energy – in a word, the sheer 'variety' of life. So far all this is familiar enough. All I have done is recognize the larger concerns of the poem in a short passage, in miniature.

What an examination of style requires is that you point to the specific verbal choices Chaucer made to bring these ideas to life. Notice, however, that I start with the overall meaning of the passage and its relation to the poem as a whole. That way I am more likely to say something genuinely significant, and so avoid the temptation simply to list features without any clear idea why. So how, in specific verbal detail, does Chaucer create a sense of 'variety within unity', 'disorder within order'? Let's start with the orderly side of things. How is order suggested in these lines? Well, one 'orderly' aspect of them is the fact that they are presented as poetry, with the lines neatly ranged down the page. And there are other signs of 'poetic' order too: the fact that words rhyme at the ends of adjacent lines, soote' and 'roote', 'licour' and 'flour', and so on. Lines that come in rhyming pairs like this are called 'rhyming couplets' and the neatness with which they rhyme suggests a particularly strong sense of order. Now look at the *line length*. In what way is this also regular and 'ordered'? To be precise we need to do a simple syllable count, and here is how you would do it for the first two lines:

```
   1     2    3  4    5    6    7   8   9  10
Whan / that / Ap/rill / with / his / shour/es / soot/e

   1     2      3      4     5      6       7    8    9  10
The / droght/(e) of / March / hath / perc(e)d / to / the / root/e
```

The only tip you need for counting syllables in Chaucer's English is that there was considerable freedom at the ends and beginnings of some words. The endings '-e', '-es' and '-ed' might not count as full syllables depending on the pace of the reading, and the same applied to adjacent vowels. These were sometimes allowed to run into one another (as they do in speech anyway) and just count as one syllable. There are examples of all these things in our two lines. None the less, one thing comes out clearly from such an analysis, and it is borne out by all the other lines in the poem: each line uses about ten syllables (it is decasyllabic). Put formally, then, the main principle of poetic 'order' in *The General Prologue* is that it uses rhyming couplets and a decasyllabic line. And that, as far as labelling goes, is all you need say about the verse form.

The next question is, 'What is the effect of the verse form?' In fact, the answer is the same as that for most poetry: it gives a basic harmony or 'music', as well as an essential unity to the language. Call it what you like, but the main function of verse is to be pleasingly harmonious in itself, as well as to provide a solid and regular framework in which the poet can explore his ideas and language. Now, on its own the verse form is not particularly interesting. It is like a piece of gymnastic apparatus, only interesting when someone is actually performing on it. What we now need to do, therefore, is look at the other stylistic features and how they add variety to the verse form.

So how, in his choice and arrangement of specific words, does Chaucer create a sense of variety? Put formally, the answer is that he does it through his wide range of *diction* and his flexible handling of *rhythm* and *sentence structure*. This may sound off-putting, but in practice these things are easy enough to spot. For instance, notice how Chaucer's opening sentence runs on for 18 lines without a full stop. That in itself provides ample opportunity for a statement which is rich and varied, yet also clearly unified. The result is a single panorama with many aspects, a single sentence with many subordinate clauses. Notice here how the larger critical issue is reinforced by a specifically stylistic point. You can say the same sort of thing about the rhythm and pacing of the passage. Notice how the sense flows over naturally from one line to the next (this is usually called 'enjambment'), and how the whole passage is freely linked by common words such as 'and', 'when', 'then' and 'that'. The effect is very much that of ordinary conversation, and there is a strong sense of the speaking voice. However, at the same time, we are constantly aware of the underlying regularity and order of the verse form, the steady predictability of the rhyming couplets and the ten-syllable line. In other words, we are yet again aware of 'variety within unity', this time in the delicate tension between rhythm and verse form.

Now look for a similar variety and tension in Chaucer's range of vocabulary. You have probably noticed a certain formality in the passage. 'Engendred', 'Zephirus' and 'inspired' are fairly long words and have an abstract, Latinate ring to them. None the less, they rub shoulders quite readily with more down-to-earth and familiar words such as 'shoures', 'soote' and 'flour'. In short, the passage is both formal and informal – both 'orderly' and 'varied'. Just as we had the orderliness of the verse form playing against the freedom of the speaking voice, so here we have formality playing against informality. Look out for signs of this throughout *The General Prologue*. It is called Chaucer's 'mixed style' and has the effect of making you see the same thing in different ways. Here, for instance, you see the spring in grandly formal terms, as a mighty and heavenly power 'engendering' and 'inspiring' growth. Notice how *personification* is also used to increase this sense of grandeur: 'Zephirus', a classical personification of the wind, is breathing sweetly, while 'the yonge sonne' is 'running' in the sky. And yet, at the same time, you also see the spring as something familiar and literally down-to-earth, expressed in terms of simple 'flowers' and 'roots'. This 'mixed style' is the natural counterpart of Chaucer's 'mixed vision'. He shows us both ideal and real aspects of the world, so he uses language to match. There is therefore no reason why you should be afraid of commenting on Chaucer's style. It is simply another, more detailed way of studying his poetic vision.

CONCLUSION

I hope that by now you have some firm ideas about what to look for in *The General Prologue* and how to go about organizing your response. It can all be reduced to a few simple tips. Start by trying to see the poem as a whole, getting a firm hold of its overall and main ideas. Then look more closely at the characters, both individually and as groups, so that you can show how they represent 'ideas in action'. When you have consolidated your analysis in this way, you can go on to elaborate and extend it. The narrator, the social and historical context, and Chaucer's style can be looked at in turn for the light they throw on what the poem is about and how it is put together. Notice that at every stage the best approach is to concentrate on a fairly short passage, interpreting it in relation to the main ideas you have already established. The result will be that your analysis will always have a strong sense of purpose and yet will become progressively more subtle and complex. In this chapter I have concentrated on *The General Prologue,* but in the following chapters it should become clear that exactly the same approach works, and works well, with any Chaucer text.

3

HOW TO STUDY *THE CANTERBURY TALES: THE KNIGHT'S TALE*

This chapter sets out a method for studying any of the Canterbury Tales, and illustrates it with a look at one of the most commonly studied Chaucer texts after *The General Prologue, The Knight's Tale*. Even if you are not studying this tale, you should still find the method and insights developed here of direct relevance to your particular tale. To help you make the connections, briefer study frameworks along the same lines are supplied in the next chapter for the most commonly studied Canterbury Tales.

The method employed here is the same as that used in the previous chapter and throughout the rest of this book. Basically, it is very simple. First, we establish what kind of work we are dealing with and get a firm sense of the poem's overall shape and main ideas. After that we concentrate on the characters, looking at both the *kind* of characters used (i.e. characterization), and the arguments they express as they react with one another. This gives us a solid critical base. It also demonstrates the fundamental critical strategy, which is to move from a general awareness of the poem into detailed analysis of specific passages, and then move back out to an awareness which is more discriminating and sophisticated. The constant illustration and testing of larger ideas is crucial. So is the fact that the analysis moves from simple propositions and observations to progressively more complex ones. Only when you have a good grasp of the poem's basic shape and argument are you encouraged to elaborate and extend your analysis. That is when you can take on board such complicating factors as the tale's relation to the teller (here the Knight), the relation of the text to actual life in fourteenth-century Europe (here the whole problem of chivalry in theory and in practice) and, finally, the precise features of the poem's style and how to go about describing them.

Of all Chaucer's tales, *The Knight's Tale* is the one students tend to find most bewildering and overwhelming. This is usually because they go at it wildly and without any clear sense of where they are going. You should therefore recognize that this is a substantial, serious poem and that it is going to demand a fair amount of hard work. However, *The Knight's Tale* is also a rich, impressive and enjoyable poem, and amply rewards the work you put in. So, let's make the job of studying it as enjoyable and effective as possible. We can start with the simple, obvious things.

STEP I WHAT KIND OF WORK AM I STUDYING?

It always helps to know in advance what kind of work you are dealing with. That way you read it for what it is rather than as something else. Like much of Chaucer's work, *The Knight's Tale* is a long narrative poem; it tells a story in verse and takes well over 2000 lines to do it. So, the first thing to expect in a Canterbury Tale is a strong narrative interest: you will be looking at characters, events, speeches and descriptions (the very stuff of novels and plays rather than most poetry). The second thing to expect is a poem which is leisurely and large-scale in its effects. There are none of the highly compressed images and densely difficult thought-clusters of much modern poetry. Everything is 'spread around'.

It will also help if you identify the 'type' of story Chaucer is using at any one time. This is much like identifying a Shakespeare play as a 'tragedy' or 'comedy' or 'history', except that the categories in Chaucer's day were different and need a little explanation. *The Knight's Tale*, for instance, uses a type of story very common at the time. It is a court romance, and other examples include Chaucer's *The Franklin's Tale* and *Troilus and Criseyde*. All feature knights and ladies and share the main concerns of medieval chivalry: tournaments, battles and romantic courtship. In fact, like most of the Canterbury Tales, all these stories are about love and violence. The main thing that distinguishes court romances is that they present love in a particularly aristocratic and refined form sometimes called 'courtly love', and their violence is also of the highly ceremonial 'chivalric' sort.

The Knight's Tale is not a 'pure' court romance, however, and in this respect it is also characteristic of Chaucer's work in general. Chaucer almost always mixes one story type with another, and the result is that his fictions are richer and more varied than they would be if using one type alone. In this case, Chaucer takes the court romance as his main base and builds onto it elements of what we call the moral tract. This type, as its name suggests, is not really a story type at all, but rather a form of openly instructive writing full of moral and philosophical distinctions on such matters as good and evil, life and death, fate and free will, and so on. You will find a fuller discussion of court romance, moral tract and the other four story types used by Chaucer in the section 'Chaucer the works' in Chapter 1 (see pp. 8–17). The only thing you need to recognize at this stage is that *The Knight's Tale* (like most of the tales) uses a combination of two types. It is about knights and ladies and their peculiarly refined forms of love and violence, but everything is given extra weight and moral seriousness because of the influence of the moral tract. The emphasis, as always in Chaucer, is on a *mixture* of materials and a *variety* of perspectives.

This sense of 'mixture' applies equally to the last large feature of *The Knight's Tale* to which I want to draw your attention: its mixture of medieval chivalry and a classical setting. You may at first be surprised to find medieval knights and ladies in ancient Athens and Thebes, and the presence of pagan gods such as Mars, Venus and Diana may also come as a shock. 'What have all these got to do with medieval Christianity and a single Christian God?' you may ask! In fact, this 'mixing' of different times (also called 'anachronism') is common in medieval literature. Chaucer's *Troilus and Criseyde* is another example. It takes place in ancient Troy, but the characters fight and love according to late-fourteenth-century ideals. For the moment, though, it is enough to reaffirm the general critical principle. Chaucer often mixes his materials (here ancient and medieval, classical and Christian), and the result is particular *variety* in the ways he looks at things.

This section has tried to set out some expectations you should bring with you when reading one of the Canterbury Tales. These expectations are few but fundamental. Whichever text you are studying, expect a strong narrative interest and know that much of the time you are going to be looking at characters and action, and at how the story as a whole is handled. You should also reassure yourself about the basic types of story Chaucer uses. These may be unfamiliar, but there are just a few and their main characteristics can be quickly picked up. Here I pointed to the fact that *The Knight's Tale* combines one story with another, as well as the fact that it combines different periods and perspectives. The same can be said of virtually all of Chaucer's poetry, and that is why I have repeatedly used the terms 'mixture' and 'variety' to try to describe the overall effect of reading his tales.

STEP 2 WHAT IS IT ABOUT?

Once you have read the poem through, the first thing you should do is get a firm grasp of the story. *The Knight's Tale*, like most of Chaucer's tales, is long and packed with incident, so what you need most urgently is a sense of the tale as a whole, without unnecessary detail. Here, for example, is a brief outline of the main events in *The Knight's Tale*. Do something similar for yourself, all the time trying to reduce your story to its essential structure and purpose. *The Knight's Tale* is in four parts, so I shall use these as a framework.

Part 1: Duke Theseus of Athens is returning home after the wars, with his bride and her sister Emily. However, the peace and triumph is short-lived, for straightaway he has to go to Thebes to avenge some noble ladies whose husbands have been deprived of burial rights. During the attack on Thebes a couple of Theban princes, the cousins Palamon and Arcite, are taken prisoner and put in a tower back in Athens. From high up in their tower they see Emily, Theseus's sister-in-law, walking in the garden below. Both instantly fall in love with her and fall out with one another. A little later Arcite is released (but on pain of death if he is ever found in Athens) and Palamon is left in prison. And that is how the first part concludes: neither of the two would-be lovers can get to Emily, and we are left with the question, 'Which of them is the worse-off?'

Part 2: Arcite returns to Athens in disguise and gets a job as a palace servant. Palamon, meanwhile, manages to escape and by chance, the two cousins meet and recognize one another in a wood. Straightaway they arrange a fight and, while this is going on, again 'by chance', Theseus comes along with his wife and Emily. Theseus is persuaded by them not to kill the two knights and decides instead to arrange a full tournament in which they will fight for Emily's hand in marriage. Both are ecstatic at the prospect of this and we are left with the question, 'Which of them is the happier?'

Part 3: is almost wholly taken up with the preparations for the tournament a year later. This includes lavish descriptions of the building of the stadium and the temples, as well as the various prayers and petitions which the protagonists deliver to their gods: Palamon to Venus, Emily to Diana, and Arcite to Mars. Part 3 concludes with an almighty row amongst the gods, and this is only finally sorted out by Saturn.

Part 4: the final part, deals with the tournament itself. Arcite wins the tournament but, again 'by chance' (and the intervention of Saturn), he is killed before he can actually take Emily's hand. The poem therefore concludes with Duke Theseus arranging the marriage of Palamon and Emily.

This is a bare-bones summary of what happens in the poem. Even this, however, is quite a lot to take in all at once, so what you now need to do is look for its overall shape. Try to make out an obvious beginning, middle and end. In this case, the story starts with the marriage of Theseus and finishes with the marriage of Palamon and Emily. So, basically, we can say that the whole action is framed by marriages. Another, more abstract way of putting this is to say that this poem opens and closes with a vision of social 'order' and 'harmony'. Marriages often have this significance in fiction, and they usually occur at the beginnings or ends of works so as to supply neat points of arrival and departure. Here we have both: a neat and 'orderly' opening and a neat and 'orderly' close. The great middle section of the poem must therefore in some way show us how we get from one marriage to another, how we move from one vision of social 'order' and 'harmony' to another. Not surprisingly, then, the bulk of the poem is going to be about 'disorder' and 'disharmony', about the stresses and strains which cause social change. If you think about it, this is true of most works of literature. They are all built round a problem, and the problem arises because of the transition from one state to another, and the disorder and chaos which is produced along the way. This is clearly the case in *The Knight's Tale*. Most of the poem is about the trials and tribulations of the lovers, and there is the constant problem, 'Who is going to win Emily? Palamon or Arcite or neither?' This, from a story point of view, is what *The Knight's Tale* is about. It can be reduced to this problem, this question. More generally, the important thing to realize is that you can start by reducing *all* of Chaucer's tales in this way. They can all be reduced to a single problem, a single question.

The next step is to restate the situation, though still using simple terms. In a narrative sense the central problem in *The Knight's Tale* is 'Who wins Emily?', but in a more general and abstract sense the central problem is obviously one of order and disorder'. To be more precise, the whole poem is built around the *tension* between order and disorder; it constantly pulls us between the two states. We start with one vision of order, which disintegrates, and only after much confusion and suffering do we reach another, differently organized vision of order at the end. Again this is a simple and initially crude reduction of the poem's meaning. None the less, you will find the idea of a fundamental tension between order and disorder extremely useful when trying to organize your response to the poem as a whole.

So far I have stressed the essential simplicity of all the Canterbury Tales, the fact that there is always an overarching shape and an underlying idea. It must be admitted, however, that the core of the tale is usually not quite so straightforward. There is often some complicating factor, some additional problem built in. This is called the *subplot*, and most of the Canterbury Tales have one. In *The Knight's Tale*, for instance, there is the whole matter of the gods and their part in the action. How do they fit into the story and what significance are we going to attach to them? What we must do, therefore, is add a rider to our initial statement as to what the poem is about. The problem in *The Knight's Tale* is basically 'Who wins Emily?', and to this we can now add the supplementary question: '... and what part do Theseus and the gods play?' Notice that this is merely a concrete way of saying that *The Knight's Tale* has a main plot and a subplot. The more general point is that you can do this with most works, especially with longer ones where there is nearly always more than one layer of plot. Notice, however, that we have not really needed to modify our basic idea of what the poem is about in a more abstract way. It is still about the tension between order and disorder. The only difference is that we now know that this tension may be more subtle and complicated than we first thought, involving the gods as well as the human protagonists. The next step is to see how all these ideas are actually fleshed out and given life.

STEP 3   LOOKING AT CHARACTERIZATION

The characters in any work are, if you like, its 'ideas in action'. They express its interests in human form, and often, of course, the interest is in the people themselves. Consequently, early on in your analysis you will need to come to terms with the characters, how you respond to them and what ideas they express. The first thing is to establish exactly what kind of characters you are dealing with. Some characters you can believe in and get involved with as if you actually knew them personally. Many characters in traditional novels are like this. Conversely, there are characters you know that you are not really meant to believe in the same way; they are simplified versions of people, made out of a few striking elements. Many comic characters are like this, and so are many other 'caricatured', 'stylized' figures in plays and novels. In fact, you will find that quite a few fictional characters are a mixture of both types. None the less, if you start by trying to sort out which of the two basic types of character you are dealing with (simple or complex, 'rounded' or 'caricatured'), you will get your bearings on the characterization very quickly.

So what kind of characters are you presented with in *The Knight's Tale* and how are you meant to respond to them? Now, your immediate impulse might be to start chatting about Palamon, Arcite, Emily and the rest in broad terms. Your comments would probably run something like this: these characters are 'thin', 'unconvincing', 'simple', 'like people out of fairytales', and so on. All these crop up regularly as initial responses to the kind of characters in this poem and, while such comments are handy in a general way, they are obviously not very precise and do not get us very far. What you need, therefore, is a way of focusing your sense of the characterization more sharply. And to do that, your first thought should be 'Look at a passage'. In this case, look at a passage which establishes just one of the main characters so that you will then be able to see *in detail* what sort of characterization the author is using. Here, for instance, you might choose a bit from where we see Palamon falling in love with Emily (ll. 1070–111). This is the first time he is presented at any length and is a handy passage because it shows him speaking at an initial turning-point or 'crisis' in his development. Such moments commonly occur near the beginnings of works, for they are the usual way in which an author establishes his main characters and gets the action rolling. Read through the following passage about Arcite, simply asking: 'What sort of character is this, and how am I meant to respond?'

> And with that word Arcite gan espye
> Wher as this lady romed to and fro,
> And with that sighte hir beautee hurte hym so,
> That, if that Palamon was wounded sore,
> Arcite is hurt as muche as he, or moore.
> And with a sigh he seyde pitously:
> 'The fresshe beautee sleeth me sodeynly
> Of hire that rometh in the yonder place,
> And but I have hir mercy and hir grace,
> That I may seen hire atte leeste weye,
> I nam but deed; ther nis namoore to seye.'
> (ll. 1112–22)

Let's start by saying some obvious things about the way this character speaks and acts. For one thing, we see him falling in love very suddenly and his initial reaction is, to say the least, extreme. This is confirmed by the extravagant language used to describe the whole experience: her beauty 'hurt' him, just as it 'wounded' Palamon before, and the result is that he speaks 'pitously', 'with a sigh'. Clearly, Arcite and Palamon don't feel things by halves! For them, love is experienced as violence; there is extreme pain about the extreme pleasure. Nor do they keep quiet about it. Immediately he is smitten by love, Arcite feels obliged to declare it in a full-blown complaint. He tells Palamon straight out, 'The fresshe beautee sleeth me sodeynly'. The only thing that will keep him alive is the 'mercy' or 'grace' of the lady. Emily, too, is an equally extravagant creation: she is tinged with spirituality and, in the eyes of these two, is more than human. A shorthand way of referring to such characters is simply to call them 'courtly lovers'. That is, they speak about human love in the kind of sublime, quasi-religious language used by a whole host of aristocratic romantics from the twelfth century onwards. So, if you like, you could simply say that the characterization in *The Knight's Tale* is much as you would expect in a court romance concerned with 'courtly love', and you might then go on to clinch the observation by pointing to particularly sublime and quasi-religious behaviour. As far as it goes, that is fine. However, the drawback is that it presupposes you know what you are talking about when you refer to 'courtly love'. And, certainly, you should not just say, 'This belongs to the "courtly love" tradition' and leave it at that. Such statements may appear at the beginning of a response, but they beg too many questions to appear at the end.

So how are you to push your understanding of the characterization further? Once you have noticed that it belongs to such-and-such a tradition, how are you to describe its effects? Let's pick up the two basic types of characterization with which we started this section. The question is, 'Which of the two types of character is Arcite here?' Is he the kind of 'rounded' person you can get involved with as if you knew him personally, or is he a simplified version of a person, made out of a few striking elements? Put like that, the answer is obvious. Clearly, Arcite, like all the other characters in *The Knight's Tale*, belongs to the second, 'simplified' type. We may believe in him, but only within the bounds of the fiction in which he appears. Alternatively, you might say that he is not an 'internal', 'psychologically convincing character', but an obviously 'external' and 'idealized' one. Or you might say that he is presented in highly abstract and generalized terms, that we know virtually nothing about his physical appearance and any idiosyncrasies he might have, and that everything is done in a few bold and largely conventional strokes. Notice that you would have come to exactly the same conclusions if you had concentrated on the initial description of Emily (ll. 1033–55). Lovely she may be, but she is an embodiment of the springtime or 'an aungel hevenyssh' rather than an actual, particular woman. Whichever character you concentrate on, the result will be a deeper and more detailed sense not just of the characterization, but of the poem as a whole. Notice, too, that you have a specific, not just a general, notion of 'the kind of work' *The Knight's Tale* is. By looking in detail at this one character, you can demonstrate exactly what you mean by a 'court romance', and exactly what you mean by 'courtly love' and 'courtly' behaviour. What you previously had to take on trust you can now explore for yourself.

This section has been concerned with characterization, how the characters are put together. We finished up with a profile of the central characters in *The Knight's Tale* as simplified, externalized, idealized and generalized, and for good measure we can add that they are 'courtly lovers'. This tells us a lot. However, you might then wonder what possible interest we could have in characters like this. They sound so lofty and empty! And the fact is that as individuals, in isolation, they cannot hold much interest for us at all. Many characters in medieval literature are like this. They are not people that anybody could get to know in the way they know their family and friends. The question therefore remains: 'What sort of interest do they have if not as individuals?' And the answer, not surprisingly, is that they are interesting for the ideas and values they represent and for the ways they relate to one another. They demand to be considered not so much in themselves but as parts of a larger argument. It is therefore to this larger argument that we must now return.

STEP 4   DEVELOPING THE ARGUMENT

You already know what *The Knight's Tale* is about as a story: 'Who wins Emily?', with a subplot about Theseus and the gods. You also know that in a more abstract sense it is about the problem of 'order and disorder', and the tensions that exist between these two states. What you now need is a deeper and more detailed sense of these problems in action. Once again the trick is to concentrate on short but significant passages. To explore the method, we shall look in detail at a fairly substantial passage. It is where Palamon and Arcite are fighting secretly in the grove, having already escaped from the tower. This is an obvious moment of crisis', for they are interrupted by the arrival of Theseus, out hunting with his wife and Emily, and the whole action takes a dramatic turn as a result. Read over these lines for yourself, trying to see how the tensions and conflicts amongst these characters give life to the general 'order/disorder' argument:

> Ther nas no good day, ne no saluyng,
> But streight, withouten word or rehersyng,   1650
> Everich of hem heelp for to armen oother
> As freendly as he were his owene brother;
> And after that, with sharpe speres stronge
> They foynen ech at oother wonder longe.
> Thou myghtest wene that this Palamon   1655
> In his fightyng were a wood leon,
> And as a crueel tigre was Arcite;
> As wilde bores gonne they to smyte,
> That frothen whit as foom for ire wood.
> Up to the ancle foghte they in hir blood.   1660
> And in this wise I lete hem fightyng dwelle,
> And forth I wole of Theseus yow telle.
> The destinee, ministre general,
> That executeth in the world over al
> The purveiaunce that God hath seyn biforn,   1665
> So strong it is that, though the world had sworn
> The contrarie of a thyng by ye or nay,
> Yet somtyme it shal fallen on a day

That falleth nat eft withinne a thousand yeer.
For certeinly, oure appetites heer,   1670
Be it of werre, or pees, or hate, or love,
Al is this reuled by the sighte above.
This mene I now by myghty Theseus,
That for to hunten is so desirus,
And namely at the grete hert in May,   1675
That in his bed ther daweth hym no day
That he nys clad, and redy for to ryde
With hunte and horn and houndes hym bisyde.
For in his huntyng hath he swich delit
That it is al his joye and appetit   1680
To been hymself the grete hertes bane,
For after Mars he serveth now Dyane.
      Cleer was the day, as I have toold er this,
And Theseus with alle joye and blis,
With his Ypolita, the faire queene,   1685
And Emelye, clothed al in grene,
On huntyng be they riden roially.
And to the grove that stood ful faste by,
In which ther was an hert, as men hym tolde,
Duc Theseus the streight wey hath holde.   1690
And to the launde he rideth hym ful right,
For thider was the hert wont have his flight,
And over a brook, and so forth on his weye.
This duc wol han a cours at hym or tweye
With houndes swiche as that hym list comaunde. 1695
      And whan this duc was come unto the launde,
Under the sonne he looketh, and anon
He was war of Arcite and Palamon,
That foughten breme, as it were bores two.
The brighte swerdes wenten to and fro   1700
So hidously that with the leeste strook
It semed as it wolde felle an ook.
But what they were, no thyng he ne woot.
This duc his courser with his spores smoot,
And at a stert he was bitwix hem two,   1705
And pulled out a swerd, and cride, 'Hoo!
Namoore, up peyne of lesynge of youre heed!
By myghty Mars, he shal anon be deed
That smyteth any strook that I may seen.
But telleth me what myster men ye been,   1710
That been so hardy for to fighten heere
Withouten juge or oother officere,
As it were in a lystes roially.'
          (ll. 1649–1713)

The first thing to do with a longish passage like this is to break it down into manageable bits. Do this much as you break down a scene in a play into separate speeches and movements. Here, the passage falls naturally into three sections: the fight between Palamon and Arcite (ll. 1649–62), a link passage on 'Destiny' and coincidences (ll. 1663–72), and Theseus's interruption (ll. 1673–1713). Then you need to think about each of these incidents in detail, in each case asking yourself what qualities or ideas are prominent, and trying to see how one character contrasts with another.

Let's look at the first incident, the fight between Palamon and Arcite. The action here is characteristically extreme. The two cousins start off by arming one another with loving care ('freendly as he were his owene brother'), then suddenly they are thrusting at one another ferociously with their spears. The prominent ideas are therefore obvious: love then hate or, if you like, peace then war. Either way, the two knights represent what we might call the two poles of medieval chivalry. What is significant, however, is that these two qualities are presented as deeply destructive and in conflict. This is particularly stressed in the imagery of wild animals: Palamon fights like a mad lion, Arcite like a cruel tiger, and both of them attack like wild boars frothing with rage. Taken as a whole, then, the meaning of this incident is fairly clear. You might want to call it 'chivalric disorder', or 'love and war in conflict'. But, whatever you call it, the point is that you would have moved from the simple narrative level (the fight to decide the question 'Who wins Emily?') to the more abstract level of the poem's argument. That argument, you can now demonstrate, is not only about a general tension between 'order and disorder'; it is more particularly about the destructive contradictions within medieval chivalry, about how, beneath the civilized surface of chivalry with its codes of knightly behaviour and brotherly love, there are dangerous and disturbing forces at work, seen in the bloodiness and brutality of fighting. Part of the problem, you can say, is the institution of knighthood itself, with its stress on physical violence, and by posing the problem in this way, you can transform a merely 'descriptive' reading into a genuinely 'critical' one. This is an important distinction, because the most common fault in students' work is mere description and 'storytelling' without getting at the larger ideas and organization of the piece.

Now you can go through the same procedure with the rest of the passage, only more briefly. Again, all you do is look for the issues expressed by the characters, the argument embodied in the action, and again you know in advance that these will in some way relate to the overall tension between 'order and disorder'. So, let's not just *describe* the rest of the passage; let's *discuss* it.

The most obvious feature to remark on is the contrast between Theseus and the two knights: he is the very image of power, dignity and control, whereas they seem no more than a pair of unruly and ineffectual hooligans. Notice the dramatic effect of Theseus's arrival. He parades onto the scene in great state and in control of a pack of hounds, and as soon as he sees the two knights knocking lumps out of one another he intervenes: what are they doing fighting so wildly and in secret 'Withouten juge or oother officere, / As it were in a Iystes roially?' Their biggest fault, it seems, is that they are fighting without due order and ceremony. The underlying tension is therefore obvious. Theseus represents power and order, ceremony and 'civilized' behaviour; Palamon and Arcite represent the reverse. All of them are knights, and yet they give us very different images of knighthood. Again we return to the poem's main ideas, but with a much richer and more discriminating sense of how they are worked out in practice.

There is one other large idea in the passage and we need, finally, to take that on board too. This is the matter of 'destiny'. It is prominent in ll. 1663–72, the linking section referred to earlier, and because these lines are already fairly abstract you will have no trouble spotting the ideas. All you need to do, therefore, is ask how 'destiny' fits into the argument. For instance, the basic message of these lines is that 'everything is for the best'. No matter how chaotic it might look, everything is 'reuled by the sighte above'. However, you may still be puzzled how this fits into the argument on 'order and disorder', so you need to take another look at the text. In fact, if you do so, you will see that the link between Theseus and 'destinee' is quite explicit: 'This mene I now by myghty Theseus'. Duke Theseus arrives not just 'by chance' or 'because of destiny', but virtually as 'destinee'. Unfortunately, most students fail to relate this idea of 'Theseus as destiny' to the other ideas in the poem, and consequently, they have a confused rather than enriched sense of its argument. And yet, if you do try to tie 'destinee' into the main issues, you finish up with a set of questions which are sophisticated and teasing rather than merely baffling. For instance, if the world is organized according to some providential or divine plan ('the sighte above'), then how come there is such disorder and conflict in the world? If everything is for the best', why is life often such a mess? In other words, to return to the terms in which we have constantly couched this debate, how can you have a notion of 'order' that embraces a notion of 'disorder'?

In Chaucer's longer and more complex tales you need to look at more than one central passage to grasp the full range of the argument. *The Knight's Tale* is such a tale, and therefore I will move forward to another passage, which comes from Part 3 (ll. 2271–365). This deals with Emily, the only major character we have not yet considered in this section, and shows her visiting the temple of Diana just before the tournament. Notice that I go through exactly the same steps as with the previous passage. First I break it down into manageable bits, and then I look for the way in which the underlying contrasts and tension are built up. In fact, Emily's visit to the temple falls readily into three sections: her preparations, her prayer, and Diana's response (ll. 2271–94, 2295–330, 2331–65). The significance of the first bit is clear enough. It establishes Emily as a devout servant of the goddess, going through the proper rituals as she should. The second bit develops this aspect. In her prayer she respectfully yet firmly asks that she may remain a maid (Diana was the goddess of chastity) or, failing that, that she may have the knight who loves her most. All this is useful because it fills out our sense of a central but otherwise shadowy figure. To the earlier image of Emily as the beautiful, springlike and merciful 'loved one', we can now add her quality of dutiful piety, as well as her independence (notice that she opts first and foremost for chastity and so far *neither* of her would-be lovers). Now look at the third and climactic section of the passage, Diana's response. What kind of tension can you see between Emily and the goddess Diana, and how is it finally resolved?

> The fires brenne upon the auter cleere,
> Whil Emelye was thus in hir preyere.
> But sodeynly she saugh a sighte queynte,
> For right anon oon of the fyres queynte,
> And quyked agayn, and after that anon
> That oother fyr was queynt and al agon;
> And as it queynte it made a whistelynge,
> As doon thise wete brondes in hir brennynge,
> And at the brondes ende out ran anon
> As it were blody dropes many oon;
> For which so soore agast was Emelye
> That she was wel ny mad, and gan to crye,
> For she ne wiste what it signyfied;
> But oonly for the feere thus hath she cried,
> And weep that it was pitee for to heere.

And therwithal Dyane gan appeere,
With bowe in honde, right as an hunteresse,
And seyde, 'Doghter, stynt thyn hevynesse.
Among the goddes hye it is affermed,
And by eterne word writen and confermed,
Thou shalt ben wedded unto oon of tho
That han for thee so muchel care and wo;
But unto which of hem I may nat telle.
Farwel, for I ne may no lenger dwelled ... '
(ll. 2331–54)

Diana's response is obviously meant to be puzzling and teasing: one altar fire dips and recovers, and then the other goes out completely. The goddess's spoken response is a bit clearer: Emily cannot remain a maid, she says, and must be married to one of the knights, though to which one the goddess will not say. In effect, then, Emily is turned down on her first petition (to remain a maid), and not much enlightened on her second (which knight she is going to marry). The overall impression is of a devoted servant of the goddess being overruled and kept in ignorance. That is the basis of the contrast in this passage and how the tension is resolved. Now think about the larger implications. What does all this tell us about the gods and their part in the poem's argument? Well, the fact is that the gods are always doing this sort of thing in the poem, expressing themselves in riddles and being generally mystifying. They also have a habit of laying the law down arbitrarily, without giving any reasons. You might therefore say that the gods play both a good and a bad part in the action, that they are, in fact, both a principle of 'order' and a principle of 'disorder'. Again, the knack is not only to know this, but to be able to *show* it from detailed analysis of a significant passage.

There are other issues you could illustrate from this brief encounter between Emily and the goddess Diana. You could, for instance, point up the contrast between her prayer and those of Palamon and Arcite to either side. In that case, you would notice a number of similarities as well as differences. Both Palamon and Arcite observe the rituals due to their respective gods, Venus and Mars, just as Emily does to Diana. The two knights also make specific requests: Palamon asks Venus to help him win Emily's 'love', while Arcite asks Mars for 'victory' in the tournament (believing that winning the tournament automatically means winning Emily). At this point, however, the contrast with Emily becomes clear. Palamon and Arcite actually get what they ask for, but Emily *does not*. Palamon does get Emily's 'love', and Arcite does get 'victory', whereas Emily *does not* get her first choice: to remain a maid and marry neither of them. Again the principle of contrast is central, and it is this that we look for, all the time trying to relate it to larger issues of the poem. The cruel edge to the gods' notion of 'order' we already know about. But notice, too, that there is something in the overall shaping of events which arranges things so that Emily can never get what she wants. The tale centres on the question 'Who wins Emily?', or the rather different question 'Who does Emily choose?' Clearly, left to her own devices, Emily would choose nobody and that would result in a totally different poem.

Now, you might think that all this is a lot of unnecessary fuss about Emily. You might insist that the poem is mainly about the men, so really there's nothing to get upset about. However, that would be to miss the critical point. For it is only by thinking of alternative ways in which the work might be organized, by thinking of *alternative* questions that the work might address, that you can really see it for what it is. A text is a kind of 'problem-solving' device, setting itself specific problems and then going about solving them. Obviously, you are going to have a much clearer idea of the specific problem and solution if you can think of slightly different problems, or even entirely different solutions. In this case, all I have done is slightly shift the premises on which *The Knight's Tale* is built. However, what shows up is that the tale is written from a male point of view ('Who wins Emily?'), and not from a female point of view ('Who does Emily choose?'). The effect is to illuminate both the issues and the organization of the poem as a whole. In fact, for many students the point at which they begin to think about alternative readings is the point at which their understanding of the work really takes off.

With a long and complex work it can be difficult to see the argument as a whole, from beginning to end. Even if you start off (as this book suggests) with a clear idea of where you are going, you can still get lost and confused from time to time. The usual thing that happens is that you may see it all in outline to start with and then, as you build in more detail and more subtlety, the outline becomes blurred. That is why it is important to draw your sense of the overall argument together at the end. Not surprisingly, the best way of doing this is actually to look at a significant passage from near the end of the text, one which seems to tie everything together. In *The Knight's Tale* the obvious choice is the final speech of Theseus. It offers itself as a grand summary of the tale and will also allow us to take a final look at the subplot and our question, 'What part do Theseus and the gods play?'

By now the procedure for looking at a passage will be becoming familiar. Break it down into manageable bits and then look for the underlying contrast or tension. Theseus's final speech is quite long and a fascinating mishmash of arguments and opinions. I suggest you read over the whole thing for yourself (ll. 2987–3098), trying to see that it is basically an attempt to reconcile two not particularly reconcilable points of view. For instance, notice that Theseus opens with the confident assertion that everything is for the best (linked by a 'faire cheyne of love' – l. 2988). However, he closes with the cynical advice to put up with things because the world is really terrible ('maken vertu of necessitee' in 'this foule prisoun of this lyf' – ll. 3042, 3061). This leaves you with a choice. Either you can choose the optimistic part of Theseus's summary and project that back onto the rest of the poem, or you can choose the pessimistic part and see the rest of the poem as basically nasty and vicious – for all its superficial order and glamour. Quite simply, Theseus leaves us with a divided summary which points to divided possibilities in the poem as a whole.

You will find a similar tension within the final marriage scene (ll. 3075–end). Marriages are a standard way of 'rounding off' fictions in that they allow the author to tie the loose ends of the story together. They suggest that a kind of social harmony has been achieved. In practice, however, the marriage scene usually veils a number of persistent contradictions as well, and again *The Knight's Tale* is a good example. At the end of the tale Emily is married to Palamon, and Theseus (as usual) plays a big part in the proceedings. If you like, you can see him as the embodiment of benevolent 'destiny' and 'order'. However, you also know that Theseus's role is more complicated than that. For instance, notice that it is not primarily a romantic consideration which prompts him to arrange the marriage between Palamon and Emily. It is political, to cement relations between Athens and Thebes:

To have with certein contrees alliaunce,
And have fully of Thebans obeisaunce.

(ll. 2973–4)

This is where the contradictions and tensions come in again. Officially, and in theory, it is an 'alliaunce' (suggesting something freely entered into); in practice it is 'obeisaunce' ('obedience' or 'servitude', the result of Theseus's conquest). The marriage between Palamon the Theban and Emily the Athenian is designed to set the seal on this. Now think again about that other apparently 'orderly' marriage at the beginning of the poem, the marriage between Theseus and the Amazon Hippolyta. This functions in a very similar way. Theseus had 'conquered al the regne of Femenye' ('conquered all the nation of the Amazons' – l. 866) and then set the seal on his conquest by marrying the Amazon queen. Thus, both at the beginning and at the end of the poem, marriage is used as a conventional sign of 'order', and yet that 'order' is really a cover for 'conquest' and the exercise of power. All this is challenging stuff. It may prompt you to think afresh about the middle of the poem. Remember how Emily visits the temple of Diana and is overruled by Diana, and she in turn is overruled by 'th' eterne word' of the other gods. The message at the centre as well as both ends of the poem is therefore clear: arbitrary power is passed off as though it were divinely ordained order; conquest is presented as though it were freely agreed to.

Such a conclusion may sound difficult and demanding – and in a sense it is. This is a difficult and demanding poem. However, notice that all we are really doing is developing and extending the argument that has been with us all the way through the analysis. Obviously the 'order/disorder' problem is not as simple as it may have at first appeared. We must therefore avoid a simplistic response, as though 'order' is necessarily good and 'disorder' is necessarily bad. For one thing, the gods complicate our view of the automatic goodness of 'order', and so does Theseus. In fact, we have just seen with Theseus and the gods that what we are really talking about is the power for both good and ill, and that therefore we need some such term to describe the problems explored in this tale.

In short, we started with an argument about 'order and disorder' and have developed it into one about 'power'. But, whatever term you choose, it should at least be clear that the analysis has developed over the course of critical reading. It has built on, and to some extent gone beyond, the premises with which we started. This is what should happen in the course of a reading which is progressively more detailed and discriminating: you return to where you started, but with an enriched sense of the work and its possibilities.

We now have the core of an analysis, so let's summarize how it has been built up. First, in Steps 1 and 2 we established the kind of work we were dealing with, its overall shape and its main ideas. In

Step 3 we got down to the argument in detail. We did this by concentrating on a central passage and trying to see the characters as 'ideas in action', looking for the contrasts or tensions and building up a sense of the argument from them. These we then related back to the larger idea of 'order versus disorder'. After that, because this is a lengthy text, we focused in Step 4 on two other crises in action. This allowed us to take in the other main characters and get a more comprehensive sense of the argument, again working through detailed exploration of tensions within small but significant passages, and again relating these back to the main ideas in the poem as a whole. Finally, in order to draw the whole argument together, we took a close look at the end of the poem. There we saw how Chaucer 'rounds off' the tale and draws his materials together. We also saw how some of the fundamental contradictions and tensions within the work persist to the very end, and that the work explores problems but does not necessarily solve them. By this stage we had become aware that the main issues within the poem were basically the same as we started with, but by no means as simple as we might have thought at first. Overall, then, the really hard work of the analysis is done. All we do now is build on this, extending and refining it in a number of ways. Following the pattern established in Chapter 2, in Step 5 we explore the tale's relationship to the teller; in Step 6, its relationship to actual life at the time; and in Step 7 we take a closer look at the poem's style.

STEP 5   RELATING THE TALE TO ITS TELLER

The Knight's Tale, like all the other Canterbury Tales, is a tale told by a fictional character. It therefore makes sense if we clarify our notion of this particular character, and then look for signs of him in the tale he tells. Doing this should throw some more light on the precise choice and treatment of material. We shall illustrate the method with the Knight, but you can do exactly the same with any of the pilgrims.

The first thing to do is turn to *The General Prologue* and see how the pilgrim is presented there. You might then look at how he or she is presented in the 'linking sections' which coordinate *The Canterbury Tales* as a whole. For instance, the Knight in *The General Prologue* is the first of the pilgrims to be described (ll. 43–78), just as his tale is the first to be told. Presumably, this is because he is highest in social rank and one of the oldest pilgrims. Once you have established the significance of the pilgrim's 'placing' in this way, you should look at the description itself. Again, you will get to the core of the passage if you look for the underlying tension, what makes the pilgrim tick. In the Knight's case you will notice that two things are emphasized: he has done almost nothing but fight in campaigns and tournaments ('he loved chivalrie'), and yet he also seems modest and pious ('as meeke as is a mayde'). These two aspects of him, his war-loving yet unassuming nature, are not altogether easy to square with one another. We might therefore say that it is this tension or contradiction which makes him interesting. Similarly, critics often point to the fact that it is not clear whether the Knight fought for his faith, or personal glory or for money. We cannot be sure whether he was an idealist or a mercenary. But, whichever way you incline, the issue remains the same. There is an underlying tension or potential contradiction in the presentation of the Knight. The impression we get of him is essentially ideal ('a verray, parfit gentil knyght'), and yet there is at least a suspicion that this may be a flawed image. You will find that a similar tension between 'ideal' and 'real' aspects underlies the presentation of most of the pilgrims in *The General Prologue*.

The next step is simply to ask if all this adds anything to our view of the tale. Obviously *The Knight's Tale*, a court romance featuring war and a tournament, is the right kind of work for a man who 'loved chivalrie'. It may also be that the emphasis on aged and patriarchal figures in *The Knight's Tale* (Theseus, Saturn and Egeus) says something about how the Knight sees himself. But, really, the main thing to hold on to is the fact that the Knight's image is basically ideal, yet also perhaps flawed and suspect. Simply transfer that insight from the teller to the tale and see what happens. You may even come to the conclusion that the image of chivalry in *The Knight's Tale* is precisely that: 'ideal, yet also perhaps flawed and suspect'. For instance, consider the description of the Knight as 'true, perfect and noble', and ask if it will also do to describe the vision of love and war we get in his tale. If you concentrate on the idealized and 'orderly' side of things, clearly everything is 'true, perfect and noble'. But if you concentrate on the 'disorderly' side of things, the arbitrary exercise of power which masquerades as law and order, then clearly it is not. Either way, you should now see that relating the tale to its teller can be both interesting and illuminating.

There is another important aspect of the teller–tale relationship you should be alert to. This has to do with 'irony' (also see Chapter 8, pp. 180–1). *Irony* occurs when you are not sure whether to take what you are being told at face value, when more is meant than meets the eye. Irony is common in Chaucer, though it is not found in every line, as some critics would have you believe. For instance, notice that the Knight says he will not describe Arcite's funeral in detail (ll. 2920–66), but then proceeds to pile detail on detail, each one prefaced by the claim that he is not doing it! Rhetorically, this sort of thing is called 'occupatio', the device of 'not saying', and here it is carried to extravagant and maybe ironic lengths. In this case, perhaps you do not agree that the teller is being ironic, or that both teller and tale illustrate a kind of 'flawed idealism'. That is fine, as long as you argue your case from the text. The main thing is that you should at least explore the teller–tale relationship and see what light it has to throw on the choice and treatment of material in your text.

STEP 6   SEEING THE TEXT IN CONTEXT

In this section we stand back from the text and try to see it in a wider literary and historical context. All the previous sections have, as it were, looked 'inside' the text, at its story, characters and argument. But it is equally important to look 'outside' the text to see how all these things related to actual life in the late fourteenth century. Such materials tend to get presented as mere 'background', so I shall suggest some ways in which they can be brought into the 'foreground' of your analysis, where they belong. In fact, the critical use of related literary and historical material is what distinguishes the 'study' of literature from a mere 'reading' of it.

What are the most obvious differences between Chaucer's treatment and that in his literary sources? What do these differences tell us about his precise focus and emphasis? Questions such as these can be addressed to any of Chaucer's texts where the sources are known and they always provide illuminating answers, as we shall see now with *The Knight's Tale*. *The Knight's Tale* has two main sources: Boccaccio's *Story of Theseus* in his *Teseide* (c. 1340), and Boethius's *Consolation of Philosophy* (sixth century). The first provides the main story for the court romance; the second provides the moral-tract material for some of the long speeches. Comparison with both of these shows clearly what Chaucer chose to cut or emphasize, and therefore throws a lot of light on his sense of what he was doing. For instance, Chaucer reduced Boccaccio's story by almost two-thirds and cut out a great deal of epic material dealing with the conquests of Theseus, especially at the beginning. The result is therefore a much sharper focus on the ethical and romantic problem: 'Who wins Emily?' Chaucer also 'flattened out' Boccaccio's characters, making them much more typical and less individual. Comparison shows that Palamon and Arcite are much less differentiated in the English version, and Chaucer's Emily is altogether more shadowy and insubstantial than Boccaccio's Emilia. In fact, this is unusual for Chaucer, whose characters are generally more, not less, individual than those in his source. The comparison with Boccaccio is therefore emphatic proof that Chaucer was more interested in ethical predicaments than individual personalities in *The Knight's Tale*.

Similar interests and emphases are confirmed by comparison with Boethius's *Consolation of Philosophy*. More information on this work and Chaucer's widespread use of it can be found on pp. 14, 209. Here it is enough to note that the Latin work is about a man in prison who eventually works through to an optimistic view of life – a belief that, despite all appearances to the contrary, everything is ultimately for the best. Speeches such as those by Arcite in ll. 1223ff. and by Theseus in ll. 2987ff. are heavily indebted to Boethius. The crucial difference in *The Knight's Tale* is that these speeches are often given a bitter or cynical edge, and that the larger pattern of events – especially the action of the gods – does not give the same ground for optimism. Again, this is an insight which both enriches and reinforces the experience of reading the text. Chaucer clearly saw the problem of 'order' as genuinely problematic, and in his framing of Boethian materials there is even more reason to doubt that 'everything is for the best'.

Now that you have a wider literary view of the poem, it makes sense to place it in its wider social and historical context. This, too, helps show up the distinctive emphases of *The Knight's Tale*; what Chaucer said, as well as what he omitted to say. All this has a lot to do with what I have called 'Chaucer the man' and 'Chaucer the narrator' in the 'Four Chaucers' section of Chapter 1, which will help you with the relevant aspects of his biography. There you will find, for instance, that Chaucer was a diplomat and senior civil servant writing with a court and upper-class audience in mind. This affected what he wrote and how he wrote it almost as much as you are affected when writing for a specific teacher or a specific exam. So, here are some precise suggestions on how to bring this 'background' material into the 'foreground' of your analysis. There are similar guidelines in Chapter 4 for other frequently studied Canterbury Tales. In each case you will see that you are invited to start with the text, move out into the context, and then move back to the text with a fuller sense of its historical significance.

Chaucer knew about chivalry in practice, as well as in theory and from books. In 1360 he was on active service as a squire in the Hundred Years' War with France. He would have been involved in battles and sieges, and was himself (like Palamon and Arcite) taken prisoner. This is significant because Chaucer had plenty of opportunity to see that medieval warfare, for all its glamour, was frequently brutal and vicious. Even court chroniclers such as Froissart had difficulty in disguising the glorified hooliganism of Edward the Black Prince (one of the sons of Edward III) and other knights as they rampaged round France in search of plunder. Prince Edward's merciless slaughter of every man, woman and child in Limoges (1370) was simply one of the more spectacular atrocities in a spectacularly atrocious war. The critical point is that *The Knight's Tale*, unlike many court romances, does not wholly disguise this brutal aspect of chivalry. Alongside the traditional image of Theseus as a 'good ruler', it gives hints of the kind of total warfare he engaged in. Thebes, like Limoges and like the towns referred to in the description of the temple of Mars, is totally devastated after Theseus's siege:

> And by assaut he wan the citee after,
> And rente adoun bothe wall and sparre and rafter ...
> And dide with al the contree as hym leste.
>
>   (ll. 989–1004)

Similarly, Theseus's official motive for conquering Thebes was to secure the return of their husbands' bodies to some noble ladies, but in practice it was little more than an excuse for plunder. Nor does Chaucer ignore the real consequences of such conquest: soldiers feverishly picking through heaps of the dead and dying in search of valuables (ll. 1005–98). Critically, it is particularly worth noting that historically convincing details such as this are not at the centre of *The Knight's Tale*. They are on its edges and picked up in passing. Consequently, they disturb but do not completely destroy the idealized image of chivalry promoted by most of the narrative. As a courtier addressing a court for whom war was a normal aspect of foreign policy, Chaucer would have been 'indiscreet' to say more – and many of his aristocratic contemporaries said less.

Obviously a court writer was on safer ground when it came to the more ceremonial and 'playful' aspects of chivalry. Chaucer was particularly well-informed in this area too. As Clerk of the King's Works between 1389 and 1391 he was responsible for furnishing royal palaces and chapels, as well as for organizing two large tournaments. Some such experience clearly informs the practical eye for painters' and carvers' skills in the descriptions of the temples in Part 3 of *The Knight's Tale*, as well as the convincing picture of the workmanlike bustle surrounding the tournament in Part 4. One other aspect of 'Chaucer the man' should be added to those of soldier and administrator in relation to this poem: Chaucer the diplomat. In 1381 Chaucer was in France engaged in marriage negotiations for Richard II and a daughter of the French king. In fact, the marriage was not concluded, but it reminds us that Chaucer was well aware of the political rather than the romantic function of royal marriages. He knew well that dynastic marriages such as those of Theseus and Hippolyta and of Palamon and Emily in *The Knight's Tale* were meant to set the seal on political 'alliances', and that these in turn were often a polite name for what was really 'conquest'. In other words, you can detect a strong undercurrent of court diplomacy as well as court romance in *The Knight's Tale*. The reasons for it are to be found in court facts, suitably trimmed with court fictions.

Here is a final observation on this text in context. It was fortunate for Chaucer that he was out of the country in 1381. He almost certainly missed the Peasants' Revolt, the main political event of late-fourteenth-century England. The passing reference to it in *The Knight's Tale* is therefore all the more interesting. In l. 2459 there is a solitary mention of 'the cherles rebellyng' ('rebelling peasants'), and this is lumped in with a medley of violent and apparently accidental disasters such as drowning and plague, as well as some, such as strangling and 'derke tresons', which are more intentional. All of these are explained as the results of Saturn's influence. They are all, including the rebelling peasants, seen as inevitably diseased and destructive. It goes without saying that this is a ruling-class view of the Peasants' Revolt. 'Cherles rebellyng' were a constant anxiety and a dangerous subject at court. The fact that they were referred to at all is a measure of the anxiety, while the fact that the reference is brief and disparaging is a measure of the danger.

Overall, then, the value of a contextual approach is that it allows you to see the wider implications of a text. In this case, it has shown that Chaucer had wide experience of late medieval life and books, but that he also worked within literary, social and historical limits. It is therefore a way of seeing both the breadth *and* the limitations of Chaucer's achievement.

STEP 7   ANALYSING THE STYLE

In a sense, all your analysis has been concerned with the style of the poem. Everything depends on a close reading of the words. However, sometimes you need to know how to describe the language itself in more detail. This section offers some guidelines for approaching the style of *The Knight's Tale* in particular, and *The Canterbury Tales* in general.

The most obvious thing about the language of *The Knight's Tale* is that it is organized as verse. In fact, like much of Chaucer's poetry, this poem is written in what are called 'decasyllabic rhyming couplets'. This may sound terrifyingly technical until you pause to work it out for yourself. For instance, here are the first four lines of the poem:

> Whilom, as olde stories tellen us,
> Ther was a duc that highte Theseus;
> Of Atthenes he was lord and governour,
> And in his tyme swich a conquerour … .

The 'decasyllabic' aspect of the verse form simply comes from the fact that there are around ten syllables to the line ('deca- from the Greek for 'ten'). The 'couplet' aspect is easy enough to spot too: 'us' / 'Theseus', 'governour' / 'conquerour' come in rhyming pairs at the ends of adjacent lines. You will find the same pattern wherever you look in the poem. It provides a pervasive music and means that all the language is fundamentally harmonious and 'orderly'. Incidentally, notice that I have picked up the term 'orderly'. This is to demonstrate that, even at the level of the verse form, you can tie the matters of style into the larger issues of the poem. 'Order' and 'disorder' were key terms when describing the overall tension within the work. They will do just as well to describe the tension within its language. The 'disorderly' aspect of the language arises from the fact that we are also aware of the variable rhythms of a speaking voice. The *rhythm* is flexible and 'disorderly'; the *verse form* is regular and 'orderly', and the play of the one against the other results in a tension. It is as simple as that. The opening lines of *The General Prologue* use the same verse form and are analysed in a similar way in Chapter 2 (see pp. 42–3).

While studying your tale, you may well come across the comment that it is written in 'high' or 'middle' or 'low' style. This, too, is not that mystifying when you get down to it. Like most medieval poetry, Chaucer's poems can be placed in so far as they are written at one of these stylistic levels, also sometimes called 'elevated' (high), 'plain' (middle) and 'colloquial' (low). In practice, Chaucer frequently *mixes* his styles, just as he mixes his basic story types. None the less, it is handy to identify which of these three styles is dominant in the text you are studying. Again the principle can be illustrated from the first four lines of *The Knight's Tale*. Would you say that the language used there is 'elevated', 'plain' or 'colloquial'? One of these you can obviously discount straightaway. Whatever else it is, the language is certainly not 'colloquial' or 'low'. It is not particularly idiomatic or chatty. Nor, you might now add, is it particularly elaborate or 'elevated'. In fact everything is fairly clear and straightforward, what you might very well call 'plain'. The opening lines of a text often set the tone for the whole in this way, and they do so for *The Knight's Tale*. Its characteristic level of style is 'middle', and in this respect it is characteristic of the most common style in *The Canterbury Tales* as a whole. Such clear, controlled and yet not especially formal language is the backbone of Chaucer's narrative art.

Having established the routine style of the poem in this way, the next thing is to look for any divergences from it. Are there any places where the style changes and becomes noticeably 'higher' or 'lower', more or less formal? Look back at Arcite's speech quoted on p. 53 and try to place that on a scale running from 'formal/elevated/high' to 'informal/colloquial/low'. In fact, the speech is so full of abstract words such as 'mercy' and 'grace', and there is such a poise and sophistication about the sentence structure, that you can only call the style 'formal' or 'elevated'. The thing to notice now is that these changes of style do not occur haphazardly. They are always accompanied by some change of content or attitude. In this case, the stylistic shift in Arcite's speech is a clear sign that he sees both Emily and himself in a sublimely idealistic way. In other words, he is an idealist and an extravagantly 'courtly lover', and you can pick that up from the way he speaks. The same applies to shifts into 'colloquial' or 'low' style in the poem. These too are accompanied by shifts in attitude. One such descent into blunt and down-to-earth language is where Theseus draws attention to the idiocy of Palamon and Arcite's secret fight in the grove (ll. 1808–10). He points out that Emily knew no more of all this wild carry-on, by God, than does a cuckoo or a hare, and the effect is obviously deflating – particularly because of the reference to traditionally daft animals. The larger critical point is that the idealism of the court romance is not immune from sceptical, even cynical, comment. And, again, all we are really doing is demonstrating that changes in style are accompanied by changes in attitude.

The whole matter of style in Chaucer's poetry can be summed up quite simply. Chaucer cultivates a 'mixed' and 'varied' vision of life because he seems to be as interested in 'disorder' as in 'order'. That is why he often mixes one story type with another, and why he also mixes styles within the same work. By and large, Chaucer favours a fairly clear and unpretentious narrative style, what we have called 'plain' or 'middle'. But he also draws on a range of 'high/elevated' and 'low/colloquial' styles, and these are always used to point up some change in attitude. Most of his stories bob along quite amiably, but they are also punctuated by passages of lofty idealism, or interrupted by some utterly down-to-earth home truth. The first sign of all this is always a change in the language, so the detailed study of style is simply another way of approaching the poem as a whole.

CONCLUSION

Students often conclude essays with a final paragraph which sounds remarkably like their first. They restate their aims and objectives, simply substituting the formula 'In conclusion, we have seen that …' for the opening 'In this essay I intend to show that …'. The result is tediously predictable, so I shall try to avoid making the same mistake. The method for approaching one of the Canterbury Tales was stated at the beginning of this chapter, and I have illustrated its detailed application to *The Knight's Tale*. It may be helpful if I conclude by summing up the whole method as clearly as possible:

1. Start by sorting out the 'kind' of work you are dealing with.
2. Get a firm sense of the tale's overall shape and main ideas early on.
3. Concentrate on one main character, trying to see what 'kind' of character it is and how you are meant to respond.

4. Develop your argument by approaching all the characters as 'ideas in action', as parts of a larger pattern of contrasts and tensions.
5. Look at the narrator and see what light this throws on the tale he or she tells.
6. Consider the literary and historical context of the work, trying to see the distinctive emphases and omissions of Chaucer's text.
7. Always base your analysis on close reading of short passages, and make sure you can analyse a passage for its style.

4

STUDY FRAMEWORKS FOR *THE CANTERBURY TALES*

The method for approaching one of the Canterbury Tales is set out in the previous chapter. There it is applied to *The Knight's Tale*, and you should turn to the sections in that chapter if you want a more detailed demonstration of any of the steps. We go through exactly the same steps with each of the following tales. The tales of the Miller, Wife of Bath, Clerk, Merchant, Franklin, Pardoner and Nun's Priest have been featured first simply because they tend to be the ones studied most often. Those of the Reeve, Prioress, Friar and Summoner are treated later as they tend to be less studied. All these tales share many concerns and strategies, which is why I sometimes invite you to look across from one to another and make comparisons. Further comparisons are invited across the whole of Chaucer's work in Chapter 8.

THE MILLER'S TALE

Step 1   What kind of work am I studying?

The Miller's Tale is first and foremost a funny story. It will therefore help if you start with a firm idea of what kind of story it is and what makes it funny. *The Miller's Tale* is basically a fabliau, a short story built round an extended joke or trick (see pp. 9–10). Like other fabliaux, it is characterized by a fair amount of raw sex and knockabout violence, all set in a context of tradesmen, minor clerics and students. In fact, Chaucer calls this story a 'cherles tale' (a churl's or serf's tale) and offers it as a lively contrast to the high-class 'noble storie' just told by the Knight. You will find that this sense of contrast and variety is also carried over into *The Miller's Tale* itself. Here Chaucer adds a dash of court romance to its traditional opposite, the low-life fabliau. The result is that we see his student and church clerk as courtly lovers, and they woo their 'lady' (a carpenter's wife) with a wonderfully improbable kind of extravagance. Overall, then, you should expect a tale which is rich, varied and funny.

Step 2   What is it about?

Many of the effects of *The Miller's Tale* depend on slick plotting and fine timing. You therefore need a particularly firm grasp of what goes on. The knack is to see that the plot is built round just two interlocking tricks. The first trick is played on old John, the carpenter, by his young wife Alison and their lodger, a student called Nicholas. They persuade the carpenter that a second Noah's flood is on the way and that they should all sleep in tubs in the loft so as to avoid drowning. Once John is asleep, Alison and Nicholas promptly sneak downstairs to make love. This is the first and main trick, and you might call it 'How the carpenter was fooled' or the 'Noah's flood trick'.

The second trick is neatly fitted into the first. It involves Nicholas, Alison, and another character called Absolon, a church clerk, and makes another 'triangle' of characters interlocking with the first. Absolon is a stylish, but rather affected individual who is also after the carpenter's wife. The very night that she and the student are in bed, Absolon comes round to woo her beneath the window, singing songs and asking for a kiss. Alison responds by sticking her backside out. In the dark Absolon kisses it and only realizes later what he has done. When he hears the general merriment in the bedroom ('Tehee!') he flies into a rage and decides to take swift revenge. Borrowing a red-hot plough-iron from a blacksmith he returns to the window and asks for another 'kiss'. Nicholas then tries to repeat the trick and sticks out his backside, but this time Absolon is ready! The result is again a lot of fun, outrage and, of course, *pain*! *You* might call this second trick 'Absolon's revenge' or the 'Kiss-my-bum trick'. But, whatever you call it, the crucial thing is to recognize that *The Miller's Tale* is built round just two extended and interlocking jokes: one played on the carpenter, and the other played on Absolon (and then 'backfiring' on Nicholas). You should also notice that both tricks are motivated by a common interest: 'Who is going to win Alison?' This gives a neat unity to the plot.

Once you have the main shape of the plot fixed in your mind, you need to get a rough idea of what it all means. What are the main ideas or themes around which *The Miller's Tale* is built? Most ideas in Chaucer's poetry turn out to be 'variations on a theme', exploring a variety of positions within an overall unified framework, and in this case, as so often in Chaucer, the controlling idea is love. The basic variations are easy enough to pick out. Nicholas is superficially 'romantic' and basically lively, whereas Alison is, if anything, less sophisticated but more lively. Absolon, by contrast, is extravagantly romantic and very idealistic. Overall, then, there is a tension between what you might call 'realistic' and 'idealistic' ways of looking at life and love.

Chaucer often expresses his ideas in religious as well as purely human terms and this happens in *The Miller's Tale* too. Notice that the biblical story of Noah's flood acts as a constant religious backdrop to the action; it ensures that we never completely forget another, more spiritual scale of values against which the human ones can be plotted. The important thing, therefore, is to recognize that Chaucer is exploring a *variety* of attitudes to what can be loosely called 'love'. There is the idealized and fashionable love of court romance and there is the physical and rawly realized love of fabliau. There is 'love of the world' and there is 'love of God'. If you mix all of these together you have a good idea of what, in a general way, *The Miller's Tale* is about.

Step 3 Looking at characterization

Now that you have a good grasp of the kind of work *The Miller's Tale* is, as well as its overall shape and main ideas, you need to see how Chaucer breathes life into his fiction. This brings us to the kind of characters he uses, the characterization. Which of the two main types of characterization is Chaucer using here? Are the characters complexly 'rounded' and psychologically realistic individuals, or are they fairly simple caricatures or 'types'? As usual, the best way of finding out is to look at a passage which establishes one of the main characters. In this case, the initial description of Alison is an obvious choice. We shall take some cues from the opening lines, and you can read the whole thing through for yourself later. Simply ask what

view of the carpenter's wife we are given, whether from the 'inside'
or the 'outside', and ask yourself whether she comes across as an
'individual' or a 'type':

Fair was this yonge wyf, and therwithal
As any wezele hir body gent and smal.
A ceynt she werede, barred al of silk,
A barmclooth eek as whit as morne milk
Upon hir lendes, ful of many a goore.
Whit was hir smok, and broyden al bifoore
And eek bihynde, on hir coler aboute,
Of col-blak silk, withinne and eek withoute.
The tapes of hir white voluper
Were of the same suyte of hir coler;
Hir filet brood of silk, and set ful hye.
And sikerly she hadde a likerous ye.
(ll. 3233–44)

The first thing that might strike you is probably the fact that this
description is crammed with detail: her fine slim body, her decorated
girdle and white apron, the black silk embroidery, and so on. And
yet notice that all this detail is really of one sort: it all focuses on her
external features, her body and her clothing. In so far as it strays
from these at all, it is into obvious and colourful comparisons with
nature (her body is as slim as a weasel's, her apron as white as morning
milk, and so on). You will find that this dual emphasis on physical
appearance and nature imagery is sustained throughout the whole
description. In terms of characterization, the conclusion is obvious:
Alison is presented physically and 'externally'. Put the other way,
you might say that we are given almost no sense of her 'internally',
her own inner thoughts and feelings. The comment on her 'lecherous
eye' is symptomatic. It is the remark of an observer, not the person
observed. Alison is therefore what is felt and thought about her, not
what she thinks and feels herself.

Alternatively, you might want to approach her characterization
from a slightly different point of view, using different terms. For
instance, would you call Alison an 'individual' or 'type'? Looked at
in one way, all the fine detail makes her appear a specific person,
someone you could pick out in a crowd. And yet notice how it all
really adds up to just one overall impression: she is a 'pretty young
thing', what might now be called a 'sex object'. Alison *appears* an
individual but is *essentially* a type. In fact, this kind of characterization
is common in Chaucer, most notably in the descriptions of the

pilgrims in *The General Prologue*. The sheer variety and wealth of detail creates the impression of a specific person, and yet, taken together, it all adds up to a comparatively simple stereotype. Look at the other characters in *The Miller's Tale* and you will find that they are all built like this: richly textured on the surface and yet fundamentally simple. John the carpenter is *essentially* a type of old and stupid husband, Nicholas a crafty and cocky young student, and Absolon a fop and a dandy. However, what makes them all really interesting is the richly textured way in which they are presented, the strong impression we are given of an actual presence. As so often in Chaucer, the result is a marvellous sense of *variety*. We have already seen that variety of ideas characterizes *The Miller's Tale* as a whole, so it should not really surprise you to find it in the characterization too.

Step 4 Developing the argument

In order to develop a more detailed sense of the argument in *The Miller's Tale*, you should look closely at a couple of passages: one from the 'How the carpenter was fooled' part of the story, and the other dealing with 'Absolon's revenge'. That way you can take a closer look at the two sets of triangular relationships the tale explores. For instance, look at the passage where the student is tricking the carpenter into believing that a second Noah's flood is on the way (ll. 3477–600). Look for the underlying *contrast* and *tension* between the two characters. On the one hand, there is the carpenter: a superstitious, uneducated man who produces a string of garbled prayers, part pagan and part Christian. On the other hand, there is the student: calculating and controlled and constantly playing on the carpenter's ignorance by displaying his own learning. The nature of the opposition is therefore clear. You might describe it as 'manual labourer' versus 'intellectual', or 'ignorance' versus 'learning' (the latter corresponds to the common medieval distinction between the 'dewed' and the 'lered', the ignorant and the learned). Either way, you have quickly identified one of the additional strands of the argument in *The Miller's Tale*. The tale is basically about different attitudes to love, but mixed in with this is an argument about different attitudes to and uses of knowledge. Notice how the two are tied together here. The student is abusing his knowledge and the old man's superstition in order to sleep with his wife. Nicholas should use his biblical knowledge for the 'love of God', but in fact he is using it for the 'love of the world' – here the love of woman! You can therefore show that the confrontation between carpenter and student, ignorance and learning, is really just a development of the main argument on love, not a departure from it.

Do the same with the two other main characters, Alison and Absolon. A mere four lines from Absolon's long 'wooing scene' will make the point. Again, simply look for the underlying *contrast* or *tension*:

> 'Ywis, lemman, I have swich love-longynge,
> That lik a turtel trewe is my moornynge.
> I may nat ete na moore than a mayde.'
> 'Go fro the wyndow, Jakke fool', she sayde.
> (ll. 3705–8)

The contrast could hardly be greater! Absolon is in full romantic flight ('like a true turtle-dove') – and then Alison tells him to get lost! In conceptual terms it is what you might call a case of 'idealism' verses 'realism'. Now look at the surrounding passage and you will find that other contrasts stand out equally clearly: the fussy fastidiousness of Absolon is set against the earthy physicality of Alison, while his fashionable 'courtly' ways are contrasted with her traditional 'country' manner. You can explore such contrasts further for yourself (also see p. 212). The point is that again attention to a short but climactic passage allows you to develop a sense of the argument quickly and in detail. In this way you can show that in addition to the supporting argument on learning and ignorance, there is one exploring the tensions between fashionable posturing and traditional directness, between pseudo-courtly ways and those of the country. At the same time, you can show that all these support one overarching theme: love. In other words, you have traced both the theme and the main variations on it, so you now have a firm yet flexible sense of what *The Miller's Tale* is about.

To see how all these variations are finally tied together, you naturally turn to the conclusion of the tale. What kind of order is finally imposed? What is the overall unity within which all this teeming variety is expressed? Now, the action at the end of *The Miller's Tale* is fast and furious, so the first thing you should do is make sure you know exactly what happens. Really, it all hinges on Nicholas bawling for water. Absolon scalds his backside and, on hearing the cry, 'Water!', the carpenter thinks the Flood has come, cuts the rope holding his tub to the roof-beams and immediately crashes through the floor. The result is chaos: 'And doun gooth al!', as Chaucer puts it (l. 3821). This kind of farcical ending is common in fabliau; everyone is literally brought down to earth with a bump and there is general merriment as a result. However, you might still be wondering what it all means. Where are we left in terms of the overall argument? If you think about the last five lines, they will tell you:

> Thus swyved was this carpenteris wyf,
> For al his kepyng and his jalousye;
> And Absolon hath kist hir nether ye;
> And Nicholas is scalded in the towte.
> This tale is doon, and God save al the rowte!
> (ll. 3850–4)

Notice that, for all the apparent confusion and disorder of the tale, everything in a sense comes out right in the end. Everyone gets a kind of rough 'poetic' justice. The jealous carpenter and the posturing church clerk get humiliated in different ways, and the cocky young student gets Alison – but a burnt bum as well. You might therefore conclude that variety exists within an overall unity, or that apparent disorder and injustice are part of a larger pattern of order and justice. Either way, it is important to recognize that the tale finishes with a generous gesture of acceptance, virtually a blessing: 'and God save al the rowte!' For all the chaos and 'sinful' goings-on, God's in his heaven and all's right with the world.

Step 5   Relating the tale to its teller

A sense of the fictional narrator, here the Miller, is obviously going to help you explain what sort of tale he tells and why. In fact there is quite a lot of information about the Miller – in *The General Prologue*, ll. 545–66, his own prologue and that to *The Reeve's Tale* immediately following. What you need most, therefore, is a good grasp of his main characteristics, the most obvious things that stand out about him. What you should *not* do is simply list his physical features: his fox-red beard, his mouth like a furnace, the bristly wart on his nose, and so on. That would be to stay at the level of describing detail. What you really need is some neat way of encapsulating everything that this detail stands for. In fact, once you look for them, it is fairly easy to pick out just two or three main strands in the Miller's characterization. There is his brutishness and his love of racy stories, and to these you might add the fact that he seems to be drunk and is deliberately rude to the Knight and the Reeve. Now all you do is look for evidence of these characteristics in the tale he tells. Obviously a fabliau laced with raw sex and violence is well suited to a brutishly physical man, especially one who has a reputation as a loudmouth and a rude storyteller ('a janglere and a goliardeys' – l. 560). The rudeness to both the Knight and the Reeve is also carried over into the tale. *The Miller's Tale* turns out to be a fairly close parody of *The Knight's Tale*, and also includes a sideswipe at carpenters (the Reeve had been a carpenter by trade). All this confirms the strong link between the Miller and his tale, and certainly accounts for the basic *choice* of material. What it does not do, however, is account for the precise *treatment* of this material. For an explanation of that you need to look elsewhere.

Now think about that other narrator who always lurks somewhere behind the fictions, Chaucer himself. Neither Absolon's rhetorical speeches nor the intellectual ingenuity of Nicholas's trick seem particularly plausible from such a thug as the Miller. However, if you think in terms of the ultimate narrator, a sophisticated poet such as Chaucer, such features are perfectly explicable. If he is skilful about it, the poet can have it both ways. He can play up the rude bits of his fabliau and then blame them on the Miller ('Blameth nat me … The Millere is a cherl, ye knowe wel this' – ll. 3181–2). Alternatively, as the occasion demands it, he can slip into his own voice and play around with more sophisticated language and ideas. In fact, much of the delight in reading *The Canterbury Tales* in general lies in gauging the extent to which Chaucer *mixes* his own voice with that of the pilgrim who is telling the tale. And again notice that all we are really doing is pointing to the essentially 'mixed' and 'varied' nature of Chaucer's poetry.

Step 6 Seeing the text in context

Here are some ways of seeing the tensions between the characters in *The Miller's Tale* as expressions of tensions within actual life at the time. The most obvious social aspect of this tale is that it deals with the lives of townspeople and non-nobles, and that all these people are presented as in some way funny. People like this (tradesmen, students, minor religious figures and country wives) were traditional figures of fun in late-medieval court literature. It is common to find them depicted in ridiculous and compromising positions. In fact, this is such a persistent feature of stories told for nobles about non-nobles that it is useful to remember that the derogatory edge was first given to words such as 'churl', 'villain' and 'peasant' at court. All these terms were capable of carrying neutral or technical senses (a 'vyleyn', for instance, was technically someone tied to a particular 'ville' or domain), but in standard court usage they all tended to be bandied about as terms of derision and contempt. To courtiers, it seems, the 'lower orders' were almost automatically funny. To this extent, then, Chaucer's 'cherles tale' conforms to literary and social type. *The Miller's Tale* is basically a fabliau poking fun at the 'lower orders'. However, there is more to it than that. Chaucer does more than offer straightforward reflections of upper-class prejudices. Just as he mixes elements of court romance with fabliau, so he presents a more mixed and less rigidly hierarchical view of medieval society. Both the student and the church clerk are presented as 'romantic heroes', and both of them in different ways ape the dress, language and manners of the court. The *historical* point is that Chaucer is very sensitive to shifts in the fabric of late-fourteenth-century society. The *critical* point is that his view of the 'lower orders' is tinged with sympathy as well as mockery, affection as well as condescension. In such simple but powerful ways, a sense of changing historical context can help you identify crosscurrents within the text.

A similar mix of affection and condescension characterizes the presentation of the only woman in *The Miller's Tale*. From one point of view, she has all the glamour of a lively young animal; from another, she is simply a woman fit for 'swyving' – a good lay for a lord, or a fine wife for a yeoman ('For any lord to leggen in his bedde, / Or yet for any good yeman to wedde' – ll. 3269–70). Obviously it is important to note that *both* the narrators (the Miller and Chaucer) are men and that Alison, like most heroines of medieval story, is literally 'man-made'. But, again, a couple of historical observations help make the critical point more forcefully. In the Middle Ages it was common for rich old men like John the carpenter to marry young wives like Alison. Men generally had much greater economic power than women, so it was usually the men who picked their partners, not the women. Similar real historical imbalances help explain the fictional male–female relationships in tales otherwise as different as those of the Knight, Clerk, Merchant and Franklin, as well as

Chaucer's *Troilus and Criseyde*.

Confrontations such as that between Nicholas the student and John the carpenter, the 'learned' and the 'ignorant', are also common in Chaucer's poetry. With less than 5 per cent of the population able to read and write, and education as a whole largely under the control of religion, such abuse of book-learning was widespread. Chaucer's fraudulent Pardoner is another, more spectacular instance of the same tendency to mystify religious knowledge for purely personal ends. Again the historical observation is simple, but helps to make a more powerful critical point. Chaucer's characters are not just 'interesting people'; they also express tensions within contemporary life and enact contemporary arguments.

Step 7   Analysing the style

This final section invites you to look back at the language of the poem and see how the study of its style is simply another way of approaching the larger issues. Once more the general principles of *variety* and *tension* will stand you in good stead. The tension between the verse form and the rhythm is common to all Chaucer's poetry and some tips are supplied in the corresponding sections on *The General Prologue* (Chapter 2) and *The Knight's Tale* (Chapter 3). Like *The Miller's Tale*, both use a ten-syllable line in couplets, so the main features are the same. More particularly, *The Miller's Tale* is famous for its 'mixed' style, so you should be alert to this. Really we have already covered it, for all that is meant by 'mixed style' is Chaucer's delight in constantly shifting between 'high' and 'low' styles – or even mixing them up completely. For instance, look again at that passage where Absolon is wooing Alison beneath her window (see p. 79). It sweeps from 'high' style to 'low', from image-filled eulogy to brutal bluntness, in the space of a line ('"Go fro the wyndow, Jakke fool", she sayde'). The description of Alison that we looked at is even more 'mixed'. It uses a lot of homely imagery, but organizes it in a rhetorically formal, top-to-toe manner. Such things are always happening in the style of *The Miller's Tale*. Describing its style is just a more detailed way of tuning into the larger 'mixed' aspects of the poem: its tendency to play the idealism of the court romance against the realism of fabliau, as well as its overall concern with competing views of life and love.

THE PARDONER'S PROLOGUE AND TALE

Step I   What kind of work am I studying?

The Pardoner is every bit as memorable as the tale he tells. The best way of approaching this text is therefore to try to see the whole thing, both prologue and tale, as a complete package from the beginning. On its own the tale is easy to categorize. It is a sermon on the theme, 'acquisitiveness is the root of all evil' ('*Radix malorum est Cupiditas*' –l. 334), and it uses a moralized story or 'exemplum' to illustrate it. This is straightforward enough. What makes the whole thing more interesting is the fact that Chaucer mixes this sermon with another kind of story material. In effect he takes the sermon and puts it inside a long speech in which the Pardoner confesses how he uses sermons to trick people for money. The result is a sermon *within* a confession. The sermon is therefore not so much a real sermon to a real congregation, but a kind of 'demonstration sermon' in which the preacher displays his skills and his selfish motives to the other pilgrims. If you get hold of this dual aspect of *The Pardoner's Prologue and Tale*, the fact that it is a sermon and confession combined, then all the other aspects readily fall into place.

Step 2   What is it about?

What you need now is a sense of the text's overall shape and its main ideas. In fact, the best place to start is with the central tale about the three layabouts, as everything else is organized round that. Here it is in outline.

Three young lads do nothing all day but drink, gamble, swear and fornicate. One day they hear that a drinking companion of theirs has met his death, so, foul-mouthed, full of drink and threatening to kill him, they set off to look for 'Death'. On the way they meet an old man and ask him if he knows anything about 'Death'. He replies that they will find 'Death' under a tree and shows them the way. Once there the three lads find a great heap of money and immediately set about deciding how to carry it back to town in secret. They decide to do this under cover of darkness, and that one of them should go to the town for food and drink while the other two keep watch over the money. This done, the two who are left behind swear a pact that they will stab the third when he returns, so leaving them with the money to split just two ways. Meanwhile, the lad in town is busy poisoning the wine for the other two, so that he can have all the money for himself. Everything goes as they plan – except that none of them gets the money. The lad returns from town and is stabbed, while the two murderers drink the poisoned wine and die a horrible death. And that is the end of them and the story.

In outline this is obviously nothing more than a neat little fable with a sting in its tail. You might call it something like 'The quest for Death', note that its ending is ironic (the lads *do* actually find 'Death', but in a way they had not expected), and leave it at that. What you now need to do, therefore, is put this story back in its wider narrative context. That way you will see that it is not just a fable but part of a sermon, and that this sermon is itself part of a longer confession. The connection between the 'quest for Death' story and the sermon is straightforward enough: the story simply illustrates the moral that 'acquisitiveness is the root of all evil'. That is why its moral dimension as an exemplum is constantly emphasized in moralizing tirades against drunkenness, gluttony, swearing, and so on. The next move is to add that outer narrative layer. The story is our core, the sermon surrounds that, and round both of them there is the confession. So what happens in the confession part of *The Pardoner's Prologue and Tale?* Well, you might say that all that really happens over the entire length of this text is that the Pardoner shows what an amazing preacher he is. It is a kind of magnificent boast. The catch is that all the time the Pardoner keeps giving the game away, admitting that he is only in it for the money. Time and again he freely acknowledges that he is totally motivated by self-interest, and that there are no genuinely pious reasons why he does anything at all. That is why the whole thing is best called a confession.

It has just been suggested that a handy way of thinking of *The Pardoner's Prologue and Tale* is as a confession containing a 'demonstration sermon', which in turn contains a moralized story. Another way of putting this is in terms of the *two* audiences for different parts of the Pardoner's performance. On the one hand, there is the audience made up of the Pardoner's fellow pilgrims on the road to Canterbury; on the other, there is the imaginary congregation to whom the Pardoner delivers his 'demonstration sermon'. Both together make up the total fictional audience to whom the text is addressed. So, whichever way you approach it, the important thing to remember is that *The Pardoner's Prologue and Tale* is basically a *mixture*. It mixes sermon and confession, and it mixes two fictional audiences. First you should try to separate these elements, and then later you will be able to see more easily how they fit together.

You will already have noticed that there are a number of recurrent ideas or themes spanning the poem. A rough list of these will put you in touch with the general content as well as the form of the text. 'Money', 'death', 'swearing', 'drinking' and 'sin' are obviously going to figure in any overview of what the poem is about. More particularly, it is useful to try to see the whole text in terms of a single issue, a single problem. You might, for example, fasten on the problem of 'deception', of things not being what they appear (whether pardons or relics or wine or people). Or you might take a slightly different line and see the whole text in terms of a tension between 'ideal' and 'real' views of religion: the Pardoner should ideally be this, but in fact he is really that; relics should ideally be used for this, but in fact they are used for that; and so on. You could then re-express the central problem of the poem as the pull between spiritual and human values, or as the abuse of the 'love of God' in favour of the 'love of the world'. Obviously there are many possibilities. But, whatever you opt for, the important thing is to get a sense of the main issues early on.

Step 3   Looking at characterization

Put the character of the Pardoner himself to one side for the moment, and think about the characters in the story. What kind of characters are they, and how are you meant to respond to them? Take the three 'riotoures', for instance: do we get to know them intimately as individuals, or do we see them more generally as types of people? The fact that they have no names, and that we never distinguish one from the other, is an obvious clue. So are the constant reminders that all of them can be described in terms of a few questionable qualities: swearing, drinking, and so on. Obviously, then, they are types, and from the point of view of characterization we look for nothing more. They represent, if you like, a broad principle of 'disorder' or 'worldliness', and they are all equally deceitful.

Now look at the old man. He is the only other main character in the story and one who attracts a lot of critical attention. What do you make of him, and is his characterization as straightforward as that of the three lads? The old man's meeting with them occupies a mere fifty lines or so (ll. 711–67), but his appearance is clearly significant and the main turning-point in the action, so you should read over this passage carefully. As usual, it will help if you look for the underlying *tension* in the scene. What kind of dramatic *contrast* is produced? Obviously there is the contrast between youth and age, as well as the fact that the lads are arrogant and bullying in their speech while the old man speaks 'ful mekely' (l. 714). But after that you might be a little puzzled. What does the old man mean by saying he can find no-one in the world 'That wolde chaunge his youthe for myn age' (l. 724)? And why does he call so relentlessly on Death, asking his 'mother earth' to take him ('Leeve mooder, leet me in!' – l. 731)? Critics have filled a lot of paper debating the significance of these lines, and so might you. However, the important thing is to keep hold of the contrast between the old man and the three lads. He is searching for Death and so are they. The point is that, in the end, they do find Death, though not as they expected, while he presumably is still desperately searching for Death and does not. There is therefore a kind of twist to the contrast, and we usually call such twists 'ironic'. Irony in a plot means that things come out neatly, but in ways that you (or the characters) did not expect. All this leaves you with a number of things you might say about the old man: that he has close associations with death but is not Death itself, that he is there to point up the youth and arrogance of the other characters by his own age and humility, and that, finally, the contrast between them is ironic. For the rest he is a mysterious and enigmatic figure. In fact, this takes you quite a long way in your view of the old man, who by now has become something of a critical celebrity. However, it must be admitted that in many respects he remains an enigma. He is ultimately the kind of character who always attracts more questions than he answers.

Step 4   Developing the argument

To develop your sense of *The Pardoner's Prologue and Tale* as a whole you need to concentrate on a couple of passages, one from the beginning and another from near the end. You already know in a general way what the text is about: 'deception', or the abuse of spiritual values for human ends. Now you need to know how these issues are explored in practice. Start by taking a close look at the first twenty-odd lines of the prologue (ll. 329–51). This will put you in touch with the Pardoner's preaching-techniques and therefore with the routine tactics of his whole performance. It will also demonstrate in detail how he goes about deceiving people and abusing religion. Here are the first six lines:

> 'Lordynges,' quod he, 'in chirches whan I preche,
> I peyne me to han an hauteyn speche,
> And rynge it out as round as gooth a belle,
> For I kan al by rote that I telle.
> My theme is alwey oon, and evere was –
> *Radix malorum est Cupiditas.*'
>
> (ll. 329–34)

Essentially, this is a summary of the form and content of Pardoner's entire performance. He says how he cultivates a 'haughty, superior' way of speaking ('an hauteyn spech'), which he declaims loud and clear. And then he says that he only ever talks on one theme ('*Radix malorum ...*'), which knows by heart ('by rote'). In other words, every aspect of what he does is calculating and contrived.

Now look over the remaining 100 lines of the prologue. Look out particularly for places where the sermon tips over into confession, where the Pardoner not only displays what he does, but also admits why he does it. Here is an example:

> Of avarice and of swich cursednesse
> Is al my prechyng, for to make hem free
> To yeven hir pens, and namely unto me.
> For myn entente is nat but for to wynne,
> And nothyng for correccioun of synne.
>
> (ll. 400–4)

Notice how this starts with a reminder of the subject of his sermon ('avarice'), then switches to the frank acknowledgement that getting money ('to wynne') is his only motive. In fact, he preaches *against* what he practices. *The Pardoner's Prologue and Tale* is full of such changes of direction, and much of the delight in studying it comes from gauging exactly how and why the Pardoner is speaking at different times. The important thing to remember is that everything results from the same basic *mixture* of materials: sermon turning into confession, and then turning back into sermon.

To see how this mixture finally comes out you should turn to the end. The crucial passage is where the Pardoner rounds off his sermon by turning to his fellow pilgrims and actually tries to sell them pardons and relics (ll. 904–68). The changes of direction here are both subtle and profound, so you should examine the whole passage in detail. Here is an outline to help you. The Pardoner has just finished his story of the three layabouts with a melodramatic denunciation of sin in general, and avarice in particular. 'Avarice' therefore provides him with the necessary excuse to address his imaginary congregation on the subject of giving away their goods to him, in return for pardons and relics (ll. 904–15). This in turn prompts him to reflect for a moment that the only genuine pardons come from Christ, not pardoners (ll. 915–18). But this is only for a moment, and then he is back to the business of trying to sell pardons and relics to his companions on the road (ll. 919ff.). The Host tells him to get lost (in a particularly obscene way) and social harmony is finally restored only after the intervention of the Knight. With this outline to refer to, you should now go through the passage yourself, noting exactly how and where all the transitions occur. At each stage ask who the Pardoner is addressing and why. Once you have done that, you then need to ask what it all *means*. Does the ending offer any resolution of the text's issues? Does it tie everything together so that you can say, 'Oh yes, *that's* what it's all about!'?

We noted earlier that the text is coordinated by a single idea, what we called 'deception' or 'things not being what they appear'. So what are we finally told about 'deception' here? In this respect the crucial lines are obviously where the Pardoner is actually switching from his imaginary to his real audience, the other pilgrims. The transition is marked by his final and most amazing confession:

And Jhesu Crist, that is oure soules leche,
So graunte yow his pardoun to receyve,
For that is best; I wol yow nat deceyve.
(ll. 916–18)

In other words, the only true pardon is Christ's, not the Pardoner's: 'That is the best, I will not *deceive* you'. Perhaps the conclusion is therefore that the Pardoner can deceive himself and us no longer. He finally has to admit that he is an utter fraud. Or you might put it another way and say that he finally acknowledges that the only true values are to be found in the 'love of God', not 'love of the world'. In itself that would be a neat and thoroughly orthodox conclusion. However, that is not quite what happens. Chaucer gives an extra little twist to his materials, and he does so by letting the Pardoner prattle on. Even though the Pardoner has just admitted that his own pardons are comparatively worthless, he still tries to sell them to the other pilgrims. Why? Critics have made much of this, but notice that again our basic terms are useful as a framework in which you can develop your own response. From one point of view, the Pardoner seems to have made a strategic error: he careers straight on from his sermon into his confession, from his imaginary to his real audience. He seems to have forgotten that his companions have heard everything, both sermon *and* confession, and can therefore see through all his tricks. In short, he seems to have 'blown it'! From another point of view, you might say that the Pardoner has finally deceived *himself*, that he is so practised in deception that he no longer has any way of telling wrong from right, illusion from reality. The final twist would then be that this is ultimately a study in delusion and self-deception. He is the victim of his own obsession. Whichever way you incline, you should at least be aware that there are a number of problems in this text, and (equally importantly) that these problems can be stated in fairly simple terms. The notion of a mixed sermon and confession helps you to come to terms with the shifting strategies of the text, and some such notion as 'deception' or the confusion of 'appearance and reality' helps you to explore its meanings. Where you go from there is very much up to you. The following sections simply suggest some other angles you might explore.

Step 5   Relating the tale to its teller

The Pardoner has necessarily figured from the beginning in our view of his tale. All we do here is look at the description of him in *The General Prologue*, ll. 669–714, and in the 'Words of the Host' immediately preceding his own prologue. Does this material throw any more light on what he does and why? As usual, there is a lot of colourful and engaging detail, you need to sort it into broad categories. What two or three aspects are stressed about the Pardoner?

In fact, the description in *The General Prologue* breaks readily into two parts: the Pardoner's physical appearance and a summary of the tricks he gets up to when selling pardons and relics. The latter simply confirms what we already know, so concentrate on his appearance. It is what you might call 'strange' or 'weird' and clearly tells us something new. For instance, the Pardoner obviously considers himself fashionable ('Him thoughte he rood al of the newe jet' – l. 682), but to everyone else his wax-yellow hair hanging in 'rats-tails' looks pretty tatty. The point, therefore, seems to be that he is unself-critical as well as ostentatious. His unnaturally smooth face and high goatlike voice also put the stamp on a presence which is, to say the least, 'striking'; and, as far as Chaucer the pilgrim is concerned, the Pardoner looks downright weird: he says that, for all he knows, the Pardoner could be a castrated stallion or a mare (l. 691; also see pp. 211–12)

Now all you do is add this impression to your view of the Pardoner in his prologue and tale. For instance, does an 'ostentatious but unself-critical' narrator help you explain the ending, where he has boasted about all his tricks and *still* tries to sell pardons and relics to the other pilgrims? Alternatively, consider the possibility that the Pardoner is drunk when he tells his tale, for that is the dominant impression left by the exchange between the Host and the Pardoner in 'The Words of the Host'. Perhaps *that* explains why the Pardoner finally oversteps the mark, that he is so fuddled with drink that he does not know what he is doing. You can argue all these points in more detail for yourself. The important thing is to see that they arise naturally from material 'outside' the prologue and tale. The materials you choose to emphasize will automatically change your perspective and therefore your interpretation.

Step 6   Seeing the text in context

The previous section treats the Pardoner as a 'rounded' individual, with personal problems which carry over into his performance. This section invites you to see *The Pardoner's Prologue and Tale* as an expression of problems within the late-medieval Church and within contemporary society as a whole. You can see the text as a product of history, not just of 'personality'. In fact, to see the text in context you need just three historical observations: about pardons, relics and eunuchs. You will see that all these bear directly on the main issues of the text (money, death, sin and deception), so in no way can they be considered mere 'background'.

Pardons and pardoners were a direct result of a 'cash-flow crisis' in the late-medieval Church. The Church had plenty of wealth tied up in land and buildings, but it was having great difficulty keeping pace with an increasingly money-based economy. It needed not just services and goods; it needed money. One of its responses was to invent pardoners, people who would go around selling the 'spiritual capital' of religion (by trading on people's beliefs), rather than selling off the Church's actual economic capital (its land and buildings). The idea was that pardoners would sell signed 'pardons' to sinners, and let them off their penance in return. For instance, you would give a certain sum of money and be let off a certain number of days fasting. As everybody was technically a sinner, this meant the potential market was vast! That was the idea anyway. In practice the selling of pardons quickly became an international scandal. It made the economic aspect of religion utterly blatant, and for many people the Church lost credibility. Official Christianity was a sham that openly perverted spiritual means for financial ends. Connecting all this to the main issues in *The Pardoner's Prologue and Tale* is obviously not difficult. To do so has the marvellous effect of showing exactly *why* money, sin and death are such a tightly bound cluster of issues in this text. Pardoners literally traded on sin, and their most powerful bargaining position was the fear of death and damnation. 'Pay now or burn later' has to be one of the most persuasive sales messages of all time! In this respect Chaucer's Pardoner may be a particularly talented individual, but the ends to which he put his talents were far from unique.

It is the same with relics. They also were a routine part of the paraphernalia of late medieval religion. They were not just a sideline of perverted individuals. In fact, claims about the magical power of holy relics abounded: all the way from alleged bits of the Cross and Christ's robes to the fingers and toenails of saints, often displayed in ingeniously constructed caskets. As with pardons, the possibilities for cheating the ignorant were huge. Hardly any relics could be proved absolutely genuine or absolutely false, so there was always plenty of room for dishonesty and deception. In this respect, too, Chaucer's Pardoner is symptomatic of a wider and deeper problem; he is as much a 'type' as an 'individual'. The historical observation again helps to reinforce or modify a critical observation already made.

The final observation relates to the Pardoner's possible status as a eunuch. The narrator in *The General Prologue* and the Host both draw attention to this aspect of him and, as we have said, it seems to be based on the simply physiological fact that the Pardoner has a completely hairless face and a high voice. In fact, in Chaucer's day this habit of judging people by their appearances was elevated into a pseudo-science called 'physiognomy'. It was founded on the fallacious belief that specific physical characteristics can be equated with specific temperaments, or even moral and spiritual dispositions. In the Pardoner's case the strong suggestion is that, because (a) he looks and sounds as he does, he is (b) a eunuch and therefore (c) depraved. This is illogical nonsense, but it was not thought so at the time. The critical point is again that the Pardoner is very definitely an expression of social beliefs in the late Middle Ages, and thus in this respect a 'type' rather than an 'individual'. His character is a way of seeing the character of late-medieval society, and vice versa. They are mutually illuminating, and that is why we look at the text in context.

Step 7   Analysing the style

Once more this is simply a different approach to what are essentially the same issues. Shifts in the poem's style correspond to fundamental shifts in its overall strategy, so the best thing is to take another look at the concluding lines (11. 895ff.). This time look more closely at the exact choices and combinations of words. For instance, notice that the sermon and confession parts of this passage tend to use language differently. On the one hand, there is the repetitious and highly abstract declamation of the preacher ('O wikkednesse! / O glotonye, luxurie and hasardrye!' – ll. 896–7); on the other, there is the conversational charm and simplicity of 'But, sires, o word forgat I in my tale' (l. 919). Look out for such modulations of style throughout *The Pardoner's Prologue and Tale*. They are the first sign that the Pardoner is up to his rhetorical tricks, and using them to persuade and deceive. In the last resort, it should only be he – and not you – who is taken in by the power of his words!

THE NUN'S PRIEST'S TALE

Step 1   What kind of work am I studying?

The sheer richness and variety of *The Nun's Priest's Tale* can make it initially confusing. For that reason it is useful to start with a firm idea of the basic kinds of material it is built from. In fact, there are just three: sermon, fable and court romance. *The Nun's Priest's Tale* is a sermon in that it is delivered by a priest and has an obvious moral point, a fable in that it uses animals acting like people to point the moral, and a court romance in that these animals are presented in terms of romantic heroes and heroines. Clearly, it is something of a 'mixed bag'. Also, as you might expect from a tale where animals mimic the ways of court, it is very funny. A trivial subject is given heroic treatment, and that is why *The Nun's Priest's Tale* is also sometimes called a 'mock-heroic' poem. So, whatever you call it, you should at least be prepared for a tale which is rich, varied and funny.

Step 2   What is it about?

There is a great deal of incidental material in this tale. However, the animal fable around which everything is built is straightforward enough, so you should start by getting hold of that. A cock and his seven wives live on a farm belonging to a poor widow. The cock has a dream that he is going to be eaten by a doglike creature, but his favourite wife, Pertelote, dismisses the dream as meaningless and tells him not to be silly. Some time later a fox comes into the yard and engages the cock in conversation. After flattering the cock about his singing (his name is Chauntecleer, meaning 'Sing clearly'), the fox finally persuades him to crow at the top of his voice. While the cock is straining to do this the fox grabs him by the throat and makes off. Immediately there is uproar in the farmyard and all the animals and neighbours set off in pursuit. Just as the fox is about to drag him into the wood, the cock suggests that the fox turn and shout some abuse at their pursuers. This the fox does, and the moment he opens his mouth Chauntecleer escapes to a tree. That is the end of the story and, as usual with a fable, it has a moral. In this case it is a double-edged one: 'Beware of flattery!' and 'Keep your mouth shut!'

Looked at this way, as a fable or cautionary tale, *The Nun's Priest's Tale* is obviously straightforward. What makes it more complicated and interesting is the fact that all kinds of other materials are incorporated in it. In particular, there is a long debate between Chauntecleer and Pertelote on the significance of dreams, and this in turn includes a couple of illustrative stories. What you finish up with is, therefore, stories within a story, and this can be confusing. However, if you keep hold of the idea that *The Nun's Priest's Tale* is basically an animal fable with bits added, you will not be confused for long.

Step 3   Looking at characterization

To see how the main characters are presented, look at the initial description of Chauntecleer and Pertelote (ll. 3647–78). Try to see the way in which this description is built up from grand images you would not normally associate with a couple of farmyard birds. The cock's voice is pleasanter than the church organ, his comb is like fine coral and edged like the battlements of a castle, his claws are whiter than the lily, and his overall colouring is like burnished gold. He is above all a 'gentil' (noble) cock and it is the same with his wives. They are not just hens but his 'paramours' (lovers), and his favourite is 'faire damoysele Pertelote', who is particularly 'Curteys ... discreet and debonaire'. Notice that by the time you have finished you see all of them in two ways. On the one hand, they are familiar farmyard animals; on the other, they are exotic figures from court romance. The result is an underlying tension in their presentation, and it is this tension (or incongruity) which produces the sense of mock-heroic.

Step 4   Developing the argument

Once you have grasped the idea that *The Nun's Priest's Tale* is a mock-heroic animal fable, you can look to see how this strategy is developed in the body of the poem. For instance, take a look at part of the long debate between Chauntecleer and Pertelote on the significance of dreams. Here is a sample of how Pertelote argues against them:

> 'Lo Catoun, which that was so wys a man
> Seyde he nat thus, "Ne do no fors of dremes?"
> Now sire,' quod she, 'whan we flee fro the bemes,
> For Goddes love, as taak som laxatyf!'
> (ll. 3737–40)

Notice that she starts with a classical authority, Cato, who set no store by dreams, and then she promptly descends to another level, telling her husband to take some laxative to stop his dreaming. This kind of thing happens throughout their debate. We are constantly tossed between the learned and the crude, from the sublime to the ridiculous, and the effect is essentially funny. In fact, rather than being *about* anything in a sustained and serious sense, *The Nun's Priest's Tale* is much more an experiment in different styles and sudden surprises. It does not have a particularly consistent argument, but it does have a remarkable capacity to change pace and even direction. You might say that, if it is 'about' anything, it is about the art of telling a story in an amusing way.

Step 5   Relating the tale to its teller

Because narrative art is so prominent an issue in *The Nun's Priest's Tale*, it follows that you should take a careful look at the narrator, the Nun's Priest. We are given some information about him in his prologue and epilogue, so you should consider what this adds to your view of his tale. In fact, two things stand out: the obvious but important fact that he is a priest, and the fact that he is by nature an extremely vigorous and physical man. It also appears that the Host insists that the priest tell a 'murie' (pleasant) tale (l. 3612). If you now transfer these insights to the tale itself, they may help you explain some of its emphases. First, the fact that the narrator is a priest means that he is probably used to preaching. Perhaps that is why there is so much moralising and, in particular, the inclusion of two moralising stories ('exempla') in the debate between Chauntecleer and Pertelote. Certainly, his status as a priest and preacher would explain why he concludes the whole tale with the exhortation, 'Taketh the morality goode men' (l. 4237). Alternatively, you might think about the priest's vigorous nature. Perhaps that explains the occasional directness and earthiness when he is talking about the animal side of things. Finally, the Host's insistence that this should be a 'murie' tale is obviously carried through in practice. The performance is nothing if not entertaining. In all these ways a knowledge of the narrator may throw extra light on his tale.

Step 6   Seeing the text in context

The Nun's Priest's Tale touches on a number of issues treated in a more sustained fashion elsewhere in Chaucer's work. Notable amongst these are the relations between husband and wife and the debate on the significance of dreams. However, there is one minor, but unique reference in this text to what was in practice a major social event. This is the reference to 'Jack Straw and his followers' (ll. 4191-4), and it refers to one of the leaders of the Peasants' Revolt of 1381. It is the only certain allusion by Chaucer to the most momentous social upheaval of late-medieval England, and it is interesting precisely because it is so disparaging and marginal. In context it simply adds a sense of chaotic colour to the chase after the fox. However, such a slight and slighting reference may lead you to a broader observation on Chaucer and his role as a court poet.

Chaucer's social sympathies may have been broad, but they did not extend to the aggrieved and exploited peasantry who took direct political action against the elite of which he was a member.

Step 7   Analysing the style

Implicit in most of the previous steps has been the assumption that the style of *The Nun's Priest's Tale* is particularly varied and 'mixed'. What you should finally do, therefore, is make sure you can identify and comment sensibly on the different styles of the poem. Look particularly for places where one style shifts to another. For instance, the story starts with a description of the poor widow's life and uses an economical 'plain' or 'middle' style. We then move into a more ornate, 'high' style with the mock-heroic description of Chauntecleer and Pertelote (discussed above). And from there we move yet again to a more sonorous and sermonizing style in the debate on dreams, characterized by weighty abstractions and appeals to learned authorities. These three styles ('plain', 'high' and 'sermonizing') roughly correspond to the three basic types of material which go to make up *The Nun's Priest's Tale*: fable, court romance and sermon. All you are doing, therefore, is confirming in detail the 'mixed' strategy of the poem as a whole. You will find further examples of all three styles in the climactic scene where the cock is finally grabbed by the fox (ll. 4119–65). Here, as throughout the poem, Chaucer seems to be interested above all in showing just how skilful he can be at presenting the same thing from different points of view. It is a poem in which narrative and sheer 'stylishness' take precedence over content. And yet, as is so often the case in Chaucer's works, the variety and energy of the language point to the diversity and complexity of experience. In this way we can say that there is a tension between the simple verities of the poem as a fable, and the untidy facts of real existence acknowledged in Chaucer's language.

THE MERCHANT'S TALE

Step 1   What kind of work am I studying?

Like most of the Canterbury Tales, *The Merchant's Tale* is made up of a rich mixture of materials. In this case it is a mixture of two main

story types: the court romance and the fabliau. It is a court romance
in that its main characters are a knight, his wife and a squire, and
because it is concerned generally with 'courtly love', the art of refined
and aristocratic courtship. It is a fabliau in that it has a comic plot
revolving round a trick, and because a fair amount of the love in the
tale is not so much 'courtly' as bawdy. So, you should expect a read
which is extremely varied: both serious and funny, idealized and yet
also down-to-earth. You will find that sometimes these elements
complement one another, and sometimes they come into conflict.

Step 2   What is it about?

There are a number of long moralizing passages in *The Merchant's
Tale*, particularly towards the beginning. As these may put you off
initially, it is a good idea to get firm hold of the basic situation and
plot. Both are essentially simple. The situation involves three main
characters: the old knight January, his wife May, and a young squire
called Damian. The plot revolves around the way in which May
manages to trick her husband and have sex with the squire. For this
to happen notice that just three events are crucial: (1) that January
goes blind and therefore cannot see what is going on; (2) that the
squire gets a counterfeit key to the private garden in which January
and May meet; and (3) that January's eyesight miraculously comes
back at the very moment that his wife and the squire are making
love in a tree over his head! The comic improbability and rudeness
of all this is what confirms it as fabliau. To this outline of the plot
only one thing need be added: the way in which January gets his
sight back. This is as a direct result of the intervention of the god
Pluto and his wife Proserpine. Pluto takes January's side, giving him
his eyesight back, and Proserpine takes May's, giving her the power
to explain everything away. The incident with the god and goddess
is therefore a subplot and it comes together with the main plot at
the end to produce the climax.

In a more general sense *The Merchant's Tale* is obviously about
'love'. And like many of Chaucer's tales, it is really just an exploration
of love from different points of view. There is idealized love, and
there is straightforward sex. There is divine love, and there is human
love. All these aspects cross and re-cross in the tale, and the result is
what we would now call an interest in 'personal relationships'. Who
should exercise the power in a particular relationship, the man or

the woman? What forms does that power take at different times? But, whatever terms you choose (whether 'love' or 'personal relationships' or 'power'), you can at least be sure that this tale revolves round just three characters and a single main issue.

Step 3   Looking at characterization

The character of the knight, January, is established in the first 20 lines (ll. 1245–65). Look at this passage and it will help you see what kind of character he is in particular, as well as what kind of characterization there is in the tale generally. In fact, just a few things are stressed about January, so you can say that the characterization is fairly simple. He is old and prosperous and, after a life of debauchery, he wants to get married. Notice, however, that even at this early stage a specific *tension* or *conflict* is built into his character. It is not clear whether he wants to get married for pious reasons, to avoid sin, or simply to have a woman at his disposal all the time. There is a spiritual and conventionally acceptable side to his view of marriage, but there is also a side which is merely lustful and selfish. You will find that these traits are confirmed in his character as it unfolds, and, as you might expect, they contribute to our view of love and marriage within the tale as a whole. Marriage is seen as something spiritual and acceptable, but it is also seen as an arrangement whereby more sinister and selfish forces can come into play.

Step 4   Developing the argument

To see how the characters relate to one another and how their relationships express different aspects of the argument, you need to look in detail at some crucial passages. For instance, look at the passage where January first catches sight of May (ll. 1577–610). The precise way in which he falls in love with her is significant. It is all presented through his thoughts as he busily reviews the possibilities and finally fixes on May. The 'fantasizing' or 'obsessive' nature of his thought is emphasized ('fantasye' figures at the beginning and end of this passage), and the overall impression is of a man locked into his own view of things. What May, the object of his desire, thought we simply do not know. In other words, the nature of the 'love' problem is deepened. Here we see more of its selfish and purely acquisitive side, and we may begin to wonder about the mental health of this aging debauchee.

If you now look at the bedroom scene on the marriage night (ll. 1818–54), the issues become even clearer. Again there is a massive imbalance between what we know of January's and what we know of May's views of the proceedings. Almost everything is seen through the eyes and mind of the old knight, 'But God woot what that May thoughte in hir herte' (l. 1851). Again, too, there is an emphasis on the superficially legitimate side of holy matrimony, and this is once more set against the crudely lustful lovemaking of the old man. The passage is full of images of food, drink and animals, as well as a knife; so you should also consider what these add to your sense of January and his attitude to love. The only hint that we have of May's attitude comes in the line, 'She preyseth nat his pleyyng worth a bene' (l. 1854). It is therefore time to take a closer look at her and her relationship with the other main character, the squire Damian.

The first meeting of May and Damian is characteristic and sets the tone for their subsequent relationship (ll. 1932–45). Notice that the squire is superficially 'courtly' (he begs 'Mercy!' of his lady), but really both he and May are extremely practical when it comes to arranging their affair. Damian slips May a letter, she promptly replies – and before you know it she has slipped him the garden key to make a copy. Their courtship observes a few polite rituals, but fundamentally it is of a direct and no-nonsense kind. All you now need do, therefore, is consider what the relationship between Damian and May adds to your view of love. Clearly, love to them is neither spiritual nor, in the last resort, particularly 'courtly'. So what is it, and how does it differ from the kind of rapacious lust January feels for May? The outline of an answer can best be seen by looking at the climax of the tale.

The conclusion of *The Merchant's Tale* is complex and needs to be read several times in detail. However, here are some suggestions for tackling it. First, notice that it is prefaced by a wrangle between the god Pluto and his wife Proserpine about the reputation of women. Pluto is upholding the traditional view of women as deceitful and sinful, while Proserpine is defending her sex against male propaganda.

Obviously this argument keys directly into the larger argument about men and women in the tale. But the god and goddess affect the action even more directly: they actually take sides in January and May's relationship. Pluto says he will literally open January's eyes to what is going on (May and the squire are up a tree making love), so Proserpine responds by saying she will give May a quick wit and good excuse. This is, in fact, what happens, and you can fill in the details for yourself. What you should particularly consider is the way in which this conclusion resolves the main tensions of the poem. It seems that Youth and Age (i.e. May and January) are finally reconciled, but only after Youth and Youth (i.e. May and Damian) have got together. Similarly, the marriage seems to have been restored to a kind of harmony – but only after there has been a sexual fling along the way. Finally, you might consider the significance of January's blindness. Is the sudden return of his sight in some way symbolic, suggesting that he has both literally and metaphorically 'seen the light'? Has he, do you think, come to a clearer understanding of himself and his wife? You will not find these altogether easy questions to answer, for this is still in many respects a problematic tale. However, if you look for the resolution of previous tensions, you can at least say to what extent the conclusion is successful in tackling them. Love, marriage, power and the nature of relationships have all been explored from many points of view. It is finally up to you to decide whether this is a happy, a sad or a bittersweet ending.

Step 5 *Relating the tale to its teller*

You may find a clue as to how to take the ending of *The Merchant's Tale* if you look at his prologue immediately before it. Reading this you can form a fuller idea of the specific narrator, and ask whether this affects your overall view of his tale. The opening lines are characteristic of him: 'Wepyng and waylyng, care and oother sorwe / I knowe ynogh ...' (ll. 1213–14). Clearly, the Merchant is a miserable man, and it soon turns out that the reason for this is that he has just got married to a woman he cannot stand. If you can transfer this insight to the tale, the ways of responding may become clearer. Perhaps the whole thing is an exercise in cynicism, a kind of extended 'moan'. Certainly, this would help you account for the lengthy and apparently sarcastic praise of women with which the tale opens. It would also explain why the god Pluto is such a cynic and, finally, it might just cast doubt on the 'happy-ever-after' nature of the ending. Perhaps January and May are only at the beginning, not the end, of a marriage of lies and deception!

Step 6   Seeing the text in context

Besides being about 'love', *The Merchant's Tale* explores the fraught relationship between an old husband and a young wife. In this sense it can be said to be about 'marriage'. In common with other tales in the so-called 'Marriage Group', *The Merchant's Tale* can thus perhaps be better understood by comparison with other Canterbury Tales dealing with love, marriage and power. You will find further information on these questions in the sections of this chapter dealing with the tales of the Clerk, Franklin and Wife of Bath and also in Chapter 8 (pp. 202–14).

Step 7   Analysing the style

The style of *The Merchant's Tale* is very rich, so you should try to develop a sense of this. Particularly notice where the poet moves from one type of language to another. For instance, the squire Damian is usually presented in a 'high' or 'courtly' style, but notice that, as in the passage referred to above, the high style is usually cut short or deflated in some way. The suggestion is therefore that his courtliness is a mere pose. Underneath, he is just a vigorous lad. Notice, too, that there are occasional passages of moralizing in the poem, full of sonorous generalizations and appeals to learned authorities. The counsellors Placebo and Justinus use this style, and so do the gods Pluto and Proserpine. So, too, does the Merchant towards the beginning of the tale. Such passages can be off-putting at first. But all they really do is add to the moral weight of the poem and provide opportunities to deal with its main issues in a more abstract way. They are all about the 'pros' and 'cons' of marriage.

Finally, at the other end of the scale from abstraction, you should look out for recurrent images. Food, drink, knives, keys, animals, and especially birds, all figure both literally and metaphorically in this poem. They make it richer in verbal texture and they usually have something to contribute to our view of the characters and the problems they explore. *The Merchant's Tale* presents us with many different views of men and women, so it naturally uses a wide range of language to do it. As usual when studying Chaucer's style, noting the wide variety of language he uses is simply another way of recognizing that he presents many different views of the same thing. In form as in content, his vision is fundamentally 'mixed'.

THE WIFE OF BATH'S PROLOGUE AND TALE

Step 1   What kind of work am I studying?

Like most of the Canterbury Tales, *The Wife of Bath's Prologue and Tale* is a composite or 'mixed' work. In this case, it is made up of two main elements, a sermon and a confession, and if you get hold of these two aspects from the beginning, everything else falls into place. Let's look at it first as a sermon. The Wife of Bath clearly sets out to give the other pilgrims a full-blown sermon with all the traditional trimmings. There are biblical quotations, illustrative stories and direct appeals to the audience, as well as a long moralized story ('exemplum') to drive home the message. All these features combine to build up an image of the Wife of Bath as a particularly vigorous and versatile preacher. However, there is a catch. The Wife is not really a preacher at all, but a prosperous widow, and her message is itself far from traditional. What she is preaching is a defence of women's powers within marriage, as well as an attack on male clerics, who usually presented women as the source of sin and strife in the world. In other words, the Wife of Bath is turning a lot of traditional sermon conventions on their head; she is preaching a kind of 'mock' or 'anti' sermon. This is obviously both fascinating and funny. However, what makes *The Wife of Bath's Prologue and Tale* doubly interesting is the fact that this 'mock-sermon' is itself combined with another device, the confession.

In the course of her preaching the Wife gives the other pilgrims an intimate account of her life and loves to date. As she has been married five times her confession makes for sensational as well as instructive reading. In fact, sex and violence figure prominently, so the whole thing turns (quite literally) into a 'blow-by-blow' account. This is the 'confession' side of the prologue and tale. Now all you need to do is think of the two sides of the work, the sermon and the confession, at the same time. The combination may be complex in practice, but it is very simple in principle. On the one hand, there is the Wife as preacher and public defender of women; on the other, there are the intimate confessions of an experienced widow and woman of the world. The two together make this one of Chaucer's richest and most fascinating tales.

Step 2   What is it about?

On a first reading the mixture of sermon and confession makes this a difficult text to follow. What you therefore need is a basic sense of what happens and when. In fact, for all the asides and illustrations, the sequence of events in *The Wife of Bath's Prologue and Tale* is remarkably simple: the Wife talks about her five husbands (three of whom were rich and old, two of whom were young and lively), and then goes on to tell a tale about a knight who raped a maiden. The knight's punishment is to find out 'What thyng is it that wommen moost desiren' (l. 905), and this he finally does with the help of an old woman, whom he then marries. The answer to the question is that women want power ('Wommen desiren to have sovereynetee' – l. 1038), and, as this is also the main idea behind the Wife's account of her five marriages, you should hold on to it. That way you can relate the whole poem to a single issue ('women's power'), and you will be able to see that both the prologue and the tale are really just different ways of exploring the same thing.

Step 3   Looking at characterization

There is a wide range of characters you need to think about in this tale: the Wife herself, her five husbands, and the knight and the old woman. The Wife is the most complex, so we shall leave her till later. Let's start by looking at the passage introducing the five husbands (ll. 193–206). Notice that the first three come across as a group rather than separate people, as 'types' rather than 'individuals'. They all fall into the Wife's category of rich, old and foolish husbands, and they are a familiar literary type. The other two husbands are more individualized. One is a young gallant who requires more subtle handling from the Wife (ll. 453ff.), and the other, her fifth husband, is an altogether stronger and more substantial character. Notice that when he is introduced (ll. 504ff.) he has a specific name (Jankin), a specific occupation ('a clerk of Oxenford' – l. 527), and elicits a much more complex response from the Wife. None the less, for all the difference, remember that all five husbands illustrate the same basic point. Rich or poor, old or young, stupid or clever, they are all examples of powerless husbands, men whom the Wife finally succeeded in taming.

Now look at the characters in the Wife's tale and the way they are introduced (ll. 882ff.). These are even more obviously character 'types': the knight is simply a 'lusty bacheler' and he rapes a maid, about whom we know nothing except that she is raped. Clearly such characters are not meant to be interesting as individuals; they are merely figures in a kind of fairytale. Their significance lies not so much in what kind of people they are as in the ideas they represent. In this instance, as with the Wife's husbands in her prologue, it is easiest to think of the knight and lady as elements in the Wife's argument. As this is an argument proposing 'women's power', obviously the rape by the knight is meant to illustrate the reverse. It is a display of brutal male power.

The 'olde wyf' in the tale is also best approached as another element in the Wife of Bath's argument (ll. 997ff.). Notice that she too has no name and is not described in great deal (in other words, she is not an 'individual'). None the less, she is the linchpin in the argument on 'sovereynetee'. It is she who gives the knight the correct answer ('Wommen desiren to have sovereynetee' –l. 1038), and in so doing she gains power over him. The approach to take, then, is to regard *all* the characters in *The Wife of Bath's Prologue and Tale* as elements in the Wife's argument. They all have a contribution to make to our view of 'women's power'.

Step 4   Developing the argument

The Wife of Bath is such a lively and digressive narrator that her argument is often difficult to see as a whole. What you should therefore do initially is concentrate on just three or four crucial passages. That will give you a detailed sense of the fundamental strategies and issues. You should also keep reminding yourself that the whole text can be reduced to a mixture of two major strategies (sermon and confession), and a single issue ('women's power').

Read through the opening lines of the poem (ll. 1–29). Notice that from one point of view this is simply a confession, a kind of autobiographical rumination from the wife based on her own experience:

Experience, though noon auctoritee
Were in this world, is right ynogh for me
To speke of wo that is in mariage ... .
(ll. 1–3)

And so she goes on to chatter about her five 'Housbondes at chirche dore'. But notice that, from another point of view, this is also the beginning of the Wife's 'mock-sermon'. She is deliberately laying her own experience of marriage against the established 'authorities' ('auctoritee') on marriage. In fact, she goes on in this sermonizing vein to pile up more and more biblical stories and quotations in support of her own attitude to marriage: this is essentially that you should marry often and enjoy sex. There are more subtle twists and turns you can trace in the argument here, such as the fact that some of her illustrations also support the opposite point of view. However, the fundamental insight remains. The Wife of Bath is treating us to a confession of her life to date, and she is also delivering a deliberately provocative sermon on sex and marriage. This holds good for all the rest of her performance.

Take another passage, the Wife's advice to other 'wise wyves' (ll. 224ff.). Again there is the combination of an intimately confessional manner ('Now listen how I went about things ...'), with a direct, sermonizing exhortation ('This is how you should speak to and treat men ...'). And both are followed up by a marvellous display of how to go about nagging an old husband! By this time you may have noticed that the effect of all this boasting and bullying is rather double-edged. On the one hand, the Wife certainly comes across as an assertive and independent-minded woman. On the other hand, she is also aggressive and blatantly dishonest, and freely admits that she herself has often told lies. Overall, then, your response is likely to be 'mixed'. Criticism of the Wife gets mixed up with admiration, and you may find yourself unsure how exactly to respond to what she says. The result is *irony*. You may be unsure whether to take what she says seriously or comically, at face value or for what it leaves unsaid. This double-edged, ironic aspect of *The Wife of Bath's Prologue and Tale* takes many forms, and yet it is always a result of the fundamentally simple mixture with which we started: a mock-sermon combined with a confession.

You will find the most dramatic display of the sermon-confession combination at the end of the Wife's Prologue (ll. 772ff.). This is where she tells us how she triumphed over her fifth and most challenging husband, the Oxford scholar, Jankin. Notice that it is the climax of her mock-sermon because she depicts herself as the heroine who has had enough of male propaganda about women. Her triumph is in getting the male cleric to burn his 'book of wikked wyves' (l. 685). Notice, too, that it is the climax of her confession because this is where she reveals her most calculating mix of physical force and cunning: she pretends she is dying from a blow given her by Jankin, only to hit him back when he comes closer. The upshot of all this is that the Wife is a shining example of what women should *and* should not be! Her public image is above reproach, but her private image is far below it. Thanks to the combination of sermon and confession we see both at once.

Step 5 *Relating the tale to its teller*

You can consolidate your view of the Wife of Bath if you turn to the description of her in *The General Prologue* (ll. 445–76). As usual in *The General Prologue*, the detail is rich and fascinating: you find out, for instance, that she is gap-toothed and a bit deaf, that she wears sharp spurs and extravagant hats, that she never allows anyone to push in front of her at church, that she has been on lots of pilgrimages, and so on. Notice, however, that all this detail can be reduced to just three dominant features. She is prosperous, bullying and highly sexed. Now all you do is consider what these insights add to your view of the Wife's prologue and tale. Her prosperity we know comes largely from a succession of rich husbands. Her bullying nature we have had abundant proof of in her performance as a whole, and we have also observed that this is usually tied in with the calculating use of her own sexuality. Another way of putting all this is therefore in terms of a fundamental *tension* in the Wife's nature. She is both amorous and aggressive, and it is the constant movement between these two states which makes her particularly formidable. You might say she works on a kind of 'love-hate' principle. In her own prologue she describes herself in astrological terms as a combination of Venus/Love and Mars/War (ll. 609–26). Her relationship with Jankin, as we have just seen, is also characterized by a similarly dynamic mixture of love and hate, attraction and repulsion. In this connection you might even wish to note that the Wife's tale is itself set in motion by a rape, the crudest mixture of sex and violence and the ultimate debasement of attraction and repulsion. Whatever terms you use ('love/hate', 'Venus/Mars', 'attraction/repulsion' or 'sex/violence'), it is clear that some such tension is at the core of the Wife's character. You may therefore find such terms useful when trying to say more precisely what is meant by 'sovereyntee' or 'power' in the Wife's prologue and tale. (Also see pp. 204–5.)

This is also a good place to remind yourself that the ultimate narrator of *The Wife of Bath's Prologue and Tale* is not a woman at all but a man. For instance, how does it affect your view of the whole performance to know that Alisoun of Bath is the creation of Geoffrey Chaucer? Perhaps, therefore, it is all a subtle piece of male propaganda! Perhaps the whole point of *The Wife of Bath's Prologue and Tale* is that it is designed to draw attention to the potential independence and assertiveness of women – only to undermine their position by revealing that the Wife is really a rogue. Whatever conclusion you come to, some serious consideration of the narrator (or narrators) of this work is clearly necessary.

Step 6   Seeing the text in context

There are many issues in *The Wife of Bath's Prologue and Tale* which a little knowledge of its social and historical context will help you to focus more sharply. Contemporary attitudes to marital disputes and to rape, the legal and financial status of widows, the fact that women were not allowed to preach – these all have a bearing on the way we see the Wife's characterization and performance. In some ways it is enough simply to mention these issues for their significance to be glaring. However, a few historical observations are clearly necessary.

By and large, as now, what actually went on within marriages in Chaucer's day went unremarked and unrecorded. None the less, it does seem that medieval marriages were frequently fraught and sometimes violent. If you think about it, it could hardly be otherwise when the usual considerations behind marriage at every level were economic rather than sentimental. Marriages of convenience were much more common than marriages of affection. The result was therefore a fairly high level of violence within marriage, and a fairly high incidence of affairs outside it. It would seem that wife-beating was allowed as long as you did not actually maim or kill your wife. On the other hand, the nagging wife or 'scold' might be publicly ducked in the village pond. Such, in its worst aspects, was the general texture of medieval marriage. Economic power also tended to be vested in men, and daughters made the best match they could. With all this in mind the behaviour of the Wife of Bath becomes understandable. Initially she has no economic power of her own and only gets some by a combination of cunning and exploitation of her main resource, her body. The Wife is therefore not just an individual, a specific woman; she also, in an exaggerated way, represents the lot of many medieval women. The same can be said of the Wife's status as a widow. Medieval widows had considerably more legal and financial independence than either married or single women. For that reason the Wife is also a particularly plausible 'type' in that she combines prosperity and independence.

The maid raped in *The Wife of Bath's Tale* can also be seen as a significant 'type'. Rape commonly went unremarked in the Middle Ages and, in so far as it was recorded, tended to get confused with 'raptus' (the legal term for abduction). Chaucer himself was accused of what was probably this latter form of 'raptus'. On both cases, the maid's rape and Chaucer's 'raptus', critics usually observe a discreet and deferential silence. You might pause to consider why, and also to think about how your reading of the tale is altered if you stress the element of sexual violence in the poem.

The other social issues raised by *The Wife of Bath's Prologue and Tale* are treated elsewhere in this book. The male monopoly of higher education and preaching obviously explains the specific power of Jankin, the Oxford scholar. Parallels can be followed up in the corresponding sections on the Miller's and Pardoner's tales. So can other treatments of 'sovereyntee' and power within marriage in the tales of the Clerk, Merchant and Franklin (other tales belonging to the so-called 'Marriage Group'). Also see Chapter 8, pp. 210–11.

Step 7   Analysing the style

The style of The Wife of Bath's Prologue and Tale is particularly rich. The best way to approach it is in broad categories corresponding to the two basic strategies used in the work as a whole: sermon and confession. For instance, look back at the opening lines of the prologue. Notice how the language shifts from a relaxed conversational and confessional style to one which is much more strident and declamatory, in fact sermonizing. In the space of a few lines we move from 'For, lordynges, sith I twelve yeer was of age ...', to 'Herkne eek, lo ...' (ll. 4–14). You should also look out for occasions where the tone suddenly becomes more lively and idiomatic. This happens where the Wife is interrupted by the Pardoner, or the Friar and the Summoner, or even by herself musing on past experience. The basic point is that this is a text full of different, highly dramatic 'voices', and all of them contribute to what is a complex performance.

To be sensitive to these shifts of tone and different 'voices' is simply a way of registering, through the style, the fundamental complexity of the Wife's characterization and the issues explored.

THE CLERK'S TALE

Step I   What kind of work am I studying?

In outline *The Clerk's Tale* is fairly simple: it is a story celebrating the supreme virtue of a saint-like figure. It therefore belongs to a common type of medieval work called the 'saint's life', or 'holy life'. In this case the heroine is 'patient Griselda', a kind of super-woman who manages to be patient despite the most horrible trials and tribulations. What complicates the whole thing is the fact that you may not be sure how to respond. On the one hand, you can read *The Clerk's Tale* as a grotesque fairytale full of fantastic displays of cruelty; on the other, you can read it as in some way about real people in situations you can sympathize with. Either way, you are likely to find yourself constantly asking, 'How do I respond? What do I make of this?' *The Clerk's Tale* is a holy life – but with some disturbing differences.

Step 2   What is it about?

The fairytale aspects of the work stand out if you summarize the plot. Essentially, it is a 'rags-to-riches' tale of a poor peasant girl who marries a marquis, is 'divorced' by him, but is finally reinstated as his wife. In the course of this the heroine is also subjected to a whole series of outrageous tests: first one, then another of her children is taken away from her, apparently to be murdered; and then, as a mere servant, she is forced to attend her husband's supposed second marriage. Overall, therefore, there is the kind of big and bold story pattern we usually associate with fairytales. You should hold on to this as it provides a simple framework around which you can build your interpretation. The main issues are equally obvious. This is above all a tale of *patience* and *suffering,* and you will find some such terms useful when trying to formulate a more abstract sense of what the work is about.

Step 3   Looking at characterization

Now look more closely at the characterization. Try to see what kind of characters you are dealing with and how you are meant to respond. For example, here are the first few lines introducing Griselda:

> A doghter hadde he, fair ynogh to sighte,
> And Grisildis this yonge mayden highte.
> But for to speke of vertuous beautee,
> Thanne was she oon the faireste under sonne;
> For povreliche yfostred up was she ... .
> (ll. 209–13)

Clearly, from a physical point of view there is little to go on. Griselda is simply 'fair ynogh to sighte' and 'oon the faireste under sonne', both of which are rather standard compliments. However, if you go on to draw up a list of her main features, you will find that these are all of a broadly similar kind. They are all related virtues. Griselda is humble, sober, chaste, obedient, hard-working, and so on. In other words, she is an essentially *idealized* figure. She is interesting not so much for how she thinks and feels as an individual, but for what she represents as an ideal. If you can keep this 'ideal' aspect of Griselda in mind, it will help you to understand the problems that arise later, when you are invited to see her in more 'realistic' ways. To start with, though, it is important that you see her as a kind of saint.

Step 4   Developing the argument

The next step is to look at the characters as a whole and to try to see what ideas they represent. As usual, detailed study of a couple of crucial passages will help you get your bearings. Take the first meeting between Marquis Walter, Griselda and her father (ll. 295–367). This is a fairly long passage, but particularly useful because it reveals the tensions between the main characters. On the one hand, there is the poor and humble Griselda; on the other, there is the rich and powerful marquis. Notice, too, that there is a contrast between the two men and the woman. It is the two men, father and prospective husband, who actually arrange the marriage; Griselda is simply asked afterwards whether she consents. In this way you can arrive quickly at a fuller sense of what *The Clerk's Tale* is about. Not only is it about 'patience' and 'suffering' in general; it is also, more particularly, about different kinds of power. There is the power of the rich over the poor, and the power of men over women. Both have their part to play in the crossing and re-crossing of issues as the plot unfolds.

A quick way of seeing how all these issues are tied together is to turn to the end. For example, look at the final 'family reunion' scene, where Griselda is reunited with her children and also told by Walter that he has not divorced her after all (ll. 1044–134). Clearly, this is meant to be some kind of 'happy ending', so it is worth asking who is happy and why. Well, Griselda is happy because she has her children back, and Walter is happy because his wife has stood up to every conceivable test he could inflict on her. You might therefore say that this is a happy ending because the suffering has stopped and patience has been rewarded. Put in more specifically social terms, the conclusion is equally emphatic. The rich and powerful know what they are doing (despite all appearances to the contrary), and men finally know what is best for their wives. There is even an explicitly religious dimension to this 'happy ending' which helps to sanctify it. The passage is full of references to God and divine benevolence, and the strong implication is that Walter should be seen as some kind of divine agent. Like God, he seems to punish the faithful, but in fact he rewards them in the end. Consequently, as we said earlier, Griselda can be seen not merely as a good wife and mother, but as virtually a saint. In fact, with Walter playing God and Griselda a saint, everything is as it should be in a medieval holy life.

Not surprisingly, many modern readers find all this holy-life stuff difficult to take. They do not see why Walter should be excused as some kind of Godlike figure, and they certainly cannot see why Griselda should have put up with him. None the less, the fact remains that this kind of thing was common in medieval works of piety. So you should at least try to understand it in those terms, even if you do not agree with them. Fortunately for us, however, it also seems that Chaucer did not wholly agree with this kind of story either.

Step 5   Relating the tale to the teller

In this case the attitude of the narrator substantially affects the way in which we respond to his tale. He invites us to see it in a specific light. The easiest way of showing this is to concentrate on the explicit comment by the narrator at the beginning of Part 3 (ll. 449–62).

This is the point where Walter decides to 'tempte' Griselda by removing their first child, and this is the reaction he provokes from the Clerk:

> what neded it,
> Hire for to tempte, and alwey moore and moore,
> Though som men preise it for a subtil wit?
> But as for me, I seye that yvele it sit
> To assaye a wyf whan that it is no nede ... .
> (ll. 457–61)

The effect is devastating. At a stroke, the whole emphasis of the story is shifted from the heroine's patience to her suffering, and with it goes a shift in our view of Walter. According to the Clerk, he is not a just and Godlike figure, but simply a human being who is cruel and wrong. This is just one passage, but you will notice others like it throughout *The Clerk's Tale*. Their combined effect is to make you think much more critically about how you are to react. They also point to the fact that this may be a holy life, but it is one which demands a particularly flexible and human response. The basic choice is therefore the same as we started with. On the one hand, there is the ideal and spiritual way of reading the tale; but on the other, there is a more immediately human and feeling way of reading it. The narrator simply reminds you not to concentrate on the former at the expense of the latter.

Step 6   Seeing the text in context

The relationship between Marquis Walter and the peasant girl Griselda obviously has a social as well as a personal side to it. It will therefore help you to focus the issues if you try to see them in a broader literary and historical context. Problems connected with the relative power of men and women also arise in the tales of the Knight, Miller, Franklin, Merchant and Wife of Bath. In fact the contrast with *The Wife of Bath's Tale* is pointed up in a kind of epilogue to *The Clerk's Tale*, the 'Envoy'. You should therefore turn to the corresponding sections dealing with other tales so as to fill out your sense of where Walter and Griselda fit into the larger argument. In addition, you should also consider the presentation of Walter's other subjects. How far do the people on his estate have a convincingly human identity of their own, and how far are they a mere backdrop to the main action – the conventionally fickle masses? Are they people or pawns? Your answer to this will again depend upon the degree to which you read the tale in human or ideal terms. All you are doing, therefore, is applying the same criteria to the 'minor' as well as the 'major' characters.

Step 7   Analysing the style

Two things should be noted in the style of *The Clerk's Tale*, and both can be illustrated from the passages referred to already. One is that the routine style of the poem is 'middle' or 'plain'; it is neither particularly 'high' and formal, nor particularly 'low' and colloquial. The initial description of Griselda is a good example in that it is clear and economical, but also rather colourless. On the other hand there are occasional passages where the style becomes more animated and colourful. You get a stronger, more colloquial sense of the speaking voice. The interruption by the Clerk is such a passage, and so is the whole of the concluding 'Envoy'. At these points the normally orderly and composed manner of the poem is fundamentally changed. Notice that these shifts in style correspond to fundamental shifts in attitudes. It is as though the narrator cannot maintain his stance of detached impersonality, and the result is a brief flash of personality and real involvement. In other words, we are reminded that there is more than one 'voice' in *The Clerk's Tale* and therefore that there is more than one way of responding. As always in Chaucer, it is this mixture of styles and attitudes which makes his work so challenging.

THE FRANKLIN'S PROLOGUE AND TALE

Step 1   What kind of work am I studying?

The Franklin's Tale is essentially a court romance, a tale about knights and ladies engaged in the highly idealized form of courtship called courtly love. However, what makes this particular court romance unusual is the fact that Chaucer mixes in with it elements of another type of story, the holy life. Holy lives are often like court romances, except that their heroes and heroines are holy people rather than knights and ladies, and the predicaments they are faced with tend to be of a specifically religious rather than broadly moral kind. In other respects the struggles of these lone individuals in hostile circumstances are remarkably similar.

Dorigen, the heroine of *The Franklin's Tale*, is primarily a courtly lady. None the less, you will also find many features of the holy life in her characterization and predicaments – in particular, an emphasis on her suffering as well as her need to take highly ethical decisions. With these two aspects of the tale firmly in mind, you will be in a good position to understand its particular emphasis. Expect a story about aristocratic courtship, and think especially about the trials and tribulations of the heroine.

Step 2   What is it about?

The story in *The Franklin's Tale* centres on a 'love triangle' made up of the knight Arveragus, his wife Dorigen and a squire called Aurelius; problems result from the squire's persistent wooing of the wife. This is a standard situation in court romance. There is also a fourth character, the magician, who helps Aurelius woo the lady, but he is fairly minor and best seen as part of a subplot.

Step 3   Looking at characterization

You can get hold of the characterization in *The Franklin's Tale* by looking closely at the presentation of Arveragus and Dorigen in the first thirty-odd lines (ll. 729–60). What kind of characters are they, and in what ways do they relate to one another? For instance, notice that you know almost nothing about them physically. Dorigen is simply and conventionally 'oon the faireste under sonne' and we have no idea what Arveragus looks like. In fact, as is common in court romance, these characters exist almost exclusively as sets of abstract postures and disembodied qualities. Arveragus is the classic 'courtly lover' and observes a standard pattern of feeling: he falls totally in love, experiences 'wo, peyne and distresse', performs heroic deeds for his lady, and finally wins her over by his 'worthynesse' and 'obeysaunce'. Dorigen then simply has to show 'pitee' on him for the love match to be complete. Some of the other terms used in this passage are not quite so standard, and you should therefore pay particular attention to them. For example, the actual marriage agreement is built round the terms 'maistrie' and 'soveraynetee' (both meaning 'power' or 'control'), as well as the terms 'gentillesse' and 'trouthe' (nobility and fidelity). The idea is that husband and wife will both act nobly and faithfully, and in particular that the husband will not assume he has power and control over his wife ('take no maistrie'). The only thing he asks is that he should keep the appearance of power ('the name of soveraynetee'). Clearly, then, what is being presented is a type of mutually respectful and in most ways equal relationship. The only condition on which the knight insists is that he should at least *appear* to be in charge. This is important, and you will need to come back to it. However, for the moment it is enough to see that we know almost nothing about Arveragus and Dorigen as individuals, but that we do perceive them as a couple, a husband and wife bound by a specific contract. They exist for us as sets of interrelated ideas rather than two fully developed people in their own right. The opening sets the tone for the rest of the tale, and it points to the fact that *The Franklin's Tale* is much more about complex ethical problems and issues than it is about complex personalities. It also suggests that we should look at all the characters as elements in an overall argument, and try not to talk about them in isolation.

Step 4 Developing the argument

Concentrate on a couple of passages in which you can explore the central triangle in greater depth. How do the three main characters relate to one another, and what do their relationships tell you about the nature of love? For instance, take the passage in which Dorigen turns down Squire Aurelius (ll. 967–1010). This is a crucial turning-point in the action and allows you to see the underlying tensions clearly. On the one hand, there is Dorigen representing faithful love *within* marriage; on the other, there is Aurelius urging her to be unfaithful and offering love *outside* marriage. The contrast is stark, but notice how the argument is resolved. It all hinges on the interpretation of her parting report. Having given the squire a firm 'no', Dorigen then adds that she would only love Aurelius when all the rocks have been removed all along the coast of Brittany (ll. 990–8). As this seems to be utterly impossible, all she may be saying in effect is 'I'll love you when pigs can fly!', that is, *never*. However, from another point of view, you might claim that Dorigen is behaving carelessly and that it is a silly thing to say in the circumstances. How you respond here is crucial. The result will be a view of Dorigen as either firm or flippant – or, if you like, both. But it is your decision on the basis of your reading.

To see how the relationship between Dorigen and her husband stands up to pressure you need to look at a later passage. The exchange between Dorigen and Arveragus on his return home is an obvious candidate (ll. 1457–92). By this time the squire has indeed arranged for the rocks to disappear. On the one hand, we have the distraught wife confessing that she has given her word to love the squire if the 'impossible' happens; on the other, we have the husband insisting that, as the 'impossible' has happened, she should keep her word and go to the squire. Again look particularly at the knight's final words and how the argument is resolved. In fact, the husband concludes that the shame is all his and forbids his wife to tell anyone 'on pain of death', and then he packs her off to report his decision to the squire. Once more you have a choice how to interpret all this. You might choose to see it from the husband's point of view, and credit him with a brilliant piece of decision-making and a wonderfully magnanimous gesture. Alternatively you might see the situation from the wife's point of view, and wonder what happened to their ideally 'equal' relationship, their mutual 'maistrie'. Arveragus is not only keeping up the appearance of 'soveraynetee'; he seems to have taken over complete control. Obviously the relationship between Dorigen and Arveragus is a complex and contentious one, and you will find it much discussed by critics. However, the underlying problem can still be expressed in basically simple terms. Under the general heading of 'love', it is an exploration of 'power' or 'control' within human relationships. These are the terms with which we started, and really all we are doing is refining them.

So what is the final situation in *The Franklin's Tale?* How are the issues of 'love' and 'power' finally resolved? If you read the last few lines (1607–24) carefully, you can come to your own conclusions. All I shall do is point to some possibilities. The magician, for example, sees the whole thing as a kind of noble 'tit-for-tat'; he stresses the fact that the knight, the squire and himself have each tried to act nobly ('gentilly'). This is the gist of the narrator's final question too: 'Lordynges, ... Which was the mooste fre [noble], as thynketh yow?' But notice that again there are basically two interpretations, depending on your point of view. On the one hand, you might see this as a 'happy-ever-after' ending in which everybody acted 'gentilly'.

You would therefore emphasize the view that the knight and the lady have a wonderfully equal relationship. On the other hand, you might wonder what has happened to Dorigen in this final round of back-patting and self-congratulation. She certainly does not figure in the magician's view of things, for it is only himself and the two other men whom he congratulates. Nor does it seem that Dorigen is included in the narrator's final question: 'Which was the mooste fre?' In this case you might say that by the end of the tale Dorigen has slipped completely out of sight!

Overall, then, you are left with two rather different ways of seeing *The Franklin's Tale*. One is that it is a straightforward justification of love within marriage, based on mutual respect and equality. The other is that it is a more complex exploration of the roles of women and men in marriage, and that the power is weighted in favour of the male. In short, you can see the relationship of Averagus and Dorigen as genuinely or superficially equal. Alternatively, you might choose to emphasize one or other of the two main story types to be found in *The Franklin's Tale*. Is it a court romance celebrating nobility and love, or is it really more of a holy life, in which the real but acknowledged 'saint' is the suffering and harassed heroine? If you opt for the latter view, then you would probably draw particular attention to Dorigen's noble complaint (ll. 1355–456). Whichever way you incline, it is finally up to you to decide how you perceive the mixture of love and power in this tale. For further discussion of this tale as a 'solution' to the supposed 'Marriage Group', see Chapter 8 (pp. 210–11).

Step 5   Relating the tale to its teller

Now think about the narrator, the Franklin, and what he adds to your sense of his tale. You should start by looking at the description of him in *The General Prologue* (ll. 331–60), as well as the material in his own prologue and the 'Words between the Franklin, the Squire and Host'. For all the detail, just one thing is stressed about the Franklin: that he is a prosperous landowner, but that he really wants to be considered a nobleman (of 'gentil' status). Now all you do is look for a similar preoccupation in his tale. To what extent is *The Franklin's Tale* also preoccupied with nobility ('gentillesse') and noble behaviour in general? You already know that these terms figure at the close of the poem, so it is worth looking at similar 'noble' words such as 'worthy' and 'worthynesse' too. In fact, you will find that all these terms and ideas figure prominently, so you might now wish to refine your view of the poem as a whole. Perhaps it is not only about 'love and power', but also an exploration of 'what it is to be noble'. For instance, is 'nobility' simply a matter of social rank, or is it (as the magician believes) more a matter of personal worth? Clearly this is an aspect of the tale's argument, and you might wish to explain it by reference to the teller. In this way each may throw light on the other.

Step 6   Seeing the text in context

The Franklin's Tale obviously has a social dimension, so some historical observations are necessary to help you see the issues more clearly and in perspective. The relevant historical context can be summed up in terms of just three aspects of late-fourteenth-century life: the decline of chivalry, the corresponding increase in non-noble landowners, and a continuing imbalance in the economic power of men and women. The first two can be taken together. Chivalry, with its emphasis on knights in single combat, was becoming increasingly impractical and irrelevant in the real warfare of the later Middle Ages. Most battles were in fact won by archers and foot soldiers. The result was that the court romance, the main literary form of chivalry, was itself beginning to look rather archaic and old-fashioned. Meanwhile, at the same time as chivalry and the court romance were in decline, another more practical and economically vigorous class was forming. These were the non-noble merchants and senior administrators, and they were becoming a very influential and extremely self-conscious section of society. Chaucer's Franklin was one of these. Now consider the critical relevance of all this to the Franklin and his tale. Here we have a narrator who is highly conscious of his own non-noble status, and who desperately wants to be considered 'gentil'. The result may therefore be that he tells a kind of 'ultra-noble' court romance in order to impress the other pilgrims. Looked at this way, *The Franklin's Tale* then becomes an ostentatious and rather overdone showpiece in an outmoded fashion. None of this really changes the issues the tale explores, but it does alter the frame in which we see them. Maybe there is something over-solemn and silly about the whole performance after all?

The fundamentally unequal economic relationship between men

and women in the Middle Ages is referred to frequently in this book. All that need be added here is that you should consider the impossible situation in which Dorigen is put as an expression of the situations in which many medieval women found themselves. With little direct power of their own they were often dependent on the whims or the decisions of men. You will find more information on the factual and fictional sides of 'maistrye' in the corresponding sections of this book dealing with the Knight's and Miller's tales. Look, too, at the treatment of similar issues in the tales of the Merchant, Clerk and the Wife of Bath, the other tales in the so-called 'Marriage Group'. In all these cases the struggle over power has a sexual as well as a class dimension, and all of them express tensions within actual life at the time.

Step 7   Analysing the style

Finally, make sure you can make sensible comments on the style of *The Franklin's Tale*. In fact, the style of this tale is quite similar to that of *The Knight's Tale*, so you should start with the corresponding section of Chapter 3, where the subject is treated in more detail. Here are some specific tips. Look again at the opening description of Dorigen and Arveragus (ll. 729–60). Try to see how the generally abstract texture of the language (full of words such as 'worthynesse' and 'obeysaunce') results in a type of characterization which is itself abstract and idealized. Notice, too, that many of the sentences are neatly balanced and produce a sense of formality. All these abstract and formal features are essential in creating the idealized world of court romance.

Reading through the poem, you will also be aware of places where its style changes. Notice these and think about why they occur. For instance, there is the melodramatic extravagance of Dorigen's complaint (ll. 1342–456). Suddenly you are presented with lots of rhetorical questions and learned examples of women who have been abused. Equally packed and formal, though in a more technical language, is the catalogue of the magician's astrological powers (ll. 1273–93). In both these cases you might simply say that such passages add to the richness and interest of the story, as does the little passage presenting Janus by the fire at new year (ll. 1245–55). However, you might also say that the Franklin is really treating us to a rhetorical fireworks-display. In his styles no less than in his story, he seems to be showing us just how 'gentil' he can be. Whatever detailed comments you make on the style of *The Franklin's Tale*, you can always relate them to larger aspects of the tale in this way. And this, really, is the secret of how to develop your analysis of any of the Canterbury Tales: start with some broad ideas, then look at the details of the text to develop your ideas, but after that return to your sense of the larger issues of the poem in order to draw your thoughts together.

FURTHER STUDY FRAMEWORKS

What follow are some guidelines for looking at four more tales. Again, they offer 'frameworks' rather than analyses, and are designed to prompt and support you in the development of your own views. The same seven-stage progression is used as with the other Chaucer tales. Here, however, it is pushed a little further so as to help you develop your own critical method too. More guidance on the exploration of current critical debates across, as well as within, tales can be found in Chapter 8.

The Reeve's Tale

Step I   *What kind of work am I studying*

Like *The Miller's Tale*, to which it is a dramatic response, *The Reeve's Tale* is a fabliau. It is a comical tale of trickery, crude sex and knockabout violence, and is set amongst what, from a court point of view, would be seen as 'the lower orders': a miller and his family and a couple of poor students. We may also see the tale as a triple-edged satire on: (1) the pretensions of tradespeople aspiring above their station; (2) 'learned' people who may not be as clever as they think; and, incidentally, (3) clergy who should be celibate and not have children (the miller's wife is the illegitimate daughter of the local parish priest). Furthermore, within the dramatic framework of *The*

Canterbury Tales as a whole, this is a particularly developed instance of a tale being told by one pilgrim in order to get back at another. The Miller has just told a scurrilous tale featuring a gullible carpenter; so the Reeve, who was a carpenter by trade, resolves to get revenge and 'quite' the Miller (ll. 3916, 4323) by telling a tale in which the butt is a cheating miller. *The Reeve's Tale* is therefore the return bout in a narrative needle match. Another pointed instance of such 'quitynge' is that between Friar and Summoner.

Step 2   What is it about?

This tale is remarkable for its economical description, brisk action and tight plotting; so it is crucial to have a firm grasp of what is going on. Knowing precisely who is where and when is particularly important during the climactic night-time episode; for here the hopping from bed to bed is at its most finely choreographed and farcically theatrical. The scene is set by descriptions of Symkyn the miller and his family, including stuck-up wife, buxom daughter (Moll) and a baby in a cradle (ll. 3925–4001). All have their parts to play in the ensuing action. This is set in motion by the arrival of two Cambridge students, Alan and John, who are bringing their corn to the mill to be ground. Despite their best efforts and their boast that the miller will not cheat them, that is precisely what he manages to do. Slipping out during the grinding, Symkyn unleashes their horse which promptly gallops off to the fens to join the wild mares. The two students spend the rest of the day catching it, during which time the miller has stolen a bushel of their ground wheat. Returning too late to get back to their college, Alan and John are obliged to ask Symkyn to sell them board and lodgings for the night. During supper, the miller and his wife get thoroughly drunk and eventually all tumble to their several beds in the one room.

At this point both the atmosphere and the plot thicken: the air with the sound of snoring and smell of farting; the intrigue with some sexual manoeuvres in the dark which require attention to appreciate fully. The initial sleeping arrangements are as follows: the two students share one bed; the miller and his wife share another (with the baby in a cradle at the foot of it); daughter Moll sleeps alone to one side. By the end, however, there has been a great deal of bed-hopping and not a little 'swyving' (see ll. 4178, 4317; the nearest modern word is perhaps 'screwing').

The first move is when Alan slips to the daughter's bed and the two set to on a long night of lovemaking (ll. 4168ff.). The second move occurs while the wife goes off to relieve her full bladder. John the other student shifts the cradle to the foot of his own bed, so that when the wife returns she gets in with him by mistake – and again the upshot is a night of 'prykinge' and 'swyving' (ll. 4214ff.). The third and final move occurs when Alan returns to what he believes to be his own bed. However, he too is misled by the shifted cradle and gets in with the miller instead (ll. 4249ff.). To make things worse, Alan promptly begins to boast of his sexual exploits with the miller's daughter in what he believes to be his fellow student's ear. A riotous brawl immediately breaks out and in the confusion the wife inadvertently cracks her husband over the head with a staff. The two students, meanwhile, manage to slip away. They even get to take their stolen wheat with them, which, the daughter has told Alan, was baked into a cake. Everything is rounded off by a moral pointed expressly at millers. The immediate target is obviously the cheating miller *within* the tale: 'A gylour shal himself bigyled be' ('A cheat will himself be cheated' l. 4321). However, the Reeve also has an eye trained on the pilgrim Miller *outside* the tale, whom he clearly gets at *through* it. As the last line reminds us: 'Thus have I quyt the Millere in my tale' (l. 4324).

Step 3   Looking at characterization

The characters are drawn with the bold outlines of caricature, but with sufficient complexity and distinguishing detail both to motivate the plot and to be engaging in themselves. Characterization is developed through a combination of description and action. Symkyn and his family, for instance, are introduced in the first 50 lines through the kind of freestanding description or 'portrait' made familiar by *The General Prologue* and *The Miller's Tale*: general type is realized through varied detail; features of physical appearance and dress mingle with aspects of behaviour and temperament, and the whole is shot through with glimpses of personal history. The keynote with the miller is that he is 'As any pecok ... proud and gay' (l. 3926) and that he is commonly known as 'deynous (contemptuous) Symkyn' (l. 3941). At the same time, a wealth of detail points to the fact that he is a bully and a cheat, and a dangerous man to cross. At first sight the miller's wife is simply an extension of his social pretensions: a prize property and adornment. On closer inspection, however, she turns out to be sullied goods and a snob: only educated in a nunnery because she is the illegitimate offspring of a priest: 'as digne (worthy) as water in a diche' (l. 3964).

Something similar may be observed of the presentation of the two students. Their characters, however, are established dramatically through speech and action rather than relatively statically through description. Alan and John are also distinguished from all the other characters, as well as from the Reeve and Chaucer, in that they come from 'fer in the north' (l. 4015; all the others are Southerners). Both students are therefore represented as using consistently Northern speech forms, for example, 'gif' for 'if', 'thair' for 'ther', 'taa' for 'tak(e)' and such dialectal variants as 'lathe' for 'barn'. The key note for the pair of them is that they are almost too clever for their own good – 'cocky' in every sense. Thus we may not easily be able to tell them apart. But we can certainly tell that their callow youth, would-be 'learning' and maybe even their very Northernness are being gently mocked.

Step 4 Developing the argument

A critical understanding of *The Reeve's Tale* as a whole requires us to bring together a variety of aspects, structural and thematic. These include descriptive, scene-setting techniques (e.g., the introduction of Symkyn and his wife, ll. 3921–4001), as well as alternations of narrative report and dramatic exchange (the grinding scene, for instance, ll. 4016–56). All these features are informed by an abiding concern with social tensions and pretensions. Therefore, for anything like a full grasp of this tale, we need to hold in mind such overarching issues as the relations between tale and teller and text and context, even while remaining attentive to such localized matters as shifts in style. This we now do.

Step 5 Relating the tale to its teller

In this case there is an unusually close and sustained relation between tale and teller. As framed, this story could only be told by the Reeve. We therefore have to weigh the 'external' relations between the Reeve and the Miller as pilgrims and personalities, even as we weigh the 'internal' representations of miller and reeve/carpenter within the tales as such. From this point of view, the individual prologues of the Reeve's and Miller's tales together with the paired description of these pilgrims in *The General Prologue* (ll. 545–622) can be seen as central rather than peripheral, essential not incidental. Crucial to this teller–tale, 'external-internal' dynamic is the fact that the miller *within The Reeve's Tale* has some pointed resemblances to the pilgrim-Miller *outside* it. Both are rough, love wrestling and tend to get drunk. A further twist is that the Reeve himself clearly knows a lot about the measuring out of grain, being wary of cheats, and the 'handling' of other people's property (see *The General Prologue*, ll. 594ff.). The implication seems to be that it takes an accomplished cheat (the Reeve) to know one (Symkyn).

But there is another twist to the tale–teller relation. For it would clearly take a far more learned and literary narrator than the average reeve to craft a tale as economical, allusive and artful as the one we have here. We must never forget, therefore, that the pervasive and in every sense *informing* presence in these tales is Chaucer: a poet, scholar, courtier and man of affairs of unusually wide – though inevitably in some respects limited – knowledge and sympathies. For how else could we account for the passing allusions to ecclesiastical and legal discourse and the parodic recognition of court manners so subtly accommodated within the tale (see below Step 7 on style)? And how else, we might add, is this so palpably a male's eye-view of women and of sex, where men decide to 'swyve' and women simply accept and even expect it? Of course, Chaucer himself could always hide behind the mask supplied by his fictional narrator – the Reeve is a self-confessed dirty old man (see ll. 3874–98).

Step 6   Seeing the text in context

Some facts will help give historical weight and critical point to the economic changes and social tensions witnessed by *The Reeve's Tale*. Reeves were stewards responsible for administering other people's property, and they constituted an increasingly influential section of 'middle men' in Chaucer's time. They were economically and socially mobile – often 'upwardly' (the Reeve, notice, has left his former trade as a carpenter behind; see *The General Prologue*, ll. 613–4). Millers, however, though pivotal in the traditional rural economy and often powerful figures in the village, were more tied to their trade and had fewer prospects. The 'estaat of yomanrye' (rank of yeoman, l. 3949) was as high as a miller might aspire to. Hence the pervasive sense of decidedly small-town pecking-orders and jealousies (ll.3951–68). Students, meanwhile, then as now, were viewed with a mixture of reverence and contempt by members of the local population. Sometimes this led to outright hostilities, as in the periodic clashes between 'town and gown' in Oxford and Cambridge. The ultimate cause was economic: disputes over college rents and city taxes. But the immediate symptom, as witnessed by the present tale, was social and personal: mutual suspicion and incomprehension between representatives of the 'lewed' (ignorant) and the 'learned': town and gown, tradespeople and scholars.

It is also clear that Chaucer composed these fictions chiefly with an audience and readership of fellow courtiers, richer merchants and senior clergy in mind. He therefore follows the general tendency in court versions of fabliau to characterize and satirize the 'lower orders' as driven by raw appetites and ridiculous aspirations – in a word as 'funny'. At the same time, evidently, members of the court could be titillated in safety. Sex and the rudely bared body might not be openly celebrated in court ceremonial and rituals, nor in court romances. But they could still be given freer, funnier play in certain kinds of 'low life' fiction. Comedy was a valve that released physical energies even as it controlled political pressures.

Step 7   Analysing the style

The display of social pretensions and a play of political tensions are also observable in the stylistic range of the tale. The Reeve promises he will 'quyte' the Miller 'right in his cherles termes' (pay him back in his own low language, ll. 3916–7; cf. *The Miller's Prologue*, ll. 3182–3). In the event, there is little swearing and no verbal obscenity. There is, however, a lively and relatively unadorned array of styles. In medieval rhetorical terms, we move from a measured 'middle' style for the bulk of the description and narration to bouts of 'low' (or at least colloquial) style for the speeches. The latter are characterized by short phrases made up of common words denoting familiar objects, all liberally sprinkled with exclamations and proverbs. A typical instance is the report of the exchanges between Symkyn, Alan and John (ll. 4016–66). For the rest, as already mentioned, the tale is further enlivened and its intellectual and literary range extended by passing gestures to other words and worlds. Ecclesiastical and legal discourses are playfully invoked by Alan as he comments on Symkyn and his family snoring their 'complyn' (evening service) and when the student justifies the 'esement' (recompense) due to him by taking the miller's daughter (ll. 4170–87). There is even a mimicking of the courtly 'aubade' (dawn song) as Alan and Moll take leave of one another after their night of lovemaking: "'Fare weel, Malyn … Now deere lemman …" … she gan to wepe' (ll. 4235–48). All these features enrich the texture but never slacken the pace in what, from first to last, is one of Chaucer's lightest satires and briskest narratives.

THE PRIORESS'S PROLOGUE AND TALE

Step I   What kind of work am I studying?

This type of tale at first seems strange to many modern readers. In general terms, *The Prioress's Tale* is a saint's life or legend and what is called here a 'miracle' (l. 691). More specifically, it is one of a whole host of stories celebrating the miraculous powers of the Blessed Virgin (Mary, mother of Christ); here as she helps and rewards a little Christian boy who is murdered for singing her praises and thereafter recognized as a child martyr. The tale is prefaced by and interspersed with instances of prayer and hymn. It may also be seen as a kind of sermon 'exemplum' illustrating the moral 'Mordre wol out' ('Murder will become known', l. 576). All these aspects confirm the basically religious nature and function of the material. And yet, in the grisly cutting of a child's throat and the hurling of his body into a latrine, today's readers may perceive similarities with sensational horror stories of the 'slasher' variety. They may also sense, with some distaste, the routinely anti-Semitic premises of the plot; for the child is murdered by Jews who here feature as the type of evil 'bogeyman' commonly found in fairy story and cautionary tale.

Overall, then, as usual with Chaucer, we are presented with a mixture of genres and a potential variety of perspectives. But it is still up to you, the individual reader, to gauge how far you are prepared to read *The Prioress's Tale* in religious or secular, medieval or modern terms; and also to determine what you understand those terms to be.

Step 2   What is it about?

In outline the story is exquisitely simple. A seven-year-old Christian boy, the son of a widow, walks through the Jewish quarter of an Asian city every day on his way to and from school. As he does so, he regularly chants his 'Ave Marie' ('Hail Mary', a Latin prayer to the Virgin) and the 'Alma Redemptoris [Mater]' ('Loving [Mother] of the Redeemer', an advent hymn). The Jews are enraged by this vaunting of Christianity so, prompted by Satan, they hire an assassin to cut the boy's throat and cast the body in a privy. The boy's distraught mother, guided by Christ, eventually discovers her slain son there. Though his throat is cut, he still sings the 'Alma Redemptoris' in full voice. Immediately, the Christian authorities are sent for; the Jews responsible are first mutilated then hanged, and the child is taken in procession to a nearby abbey. He may only stop singing, he informs the abbot, once a 'greyn' (most likely a pearl) placed on his tongue by the Virgin at the time of his murder, has been removed. This the abbot does, whereupon the boy promptly falls silent and dies. Thereupon, he is placed in a marble tomb and celebrated as a child martyr.

Several things give this essentially simple 'miracle' both variety and breadth. The prayers and anthems lend it a ceremonial pace and celebratory ring. Meanwhile, the narrative texture varies from the domestic realism of the exchange between the younger and older schoolboys (ll. 525–50), through the shocking brevity of the accounts of the boy's murder and the execution of the Jews (ll. 570–1, 633–4), to the luxuriant pathos of the agonized mother (ll. 586–606). There is also, at the close, an extended reference to 'yonge Hugh of Lyncoln' (ll. 684–6), another specifically English child martyr who was supposedly murdered by Jews. The main thing to bear in mind, however, is that all these aspects reinforce, embellish and sometimes complicate what is essentially a simple story: a 'miracle' that is by turns pious, sentimental and sensational.

Step 3   Looking at characterization

In such a brief, miraculous tale it is obviously unwise to look for psychological characterization and for character development. Instead, we need to look for the contribution the figures make to an overall narrative pattern and moral scheme, and to recognize the various roles they play in the genre in hand. On closer inspection, these turn out to be a range of roles in a variety of genres. Thus in basic narrative terms the boy's mother is simply a 'povre wydwe' (poor widow, l. 586), alone and vulnerable. At the same time, in specifically religious terms, she is represented as a counterpart of Mary mother of Christ. In particular, her display of 'moodres pitee' and her pathetic agony at the sight of her dead son (ll. 593–600) strongly recall the 'mater dolorosa' (grieving mother) of the Christian tradition, and even more particularly the *pieta* figure of Mary lamenting over the body of *her* dead son, Christ. (For a further parallel, see the presentation of Griselda and her child in *The Clerk's Tale*, ll. 547–72.)

And yet, at another moment and from another point of view, the child in the present tale is presented as neither more nor less than a little boy asking a slightly bigger boy for help with some especially difficult homework – the learning of the 'Alma Redemptoris' (ll. 516ff.). Overall, then, characterization is controlled by the demands of plot and doctrine, and here by a palpable desire to wring certain kinds of emotional response from readers and audience. The characters as such mean little or nothing outside the world of the 'miracle' they embody.

Step 4   Developing the argument

As usual, it is a good idea to concentrate on at least three passages (from beginning, middle and end), and then to see how issues have developed over the course of the text. Also as usual, there are choices. One choice of first passage might concentrate on the scene-setting within the tale (ll. 488–511). This establishes the Jews who practise 'usure' (usury, moneylending) 'hateful to Crist' in the background, and the Christians – notably the 'sely' (innocent) child and his mother the poor widow – in the foreground. In addition, this passage introduces 'Oure blisful Lady', the Virgin Mary, implicitly linking her with both the widow and the Prioress herself (note the use of 'Oure'), and at the same time sounds the dominant note of song and celebration. A different choice of first passage might concentrate on the teller of this tale as revealed in her prologue (especially ll. 481–7). The critical aim then might be to gauge how far the Prioress, and by extension her tale, are to be taken 'straight' or satirically: as open celebrations of profound piety and heartfelt pathos, or as covert criticisms of shallow sentiment and casual sensationalism. Either way, the opening move should lay the textual and critical grounds for your approach.

A second, central passage would be selected accordingly. For instance, you might feature the representations of grieving mother and murdered child already referred to (ll. 579ff.). Attention could then be drawn to the construction of the latter in terms of the Blessed Virgin and the martyred Christ, and analysis could concentrate on the articulation of the scene for maximum affective power. Alternatively, you might choose to highlight passages which legitimize violence as the necessary fitting of punishment to crime (ll. 567ff., 627–34). The issue then might be how far we are to condemn the death of an innocent Christian while condoning the deaths of guilty Jews. Or are the moral and religious sentiments merely pretexts for a spectacular display of violence?

The choice of final passage would largely depend upon those chosen previously. A religiously orthodox reading would be likely to play up the apotheosis of the innocent child and his ritual transformation into an enshrined martyr. In this respect a highly effective, and deeply affecting, passage is the one where the abbot removes the 'greyn' from the boy's tongue (ll. 670–83). This action is at once personally tender and institutionally sanctioned; the abbot comes across as a kind, concerned man as well as a devout senior cleric. A more secular and sceptical reading, however, would be likely to draw its conclusion from the final verse of the tale (ll. 684–90). The reference to 'Hugh of Lyncoln, slayn also / With cursed Jewes' reminds us that from beginning to end the angling of this story is routinely anti-Semitic (compare ll. 489–92, 558ff.). But even so, we are still left with questions about whose views of Jews are in play. For instance, are Chaucer's own views to be aligned with those of the Prioress? Or are both (or neither) of them to be blamed (or excused) for views that at the time were considered unexceptionable – though they can certainly give offence today? Either way, 'developing an argument' means precisely that: gradually gathering and carefully weighing evidence from outside as well as inside the text (see below) – not simply jumping to conclusions.

Step 5   Relating the tale to its teller

Here the pressing question is how far we carry over the apparently critical attitude towards the Prioress in *The General Prologue* (ll. 118–64) into a reading of her individual prologue and tale. Certainly the representation of her as a pilgrim carries clear traces of heavy irony, if not of outright satire. She sang the divine service 'ful weel', but with an affectedly nasalized intonation. She was demonstratively 'charitable and pitous' and 'al was conscience and tendre herte', but such qualities were reserved for small trapped animals and lavished on her lapdogs! At the very least, we may begin to wonder precisely how we are meant to respond to the Prioress's treatment of this 'miracle'. Is it perhaps being set up as a mere display of pious sentiment: an excuse for a series of superficially religiose gestures rather than the expression of a genuinely religious experience? Melodramatic pathos rather than heartfelt compassion? Clearly, much also depends upon how we respond to the Prioress's confession in her own prologue (ll. 481–7). There she complains that 'My konnyng is so wayk ...' and compares herself to a 'a child of twelf month oold or lesse'. If we take this as a personally authentic and doctrinally authoritative declaration of humility and self-deprecation, we underwrite a sympathetic view of the Prioress. If we see this as unwitting acknowledgement – or even sincere admission – of her emotional immaturity and superficial piety, we underwrite more critical views of her and, by extension, of the tale that follows. In any event, the relation between tale and teller is vital but vexed.

Readers alert to gender-stereotyping may be especially vexed that all these images of woman, whether human or divine, have a distinctly 'man-made' feel to them. They may also point out that the ultimate teller of this tale and the person with overall responsibility for all these constructions of women is 'Chaucer the man'. Even then, however, we still need to ask how far this particular medieval male author aligned himself with or against the various more or less patriarchal traditions he inherited.

Step 6   Seeing the text in context

The crucial historical issue here is the treatment of Jews. This has already been mentioned, but requires further elucidation if critical points are to have force. Three things need to be known. Firstly, in England between the thirteenth and seventeenth centuries there was, in fact, *no* 'Jewerye / Sustened by a lord of that contree / For foule usure and lucre of vileynye' (ll. 489–91). There was therefore in

Chaucer's London *no* Jewish quarter or ghetto, such as the one located in Asia in the tale and such as those actually existing in other late medieval European countries, Italy and Germany, for instance. Secondly, the 'yonge Hugh of Lyncoln' referred to at the close of the tale (l. 684) was not in fact murdered by Jews in 1255, but by someone else, perhaps accidentally, in a still unsolved crime. All this may go some way towards mitigating casual charges of anti-Semitism that may otherwise be levelled at Chaucer's contemporaries and predecessors. A third fact should be added, however. Though not publicly encouraged or officially licensed, individual Jews were used by Chaucer's contemporaries as moneylenders. They were thus viewed with a mixture of envy and suspicion and sometimes downright hostility. In any case, it was rarely forgotten by a massively Christian community that Jews were partly responsible for the death of Christ. Hence the common formula and persistent image of the 'cursed Jew' found in popular romance and sermon alike (cf. *The Prioress's Tale*, ll. 570, 574, 685). Some such indiscriminate process of 'scapegoating' was doubtless at work in the attribution of Hugh of Lincoln's murder to Jews. Erroneous or not, it was widely believed in Chaucer's day. The Prioress can thus allude to the event as a well-known fact ('as it is notable', l. 685).

Overall, then, the historical record does not underwrite overt and systematic anti-Semitism in Chaucer's England – but it does support a sense of suspicion and stereotyping, especially if projected abroad ('in Asye', for example). Of course, none of this settles whether the Prioress is being criticized for her attitudes or, indeed, whether the 'cursednesse' of Jews is simply a premise that enables the narrative to operate. But it does oblige us to be circumspect rather than doctrinaire in our interpretation of the text in context.

Step 7   Analysing the style

This is an extraordinarily poised and pointed tale. Chaucer's narrative economy in scene-setting can be traced in the introduction of the young boy and his mother (ll. 495–512). Persons, places, time, habitual actions, characteristic attitudes and the main themes are all established with efficiency in less than 20 lines. This is all the more impressive in that everything – whether speech, description or action – is delivered in an elegantly complex seven-line decasyllabic stanza form rhyming *ababbcc* (called 'rhyme-royal' and also found in *Troilus and Criseyde* and *The Clerk's Tale*). The overall effect is one of strong story communicated through intricate verbal music.

Rhetorically, the staple style would be termed 'middle': neither baldly colloquial nor luxuriantly ornate. At certain well-defined points, however, the manner becomes noticeably more formal as the matter becomes more overtly liturgical. These are the occasions where the Prioress in her own voice or her characters in theirs move into the mode of prayer, chant and anthem. Typically, the onset of such rhetorical flights is marked by the appearance of an 'O ...': 'O Lord, our Lord ...', 'O mooder Mayde ...', 'O martir sowded to virginitee ...', 'O grete God ...' (ll. 453, 467, 579, 607). The narrative thereby shifts dramatically from third-person report to second-person address. Passages of this kind punctuate the action and give a renewed sense of the Prioress speaking in her consciously religious role. However, we may still wonder whether they lend genuine religious gravity and aesthetic sublimity to the tale or are to be viewed as the merely mannered gestures of a shallow show-off.

THE FRIAR'S TALE

Step 1   What kind of work am I studying?

The Friar's Tale is in general terms a sermon, and more particularly a satire, against the sin of 'simony': the clerical abuse of church office for bribery and corruption. The main vehicle for this is a cautionary tale of low-life greed and trickery (a fabliau) that backfires on the perpetrator. Parts of the tale can even be seen as a kind of grotesque 'mock-confession' (somewhat like those of the Wife of Bath and the Pardoner in their prologues). The summoner within the tale virtually boasts about the viciousness of his life. Taking the Friar's prologue and tale together, it is also clear that the Friar is delivering the opening shot of a 'tit-for-tat' or 'insult-trading' competition (a 'quytynge') with the Summoner. Though less well known, it ranks in every way with that between the Miller and Reeve.

Step 2   What is it about?

In outline the story is simple: it is about a corrupt summoner who at first seems to be too clever and is finally too stupid for his own good. However, this is a remarkably intricate and beguilingly subtle tale, so its speeches and actions need to be plotted attentively and in detail. We first meet the summoner on his way to extort money from a poor widow. Almost immediately, he – and we – meet another wayfarer who is dressed like a yeoman, but who readily reveals himself to be a devil in one of their many disguises. This yeoman/devil then proceeds to present himself as a kind of bailiff whose job it is to collect souls for his master Satan. Because the summoner and the devil seem to be in similar lines of business, the latter proposes that they swear an oath of 'brotherly' loyalty and share one another's trade secrets: 'deere broother, / Thou art a bailly, and I am another ...' (ll.1395ff.).

The body of the tale is then devoted to the exchanges between the summoner and the devil as they travel along. While the summoner delights in boasting how he cheats and exploits all and sundry, the devil confides that he can only actually take people's souls to hell if they are hardened sinners and it is their deliberate intent ('entente') to do ill. This is put to the proof when the summoner and devil come across a carter furiously cursing his horses for not pulling the cart out of the mire. Though the carter wishes the whole lot would go to hell ('The devel have al, bothe hors and cart and hey', l. 1547), the devil counters the summoner's encouragement to 'collect' on the spot by pointing out that 'It is nat his [the carter's] entente, trust me weel' (l. 1556).

The dramatic climax and moral point of the tale come together when the summoner and devil reach the house of the poor old widow. Intent both on cheating her and on displaying his skills to the devil, the summoner goes through his standard routine of trumped-up charges and appeals to fraudulent documents. But in this case his attempt to extort 12 pence and a new pan is a catastrophe. The widow stoutly maintains her innocence and wishes the summoner would go to hell – and take her pan with him! The devil promptly picks up on this and makes quite sure the widow meant every word she said. This she readily confirms, though she is careful to add that the summoner might still repent ('but he wol hym repente', l. 1629). The summoner rashly refuses to do this: 'that is nat myn entente ... for to repente me' (ll. 1630-1) – and the immediate result is that the devil snatches up both summoner and pan and takes them off to hell.

Step 3 *Looking at characterization*

Much like the portraits of pilgrims in *The General Prologue*, the opening of this tale (ll. 1321–74) is devoted to establishing the vicious character of the summoner in a free-standing yet dramatic way. This is done chiefly though interspersing dramatic glimpses of habitual behaviour (e.g., 'Thanne wolde he seye, "Freend, I shal for thy sake …"') with forthright denunciation of 'this fals theef, this somonour'. However, it is in the exchanges between the summoner and the devil and, later, both of them and the old widow that we fully see character in action. We also become aware of more subtle shades in the make-up of each figure. The yeoman/devil appears open but is cunning; the summoner thinks he is clever but is stupid.

Consider, for instance, the remarks thrown out by the devil as to how the summoner will find him in future:

> … fer in the north contree,
> Wheras I hope some time I shal thee see.
> *Er we departe, I shal thee so wel wisse [guide]*
> *That of myn hous ne shaltow nevere mysse.*
> (ll. 1413–6, my emphasis)

At first this seems amiable and casual – but in the event it turns out to be ominous and calculating A similar point is made later (ll. 1513–22), when the summoner asks what hell is like and the devil tells him he will find out 'by thyn owene experience'. Again this is done in a dramatically ironic way. We as readers may get the point, but the summoner – to his cost – does not. There is a similar attention to verbal detail and character type in the encounter with the poor old widow (ll. 1583ff.). For she, too (like the devil, but unlike the summoner), is aware of the need to choose one's words carefully. Her cursing of the summoner is no casual outburst but is tempered by a pious sensitivity to the possibility that he may still repent ('but he wol hym repente!', l. 1629). The fact that the summoner has absolutely no intention of repenting is not only another proof of his rash and irredeemably reprobate character. It is also the key to the main issue of the tale as a whole.

Step 4   Developing the argument

Tracing the increasingly insistent references to people's intentions ('entente') and what they intend ('entende') is the surest way of registering the main doctrinal and moral point of the tale (see e.g., ll. 1374, 1390, 1452, 1478–9, 1499, 1556, 1630). For time and again it is stressed that each of the human characters – summoner, carter and widow – has individual agency and is responsible for his or her actions. In theological terms this would be called 'free will' and it is crucial if we are to see sin as an act of commission (what people deliberately do), not simply an act of omission (what they neglect to do). Closely related to this is the use and abuse of kinds of 'swearing' and 'cursing', as well as their religious converse, kinds of 'blessing'. (This is ironically significant in that the Summoner in *The General Prologue* declares, 'Of cursyng oghte ech gilty man hym drede / For curs wol slee right as assoilyng (absolving, blessing) savith', ll. 660–1.) Thus not only is the summoner in the present tale habitually foul-mouthed, he also deliberately trades upon the church's ultimate and legitimate form of cursing, excommunication ('Up peyne of cursyng, looke that thou ...' l. 1587). By contrast, the carter first curses then blesses his struggling horses (ll. 1542ff., 1561ff.), while the widow does the reverse. Her first words to the summoner are a pious greeting and blessing ('benedicitee! God save you, sire', ll. 1584–5); but once she finds out what he really intends, her last words are a curse in earnest (ll. 1622–9).

Step 5   Relating the tale to its teller

Clearly, from start to finish, this whole tale is framed as part of an attack by the Friar on his fellow pilgrim, the Summoner. This is plainly announced in *The Friar's Prologue* and confirmed by the Summoner's indignant interruption of the tale itself (ll. 1332ff.); also by the continuing insult-trading in the latter's own prologue. Notice, too, that there are pointed references to 'this somonour' and 'thise somonours' scattered throughout *The Friar's Tale* – right up to the penultimate line (see ll. 1338, 1376, 1417, 1456, 1548, 1631, 1646, 1663). Many of these can readily be construed as double-edged swipes at the Summoner *outside* the tale as well as the summoner *within* it. In fact, many of them are virtually 'triple-edged' in that most of the damning remarks made by the Friar about clerical cheats such as the Summoner are made elsewhere about friars in general, as well as this particular Friar (see *The General Prologue*, ll. 208–69, notably the observation that he, too, would wring a farthing from a poor, shoeless widow).

Step 6   Seeing the text in context

The late medieval Church was a palpably economic as well as a purportedly spiritual institution. It is precisely the perversion of spiritual means for economic ends that makes the representations of the Friar and Summoner historically topical as well as perennially suggestive. Moreover, by Chaucer's day the Church had become remarkably profuse in its personnel and correspondingly pressing in its demands. Amongst the clergy there were now friars as well as priests and monks, while amongst clerical officers there were summoners as well as pardoners. All were ultimately chasing the same sources of revenue, chiefly in the forms of individual alms, donations and bequests, as well as statutory tithes, rents and fines. The result, inevitably, was intense inter-clerical competition. As far as many external critics could see, it involved an unseemly – often downright unholy – dash after cash. Such figures were also relatively safe targets for Chaucer. He was of merchant stock and depended for his livelihood upon civic and court – not religious – posts and patronage. In addition, there was increasingly acute competition for revenue and influence between Church and State at this time. It was therefore probably expedient, as well as entertaining, for a courtier to be critical of the acquisitiveness and worldliness of the clergy.

Step 7   Analysing the style

Though the basic stylistic level of this tale is 'middle' or 'plain' (i.e. neither 'high' romantic and sublime nor 'low' rude and comic), we may clearly discern modulations within and between passages. Thus we move from the Friar's declamatory sermonizing (e.g., ll. 1338ff., 1645ff.) to the more delicate theologizing of the devil (especially ll. 1483ff.). Meanwhile, over the course of the tale, we are treated to a poised and increasingly pointed alternation of dramatic dialogue and narrative report. The belligerent gullibility of the summoner, the cool calculation of the devil, the pious resilience of the widow, even the judgemental self-righteousness of the Friar – these are all as much matters of style as they are of characterization and doctrine. All can be conveniently traced in the passage where the trap fatally springs shut and the 'plot', in every sense, is finally resolved (ll. 1584ff.).

THE SUMMONER'S TALE

Step 1   What kind of work am I studying?

Like *The Friar's Tale*, to which it is a dramatic response, *The Summoner's Tale* offers a rich mixture of genres. In its emphasis on trickery and its decidedly anal humour it is a fabliau. In that the main butt of the joke and the focus of moral censure is a hypocritical friar it is a satire. In so far as the Summoner tells this tale in revenge for a tale told against summoners by his fellow pilgrim the Friar, it is another instance of a 'quytynge' (a tit-for-tat, insult-trading tale) – much like those told by the Miller and Reeve at one another's expense. Meanwhile, over the course of the tale as such, a number of familiar medieval genres are picked up in passing: a sermon on anger and fasting (ll. 1832ff.); the offer of a confession in return for a donation (ll. 1992ff.); and, to round it all off, a parodic lecture combining the laws of physics and theology with the lore of farts (ll. 2253ff.). A rich and heady mix indeed!

Step 2   What is it about?

In general terms, we are treated to an attack on the sin of 'simony' (abuse of church office) and an exposé of the ways in which pious posturing may be a cover for mercenary motives. In terms of events, the crucial thing to grasp is that the whole thing is held together by three episodes involving friars and farts. The first episode, in the prologue, sets the scene with a vision of hell in which a friar is shown his colleagues living up the devil's backside. The second episode, in the tale proper, shows a friar attempting to extract a donation from a sick man; but he is given a fart instead and told to divide that in 12 amongst his 'brothers'. The third and final episode takes place in a kind of narrative coda ('The wordes of the lordes squier ...') and supplies an ingenious solution as to how this may be done. The squire of the local lord, from whom the friar has sought redress, suggests that 12 friars be positioned, on a windless day, round the spokes of a cartwheel. Meanwhile, the present friar is to make the thirteenth and take pride of place beneath the hub. Once everyone is in position the offending 'cherl' is to let rip with the loudest, smelliest fart he can muster and thus, the squire maintains, the fart will be equally divided amongst all the friars present. In this way the problem is solved, the story is resolved. The Summoner has also got his own back on the Friar who whisked a cheating summoner off to hell in *his* story.

Such in outline is a tale which most people find outrageously funny and some find shockingly distasteful. Either way, we need to take a closer look at what makes it much more subtle and searching than a mere string of dirty jokes.

Step 3   Looking at characterization

The method of establishing character is very much like that practised in *The General Prologue* and in a number of the other fabliaux. The friar's routine of preaching and begging is set up in the first 50 lines (ll. 1709–65). This is dramatically enlivened by snatches of ecclesiastical Latin jargon ('*qui cum patre ...*' [who with the father...]) and samples of his characteristic spiel ('"Delivereth out", quod he, "anon the soules!"'). The scene is also made concretely particular by reference to the wax writing tablets on which the friar duly inscribes – and from which, once out of sight, he promptly erases – the names of all those who have made donations.

Such verbal facility, alternating smooth-tongued flattery with sharp-tongued threat, is then shown at work on a particular husband and wife in the body of the tale. With the compliant wife he is shown to be adept at currying favour and wheedling food; also, more disturbingly, consoling her for the death of her child with a sham vision of all the friars praying for its soul (ll. 1837ff.). With the sick and cynical husband, the aptly named Thomas (after the biblical 'doubting Thomas' referred to in l. 1980), the friar is driven to draw on progressively more severe rhetorical resources. As Thomas modulates from sceptical reserve to downright refusal, so the friar shifts from mild chastisement to full-blown denunciation (ll. 1954ff.). In all of this the underlying formula is: learned and verbally facile cleric meets – and meets his match in – simple but far from stupid layman. This dynamic is sustained in the clever worsting of the friar by the squire at the close of the tale.

In both cases, notice, the climax may be as literally and farcically explosive as a fart. But it is prepared with a narrative and dramatic precision of character and situation that may justly be termed novelistic as well as theatrical. Thomas's resistance is fuelled by sickness and a whole history of useless confessions and donations. The squire is motivated by a desire to show off before his lord and lady, as well as the promise of a new gown. Subject to each in turn, the friar is ultimately, ironically, deprived of his only weapon: speech (ll. 2169, 2287).

Step 4   Developing the argument

Here it makes sense to concentrate on passages from the beginning (including the prologue), the middle of the tale, and the end (including 'The wordes of the lordes squier...'). This helps demonstrate that there are certain recurring themes informing the performance as a whole. The most fundamental topic is the association between friars and devils, and both of them and the lower bodily functions. All together contribute to a kind of running commentary – virtually a running sewer – on the abusers of religion. There is thus a constant undercutting of words and gestures by bodies and deeds, holy surfaces by diabolical depths. The keynote, ringing throughout the tale, is struck by the early line about the devil's arse always being in the friar's mind ('So was the develes ers ay in hys mynde', l. 1705). Such resonances are clearly sustained in the scene where Thomas offers his grotesque substitute for a donation (ll. 2124ff.).

We should be aware of a gradual thickening of the tale's theological atmosphere too. 'What is a ferthyng worth parted in twelve?', complains the friar (l. 1967) when Thomas informs him he has made donations to other friars. This neatly anticipates the squire's solution to the problem of the twelvefold division of the fart: 'Lat brynge a cartwheel ... Twelve spokes hath a cartwheel communly. / And brynge me thanne twelve freres' (ll. 2255–7). In fact, there is a parodic allusion as well as a doctrinal subtlety here. These must be noted if the theological flavour as well as the scatological savour of this scene are to be fully appreciated. The allusion is to the Pentecostal image of the 'divine afflatus' whereby, according to Acts of the Apostles (2.1), God's spirit was distributed equally to the 12 apostles. The distribution of the fart is a palpably physical, parodic inversion of this. The complication is that the 'thirteenth apostle', corresponding to the friar himself at the hub of the wheel, was traditionally identified with Judas Iscariot – the one who betrayed Christ in return for gold. With all this in mind (including the fact that 'the develes ers' was 'ay in hys [the friar's] mynde'), we may recognize that the argument of *The Summoner's Tale* is indeed much more coherent and sophisticated than the loosely knit string of unsavoury anecdotes it may at first appear. It is a carefully plotted and theologically informed satire on church abuse in general, and false and mercenary 'apostles' (followers and preachers of Christ's word) in particular.

At the same time, this tale offers a finely double-edged exposure of the practice of 'glosynge'. 'Glosynge' meant both 'supplying an interpretation' (compare modern glossary) and 'cheating, deceiving with flashy appearances' (hence glossing over a problem). Thus when the friar declares that 'Glosynge is a glorious thyng, certeyn' (l. 1793) he in effect alerts us to his own favoured mode of cheating: the studied corruption of biblical authority for personal gain, interpreting the letter of scripture so as to pervert its spirit. He also anticipates his own palpably hypocritical practices of 'glosynge' later, especially in the copiously illustrated mini-sermon on 'fastynge and 'ire' (ll. 1832ff.). This is interrupted, we should observe, by the friar's request for food and followed by his display of rage. The argument is thereby embodied dramatically as well as in more abstract terms.

Step 5   *Relating the tale to its teller*

If we now turn to the presentation of the Summoner himself in *The General Prologue* (ll. 623-69), it becomes clear that his censure of the Friar is in fact double-edged. It cuts the teller as much as the butt of the tale. For the Summoner, too, is a mouther of religious platitudes and an abuser of church office. He is also, like his 'freend and compeer' the Pardoner, the very image of a lost soul and a body in dissolution. Seen in this light, the whole performance shows up as a process of *self*-exposure as well as an act of revenge upon another. We are thereby constantly aware that the Summoner, like the Friar before him, is being set up for a fall by Chaucer. The keenly anti-clerical edge and general intellectual sharpness of the whole thing clearly cannot be attributed to the semi-ignorant Summoner. And the latter, finally, is the dramatic and satiric creation of an author with quite distinct social frames and moral aims in mind.

Step 6   Seeing the text in context

In general terms, the figures of Summoner, Friar and Pardoner should be considered together. As a body of minor clerics who abuse church office for personal gain, they neatly underwrite a court agenda that increasingly saw the Church as a rival for revenue and recognized exposure of corruption as a good way of discrediting ecclesiastical motives and methods. The corresponding sections on *The Friar's Tale* and *The Pardoner's Prologue and Tale* should therefore be consulted at this point; also the comments on this group of pilgrims in *The General Prologue* (see Chapter 2).

All that need be added here is some further information on friars. At their inception in the previous century, friars had been conceived as a radical alternative to the regular monastic orders and parish priests. Like their founders and models, notably Saints Francis and Dominic, they were supposed to get their living solely by begging and fasting and, subsequently, by preaching and the ministering of confession (hence the emphasis upon all these activities in *The Summoner's Tale*, especially in the friar's sermonizing of Thomas, ll. 1879ff.). By Chaucer's day, however, friars had settled in communities with large buildings and had correspondingly large demands for support and maintenance (hence the friar's especial emphasis upon these aspects, ll. 2099–110). At the same time, friars were famous for their intellectual versatility as well as their verbal virtuosity. In part this was a result of having to live off their wits and words rather than settled estates (like monks) or fixed incomes (like parish priests). Indeed, from the first, friars had adopted – even if later they only affected – a radical stance towards learning. They were famous – or infamous – for their racy styles of teaching and preaching.

Taking all these 'background' elements together, it will now be obvious why the friar in the 'foreground' in *The Summoner's Tale* is constructed precisely along the lines that he is. He is a perfect model (or rather an imperfect anti-model) of one who has fallen away from former ideals but who persists in exploiting and perverting them. His is a beguiling combination of smooth talking and quick knowledge. But, of course, by the close of the tale he is beguiling no-one. His cover is in every sense 'blown', both by a churl's fart and the still quicker wits of a squire. This, then, is some measure of the disrepute that friars had fallen into by Chaucer's day: perhaps among the populace at large, certainly amongst Chaucer's own court circle.

Step 7 Analysing the style

Rude but far from rough, disgustingly gutsy yet also delightfully witty – these are the keynotes sounded by this tale. In terms of genre, it ranges from fleshed-out fabliau to spoof theological treatise. The task of stylistic analysis is thus to follow the verbal traces of such features in the detailed texture of the writing. Take the central exchange between the friar and Thomas, for instance (ll. 1770ff.). This eventually works round to a palpably 'low' fabliau style characterized by simple syntax, monosyllabic vocabulary and the animal imagery of farming and farting (ll. 2149–51):

> Amydde his hand he leet the frere a fart;
> Ther nys no capul [horse], drawynge in a cart,
> That myghte have lete a fart of swich a soun.

Immediately before that, however, we have been treated to an array of different styles from the friar. While his language is generally inclined to the formal and polysyllabic, with a professional penchant for rhetorical questions, exclamations and artfully suspended syntax, his tone can modulate at need from the confiding and wheedling to the declamatory and bullying. He also delights in spicing his English with snatches of Latin for ecclesiastical authority (ll. 1733, 1770, 1865, 1934, 2075, 2192) and French phrases for romantic charm (ll. 1832, 1838). All of these features can be traced in the passages already cited with respect to characterization (ll. 1832ff; see above).

But perhaps the most pointedly artful conflation of styles, overtopping even those of the friar, comes in 'The wordes of the lordes squier...'. For there we move with a combination of scholastic precision and teacherly skill to an object lesson in the dividing of a fart in 12 – or, to be mathematically and theologically precise, 13. As the lord warns us immediately before, this is indeed a teasing problem – and in the event a fitting solution – in 'ars-metrike' (l.2222). Yet only in retrospect or on a second reading are we likely to get the full theological flavour and scatological savour of that last pun. Here it means both 'the art of measurement' and 'arse-measuring'!

5

THE PARLIAMENT OF FOWLS
AND THE 'DREAM POEMS'

STEP I   WHAT KIND OF WORK AM I STUDYING?

The poems dealt with in this chapter may at first strike you as odd. However, just a few preliminary remarks on the kind of work to expect will help you get your bearings. *The Book of the Duchess*, *The House of Fame*, *The Parliament of Fowls* and *The Prologue to the Legend of Good Women* are all basically court romances: that is, they are all about highly idealized forms of love in a court setting. In this respect they also have much in common with *The Knight's Tale*, *The Franklin's Tale* and *Troilus and Criseyde*. All of these texts present life in general, and love in particular, as an elaborate ritual, and they do so from a largely aristocratic point of view. But that is not all. You will probably know from other Chaucer texts that he rarely sticks to just one type of material, that he usually mixes in others to make his treatment more varied. That is what he does here too. For instance, *The Parliament of Fowls* is not simply a court romance; it also includes elements of a moral tract called 'The Dream of Scipio' ('Somnium Scipionis'). The subject of this moral tract is 'the common good' and it acts as a weighty preface to Chaucer's main story. The middle of the poem is also interrupted, this time to accommodate a bout of low-life comedy. The result overall is therefore a poem which is richer and more varied than a court romance would be on its own. Similar observations can be made about *The Book of the Duchess*, *The House of Fame* and *The Prologue to the Legend of Good Women*. In all these cases you should expect a read which is varied, capacious and leisurely. Chaucer usually finds time to talk about many other things apart from his main subject and, if you are to understand these poems, you will have to approach them in a sympathetic way, ready to enjoy their diversity.

STEP 2   WHAT ARE THEY ABOUT?

The main subject of these poems usually makes an appearance after several hundred lines (in the case of *The House of Fame* after more than a thousand lines). Before reaching it you are treated to all sorts of preparatory material in the form of personal and philosophical musings from the author, incidental stories, and so on. In short, all these poems have a slow start. It is therefore a good idea to remind yourself that they do, in fact, have a main subject, and that everything else is built on and around that. For instance, *The Parliament of Fowls*, as its title suggests, is basically about a parliament held by the birds, and the main item on their agenda is how they are going to choose their mates. However, before you get to this parliament, there is a whole barrage of other material you must negotiate. First, you meet the poet talking about his love life and the fact that he has difficulty sleeping. Then he starts to tell you about a book he was reading in bed, 'The Dream of Scipio', and the dream he had about it later. Then this dream melts into another dream in which the poet is shown the temple of Venus and the goddess Nature upon a hill of flowers. And finally, after all that, you get to the 'parliament of fowls' itself. Not surprisingly, many modern readers have not got the faintest idea what is going on! However, the situation is not as desperate as it first seems. In the first place, notice that much of the poem takes the form of a dream. This alone should make you readier to accept the sudden yet apparently natural, dreamlike shifts from one scene to the next. Secondly, notice that all the materials of the poem are bound together by a single idea, 'love'. All that is happening is that you are being presented with different views or versions of love. There is the poet's personal love, the grandly selfless love talked about in 'The Dream of Scipio', the romantic view of love in Venus's temple, and finally the whole range of attitudes to love expressed by the birds in their parliament. In other words, what at first looked like so many disconnected fragments are, in fact, linked by a common theme.

Once you get hold of this coordinating idea, all the bits start to fall into place.

Exactly the same thing applies to the other 'dream poems'. What initially looks bewilderingly bitty and disjointed is, in fact, held together by an overarching idea. In *The Book of the Duchess* there is another complaint about sleeplessness from the poet and reference to another book he is reading (this time the story of the two lovers, Ceyx and Alcyone), and yet again this melts into the fabric of a dream. Only after all this do we meet the main subject of the poem, a mysterious man in black bewailing the death of his wife. And only later still do we find out this woman is the Duchess commemorated in the title. If this is so, you may ask, why does it take the poet so long to refer to her directly? However, the more you read *The Book of the Duchess*, the more you realize that its organization is not really chaotic but artful and successful. The death of a wife is clearly a sensitive subject; it needs to be approached discreetly and if possible, indirectly. And, it turns out, that is precisely what Chaucer does. First, he gives us a whole array of oblique references to love and death, and only later does he, in fact, tackle the matter of the Duchess's death directly. Once more the trick is to see that there is a single idea in *The Book of the Duchess*, but that it is expressed in different ways.

The same applies to the two remaining 'dream poems'. The dominant issue in *The House of Fame* is 'fame', how it is gained and how it is lost. If you keep this in mind, it will help you make sense of the lengthy preamble dealing with the story of Dido and Aeneas. There are many ways of treating this story, but notice that Chaucer chose to emphasize the loss of reputation to both the lovers when Aeneas failed to return. This emphasis on lost fame ensures that the whole poem hangs together. Similarly, in *The Prologue to the Legend of Good Women* it can prove difficult initially to see what Chaucer is driving at. Is this just a preamble to a collection of stories about noble women, or does it have something to say in its own right? My suggestion is that you approach it as an exploration of the problems faced by a medieval writer when one of his previous poems has caused offence. The whole thing then becomes fascinating as a display of the writer's skill in defending himself. Like so many of Chaucer's poems, *The Prologue to the Legend of Good Women* is ultimately about the art of writing itself.

STEPS 3 AND 4 LOOKING AT CHARACTERIZATION AND DEVELOPING THE ARGUMENT

Chaucer's dream poems are not much concerned with 'character' as such. They are much more concerned with ideas and attitudes, and the ways in which fairly abstract problems can be presented. Consequently, to understand any of these texts in greater depth, it makes sense if you concentrate on the significance of clusters of characters at climactic moments. We shall use *The Parliament of Fowls* as an example. For instance, look at the passage describing Venus and Nature (ll.260–378). Notice that there is a fundamental contrast between these two deities: Venus is lounging in her dark temple surrounded by swooning and dying lovers, while Nature is 'in a launde, upon an hil of floures', out in the open air surrounded by chirruping birds. Clearly, one expresses the dark and sensual side of love, while the other expresses its light and freedom. Now all you do is relate this to the larger meanings of the poem. Look for passages where a similar contrast is made and ask what they contribute to an overall view of love. For example, you might then notice that the dreamer was earlier faced by a choice of two inscriptions over the gate into the garden: one promised despair and the other hope (ll. 120–40). Later, too, you will see that similar contrasts are sustained in the parliament itself. In all these cases we are simply given different views of the same thing, love, and at each stage our understanding is slightly modified and deepened.

To understand the full range of attitudes to love expressed in the poem, you need to weigh the position taken up by each of the birds in the parliament. However, the principle of contrast is pervasive and it can be illustrated from the speeches of the three eagles (ll. 414–90). Notice that they express their love on a kind of 'sliding scale'. The first eagle is extravagantly courteous and every inch the ideal courtly lover; the second is less courteous and more direct, and the third is so blunt as to be brutal. All of them offer themselves as suitors for the female eagle, and yet each of them has a different view of what his suit entails. You will find similar gradations amongst the other birds. Simply ask how you would characterize the positions taken up by the goose or the cuckoo or the turtle-dove, and then try to see what their individual voices contributes to the overall variety of the poem.

To see how all this variety is finally resolved you should turn to the conclusion (ll. 659–end). Is there any final weighting or emphasis that Chaucer gives to the poem? Does he imply that one attitude to love is better than another? As usual, notice that it is ultimately up to you to choose. On the one hand, there are the three eagles who took up so much time pleading their cases that they wasted most of the day. A final decision and the consummation of their love has been postponed for a year. On the other hand, there are all the other birds, who did not go through such a laborious courtship. They are allowed to get on with their mating and to celebrate the coming of summer with a song and a dance. Perhaps then, the conclusion is that the best kind of love is natural and spontaneous, without the elaborate courtship of the three eagles. Or is it that one must wait longer for the maturing of a really noble love? Either way, the final decision is yours and it can best be made when you have thought about the ending and its relation to similar contrasts earlier in the text.

STEP 5   RELATING THE NARRATOR TO THE NARRATIVE

The nature and function of the narrator in these poems is discussed under 'Chaucer the narrator' in Chapter 1 (see pp. 17–19). There I focused attention on the poet's presentation of himself (his 'persona') in *The Book of the Duchess*, but as this persona is virtually identical in *The Parliament of Fowls*, little need be added here. The crucial point is that Chaucer presents himself as a shy and unassuming figure. He never imposes his views on the reader. That is how he can offer us such a variety of perspectives and attitudes without seeming to come down in favour of one himself. The final decision is always left with us. For instance, look again at the way in which he presents his reaction to the two inscriptions over the gate (ll. 141–68). The poet is a character in his own dream but uncertain how to respond to it. See how he dithers about until, finally, it is the guide who makes his mind up for him and hustles him into the garden. Or look again at the end of the poem. It is the same there. The parliament is finished and we may still be wondering what it all means – but the poet simply wakes up! He does not tell us what he thinks and would rather, with the sound of birdsong still ringing in our ears, leave us to come to our own conclusions. In fact, this is the role of Chaucer the narrator in nearly all his poems. He provides us with the framework for a response, but usually withdraws from explicit judgement himself. (Also see pp. 192–3.)

STEP 6   SEEING THE TEXT IN CONTEXT

It is particularly important that you try to see *The Book of the Duchess* and *The Parliament of Fowls* in context because they were both prompted by specific occasions. That is why they are sometimes called 'occasional' poems. *The Book of the Duchess* was written to commemorate the death of Blanche of Castile, the first wife of John of Gaunt, in September 1369. *The Parliament of Fowls* was written for a St Valentine's Day celebration at the court of Richard II, probably in 1383, and may refer to a specific courtship rivalry, though which it is now difficult to say. With both poems this contextual information is of more than background interest. In the first place, it should remind you that these are very definitely court poems, by a courtier and for other courtiers (including a duke and a king). This alone helps explain the 'courtly', refined atmosphere of both texts. Secondly, you should notice that the context largely conditioned the image of himself that Chaucer could project. When dealing with the sensitive matter of a wife's death the poet had at all times to be discreet and considerate. And even in the freer atmosphere of a St Valentine's Day celebration the poet obviously still had to retain some respect and decorum. Most members of the audience were of superior social status to Chaucer, and not to be treated lightly. Finally, it is worth remembering that the context helps explain both the tone and even the structure of these poems. Chaucer almost certainly read them aloud and in person. The result is therefore a tone which is respectful but also relaxed and chatty. You might even say that the context affects the shape of the poems as a whole, that they are relaxed and leisurely in their presentation of materials. In any case, even on a first reading, it is not difficult for a modern reader to start building up an image of a specific poet performing at specific times for specific groups of people. These are 'occasional' poems and they quickly recreate their own sense of 'occasion'.

STEP 7   ANALYSING THE STYLE

In the two previous sections we have discussed how to approach these texts in terms of their narrator and the context in which he operated. In both cases you will have noticed that we worked round to a fuller sense of the poems' tone or style. This is the final aspect that you should concentrate on and, as you will see, it helps you to coordinate all the others. For instance, look at the first two verses of *The Parliament of Fowls*. Notice how they establish a cultivated yet conversational tone, starting with a formal 'sententia' ('The lyf so short, the craft so long to lerne ...'), and then loosening up with chattily personal asides ('iwis, that whan I on hym thynke, / Nat wot I wel ...'). This is the routine style of the poem and it acts as a norm against which you can gauge significant shifts in style and attitude. And this is the nub of the matter, for all you are really doing is recognizing that the variety of attitudes expressed in the poem is accompanied by a corresponding variety of styles. You can confirm this by turning back to the speeches of the three eagles (ll. 414ff.). Each of them speaks in a progressively 'lower', more colloquial style. The first and most noble eagle is so verbose that he says the same thing three or four times over in different ways, all the time sprinkling his speech with the extravagantly spiritual terminology of courtly love ('merci', 'grace', 'my lady sovereyne', and so on). The second eagle is altogether more abrupt and down-to-earth ('That shal nat be! / I love hire bet than ye don, by seint John'), while the third actually goes out of his way to dismiss the conventional phrases of courtship ('Of long servyse avaunte I me nothing!'). The stylistic range here is therefore wide. It runs from 'high' to 'low', from formal to colloquial, and in each case there is an attitude to match. You can apply the same criteria to all the language in the poem. On the one hand, there is a formality expressing the more highly wrought and artificial side of love (for example, in the description of Venus, ll. 260ff.). On the other hand, there is a racy colloquialness expressing the more natural and sometimes brutal side of love (in the speech of the 'lower' birds, for example: '"Have don, and lat us wende!" ... "Com of", they criede ... "Kek kek! kokkow! quek quek!"' – ll. 492–9). In short, there is everything between high-flying rhetoric and inarticulate squawking. Perceiving and enjoying such spectacular shifts in style is simply another way of responding to the rich variety of attitudes in the poem.

Finally, it should be noted that the poem is essentially unified in form as well as in context. Just as the whole thing is an exploration of different attitudes to a single issue, 'love', so all the different styles are bound together in a single verse form. Pick out any two stanzas of the poem at random. In every case, whether it is an eagle speaking or a duck, a description of Venus or Nature, you will find that each line has around ten syllables and every stanza has seven lines rhyming *ababbcc*. This is what is meant when it is said that ultimately the form and content of a text cannot be separated. The context of *The Parliament of Fowls* is both varied and unified, and so is its style.

6

TROILUS AND CRISEYDE

STEP 1 WHAT KIND OF WORK AM I STUDYING?

Troilus and Criseyde is a long and complex work and may initially seem forbidding. However, many people (including me) think that this is also Chaucer's greatest work and you will find that it more than repays serious consideration. Here are some preliminary definitions to help you get your bearings. First, *Troilus and Criseyde* is a medieval court romance in that it presents a chivalric view of love and war. The action may be set in classical times, during the siege of Troy, but, really, the characters are medieval knights and ladies, and their behaviour is basically 'courtly'. *The Knight's Tale* is another example of a court romance which mixes classical setting with medieval characters. Second, *Troilus and Criseyde* is altogether weightier and more philosophical than most court romances in that it includes substantial elements from a moral tract called *The Consolation of Philosophy*. Third, the story of Troilus and Criseyde is a 'tragedy' in that it shows the rise and fall of its protagonists' fortunes and invites us to share their joy and pain along the way. In other words, for all its size and variety, this poem is still definable in fairly simple terms. *Troilus and Criseyde* is a medieval romance set in classical times and it deals with the tragic fate of its main characters in a morally serious way. Such a definition may not get you far, but it will get you started.

STEP 2 WHAT IS IT ABOUT?

The next step is to say in more detail what actually happens, as well as to identify the poem's main ideas. Unfortunately, this is not as easy as it sounds. This is because you can tell the story of *Troilus and Criseyde* in two quite different ways, depending on what you want to emphasize. What I shall do therefore is give you *both* versions of events and you can decide for yourself which you prefer.

Version A. Troilus, a young prince of Troy, falls in love with a young widow called Criseyde. With the help of Criseyde's uncle, Pandarus, Troilus manages to declare his love and she eventually gives her love in return. Meanwhile, Criseyde's father (who has previously defected to the Greeks) wants his daughter with him in the Greek camp. This is arranged and Criseyde is duly exchanged for Antenor, a Trojan prince who had been taken prisoner. Once in the Greek camp, Criseyde goes back on an earlier promise to return to Troilus and lives with a Greek called Diomede. Finally, Troilus falls into despair and is killed in battle shortly afterwards.

Version B. Criseyde, a young widow, is loved by a young prince of Troy called Troilus. As a result of the combined pressure of Troilus and her uncle Pandarus, Criseyde eventually accepts Troilus as a lover. Meanwhile, Criseyde's father (who has previously defected to the Greeks) wants his daughter with him in the Greek camp. This is arranged and Criseyde is duly exchanged for Antenor, a Trojan prince who has been taken prisoner. Once in the Greek camp, Criseyde finds it impossible to return to Troilus and reluctantly agrees to live with a Greek called Diomede. Finally, Troilus falls into despair and shortly afterwards is killed in battle. We do not know what happens to Criseyde.

If you look back over these two versions, a couple of things stand out. One is that the overall structure of events remain the same: Troilus and Criseyde come together and then they are separated. The other is that the actual *reasons* why this happens are put very differently. In Version A the emphasis is on Troilus and Criseyde falling in love with one another and on Criseyde failing to keep her part of the bargain by returning. In Version B the emphasis is profoundly different. There it is stressed that Criseyde only gave in to Troilus after intense pressure from him and her uncle, and that it was impossible for her to return – not that she did not want to. All this makes a big difference not so much to the general shape of events, as to how you choose to relate them. In short, you can build your account of *Troilus and Criseyde* round Troilus and throw all the blame for what happens onto Criseyde. Or you can build your account round Criseyde and take a more sympathetic view of her and the circumstances in which she is placed. Either way, you are left with a fundamental choice about how exactly to tell the story.

It is the same with the main ideas around which the poem is organized. These, too, can be presented in different ways. Obviously *Troilus and Criseyde* is fundamentally concerned with matters of 'love' and what might be called 'the fortunes of love and war'. You might say that the whole thing is built round the rise and fall of a relationship. However, the way in which you actually formulate these ideas will depend very much on how you choose to tell the story. Terms such as 'love' and 'fortune' (or 'fate') are handy when you start to talk about the overall themes of the poem, but you may well find yourself searching for other terms as soon as you try to identify its underlying tensions. If you opt for Version A and a traditionally moral view of Criseyde, then you would say that the poem is about her failure and fickleness; that it is ultimately about her 'blame' and 'shame'. In more specifically Christian terms, this means that it is about 'sin' and human fallibility. On the other hand, if you opt for Version B and the more sympathetic view of Criseyde, you would say that the poem is about her 'suffering' and 'innocence'; in more specifically Christian terms, that it is about the 'pity' of being human. None of these ideas alone is sufficient to account for the overall effect of *Troilus and Criseyde*. However, taken together, you may find them useful as a framework round which you can organize a response. 'Love' and 'fortune' are bound to figure centrally in any view of what the poem is about. But the degree to which you concentrate on the 'blame' and 'shame' or the 'suffering' and 'innocence' will be up to you.

STEP 3   LOOKING AT CHARACTERIZATION

Just as there are different ways of telling the story and formulating the main ideas in *Troilus and Criseyde*, so there are different ways of looking at the characters. You can look at them from the 'outside' and then judge them against some kind of external standard, or you can look at them from the 'inside' and so sympathize with them from their own view. Of course, you can also do both. The point is that with all the characters, you need to establish what kind of distance you are from them and their problems. Are you remote or close – or both at different times? For instance, this is how Criseyde is introduced:

> Among thise othere folk was Criseyda,
> In widewes habit blak; but natheles,
> Right as oure firste lettre is now an A,
> In beaute first so stood she, makeles.
> Hire goodly lokyng gladed al the prees.
> Nas nevere yet seyn thyng to ben preysed derre,
> Nor under cloude blak so bright a sterre
>
> As was Criseyde, as folk seyde everichone
> That hir behelden in hir blake wede.
> And yet she stood ful lowe and stille allone
> Byhynden other folk, in litel brede,
> And neigh the dore, ay undre shames drede,
> Simple of atir and debonaire of chere,
> With ful assured lokyng and manere.

(I. 169–82)

Notice that the passage is full of contrasts and tensions. Criseyde is in widow's black yet she is also beautiful; she is standing humbly and apart by the door ('ful lowe and stille allone'), yet she also has a very assured look about her ('with ful assured lokyng and manere'). You may also find it difficult to say precisely what distance you are from her. For the most part she is presented from some way off, by the door, but you may also have picked up a sense of what she is feeling; otherwise how could you know that she is standing with a constant fear of shame ('ay undre shames drede')? Clearly, Criseyde is a complex character and can be seen from different points of view. None the less, the underlying principle of her characterization is essentially simple. She is built out of tensions between potentially contradictory states, and she is presented internally as well as externally. The result is that we can sympathize with her as well as judge her.

You can extend this observation to all the main characters. Criseyde is the most complex and elusive, but you will find similar tensions and mixtures of perspective in the presentation of both Troilus and Pandarus. For instance, look at the passage where Troilus first catches sight of Criseyde (I. 267–80). First, we see him from afar as he weighs up all the women standing round the temple. Then, suddenly, he notices Criseyde and we are given a direct insight into the confusion of his emotions. Finally, after a few moments and with some effort, he resumes his calm manner and we again see him from the outside, as he appears to others. The strategy is simple: one thought or emotion followed by another to counter it. A view from the 'outside' followed by one from the 'inside'. The actual effect, however, is infinitely variable and potentially very sophisticated. Look at the introduction to Pandarus and you can confirm this for yourself. Our first sight of Pandarus is when he bustles into Troilus's room and finds his friend stricken by undeclared love for Criseyde (I. 547ff.). The effect on Pandarus is characteristic. On the one hand, he is joky and tries to cheer Troilus up with some good-humoured banter (he says that the Greeks must be really getting on Troilus's nerves if he has to mope about in his room). On the other hand, Pandarus shows genuine concern for the young prince and clearly wants to find out what is troubling him. These two elements, his jokiness and his genuine concern, are constant elements in Pandarus's make-up. They provide the fundamental tension that makes him both convincing and interesting as a character. Overall, then, the characterization is complex. You are always given more than one way of responding to the main characters and always invited to see their actions as the result of mixed motives. The next step is to relate the complexity of these characters to the complexity of the issues in the poem as a whole.

STEP 4   DEVELOPING THE ARGUMENT

You already know that *Troilus and Criseyde* is generally about 'love' and 'fortune'. You also know that the story can be interpreted in different ways to bring out either the 'sin' or the 'suffering' in what happens. To get a stronger sense of these issues in action you now need to look at some climactic passages. The passage in the middle of the poem, where Troilus and Criseyde finally consummate their love, is an obvious choice (III. 1086–113) . At this point Criseyde has been detained at Pandarus's house by a storm, so Pandarus takes advantage of the situation by arranging for Troilus to come. Even such a short scene is remarkably complex and you need to read it in detail for yourself. However, the main sources of conflict and tension stand out clearly enough. On the one side, there are the two men who between them have engineered the situation. On the other side, there is Criseyde, the object of all their scheming. Notice that the two men are further distinguished in that Pandarus is busy fussing around while Troilus is helplessly submissive (in fact, he faints). Criseyde, however, is many things at once and goes through a whole range of emotions in quick succession. At first she is angry, then she softens and comforts Troilus, and finally she agrees to give him her love. Obviously the overall effect is highly dramatic. But what does it all mean, and what does it contribute to your understanding of the poem as a whole? Well, for one thing it confirms the fact that the characters react with one another in complex ways. There is no way of talking for long about one of them without relating him or her to the others. For another thing, this passage shows that you can apportion blame or praise for what happens in very different ways. On balance you might say that the final responsibility rests with Pandarus, and yet you might also say it rests with Troilus for going along with him, or even with Criseyde for finally giving in. At any rate, what you are left with is a much fuller sense of both 'love' and 'fortune'. Both are the result of complex interactions between people and circumstances, and there is no easy way of apportioning praise or blame.

Now examine the situation at a later stage of its development. If you turn to the opening of Book V, you will also be able to take in the fourth major character, the Greek knight Diomede. Again a small extract will serve to focus the issues (V. 78–98), and again you should read the passage through carefully to pick up the many nuances. The major contrasts and tension are fairly easy to spot. At this point of the story the Trojan parliament has decreed that Criseyde will be exchanged for Prince Antenor, and Troilus is accompanying her for the hand-over. The dramatic contrast could hardly be sharper. On the one side, there is Troilus looking heartbroken at the weeping Criseyde and reminding her of her promise to return. On the other side, there is Diomede, who promptly grabs Criseyde's horse by the reins and leads her to the Greek camp. You will find that this is symptomatic of the contrast between the two men as the final book develops: one is essentially passive, while the other is essentially active. They represent, if you like, two opposing principles in men's dealings with women.

But what about Criseyde? Where does the 'hand-over' leave her, and what are you to make of her role in this encounter? The prosaic answer is that it leaves Criseyde in the Greek camp without her in any way wanting to be there. Everything was decided by the Trojan parliament without consulting her. But more abstractly, however, you might say that all the power over Criseyde's life has been taken out of her hands. Passed from one man to another, from Trojans to Greeks, her capacity for independent action has been virtually denied. Notice, too, that she does not speak at all during this exchange; all she does is cry. Her role here is even more passive than that of Troilus. How, though, does this incident deepen your overall sense of the poem's issues? For instance, to what extent does this encounter make you even more aware of the power of the men over the woman? Before it was Pandarus and Troilus who organized things, and now it is Troilus and Diomede, but in both cases Criseyde's choice is severely limited. In other words, is there a specifically male–female aspect to the exploration of 'love' and 'fortune'? Following on from this, do you have any firmer idea of who is responsible for what happens in this story, who should be blamed or praised? These are questions which naturally arise as you go further into the poem, and by the end they are crying out for an answer. That is where you should now turn – to the end.

Look at the last 60 or so lines (V. 1807ff.) For many readers the ending is a surprise, so you should particularly consider whether the surprise is satisfying or disturbing. At the end Troilus is killed in action and whisked up to the heavens. From there he has a panoramic vision of 'This litel spot of erthe' and can see all the trials and tribulations of humanity. With a chilling laugh he dismisses them all as petty and vain. The final moral is in the same chilling vein: it urges 'yonge, fresshe folkes' to reject earthly love as mere vanity and turn instead to the enduring love of Christ. Critical responses to this ending vary hugely. However, the important thing to realize is that this is simply an emphatic way of settling the issues raised during the poem. In effect what happens is that the final interpretation is tilted towards a 'sinful' reading, stressing the 'blame' and 'shame' aspect of things. In one sweeping gesture everything is dismissed as a story about pagan people and earthly love. Clearly, this is a decisive solution and for some people (who thought the poem was all about 'sin' anyway) it is a satisfying one. Others, however, do not like the ending at all. They point to the fact that we get very involved in the human action, and that we come to have a great deal of sympathy for these 'pagans'. They insist that they and their problems should not be dismissed so callously. For such people the final solution is deeply disturbing. It is a crude attempt to gloss over a set of human problems that orthodox religion cannot cope with. But whichever way you react to the ending (for it, or against it, or a mixture of both), you obviously have to think about it carefully. To do so, you will need to look back over the text and review it in the light of what happens. That, from a different point of view, is what we do next.

Step 5   Relating the narrator to the narrative

Just as modern readers have a mixed response to what happens in *Troilus and Criseyde*, so does the narrator. He, too, becomes less and less sure how exactly to tell the story. Is he to narrate from a detached and straightforwardly moral point of view, as in our Version A? Or is he to become more humanly involved with his characters, especially Criseyde, and tell it more like our Version B? Or can he, in fact, do both, mixing the two versions over the course of the whole poem? The easiest way of plotting how the narrator's attitude changes is to look at the prologues to each of the five books. In the prologue to Book I Chaucer presents himself as a 'servant of the servants of love' (I. 15), a mere attendant in the elaborate ritual of courtly love. Book II opens in the same unassuming way. The narrator claims that it is not up to him either to praise or to blame his characters; it is his job simply to translate ('For as myn auctour seyde, so sey I' – l. 18). Nevertheless, after this the narrator's projection of himself begins to show signs of strain. The prologue to Book III, in which Troilus and Criseyde consummate their love, shows distinct signs of excitement from the narrator; while Book IV opens with his depressed realization that from now it is downhill all the way. Chaucer openly admits that it is harder to write about lovers parting than about their coming together. In fact, Book V as a whole is full of such anxieties and misgivings, and by now the narrator is a long way from the cool detachment of Book I. Approached like this, it is a fairly simple matter to plot changes in the narrator's attitudes over the course of the poem. It is as though he gradually switches from our Version A to Version B, from blame to sympathy. In fact, if you now look again at the earlier books, you will find that this sympathy is sporadically expressed even before the middle of the poem. Look at II. 666–86, for example, where the narrator openly jumps to Criseyde's defence in case the reader feels inclined to criticize her. This is just one of many instances where there is a tension between the story and the different ways in which it can be told.

For all these reasons the intensely moral ending of the poem often comes as a shock. Suddenly, all the humanity and compassion generated by the narrator are swept aside and you are asked to see everything as the misguided behaviour of a bunch of pagans. It is as though the coolness and detachment of the poem's opening is reasserted with a vengeance, and now with the added force of orthodox religion. Once again, therefore, you are left with a big question: 'What, finally, am I to make of the work?' However, looking closely at the narrator's own changing reactions will help you tackle this question, even if you do not come to any firm conclusion.

STEP 6 SEEING THE TEXT IN CONTEXT

Troilus and Criseyde is obviously a complex and contentious work, so you need to draw on as many kinds of material as possible when forming a response. At this stage some awareness of the poem's relation to its literary sources as well as its historical context can be particularly illuminating. For instance, it helps to know that Chaucer massively modified the characters he found in his source, Boccaccio's *Il Filostrato*. The basic shape of the action remains the same, but all Chaucer's characters are more sympathetically presented and more 'psychological' than Boccaccio's. The latter's Criseida is straight-forwardly sensual (quite unlike the thoughtful and sensitive Criseyde), while Boccaccio's Troilo is much more of a gallant and less of an idealist than Troilus. Perhaps the biggest change is in Chaucer's Pandarus. In Boccaccio Pandaro is just another gallant, the friend of Troilo and the cousin of Criseida; in Chaucer he is older, more mature and the heroine's uncle – an altogether more complex and persuasive figure. Now all you do is ask what light these modifications throw on the critical issues. Clearly, Chaucer was more interested in character and the complex human side of things than his source, and yet, equally clearly, he felt unable actually to change the fateful course of events. The characters change but the story remains the same. The result is therefore a tension in the work as a whole, and again notice that all we are really doing is exploring the tension between Versions A and B noted earlier. Only, this time, we are doing it with the support of source material.

It is the same with the more specifically social and historical tensions expressed in the poem. Just a little knowledge of context can substantially enhance your understanding of the text. For instance, it helps to know that Chaucer wrote *The Legend of Good Women* partly as an apology to certain women at court for his presentation of Criseyde. It seems that, despite all his shows of sympathy, Chaucer still managed to offend a powerful body of women at court. Now, at first this may appear a mere sidelight on *Troilus and Criseyde*. However, if you recreate this kind of contemporary atmosphere and place the poem within it, a number of important things stand out. Most obviously, the context explains the complexity of the narrator. Here is a poet acutely aware of the tastes and attitudes of his audience. Neither the audience nor their attitudes were totally uniform, so he had to tread a precarious path between engaging and offending different people at different times. It was not easy, and the precise tensions within the poem are a fair indication why. On the one hand, there was an intensely secular side to the court, people interested above all in human relations and the elaborate expression of human courtship called 'courtly love'. On the other hand, there were senior clergy, sworn to celibacy and the upholding of orthodox Christian values, people whose views had also to be accommodated in some way. If you imagine these two extremes together in one audience, it is much easier to understand the mixed 'human' and 'religious' appeals of *Troilus and Criseyde*. The men and women of the court did not always agree either, and this, too, seems to have left its mark on the poem. There are plenty of instances of court attitudes polarizing around issues of male or female power (Chaucer's word was 'soveraynetee') and the apology in *The Legend of Good Women* is just one of them. In fact, a lot of the Canterbury Tales are focused on precisely this issue, how men and women are to be presented and what their roles should be (see also Chapter 8, pp. 202–14). Again, if you project these tensions back on to the text, they help explain why Chaucer wrote as he did, and why, in particular, he found it difficult to present just one attitude to his heroine. Poems dealing with morality and immorality, with men and women, were always potentially problematic. Studying *Troilus and Criseyde* in context allows you to see both the inherent problems of the subject, as well as the considerable resource of the author in presenting it to a mixed and demanding audience.

STEP 7   ANALYSING THE STYLE

The two previous sections encourage you to get an overview of the text in terms of its narrator and its literary and social contexts. Finally, you should look at its style. In this way you can reconnect with the poem's verbal detail while still relating it to the larger issues. For instance, look again at the central passage where Troilus faints and Pandarus presses Criseyde to show pity:

'Nece, but ye helpe us now,
Allas, youre owen Troilus is lorn!'
'Iwis, so wolde I, and I wiste how,
Ful fayn,' quod she; 'Allas, that I was born!'
'Yee, nece, wol ye pullen out the thorn
That stiketh in his herte,' quod Pandare,
'Sey "al foryeve", and stynt is al this fare!'
(III. 1100–6)

The first thing you will notice is that most of this passage is speech; it is a dialogue. In fact, this is characteristic of much of the poem and it should remind you that the dominant interest in *Troilus and Criseyde* is *dramatic*. We are, above all, interested in the speeches, thoughts and reactions of the characters. This is a simple point, but in a stylistic way it underscores the essentially 'human' side of the poem. Set against this is the fact that the passage is, of course, in verse. The language is dramatic, but it is also ordered and formally organized. In this case, as throughout the poem, there is a basic pattern of ten-syllable lines rhyming *ababbcc*. Now all you do is think about the combined effect of dramatic speech with a sophisticated verse form. Clearly, there is a tension, and this can be readily related to tensions in the poem as a whole. On the one hand, there is the varied 'humanity' of the dramatic speeches; on the other, there is an underlying sense of order and control. We respond to the variety of the individual voices, but we are also aware of a constant purpose or design. This can be put in many ways, in terms of a tension between human sympathy and moral purpose, or 'free will' and 'fortune'. But, whatever terms you use, the essential relation between localized style and larger issues remains.

Now think about the different ways the characters speak and think, their *individual* styles. All of them have different attitudes to life and love, so it is reasonable to expect this to be expressed in their language. For instance, look at the difference between Pandarus's and Criseyde's speeches in the above extract. Pandarus dominates the conversation and you can actually list the wide range of verbal strategies he employs. There is direct appeal ('Nece, … Yee, nece, …'); the implication that he identifies totally with the lovelorn Troilus ('but ye helpe us now'); a touch of metaphor ('wol ye pullen out the thorn / That stiketh in his herte'), and even an attempt to put words into Criseyde's mouth ('Sey "al foryeve"'). Given this verbal onslaught, it is not surprising that Criseyde succumbs. Notice, however, that she does so in a peculiarly broken and distracted way ('Iwis, so wolde I … Allas, that I was born!'). Thereupon she sets about trying to revive Troilus, who is in a characteristically supine and helpless state. None of this analysis really says anything you do not know already. There is a complex interplay of relationships and the result is a dramatic climax. What it does, however, is remind you that the tensions of the whole text can be explored in quite small extracts. Close attention to style is simply a detailed way of showing what the work is about and how it is put together. And this, in essence, is also the way to approach writing an essay on Chaucer, the topic of the next chapter.

7

WRITING AN ESSAY ON CHAUCER

This book so far has suggested how to go about building a critical response to the particular Chaucer text you are studying. What follows are some suggestions about how you might organize that response so as to answer specific questions in an exam. There are many ways of answering exam questions, just as there are many ways of forming a critical response. However, there are more and less effective ways of doing both. For instance, here is a standard question on *The General Prologue*. Even though you may be studying another Chaucer text, try to see the different ways in which this particular question can be tackled. The principles are the same, whatever the question and whatever the text.

> 'Chaucer laughed at human weaknesses rather than denounced them.' Consider this remark with reference to *The General Prologue*.

Where should you start with a question such as this? Well, the first thing you should do may sound so obvious it does not need saying. However, because failing to do it is by far the most common fault in exam answers, it is worth stressing it here:

START WITH THE QUESTION

You do not start a journey between A and B at C, so do not try to start an exam question anywhere you fancy. For instance, if you began answering the above question by saying 'Chaucer is one of the great poets of English literature, and that is why he has been called the "father of English poetry"', you would be starting in the wrong place. The statement suggests that you will not get round to the question till the middle of next week. Here is a better place to start: 'Chaucer certainly makes us laugh in *The General Prologue*, but there is usually also some moral point to what we laugh at. Humour and morality often go hand-in-hand in this poem ... .' Notice that all I am doing is starting with the actual terms of the question ('Chaucer laughed at human weaknesses rather than denounced them') and showing that I understand the *issue* they address. Essentially, the issue revolves around the relationship between 'laughter' and 'denunciation', and that is why I continued by referring more conceptually to 'humour' and 'morality'. Consequently, in the first couple of sentences I have connected firmly with the actual words of the question and shown that I understand the basic terms of the argument. This is what is meant by 'getting straight down to the question', and it means that the examiner does not have to groan and get irritated while you wander around looking for the actual issue. Incidentally, notice that this question (like nearly all questions) is built round a *contrast* or *tension*: here 'laughter' and 'denunciation'. Looking for a contrast or tension is something you have been encouraged to do throughout this book, whether dealing with characters or themes, so all you are doing is applying the same technique to the question. In this way you can quickly identify the crucial terms that will give shape and direction to your argument.

Another example, this time on *The Knight's Tale*, will confirm the usefulness of starting with the question in this way. Here is the question:

> 'By contrast with the gods, the human actors acquire a certain tragic dignity.' Discuss this comment on the human and divine figures in *The Knight's Tale*.

This question is a little more complicated than the one on *The General Prologue*, but notice that it also gives you more help. Here you are actually invited to 'discuss' the 'contrast' between the gods and the humans in *The Knight's Tale*. Words such as this (others are 'consider', 'examine' and 'compare'), along with phrases such as 'how far' and 'to what extent', are always there to help you construct an argument. In this case you are asked to 'discuss' and 'contrast' with very specific terms in mind. The humans, it suggests, 'acquire a certain tragic dignity', whereas the gods presumably do not. You therefore know straightaway not only that you are going to be contrasting one set of figures with another, but also that you are going to be doing this according to some notions of what constitute 'tragedy' and 'dignity'. Consequently, you would be wise to offer provisional definitions of these terms early on, or at least to suggest that they are in some way uncertain or problematic. (Alternatively, of course, you could wheel on our old faithful 'Chaucer is one of the great poets of English literature ...' and so signal to the examiner that you have very little idea of what is going on.) Once you have made a good start with the question, and shown that you know where you are going, the next step is to go there. That is what we look at next.

DEVELOP AN ARGUMENT

Solid and systematic preparation is the basis for any good essay. If you have not sorted out your critical response in the first place, you will hardly be able to form one under pressure in an exam. However, there is a particularly strong reason why you should study *systematically* from the beginning. The more clearly you have organized your ideas and materials beforehand, the easier it will be to select and re-sort them when faced by a specific question. Identifying the actual issues focused by the question is your top priority; after that you need to apply them to the text and show that you can sustain a logical and purposeful argument.

The basis for a good performance may be good preparation, but it is obvious that you cannot just reproduce everything you have prepared in the vague hope that it will somehow cover the question. This is like emptying a lorry load of sand just to fill a bucket: you may fill the bucket, but you will waste a lot of sand – and probably not be able to find the bucket either! Clearly, there needs to be some process of selection and control, some way of ensuring that you apply just enough and the right kind of knowledge at the right time. In short, you need to organize a *specific* argument for a *specific* essay. This is not as daunting as it may sound, nor is it really all that new. All you will be doing, in effect, is taking the method we have used throughout the book and modifying it for a given question. The method is organized in seven 'steps', and so far we have applied these fairly rigorously – even rigidly. The trick now is to see that, once you have formed a response, you can go through these steps in any order. You can start with Step 7, the style, or with Step 5, the relation of the narrator to the narrative, or with Step 3, characterization, and you can then proceed to the others in almost any order you choose. In fact you will soon find that what looked like a steady march from Steps 1 to 7 quickly turns into a kind of 'dance'. And it is a dance at a pace dictated by you and your response to the question.

First you need to remind yourself of the basic steps, so here they are in their familiar order:

1.   What kind of work?
2.   What is it about (story and main ideas)?
3.   Looking at characterization
4.   Developing the argument
5.   Relating the tale/narrative to its teller/narrator
6.   Seeing the text in context
7.   Analysing the style

These seven steps allow you to approach the work from every major point of view. All you do now is decide which is the *best* point of view for your specific question. Take the question on *The General Prologue*, for instance: '"Chaucer laughed at human weaknesses rather than denounced them" ... .' You have already established that your argument is going to revolve round such terms as 'laughter' and 'morality' or 'entertainment' and 'instruction', so what is the best way to develop it? Well, looking over the seven steps, you could start in a number of places. In fact, you might start with Step 1, the kind of work *The General Prologue* is. If you pointed to the fact that this poem is an 'estates satire', and that such texts were traditional ways of both criticizing and ridiculing different sections of medieval society, then you would immediately relate the question to larger matters of form and convention. You might then, rather than just plodding on through Step 2, skip a step and talk about the characterization (Step 3). In what ways can you talk about the characterization in *The General Prologue* so as to develop this 'estates satire' notion of criticism and ridicule combined? Here you could point to a couple of characters, such as the Prioress and the Pardoner, and show the ways in which they are (in words of the question) 'laughed at' or 'denounced'. Comparing these two in detail, you might well come up with the simple, but very useful observation that Chaucer is sometimes more gentle in his 'denunciation' than he is at other times. The Prioress is treated ironically and affectionately, whereas the Pardoner is more emphatically blasted by the narrator's censure. This last point, referring to the narrator, might then lead you to think more particularly about the role of the narrator in the poem, and what light this throws on the question. You could then draw on materials you had already thought about in Step 5, the narrator's relation to the narrative. And so you might proceed.

At each stage you would decide which was the next most logical step in your argument, and at each stage you would look for some way of tying the issues into specific pieces of the text or other evidence. For instance, in the case of Step 6, seeing the text in context, you might refer to the fact that late-fourteenth-century society was in a state of flux. This meant that it was particularly difficult for writers to adopt a single, consistent attitude to moral problems, and they were often obliged to cultivate a more ironic, less obviously dogmatic stance. Notice that such an observation throws light on the issues as well as demonstrating that you have thought around the text and can see it as part of a larger historical experience. The point is that in all these ways, and in others you can explore for yourself, the argument can be developed and substantiated. The precise sequence of steps is up to you, but it is very important that your essay should have some kind of shape or pattern and that this should relate closely to both the question and the text.

To help you see just how important these aspects of your essay are, here is a standard statement on the 'major criteria' required by examining boards:

> Examination candidates are expected to reveal a detailed knowledge of the text, to answer the question as set, and to write a coherent essay.

Keep these criteria in mind when selecting and sorting your material and you will not go far wrong. If you think particularly about the seven possible aspects of your argument, where to begin and how to proceed, you will be well able to fashion an argument which is as individual as it is effective.

To illustrate with another example, here is the outline of a possible answer to the question on *The Knight's Tale* ('"By contrast with the gods, the human actors acquire a certain tragic dignity" Discuss ...'). In this case, picking up the underlying contrast between the gods and the humans, you might start with the characterization (Step 3). How are these two sets of figures presented and is there any noticeable difference between them? In general the gods are powerful but petty, while the humans are powerless but well-meaning. You would clinch this point by comparing a couple of passages. Once you had got your bearings with the characters in this way, you might then focus on the 'tragic dignity' part of the question. To what extent is *The Knight's Tale* a 'tragedy', and in what sense – medieval or modern? (You would have already thought about this under Step 1, the kind of work.) With these notions in mind, you might then proceed to look at the way in which the 'tragic' action is actually developed in this text (Step 4). Does this throw a more, or less, flattering light on the interventions by the gods? Do they or the 'human actors' gain in 'dignity' as the plot unfolds? At this point you might even pick up the implication of the human characters as 'actors' in a kind of 'play' which the gods have written, a play they are forced to act out in ignorance of the overall design. From there you might push your argument in various directions: towards the Knight and *his* apparent view of the human and divine figures (i.e. Step 5); or towards Step 2 and some overview of the text's main ideas in terms of human 'free will' and divine 'predestination'. These are all issues which obviously have bearing on the 'tragic dignity' of the characters. The possibilities are virtually infinite. But whichever you chose, you would need to make sure that some coherent pattern emerged in your argument.

When you have developed your argument, do not just stop writing. Try to round off your argument, showing that you are still in control and have not simply run out of ideas. It is often a good idea to remind the reader (and yourself) of the actual terms of the question; you can then demonstrate how these have been challenged or extended by the body of your essay. Incidentally, try to avoid a final paragraph which begins 'In conclusion, it has been shown that ...' and then proceeds simply to repeat all your main points. A good essay will have kept these in mind all the time. A couple of summary remarks addressed directly to the question will do.

How to quote

Quoting is easy to do well and yet often done badly, so here are some tips on when to quote and how:

(i)   Quote when you need to substantiate a specific part of your argument.

(ii)   Quote briefly: often a single phrase or a line will do.

(iii) Quote accurately.

Quotation is there to substantiate an argument, not as a substitute for it, so do not stuff your essay full of ten-line quotations hoping that they will 'pad it out' and make it more impressive. Examiners want to know why a particular phrase or line is chosen and how exactly it supports your argument. They are not at all impressed by brute demonstrations of power to regurgitate massive chunks of a text at will. For instance, you might want to support the point that Theseus rounds off *The Knight's Tale* with a contradictory and problematic speech on the subject of universal harmony. Sometimes he seems to be saying that everything in life is for the best, and sometimes he seems to be saying the opposite. Now, writing out the whole speech (which is over a 100 lines long) might pass the time and fill a couple of pages, but it would do precious little else. On the other hand, if you said something like the following, you could make your point *and* support it in the space of two or three sentences:

> Theseus's long concluding speech starts off with an optimistic celebration of the 'faire cheyne of love' which seems to bind the universe together harmoniously. However, by the end he is making much more ominous noises about the 'foule prisoun of this lyf' and having to make 'vertu of necessitee'. There is therefore a contradiction, or at least a difference of emphasis, and the result is that we do not really know whether everything is for the best or not.

Presenting the materials like this, the argument is supported by the quotations and the quotations are explained by the argument. You are not offering one as a substitute for the other, hoping that they will justify or explain themselves. Incidentally, it would have seriously undermined the effect of this argument if I had misquoted. Talking about the 'faire cheyne of *life*', say, rather than the 'faire cheyne of *love*', might be an understandable slip, but it also suggests you do not know the text very well. So quote accurately, quote briefly and quote every time you have a specific point to substantiate.

How to write commentaries

You may be required to comment on a short extract from your text.

If this is so, you should make sure that you actually provide what is asked for rather than ramble on about whatever you fancy. An extract for commentary should not be used as an excuse to reproduce everything that you know about the text and the author, whether relevant or not. In fact, as with an essay, the essence of a good commentary is selection. For instance, at the most obvious level, if you are asked to translate specific lines into good modern English, do just that. Do not translate the whole passage or put it into verse in the hope of showing off. You will not get any more marks, and may well get less. Equally, if you are asked to comment on a passage 'for what it shows about Chaucer's method of characterization', or 'for the light it throws on the main issues of the tale', do just that. Talking about 'characterization' means more than simply describing the character in general; it means showing how a particular character is constructed, what different kinds of material the character is built from, whether he or she is simple or complex, a 'type' or a 'rounded' individual. All of this should be demonstrated from the passage on which you have been asked to comment (though you can bring in relevant supporting evidence). Similarly, commenting on 'the light the passage throws on the issues' means looking for the contrasts or tensions in the extract, and then relating those to the issues in the rest of the text. It does not mean writing a mini-essay on the text's issues, and only referring to the extract as an afterthought. This last point is the nub of the matter. Your commentary should use the actual words in front of you to substantiate a more general point. Essentially, it is the same as using quotations to support an argument in your own essay. The only difference is that the 'quotation' is chosen for you, and you are asked to explore it in specific ways. That is why writing commentaries ought to be much easier than writing essays; much of the selection has already been done for you. Strange to relate, therefore, that commentaries are often done much worse!

CONCLUSION

The aim of this chapter is to help you write good essays and commentaries on Chaucer. You may find the following summary handy when preparing a piece of work – or when you are halfway through one and cannot work out what is going wrong:

(i)   Read the text carefully, using the methods outlined in this book to help you organize your own response.

(ii)   Start with the question, trying to see how it provides
       you with the basic terms for your argument. Look
       particularly for the contrast implicit in the question or
       terms which need challenging and defining.

(iii) Structure your answer by deciding on the best points
       of view from which to tackle the argument. You already
       have seven steps for approaching a text (ranging from
       the kind of work it is to the style), so think which step
       you should start with, which step follows on most
       logically in the circumstances, and so on.

(iv)   At every stage of your argument try to support it by
       detailed reference to the text and brief quotation.

(v)   At the beginning of every paragraph, and especially
       the last one, make sure that you are still answering the
       question.

8

COMMON TOPICS AND
CURRENT DEBATES

The aim of this chapter is threefold: (1) to help identify central and recurrent topics in Chaucer's writing; (2) to encourage discussion and reflection across a number of his works, thereby offsetting the concentration earlier on individual tales and including some less-studied texts; (3) to connect in accessible ways with relevant debates in contemporary literary criticism and theory in general, and Chaucer criticism in particular. All the topics are presented in clusters in a similar way and may be approached in any order. Each is introduced in terms of a *Key issue* followed by extended definitions, explanations and illustrations. And each is rounded off by *Specific questions and suggestions* that can be put to any Chaucer text you are studying, along with *Further reading* keyed to the bibliography.

AUTHORS AND AUTHORITY, EXPERIENCE AND EXPERTISE, KNOWLEDGE AND POWER

KEY ISSUE

- How Chaucer handles the relation between received authority and observed experience, and thereby explores the nature of knowledge and power.

Chaucer's writings are full of influences from and references to other authors and their works, ancient and modern, secular and religious.

This apparently extraneous knowledge can be off-putting as well as awesome for the beginning reader ('Why does he keep going on about X? Or off on a tangent about Y?'). With just a little patience and application, however, such material can be recognized as a fascinating challenge rather than a frustrating obstacle. So can a grasp of Chaucer's sources and what he does with them. In fact, most of the information you need is available in the notes of a good edition. Equipped with this, you quickly become aware that Chaucer's reading, though wide and various, is to some extent recoverable even if it is not completely knowable. What's more, on further inspection and reflection, it turns out that he often draws on much the same range of writers and writings. Basically, we may distinguish five kinds of material in play:

1. *Works by classical philosophers, poets and historians* such as Socrates, Ovid, Vergil and Boethius, chiefly known to Chaucer and his contemporaries through later adaptations and anthologized extracts in French and Italian as well as Latin (not Greek).
2. *Biblical stories from the Old and New Testaments*, again often in extracted and adapted forms of sermon and moral treatise, including commentaries by the Church Fathers and others.
3. *Romances, heroic poems and lyrics by more modern writers* such as Guillaume de Lorris and Jean de Meung, the French authors of *Le Roman de la Rose*, and more nearly contemporary Italian writers such as Dante, Boccaccio and Petrarch.
4. *Learned epigrams (sententiae) and their colloquial folk equivalents (proverbs)* drawn from a wide variety of sources – bookish and popular, literary and oral.
5. *'Expert' and specialized knowledges* in such areas as astrology, alchemy, law, medicine, mathematics and music, again drawing on ancient and modern sources.

Chaucer was so engaged with some of these works that he translated them into English, thereby earning the accolade of 'Grand translateur' from his French contemporary, the poet Eustache Deschamps. Thus we have Chaucer's translation of Boethius's hugely influential *Consolation of Philosophy* (*Boece*) and his *Romaunt of the Rose*. Still other works Chaucer adapted as the basis for his own retellings. Hence the readily identifiable sources for parts of *The House of Fame* and *The Parliament of Fowls* (Dante), *The Clerk's Tale* (Petrarch), and *The*

Knight's Tale and *Troilus and Criseyde* (Boccaccio).

Taken together, all of the above materials (1–5) were what Chaucer and his contemporaries referred to as 'auctoritees' (authorities). They were called this because they were by recognized and revered 'auctors' (authors) or drew upon anonymous works of a generally approved and admired kind. Chaucer evidently had an avid and omnivorous appetite for reading. This taste is attested throughout his work. The crucial point to note, however, is that Chaucer's passion for reading is invariably framed in terms of a tension and potential conflict: between the rich promise of book-learning on the one hand and, on the other, what can (or cannot) be learned from personal experience and observation. The opening of the prologue to *The Legend of Good Women* (F-text, ll. 1–39) offers the most extended of many ruminations on this theme. It is worth weighing carefully because it supplies a handy key to many of the issues encountered elsewhere. The prologue opens with Chaucer in his role as dream-narrator reflecting that there are many more things in heaven and hell and on the earth (including heaven and hell themselves!) that he believes, even though he has no direct knowledge of them:

> A thousand tymes have I herd men telle
> That ther ys joye in hevene and peyne in helle,
> And I acorde wel that it ys so;
> But, natheles, yet wot I wel also
> That ther nis noon dwellyng in this contree
> That eyther hath in hevene or helle ybe,

This knowledge of things unseen but believed the poet gratefully puts down to the influence of books. He celebrates books as a kind of benign extended memory (*remembraunce*) which we must be careful not to lose: 'And yf that olde bokes were aweye / Yloren [lost] were of remembraunce the keye' (ll. 25–6). At the same time, he points out that this knowledge is still to some extent conditional. We can only give 'credence' (belief) to 'these olde approved [approved, tried and tested] stories' where they treat of things of which otherwise we cannot possibly know, either because they relate to what is past and gone or to matters of a spiritual and invisible nature: 'Wel oughte we thanne honouren and beleve / These bokes, *there we han noon other preve*' ('… where we have no other proof/experience', my emphasis). Such distinctions and qualifications and the terms in which they are couched are significant: 'olde bokes' and 'olde appreved stories' may be readily believed in; but this is precisely because they are tried and tested ('appreved') and in the absence of other 'pref' (proof, experience).

Another passage worth weighing carefully here, also with implications for Chaucer's work as a whole, is the opening of *The Wife of Bath's Prologue*. When the Wife announces that she sets store by her own 'experience' of marriage, not by any 'auctoritee' on the subject, much more is meant than meets the eye:

> Experience, though noon auctoritee
> Were in this world, is ryght ynogh for me
> To speke of wo that is in mariage ...

The fundamental complication is that all the features of married life that the Wife goes on to attribute to 'experience', and all the passages from classical and biblical texts that she cites to support her case, are themselves drawn from existing texts. In other words, the Wife attacks 'auctoritee' in general, and male clerical authority in particular, but her assault is itself grounded in those very authorities she claims to dismiss. Her much-vaunted independence is still in some sense dependent. Her claimed female 'experience' is still man-made.

Similar double-binds recur throughout Chaucer's writing. There is the persistent possibility that what poses or is passed off as 'experience' from one point of view looks suspiciously like 'auctoritee' from another. In the 'Dream Poems', for instance, we keep company with a series of curiously bookish and naïvely inexperienced dream-narrators. It is chiefly through them that we meet and interact with a variety of figures who are at once more learned and more experienced than the dreamer himself: the lovelorn man in black in *The Book of the Duchess*; Scipio the astrologer, authority on dreams and political philosopher in *The Parliament of Fowls*; the teacherly eagle with his knowledge of mathematics and physics in *The House of Fame*, as well as the artfully unfulfilled promise of 'a man of greet auctoritee' in the poem's last line; the augustly omniscient God and Goddess of Love in the *Prologue to the Legend of Good Women*. On each occasion the result is a teasing interplay of kinds of (in)experience with kinds of (lack of) authority and power(lessness). Something similar – but again different – is going on with the ingenuously unassuming figure of the pilgrim-narrator in *The General Prologue to the Canterbury Tales*. He ceaselessly picks up and pricks at, even if he does not always puncture and deflate, all that is distinctive about the actual behaviour and claimed authority of each of his fellow pilgrims.

In religious terms the most authoritative book was, of course, the Bible, the ultimate 'author' of which was reckoned to be God. However, it was also recognized by scholars and theologians that the Bible existed in two rather different Testaments, 'Old' (Jewish) and 'New' (Christian), and that it drew upon a highly heterogeneous range of writers and kinds of writing. One of the main aims of biblical commentary, therefore, was to present the Bible as a single book underwriting a single, albeit various, doctrine. At the same time, virtually by definition, anyone who interpreted and 'glosed' (glossed, commented upon) the Bible implicitly acknowledged and explicitly demonstrated that it was open to literally endless interpretation and debate. By Chaucer's day theological dispute was rife and not only amongst the clergy themselves in the relative obscurity and security of Latin. Debates were also being aired in sermons in English, notably from such religious and potentially political radicals as the followers of John Wycliffe and the 'Lollards'. The situation became all the more explosive with the prospect, around 1380, of Wycliffe's translation and widespread circulation of the Bible in English. Indeed, it is precisely the interface between Latin and English that is at issue here. Once it became permeable, questions flowed thick and fast. How, why, when and to whom should the Church 'translate' its specialist, expert language and knowledge? Would a Bible in English effectively put God's word in the hands and mind of anyone who could read at all? Could it undermine the power, prestige and authority – even the very existence – of the clergy as specialized mediators and interpreters? After all, if everyone knew what God said, why would they bother to consult a priest ? Why should priests exist at all?!

It should be stressed, however, that the argument was not so much about the divine origin and authority of the Bible as such (for most people that was not in doubt), but about the ever thicker, darker and more complex canopy of commentary that threatened to engulf it. People were becoming sceptical not so much about what the original, divine author supposedly said, but about what later, human authorities *said he said*. In some circles, therefore – Chaucer's included – scriptural interpretation in general and 'glossing' (*glosynge*) passages in particular, were commonly viewed with scepticism, and sometimes downright cynicism. This resistant turn of mind was especially prevalent amongst the steadily increasing numbers of secular professionals such as lawyers, physicians and court administrators (of whom Chaucer was one). The education of such groups was sophisticated, highly literate and sometimes remarkably literary – but it was not primarily or particularly religious.

The resonances of these debates, doubts and disputes can be felt everywhere in Chaucer's work. In general terms they take the form of a sceptical or satirical attitude to clerical 'auctoritees' at large. Belief in the word of God may be absolute; but belief in the word of men and women of God is conditional. Sensitivity to such stresses and strains is everywhere apparent in the descriptions and tales of such figures as the Pardoner, Friar and Summoner. There we are shown scoundrels who trade upon the words of God for their own purposes. They abuse and pervert holy means for vicious ends. What ideally should be authorit*ative* is really authorit*arian* – and ultimately both a sin and a crime.

The study of Chaucer's major narrative sources is another revealing way of gauging his handling of known 'auctors'. In *The Clerk's Tale*, for instance, the main issue can be expressed in terms of how far we judge Chaucer to be: (1) going along with the traditional tale as told by Petrarch, with its ostensibly simple morals of wifely patience and obedience to God; (2) identifying with the indignant objections of the Clerk, a narrator apparently sympathetic to the persecuted heroine; (3) setting up the whole thing as an ironic rejoinder to the prologue and tale he had put in the mouth of the Wife of Bath; (4) doing all three with varying emphases at different points. *The Knight's Tale*, meanwhile, looks decidedly authoritarian and not particularly concerned with the experience of individuals, especially if we compare it with Chaucer's source, Boccaccio's *Teseida*. And yet it looks markedly more philosophical than Boccaccio if we emphasize the influence of Boethius's *Consolation of Philosophy*. Conversely, Chaucer's *Troilus and Criseyde* seems much more subtle and sensitive and tuned to individual experience than its source in Boccaccio, not least because Chaucer's narrator (like the Clerk above) is openly sympathetic to his heroine. But still the final word is left to the most severely dogmatic and unsympathetic of religious and moral authorities (see V, ll. 1828ff.). Clearly, then, critical comparison with sources can be very valuable. But it still leaves the question open of which source is to be emphasized and what the critic's own aim is in making the comparison. In this respect, critics are simply authors like any other. They too may use – and potentially abuse – their academic authority and scholarly resources.

In all these ways Chaucer explores a tension between different kinds of received authority on the one hand and different kinds of observed experience on the other. The fact that authority and experience are themselves plural and often change hands (indeed, they sometimes change into one another!) means that we too must be alert and agile, as well as responsive and responsible when handling interpretations of Chaucer's work.

QUESTIONS AND SUGGESTIONS TO RELATE TO YOUR CHAUCER TEXT(S)

1. Reread the text noting the specific authors mentioned and the general kinds of authority and knowledge in play (classical; religious; philosophical; scientific; courtly; etc.). What do these contribute to the overall 'feel' of the piece? And what light do they throw on the attitudes and values of the various narrators or characters? (For instance, do any of the *auctoritees* invoked seem to be challenged or confirmed, used or abused? By whom?)

2. Look out for contrasts and possible conflicts between kinds of 'expert' knowledge and kinds of ordinary 'experience', specialist argument and common sense. How far are the former being underwritten or undermined by the latter? And how *ordinary* is the experience and *common* is the sense anyway?

3. Beginning with the introduction and notes in a good edition of the text, find out as much as you can about Chaucer's sources. What, on balance, does he seem to be doing with them? Back up your general observations with some detailed comparison where possible.

4. List the main ways in which your own experience and knowledge of the world seem to be (a) different from and (b) similar to that represented in Chaucer's text. What authorities (academic subjects; figures; personalities; books; TV programmes; films; etc.) might *you* invoke to justify your views? And are these demonstrably truer or more powerful than those invoked in Chaucer?

FURTHER READING: Ellis 1996: pp. 17–24; Rigby 1996: pp. 1–17; Ashton 1998; Bryan and Dempster 1941; Windeatt 1982; Bronson 1960.

IRONY AND SATIRE, COMEDY AND CARNIVAL

KEY ISSUE

• How Chaucer handles various kinds of humour in his work, to what critical and moral ends, and how far modern readers are prepared to laugh along.

Chaucer has a wide and deserved reputation as a comic writer. The phrase 'a Canterbury tale' has long had a popular association with laughter, often of a rude and knockabout kind. And clearly there is some truth in this view if one concentrates on parts of the low-life fabliaux of the Miller, Reeve, Summoner and Shipman. However, even in these tales there is a persistent tension between seeing them as 'ernest' (in earnest, serious) and as 'game' (in sport, playful). In fact, it is precisely this possibility that Chaucer the pilgrim both alerts us to and disclaims in *The Miller's Prologue* (ll. 3185–6): 'Avyseth yow, and put me out of blame; / And eek men shal nat maken ernest of game'. In the event, not only are many of *The Canterbury Tales* serious by any standards (and a few such as *The Parson's Tale*, *The Man of Law's Tale* and *Melibee* are arguably solemn), some of the avowedly comic tales may appear to us 'funny peculiar' (inducing unease) rather more than 'funny ha ha' (inducing laughter). Some questions persist, therefore. How far is Chaucer inviting his contemporary audience to laugh *at* or *with* the butts of his humour? And how far are modern readers in every sense 'prepared' to recognize that these are 'laughing matters'?

But first, we need to distinguish the various kinds of humour in play. Do we see a particular tale or part of a tale as, say, *ironic* or *satiric*, *comic* or *carnivalesque*? As we'll see shortly, some such terms are needed if we are to gauge the precise effect of specific devices and strategies. At the same time, it must be recognized that the medieval concept of 'humour' is itself based upon a view of human beings very different from that commonly held today. In the Middle Ages four 'humours' were recognized, each of which represented a distinct psychological and physiological 'type' and was associated with a particular element. These types can be found throughout Chaucer, notably in *The General Prologue*, and they are reviewed at length in *The Nun's Priest's Tale* (ll. 3720–37). The melancholic person was reckoned to be cold and dry and identified with earth; the phlegmatic was cold and moist like water; the choleric was dry and hot like fire; the sanguine was warm and moist like air. In this way, 'humours' were tied in with the physical side of human beings: their bodily flows and drives. Though they were not initially 'humorous' (i.e. amusing, funny) in a modern sense, it is not hard to see how this latter meaning gradually evolved from a focus on bodily functions. Significantly, 'the body' is a crucial concept in modern theories of comedy — especially the body engaged in open expressions of sex, eating, drinking and defecating.

Irony can be simply defined as 'meaning more than meets the eye' or 'saying one thing and meaning another'. More subtly, we might say that 'being ironic' entails a humorous and critical interplay between what the writer indirectly implies (but does not say outright) and what the reader may infer (but cannot prove for sure). Either way, irony is very handy when you don't care, or dare, to deal in plain-speaking. For instance, saying 'What a lovely sunny day!' on a visibly rainy one is heavy irony. However, saying 'What a lovely dress!' to someone who half- (but only half-) suspects you don't really mean it is somewhat lighter irony. Comparatively obvious and unproblematic instances of irony include the numerous approving comments on palpably vicious characters made by Chaucer in his role as ingenuous narrator in *The General Prologue*. For instance, the remark 'He was in chirche a noble ecclesiaste' (l. 708) when applied to the depraved Pardoner is clearly ironic. At the same time, it catches how the vain Pardoner sees himself, or at least wishes to be seen. Similarly ironic remarks are made at the expense of many of the pilgrims. Telltale signs are the use of such words as 'ful wel', 'the best', 'gentil' or 'noble' when referring to figures who, from the rest of their description, appear anything but. In this respect, we may view the overall ingenuousness and impressionability of Chaucer the pilgrim-narrator as a consistently ironic device. The audience is thereby encouraged to smile knowingly at the objects of his naïve enthusiasm and artfully misplaced praise. The narrator in the 'Dream Poems' is another such figure: well-meaning but obtuse, earnestly bookish yet awkwardly inexperienced. The narrator of *Troilus and Criseyde* is similar, albeit more subtle and elusive. In all these cases the effect on the reader's view of things is likely to be in some measure ironic. Less is said but more is meant than meets the eye – whether the subject be death, love, fame or an individual figure such as Criseyde.

It must be admitted, however, that the very indirectness and implicitness of irony make it a tricky substance to deal with critically.

Its presence is easy to claim but difficult to prove. It can also be uncertain precisely who or what is being got at. Take the prologue of *The Wife of Bath's Tale* and the opening of *The Merchant's Tale*, for instance. The Wife may declare, 'Experience, thogh noon auctoritee / Were in this world, is right ynogh for me / To speke of wo that is in mariage' (ll. 1–3), just as the Merchant may declare, 'Wepyng and wayling, care and oother sorwe / I knowe ynogh ... and so doon other mo / That wedded been' (ll. 1213–6). But we still have no sure way of knowing exactly where Chaucer himself stands with respect to women and men, inside or outside marriage. All we can say is that he sets up the dramatic circumstances whereby we, as audience or readers, are obliged to make decisions and judge for ourselves. Irony opens up a play of difference and possibility between authors and their narrators and characters. But it does not absolutely determine emphases and preferences.

That brings us to the differences that open up over time between a text and its readers. For the fact is that a text may be read ironically at some later date (or in some other context) even though in its initial moment and context no irony was intended or understood. Modern readers, for example, are especially prone to read as ironic any text which expresses extreme forms of idealism in matters of romantic love or religious devotion. The elaborate courtship rituals in *The Knight's Tale* and *The Franklin's Tale*, like the extravagant displays of piety in *The Prioress's Tale* and *The Clerk's Tale*, have all been subjected to sustained ironic readings by contemporary critics. But this may in part be simply because *they* find such things inherently implausible or ridiculous. It remains a moot point whether Chaucer and *his* contemporaries would have agreed.

Satire, not irony, is the term we tend to use when humour is driven by an explicit moral aim. Satire entails an intent to ridicule combined with a sense of righteous indignation. It wields a sharp weapon (cutting wit) against a readily recognized enemy (corruption, stupidity, vice, sin). In this respect, it is important to observe that most of Chaucer's pilgrims and not a few of his characters within tales (especially friars, summoners, students, millers, merchants and minor gentry) draw on traditions of 'Estates Satire'. Such figures rehearse more or less standard, even if not entirely stereotypical, views of whole sections of medieval society. Chaucer's position is then discernibly that of a duly amused or properly appalled member of his own social group: a blend of highly educated courtier and senior civil servant. In short, his satire has

distinctive but still partly predictable targets. In short, he knows who
to laugh *with* as well as *at*.

Comedy is by definition easier to spot than irony. It is distinguished
by obvious improbabilities of situation and marked incongruities of
speech and behaviour. It also tends to prompt spontaneous laughter:
a hearty belly laugh at what is palpably ridiculous, rather than the
sly and knowing smiles of irony at what is merely intimated. Most
of the outright comedy in *The Canterbury Tales* is associated with
the genre of fabliau. It therefore draws on a stock cast of relatively
low-life characters such as millers, carpenters, friars, summoners and
poor students, as well as middling kinds of merchant and morally
'errant' kinds of knight. In fact, as is common in comedy from
classical times through Shakespeare to many a modern 'situation
comedy', there is a deeply ingrained convention of identifying those
low in social status with the physically rude and morally lax side of
humanity. The positive side of this is that such people also tend to
be seen as resilient and irrepressible. Indeed, for better and worse,
such figures often represent a kind of common human nature and,
in outlook, common sense. Typically, this is expressed in the form of
popular proverbs and folk wisdom. Pandarus fills just such a role as
commonsensical counsellor and cynical pragmatist in *Troilus and
Criseyde*.

The plots of comedy are usually extended tricks or jokes involving
a mix of raw sex, stupidity, cunning, cheating and naked
acquisitiveness. The ending invariably entails a sense of 'poetic justice'
or, more informally, 'tit for tat'. The difference in Chaucer is that all
these ingredients, while there in abundance, are also spiced and raised
by the stirring in of other materials of a more intellectual and
sophisticated nature. There is invariably a serious, though never a
solemn, flavour to the cultural tastes (references, allusions, world-
views) in the background. There is 'ernist' in the 'game'.

The Shipman's Tale (not treated elsewhere in this book) may be cited
as a characteristically Chaucerian comedy and a classic fabliau in all
the above respects. It features a grasping yet gullible merchant, his
extravagant and sexually available wife, and a smooth-talking, wheeler-
dealing friar. The plot revolves around a trick over the payment of a
debt and a play on the richly ambiguous term 'taillynge'. The latter
meant: (1) 'keeping financial accounts all square' (a tally was a wooden
and later a paper accounting device; hence 'keeping a tally'); (2) by
extension, generally 'getting one's own back'; and (3) colloquially,

'having sex', 'getting some tail'. What happens in the 'taillynge' as told by the Shipman is this. The merchant's wife has sex with the friar in return for a 'gift' of money to pay off her shopping debts – a gift which in reality she knows to be a loan from the merchant to the friar. The wife finally gets away with everything, however, by claiming she thought it was a gift from her husband (not the friar), and in any case she promises to pay her spouse back in bed 'with interest'. In the foreground, then, is a racily well-crafted tale of sex, lies and tit for tat. In the background, however, is a more serious – in places almost sinister – exposure of the insidious relation between property and sex: the exchange of money standing in for an exchange of bodies. Thus, though obviously a fabliau built on traditional lines, *The Shipman's Tale* is also a thoroughgoing critique of what might now be called 'the commodification of human relationships'. It is a text that draws on long-standing comic tradition even as it bears witness to its own historical moment, notably the shift from a feudal to a commercial economy. In other words, funnily enough, it is a deeply complex as well as a delightfully simple tale of 'taillynge'!

Some such simple/complex, comic/serious richness of perspectives characterizes all of Chaucer's overtly humorous work. From one point of view, *The Parliament of Fowls* presents an uproarious free-for-all in the choosing of sex-partners; from another, it represents part of an ongoing reflection on the possibility of 'commune profit' (the common good, consensus) in the late medieval body politic. *The Miller's Tale* and *The Reeve's Tale*, meanwhile, though openly sporting with assorted bums, farts and sexual escapades, also sustain critiques of the petty politics of social climbing. *The Friar's Tale*, however, is perhaps best described as darkly and dramatically ironic; so subtle is the suspense created by the growing gap between what the reader sees and what the summoner so conspicuously fails to see. *The Summoner's Tale*, on the other hand, responds in full comic measure but in quite a different vein. The undercover antic of a 'cherl' farting in the hand of a grasping friar is also the vehicle for a sophisticated parody of theological debate. *The Nun's Priest's Tale*, on yet another hand, combines extravagant rhetorical display with the uproarious farce of a farmyard in pursuit of a fox too mouthy for his own good. It also, like all the above tales, carries implications for our views of social order – and especially disorder – which go far deeper than casual notions of comedy as mere 'entertainment' or 'light relief'.

Carnival (the adjective is **carnivalesque**) is the term most often invoked nowadays when dealing with the more politically charged functions of comedy. This approach draws on Mikhail Bakhtin's work on the blending of popular and learned elements in late medieval and early Renaissance culture, especially in Rabelais's comic epic *Gargantua and Pantagruel*. Carnival was the Shrovetide festival in which Christians feasted and revelled before the enforced period of abstinence in Lent (the term derives from Italian *carne-vale* – 'farewell to flesh'). In Europe during the Middle Ages, as in South America and many other countries now, carnival was an occasion for street parties and pageants. Sometimes these became politically charged and led to riots and uprisings. This is how Bakhtin introduces 'carnival' as a critical concept in *Rabelais and his World* (1968: p. 10):

> **Carnival celebrates the temporary liberation from prevailing truth and from the established order: it marks the suspension of all hierarchical rank, privileges, norms and prohibitions.**

He then goes on to explore carnival as an expression of popular culture opposed or alternative to an official elite order that it inverts and sometimes subverts. Physically, this involves an exaggerated and often grotesque celebration of the human body – especially the bodily functions of sex, eating, sleeping and defecating. These conventionally 'taboo' subjects are braced against all that habitually constrains or conceals them. The latter includes everything from clothing and polite manners to elevated forms of courtship and worship. Intellectually, and by extension politically, 'carnival' is a utopian ideal of universal freedom – a kind of gigantic 'holiday' or 'party-time'. Bounded and contained as they are by the pressures of workaday life and routine morality, carnivalesque expressions of holiday/party-time may be considered a merely temporary and relatively harmless escape-valve. Alternatively, they may point to more permanent and radical possibilities. Either way, the emphasis of modern commentators will depend upon their sense of the tension between what we might now call physical (especially sexual) expression and political suppression (or freedom).

Potentially 'carnivalesque' instances of comedy are not hard to find in Chaucer. Interpreting precisely what they mean is more contentious. Episodes and passages that readily spring to mind include the frank expressions of sexuality in *The Miller's Tale* (ll. 3730ff.), *The Reeve's Tale* (ll. 4193ff.) and *The Merchant's Tale* (ll. 2350ff.). The two former tales are also famous (or notorious) for freely sporting with the bodily functions of 'pissing' and 'farting' – and in precisely those terms. However, the grandest and most grotesquely anal of Chaucer's tales is without doubt *The Summoner's Tale*. The glimpse of friars swarming from the 'devil's ers' in its prologue and the thirteenfold division of the fart in the tale itself have duly delighted or disgusted all those who have read it. (Unfortunately, the latter are relatively few as the tale is seldom set – presumably precisely because it is felt improper.) Meanwhile, clamorous and potentially riotous behaviour of one kind or another, often verging on the farcical, can be found in *The Nun's Priest's Tale* (ll. 4172ff.), *The Wife of Bath's Prologue* (ll. 788ff.) and *The Parliament of Fowls* (ll. 491ff.). In all these very various cases, the uproar is finally contained within some conventional moral, religious or social frame.

It remains a moot point, however, just how sensitive or sympathetic Chaucer was to the political, as well as the aesthetic, dimensions of the carnivalesque in comedy. The passing reference linking farmyard uproar to social unrest in *The Nun's Priest's Tale* (especially that to the peasant rebels 'Jakke strawe and his meynee', ll. 4190–4) is both unique and tantalizingly enigmatic. Darker visions of popular uprising as a threat to social order figure in *The Knight's Tale* (l. 2419) and *The Clerk's Tale* (ll. 995–1001). Boozing, overeating and sexual indulgence, meanwhile, have at best an initial or merely superficial glamour amongst Chaucer's pilgrims (in the persons of the Miller, Summoner, Monk and Pardoner, for instance). At worst they are clear signs of depravity. Thus personal 'riot' in the forms of drinking, cheating and fighting promises to get short shrift in the unfinished tale of 'Perkyn Revelour' (Peter the Reveller) in *The Cook's Tale*. And this is precisely what happens to the boozers and ne'er-do-wells in *The Pardoner's Tale*. All three come to a sticky and very dead end that has absolutely no suggestion of carnivalesque celebration about it. Overall, then, Chaucerian comedy may occasionally be characterized as 'carnivalesque'. But there is still much disagreement about how far it was – and is – a laughing and/or a serious matter.

QUESTIONS AND SUGGESTIONS TO RELATE TO YOUR CHAUCER TEXT(S)

1. Would you describe the overall feel of the tale(s) you are studying as serious or humorous? If the former, are there still aspects that may be considered in some way playful (narrative perspective,

characterization or style, for instance)? If the latter, how far do you consider the humour to be ironic or satiric, comic or carnivalesque?

2. How far is the tale inviting you to laugh or smile *at* or *with* particular characters, attitudes and events? And how far are you prepared to go along with it?

3. How might you make the tale more humorous (if it is serious) or more serious (if it is humorous)? Consider systematic changes in such areas as: narrator, narrative strategy, plotting, characterization, action, speech and style. Go on to reflect upon what this activity shows about the relative seriousness and/or humour of the tale as you found it. Are such categories that stable after all?

FURTHER READING: Boitani and Mann 1986: pp. 124–42; Pearsall 1985: pp. 166–243; Kendrick 1988; Ellis 1996: pp. 40–8; Brewer 1998: pp. 276–92.

NARRATIVE AND RHETORIC, STRUCTURES AND STRATEGIES

KEY ISSUE

● How Chaucer structures his narratives and develops them through a range of rhetorical strategies and devices.

Chaucer is renowned for his skill in telling stories: pacy and action-packed, elegant and elaborate, or a blend of both. Significantly, the words 'tale' and 'prologue' are the two most prominent features in any listing of Chaucer's works: The Canterbury *Tales*, The General *Prologue*, The *Prologue* and *Tale* of the Wife of Bath (or Miller, or Merchant, or Friar ...), The *Prologue* to the Legend of Good Women, and so on. This fact alone confirms just how preoccupied Chaucer was not only with stories as such, but also with the whole business of introducing, framing and generally telling them. For prologues offer specific kinds of tale–teller relationship and help establish rapport with specific kinds of audience and readership, real and imagined. Moreover, it is axiomatic that most of Chaucer's works feature stories within stories: *The Canterbury Tales* is itself one big 'frame story' within which other stories are placed. So are the 'Dream Poems'. Indeed, there are also plenty of instances of stories within stories within stories. The tales of the murdered pilgrim and of Saint Kenelm within *The Nun's Priest's Tale* (ll. 3782–861, 3907–18), which itself is told within the frame of the Canterbury pilgrimage, are simply two of many that might be cited. In addition, some of Chaucer's pilgrims use stories as weapons and tell tales at one another's expense. This kind of 'quytynge' (getting one's own back) is fundamental to the relations between the Miller and Reeve, the Friar and Summoner and, perhaps, the Wife of Bath and Clerk. Before proceeding, however, we need to define some key terms.

Narrative can be understood in two ways: (1) as the activity of telling stories, sometimes called the process of **narration**; and (2) as what results, the story as told, the finished product. Both aspects need to be grasped for a full understanding of storytelling as both literary object (story) and communicative event (telling). In addition, it is necessary to identify the figure who tells the story, the **narrator**. The narrator may be a full-blown fictional character (e.g., Knight, Pardoner, Friar) or be a projection of the author her- or himself, hence 'Chaucer the narrator' in his role as pilgrim or dreamer (the latter is also called the authorial 'persona' or 'mask'; see Chapter 1). But stories are also told *to* people; they have audiences and readerships, whether real or imagined. We must therefore recognize and for each tale identify a range of receivers of the narrative. These receivers, sometimes called **narratees**, are basically of two kinds: (1) imaginary and dramatized within the narrative (e.g., the audience of pilgrims); (2) real and actual outside the narrative (e.g., Chaucer's contemporaries at court; us now).

Rhetoric is a term with negative and narrow connotations nowadays; hence the pejorative ring of the phrase 'merely rhetorical' or the notion of a 'rhetorical question' as being superfluous or calculating, a question to which the speaker already has the answer. However, in Chaucer's day – and indeed long before and long after – rhetoric was nothing less than the art of persuasive and effective public speaking. By extension it came to designate the art of composition in general, written as well as spoken. There were also highly systematized and widely disseminated rhetorical models of, as well as treatises on, the composition of everything from sermons and letters (the arts of preaching and formal correspondence) to the making and imitation of verse (the arts of poetry). In fact, along with Grammar and Logic, Rhetoric was one of the three fundamental subjects of the medieval school curriculum (the Trivium).

Readers of Chaucer are treated to the demonstration of rhetorical skills – and sometimes their studied display – at every turn. The main features to look out for, ranging from larger structural elements to localized verbal devices, are:

- *inductions* (prologues, proems, preambles), where the speaker or writer establishes a relationship and rapport with audience or readership, real or imaginary.
- *choice of appropriate style*, also variations upon it, where the basic style is tuned to the speaker, matter and occasion: 'high' style for sublime matters and noble speakers; 'middle' style for plainer, persuasive speaking, often about moral matters; 'low' style for a colloquial flavour and often a humorous appeal (shifts and switches between styles usually signal some change of perspective and evaluation).
- *exempla* (illustrative stories, 'ensaumples') added to the main story or situation and designed to point a moral or underscore an issue – often in an interlinked series and typically drawn from classical, biblical or popular sources.
- *sententiae* (learned maxims or colloquial proverbs) characterizing the speech of, respectively, the educated or uneducated – again often in a series and giving further authority to an opinion or argument.
- *top-to-toe descriptions of people*, whether abstractly generalized in terms of beauty, virtues and vices, notably in the court romances (e.g., Blanche in *The Book of the Duchess*, ll. 855–960); or physically particularized in terms of dress, features and behaviour, notably in the fabliaux (e.g., Alisoun in *The Miller's Tale*, ll. 3233–70 and many of the descriptions in *The General Prologue*).
- *set-piece descriptions of places* such as gardens, forests, rooms, temples and palaces (e.g., *The Parliament of Fowls*, ll. 183ff.); and *occasions* such as meals, tournaments, courtship, judgements (e.g., *The House of Fame*, ll. 1420–519; *The Knight's Tale*, ll. 2483ff.).
- *extended lists* of everything from trees and birds to suffering women and unfaithful lovers, again typically drawn from classical or biblical sources (e.g., *The Parliament of Fowls*, ll. 330–71; *The Franklin's Tale*, ll. 1364ff.).

- *encyclopedic displays of technical knowledge* – medical, astrological, alchemical, theological, and so on (e.g., *The General Prologue*, ll. 429–34; *The Canon's Yeoman's Tale*, throughout).
- *apostrophes* – prayers, invocations and complaints to God(s), Nature, muses, authorities – typically prefaced by 'O! ... O! ...' (e.g., *The Prioress's Prologue*).
- *similes or metaphors*, explicitly or implicitly talking of one thing in terms of another – and perhaps another and another (e.g., *Troilus and Criseyde*, I, ll. 215–25; *The Merchant's Tale*, ll. 1821–5).
- *repetition with variation*, saying the same thing in various ways, also called parallelism (e.g., *The Nun's Priest's Tale*, ll. 3187ff.).
- *negations and antitheses* – pairings, oppositions and series built round such formulae as 'No ... ne ... ne' (e.g., *The Book of the Duchess*, ll. 563ff.).
- *'occupatio'* – the 'not to mention that ...' formula – when mentioning is precisely what you proceed to do (e.g., *The Squire's Tale*, ll. 63–75).

As can be seen from the foregoing list, medieval rhetoric was chiefly concerned with the elaboration and extension of pre-existing material – what was called *amplificatio*. Its main aim was to reinforce and ornament rather than strip down and streamline. The latter process was called *abbreviatio* and tended to get much less emphasis in both the theory and practice of medieval rhetoric.

To be sure, Chaucer is adept at abbreviation and compression when his material and purpose demand. He can accelerate the action of a story or resist the seemingly ever-present temptation to multiply illustrations and morals. Hence the regular recurrence in his work of such formulae as 'Shortly I seye ...', 'Now wol I retourne ...', 'But now to oure matere ...', 'Passe we over until efte ...'. But even then such gestures are themselves time- and word-consuming, and may or may not be carried through in practice. One explanation of such overt attention to structure is subtle irony or downright satire at the expense of verbose preachers and clumsy storytellers. This certainly accounts for many of the over-wrought effects of the Wife of Bath, Pardoner, Nun's Priest and even Chaucer the pilgrim as the narrator of *Sir Thopas*. All these fictional narrators in various ways draw attention to their garrulous sermonizing, inept narration or rhetorical excess. All can therefore be enjoyed as well as explained as instances of parodic self-exposure. But the fact remains that for many modern readers, especially at a first reading, Chaucer has an infuriating tendency to 'pad out' rather than 'slim down'. And it is only on subsequent, better informed and more careful readings that we begin to perceive just how artful and even calculating he can be in the deployment of such apparently excessive and extraneous matter.

The challenges of such a capacious and, by and large, leisurely approach to narrative are well caught in *The Squire's Tale*. Some 400 lines into the tale the Squire is still anticipating the main point and plot complication ('the knotte') of his tale. This has been delayed, it seems, by much preliminary information on a magic horse, mirror, ring and sword – and we are still not sure why Canacee, the heroine of this particular Romance, is walking in a garden (ll. 401–8):

> The knotte why that every tale is toold,
> If it be taried til that lust be coold
> Of hem that han it after herkned yoore,
> The savour passeth ever lenger the moore,
> For fulsomenesse of his prolixitee;
> And by the same resoun, thynketh me,
> I sholde to the knotte condescende,
> And maken of hir walkynge soone an ende.

Interpretations of this passage, as of *The Squire's Tale* as a whole, vary widely. Is this simply a piece of inept storytelling, a Romance that meanders on till it runs out – unfinished because unfinishable? Or is it a finely gauged parody of the never-ending Romance genre itself – unfinishable and therefore left artfully unfinished? Put another way, is it a naive piece of overstuffed rhetorical self-indulgence, perhaps based on one of Chaucer's early and abandoned assays at the genre? Or is it rather a neat exposure of rhetorical self-consciousness and studied mannerism in an eager but inexperienced would-be poet, the young Squire himself? To be sure, *The Squire's Tale* is a particularly vexatious example. Its manner and matter both fascinate and frustrate. None the less, it does succeed in underscoring some fundamental questions about Chaucer's way with narrative and rhetoric. Is he serious or playful – simultaneously or by turns? Does he succeed or fail – and in whose terms? Is he ultimately more interested in *how* things are said (formed, structured, performed – the telling) rather than *what* is said (meant, understood, represented – the told)? Answers vary from tale to tale or from one group of tales to another. They may also vary over the course of the same tale. Some further distinctions and discriminations therefore need to be made.

One handy distinction (following Pamela Gradon, *Form and Style in Early English Literature*, 1971) is between narratives that are 'plotted' and those that are 'patterned'. *Plotted* narratives are those primarily dependent on fast-moving action, character motivation and a tightly knit sense of cause and effect. Instances would be the tales of the Miller, Reeve, Shipman and Pardoner. Such tales may not be wholly realistic in a modern sense, but they give a strong impression of being propelled by their own internal story dynamic. Things happen for clearly identifiable, substantially human reasons. *Patterned* narratives, on the other hand, tend to unfold according to a logic which is more obviously formal and shaped by aesthetic or moral considerations. Often the action seems to be determined by external, perhaps divine or diabolical, forces. Or it takes place in a dream or fairytale domain where things can happen suddenly for magical or mysterious reasons. As the name suggests, patterned narratives are characterized by bold patternings of event, with much emphasis on pairings and groupings, balances and contrasts, symmetries and hierarchies. Instances include the tales of the Knight, Franklin, Prioress, Clerk, Summoner, Man of Law and Second Nun; also all the dream poems.

But, of course, Chaucer's work is so richly various that it never fits neatly into a single category. *The Merchant's Tale*, for example, is from one point of view tightly 'plotted': action is clearly motivated in human terms and there is a palpable sense of cause and effect in the antics of husband, wife and lover. From another point of view, however, there is much that is overtly patterned. The initial debate between Placebo and Justinus over the pros and cons of marriage is formally and morally framed and dramatically static. So, in an under-worldly way, is the later wrangle between Pluto and Prosperpine – the upshot of which cuts across the human action. We are therefore aware in this tale of externally imposed pattern as well as internally generated plot. The same might be said of *Troilus and Criseyde*, where we become intensely involved in the dense texture of human emotions and the real consequences of people acting (or failing to act) in certain ways. The plot grips us. But we also never forget the overarching and, to some extent, pre-set pattern of events whereby the 'double sorwe' of these two lovers will be run out to its tragic and known conclusion. Troilus and Criseyde must, finally, act according to type and fit into the pattern. Some such qualifications, observing the 'plotted' as well as the 'patterned' dimensions of the narrative, would need to be made about most of Chaucer's tales. None the less, as a point of departure, the distinction proves serviceable.

Another handy distinction (following Tony Davenport's *Chaucer and his English Contemporaries*, 1998) is that between 'well-made' and 'wayward' narratives. Again, we may anticipate that any given Chaucer tale is likely to be judged more or less 'well-made' or more or less 'wayward', depending upon the part highlighted and how. That said, some such tendencies are certainly discernible and one or other is dominant at any one time. *Well-made narratives* are characterized by the following features, and in this order:

- fully established rapport with narrator (optional)
- early indication of main characters and setting
- purposeful development of plot and argument through combination of action, speech and description
- marked climax to story
- firm pointing of moral
- leave-taking and signing-off by narrator (optional)

The first and last features, to do with the narrator, are in a sense optional because they are dependent upon whether we focus on the teller or the tale. For the rest, the lineaments of well-made narrative are not difficult to pick out. Instances meeting all of these criteria include the tales of the Miller, Reeve, Franklin, Prioress, Pardoner, Clerk and Nun's Priest. The fact that many of these tales also incorporate other, large-scale features (including whole extra stories and extended bouts of moralizing) does not invalidate this observation. All the above 'well-made' elements are still in evidence and in that order. It's just that other materials intervene – sometimes very noticeably. One classic instance is the complaint about 'Friday' and the celebration of the rhetorician Geoffrey de Vinsauf which punctuate the climax of the cock and fox story in *The Nun's Priest's Tale* (ll. 4138–51). But similar things happen in all of Chaucer's 'well-made' narratives.

Wayward narratives, as the label suggests, are those which repeatedly wander away from the straight and narrow of the well-trodden story. They push out in different directions, and they manage in various ways to supplement, subvert or simply ignore the conventional proprieties of a story with clearly defined beginning, middle and end. Not surprisingly, there is much debate about how deliberate or accidental, radical or naive – ultimately how successful or otherwise – Chaucer's efforts in these areas are. Judgements basically depend upon two things. One is the reader's awareness of the full array of medieval textual practices, including modes of argumentation and illustration associated with genres such as sermon, confession, prayer and complaint – not only narrative as such. The other is the reader's experience and expectations of later narrative modes: realist, 'stream of consciousness', children's story, documentary, even soap opera, cartoons and feature films. Contemporary TV and film, advertising and pop are full of narratives – large and small, fully formed and artfully or artlessly fragmented. These, too, offer rich resources for comparison and contrast. They immediately influence what modern readers/viewers/audiences judge to be legitimately or illegitimately 'well-made' or 'wayward' – familiar or innovatory, exciting or confusing. All that said, a brief profile of 'wayward' narrative in Chaucer looks something like this:

- a highly or slightly developed narrator figure, who either dominates or detracts from the narrative
- an inordinately long preamble which may appear to bear uncertain relevance to the main body of the tale
- continuing uncertainty as to where the main body of the tale actually *is* and, indeed, whether it has one or many
- evident preoccupation with the mechanics of story telling and the display of rhetorical resources
- repeated bouts of moralizing and illustration ostensibly devoted to expanding and reinforcing – but also potentially diffusing and weakening – the main point(s)
- interrupted, open-ended or simply unfinished conclusion

Instances of 'wayward' narratives that are generally held to be successful, or at least suggestive, include: *The Wife of Bath's Prologue and Tale*, *The Pardoner's Prologue and Tale*, *The Merchant's Prologue and Tale* and, perhaps, *The Prioress's Prologue and Tale* (all with concerted attention to their prologues and preambles); also *The General Prologue* itself and all of the dream poems. *The Nun's Priest's Tale* is reckoned to combine a virtuoso display of rhetoric with a parody of dream lore, thereby expanding a simple animal fable up to, and even beyond, bursting point. Meanwhile, the tales of the Squire (as mentioned), Chaucer's own tale of *Sir Thopas*, and *The Physician's Tale* are all, for various reasons, found wanting in some aspect or other. Here again, however, the possibility of parodic intent is often invoked as a mitigating circumstance and even the underlying rationale. In any event, we must strongly resist any tendency to treat 'well-made' narratives as good and 'wayward' narratives as bad. The question still remains good or bad at what? And answers vary depending upon the particular models and methods of narrative (or argument, or sermon, or confession, etc.) judged to be in play; also upon how the differences and similarities between medieval and modern modes of text production are negotiated. Indeed, the tales of the Parson and Monk and Chaucer's own tale of *Melibee* are to most people now 'tales' in name only. They are sparely dramatized and barely disguised moral tracts: arguments more than actions. None the less, though rarely to the taste of modern readers, the distinctive structures and strategies of these, too, are well worthy of study.

Questions and suggestions to relate to your Chaucer text(s)

1. Try summarizing the text in two ways: (a) in a sentence of no more than 20 words; (b) in a paraphrase of 100 words. At each stage consider what you have kept in or left out. What, then, do you reckon to be central or marginal to the text? And does a distinction between, say, main narrative and rhetorical amplification help in gauging this?

2. How far would you describe the text as: (a) *plotted* or *patterned*; (b) *well-made* or *wayward*? (Allow for the possibility that it may be all of these in some measure at particular points.) Go on to consider other ways in which you might analyse the text's structures and strategies – through notions of genre or of monologue and dialogue, for instance, or combinations of description, action and speech.

3. How might you retell the text with one or more of the following in mind: (a) a different narrator (perhaps one of the other pilgrims, another dreamer, some version of yourself); (b) a change of genre or medium (romance as fabliau, for instance, or an updated version as TV soap opera or newspaper report); (c) a change of ending (opening up and closing down issues differently)? Go on to consider what light this activity throws on the organization and operation of the text as you found it.

FURTHER READING: Muscatine 1957; Bronson 1960; Gradon 1971; Miller 1977: pp. 39–92; Kolve 1984; Windeatt, in Boitani and Mann 1986: pp. 195–212; Pearsall 1985; Jordan 1987; Ashton 1998: pp. 7–42; Davenport 1998.

SPEAKERS AND AUDIENCES: MONOLOGUE, DIALOGUE AND DRAMATIC 'VOICE'

KEY ISSUE

● How Chaucer explores the shifting relations between speaker and audience (and by extension writer and reader) through manipulation of dramatic 'voice' and combinations of monologue and dialogue.

There are many kinds of speaker and audience in Chaucer, and at various levels of the text: Chaucer as pilgrim or dreamer; other pilgrims and dream figures; characters within the tales. All speak, listen and often respond to one another. In addition, in the foreground or background (depending how we 'place' him), we must imagine Chaucer himself actually reading his poems aloud at court and amongst friends. For that, it seems, is how most of them were initially 'published' (i.e. made public) – in live reading to an audience made up of a relatively small and familiar circle of peers and superiors. Thereafter, once these materials circulated in manuscript and eventually print, we may more properly speak of 'texts' and of the various speakers as kinds of *imagined* dramatic 'voice'. Of course, we now tend to approach Chaucer as a writer, through silent and probably solitary reading. None the less, we can gradually learn to '*hear*' Chaucer in imagination, and through him the speech of his various narrators and characters. In fact, once you grasp this spoken and performed aspect of his verse, many things fall into place as the products of a single and continuous yet flexibly modulated and finely tuned voice. You also become more aware of the musical harmonies and expressive rhythms of his verse *as verse*. In short, we must learn to read Chaucer with our ears as well as our eyes. This process is greatly eased, as well as enhanced, by listening to readings in one of the many available recordings (see bibliography).

The overall situation with respect to speakers and audiences (and by extension writers and readers) may be represented in the form of a list. This list is in two parts. The first part distinguishes the various 'voices' in play at different levels of the text. The second part distinguishes the various 'responses' amongst audiences or readers at different moments of production and reproduction.

- Voice of Chaucer as author actually reading out his work
- Voice of Chaucer as projected narrator (dreamer, pilgrim)
- Voices of other narrators (dream-figures, pilgrims)
- Voices of characters within tales
- Responses of Chaucer's contemporary audience
- Responses of later readers (editors, critics, commentators)
- Responses of ourselves as contemporary readers

Notice that you can read this list top downwards or bottom upwards. It all depends whether you want to start with Chaucer as the ultimate speaker/writer or yourself as the immediate audience/reader. You can also, of course, concentrate on any level of 'voice' or 'response' at any time. But whichever way we read it and whatever level we concentrate on, it is important that we 'listen' as well as 'speak' to Chaucer's work. There's therefore a kind of dialogue that opens up across time, space and cultures. This brings us to some further ways of framing interpretations.

Chaucer's works represent and explore many kinds of communication and interaction: speech and writing, conversation and books, drama and narrative. For analytical convenience, in order to make this multiplicity manageable, we may distinguish two main models of communication and interaction: the one-way process of **monologue**; and the two- or many-way process of **dialogue**. Both occur, simultaneously or by turns, throughout Chaucer's work, and together they offer a sure way of grasping the structures and strategies in play.

By **monologue** is meant speeches such as lectures, sermons and political presentations, where there is a single speaker and continuous delivery to a more or less silent audience. (The word *mono-logue* derives from Greek for 'single-speech' or 'speech-by-one'.) By extension, we may refer to any mode of communication as 'monologic' in so far as it is predominantly 'one-way': from writer to reader, or presenter to viewer, as well as from speaker to audience. Examples of extended monologues in Chaucer are the prologues of the Wife of Bath and the Pardoner; for there, even though these speakers are on occasion briefly interrupted (and to highly dramatic effect), they hold the floor and command attention almost all the time. In effect, the Wife and the Pardoner offer full-blown and partly parodic realizations of two of the dominant religious forms of medieval monologue: the *sermon* and the *confession*. Another, less dramatic and more straightforward instance of religious monologue is *The Parson's Tale*, which is, finally, perhaps more of a moral tract than a sermon.

The dominant, specifically secular forms of medieval monologue represented in Chaucer are of two kinds: the lover's or victim's 'complaint' or 'plainte' (from Latin *planctus*); and what may be called 'the noble pronouncement' or 'the judgement', often by royalty or some equally august allegorical figure such as Dame Nature or Philosophy. Extended examples of the 'plainte' can be found in *The Parliament of Fowls*, ll. 413–83; *The Knight's Tale*, ll. 1095–122, 1221ff; *The Franklin's Tale*, ll. 1352–458, and *Troilus and Criseyde*, IV, ll. 260–336. Extended examples of the noble pronouncement are *The Parliament of Fowls*, ll. 379ff.; *The Knight's Tale*, ll. 2450–78, 2987ff.; *The Prologue to the Legend of Good Women*, F-text, ll. 481ff., and those parts of *Boece* which feature the pronouncements of Dame Philosophy. A third kind of secular monologue may also be recognized, especially in the present educational context. This is the formal lesson or academic lecture, a classic instance of which is the instruction on the physics of sound-waves by the pedantic eagle in *The House of Fame*, II, ll. 725–874.

In all the above areas, then, we repeatedly meet kinds of monologue. An ostensibly single voice is continuously telling someone else (who is more or less silent and apparently acquiescent) something deemed to be important: sermonizing, praying, complaining, confessing, moralizing, instructing, informing. Chaucer and his contemporaries were thoroughly familiar with these modes of communication, both outside and inside literary texts, in fact and in fiction. Such genres recur in endlessly permutated forms in medieval writing at large. Medieval authors and their audiences evidently had a developed taste for such things. This is therefore a taste that we, too, as students of Chaucer must seek to develop and understand, even if we do not initially share or enjoy it.

What's more, on closer inspection, it turns out that Chaucer himself did not always enjoy or care to endure concerted monologues. He was not easily impressed or persuaded by, or prepared to put up with what he was simply *told*. One-way communication has its strengths and uses. But it also has its limitations and potential abuses. Chaucer evidently recognized this. In fact, he realized this problem dramatically. And that is where dialogue comes in.

Dialogue is in play every time the communication becomes two- or many-way (the term derives from Greek for 'across-speech'). Obvious kinds of spoken dialogue range from informal conversation to formal debate, and from passing exchanges to concerted interview or interrogation. Again, by extension, dialogue can refer to all sorts of exchanges and two- or many-way transactions: correspondence by letters or e-mail or even exchanges in print (in the letters or reviews sections of newspapers and journals, for instance). In this sense, the essay you write on a Chaucer text is part of a dialogue with that text; as is the comment on that essay you get back from a teacher or tutor. All are dialogues in that they involve communication which is more than one-way. There is a dynamic of 'to-and-fro', and maybe even 'give-and-take', which is fundamentally different from that in monologue. Another way of putting this is that whereas monologue involves the transmission and potential imposition of information, dialogue involves the transformation and potential negotiation of meaning. In monologue authority is asserted or at least assumed. In dialogue it is negotiated and maybe challenged.

Dialogues are everywhere in Chaucer. In fact, they often supply the overall framework within which monologues operate, or they act as the dramatic counterpoise which in some way shifts and reorients the monologue in question. *The Canterbury Tales* as a whole is of course framed as an interlocked, albeit incomplete, series of dialogues. The pilgrims tell one another stories and often these stories occasion reactions and responses – kinds of 'criticism', if you like. This occurs most obviously in the various prologues and epilogues linking the tales. But a kind of critical dialogue also breaks through (often to highly dramatic effect) whenever the pilgrims interrupt one another in the course of their tale-telling. A notable instance is when the Pardoner cuts across the Wife of Bath in her prologue to compliment her, probably sarcastically, on her preaching skills: 'Up stirte (jumped) the Pardoner ... "Ye been a noble prechour ..."' (ll. 163ff). Whereupon the indignant Wife promptly slaps him down for his drunken impertinence: '"Abyde!" quod she, "my tale is nat bigonne, / Nay, thou shalt drynken of another tonne / Er that I go [you'll drink from a very different barrel by the time I've finished]."'

Sometimes the antipathies between one pilgrim and another are expressed in still larger, structural ways. They tell tales at one another's expense. Then the narratives themselves become weapons in an exchange of blows: parts of a pointed dialogue that is clearly meant to distress the victim even as it delights and instructs the rest of the audience (including us). Examples of this tale-telling 'tit for tat', what Chaucer called 'quytinge' (requiting, pay back), are the paired tales told by the Miller and Reeve, and the Friar and Summoner. Each features a foolish or vicious version of the other: the Reeve a foolish Miller (and vice versa); the Friar a vicious Summoner (and vice versa).

But there are still other, less overt yet sustained ways in which some of the tellers and tales of *The Canterbury Tales* 'answer back' and are in dialogue with one another. *The Miller's Tale* clearly both mirrors the matter and inverts the manner of *The Knight's Tale*. The latter is a noble love-triangle after the manner of court romance; the former a low-life sex-triangle after the fashion of fabliau. Read as a pair, the effect is parodic. Moreover, many critics have followed Kittredge in his influential argument that Chaucer designed some of the tales to contribute distinctive voices and positions to a full-blown 'Marriage Discussion' (see Brewer 1978: vol. 2, pp. 305–28 and the section on 'Women and men ...' below). In fact, when studying any of the tales, it is important to keep at least one eye and ear trained on the overall dramatic framework of *The Canterbury Tales*: to attend to the prologues and other links (not treat them as optional extras), and sometimes to explore resonances and responses in other tales. For it is precisely these materials, along with the descriptions of the various pilgrims in *The General Prologue*, which invite us to grasp both tales and tellers dramatically, as voices and positions in a continuing – albeit incomplete and interrupted – series of dialogues. Conversely, to concentrate on each tale in isolation may reduce it to a single-voiced monologue: just one person's 'voice', a narrow point of view and a sole authority.

In fact, in nearly all his writings Chaucer exposes monologic, one-way, potentially authoritarian discourses to the stresses and strains, exchanges and changes of dialogue. His narrators, characters and authorities rarely stand alone, solemn and unchallenged. There is nearly always a plurality of voices and positions in play. In the 'Dream Poems', for instance, we meet a series of dream-narrators who converse with a variety of authority figures. At the same time, there is invariably another dramatic action unfolding within the dream, and this too has its distinctive voices and presences, debates and disputes – often counterpointing those introduced earlier. Thus no single voice is allowed, in any sense, to 'have the last word'. Indeed, almost everywhere in his work Chaucer ensures, that ostensibly 'imposing' monologues are either interrupted or in some way framed so as to transform our view of them. Often he reminds us that they are being used – and therefore potentially abused – by a specific speaker (character or narrator).

Chaucer's exploration of the use and potential abuse of 'authors and authorities' is treated at length in that section (see above). All that need be added here is that Chaucer often exposes – and sometimes explodes – authorities precisely through the 'dialogizing' of monologue. He realizes dramatically (and thereby encourages his audience or reader to realize critically) that what is ostensibly a single-voiced authority invariably turns out, on further investigation, to be many and various. Given such plurality and changeability, it is arguably not a single authority at all. Extended examples of this, the prologues of the Wife of Bath and the Pardoner, have already been mentioned. But even a single line can be fraught with contrary pressures, and the author can be caught in dialogue with himself. Towards the close of *Troilus and Criseyde*, for instance, at the point where Criseyde appears to have transferred her allegiances from Troilus to Diomede, the narrator feels obliged to add that 'Some say – I don't know – that she gave him her heart' ('Men seyn – I not – that she yaf hym hire herte', V, l. 1050). In context that little inserted phrase 'I don't know' (*I not*) speaks volumes. Chaucer as narrator appears to be making one last, perplexed and distressed attempt to distance himself from the near-total calumny traditionally visited upon Criseyde. This is the trace of a narrator divided against himself. An interesting variation on this strategy occurs in *The Clerk's Tale*, ll. 455–61, when the Clerk in effect interrupts his own tale to make indignant comments on the cruelty of Marquis Walter.

All the above are instances of what the critic Mikhail Bakhtin would call, in a special sense, 'dialogic speech'. He defined this as 'another's words in one's own language' (Bakhtin, *The Dialogic Imagination*, 1981: pp. 303ff.). This basically means that whenever we *adopt* someone else's words we thereby *adapt* them for our own purposes. The result is that in language there is always what Bakhtin terms a 'double-voiced discourse': the resonance of its earlier use chiming or jarring with the note it is made to sound at the time. Put another way, every time a text is *cited* (quoted, referred or alluded to) it is in effect *sited* and *sighted* differently. Indeed, it is precisely the artful manipulation and deployment of such resources that distinguishes literature from more routine language use. Hence the possibility for calculatingly complex and ambiguous effects of 'irony, satire and comedy' (see that section above).

But there are apparent exceptions, even in Chaucer. For instance, it is arguable that in *The Parson's Tale* it is precisely the *absence* of a consistently dramatized speaker and the studied *im*personality of the address which ensure the texts's acceptability as orthodox dogma. It succeeds in being a monologue – but only at the expense of any dialogic dynamic. It may offer itself as truly authoritative – but to many modern readers it comes across as dully authoritarian. This is also the usual judgement nowadays on Chaucer's 'Retraction' at the ostensible close of *The Canterbury Tales*, and the general view of the unequivocal moral at the end of *Troilus and Criseyde* (V, ll. 1835ff.). And yet, even then, though these texts or parts of texts may be designed and offered as monologues, it is still up to particular readers to accept or reject them as such, or at least to negotiate their position in relation to them. In other words – and there is always the possibility of 'another's words in one's own language' – the critical dialogue continues.

QUESTIONS AND SUGGESTIONS TO RELATE TO YOUR CHAUCER TEXT(S)

1. Consider all the ways in which the text, as a whole or in parts, may be conceived as a *monologue* (one-way act of communication) or a *dialogue* (two- or many-way act of communication). What is the critical effect of viewing it as both, simultaneously or by turns?

2. Using the list at the beginning of this section, identify the various kinds of '*voice*' (author, narrator, pilgrim/dreamer, character) in play in and around the text(s) you are studying. Go on to consider – and if possible find out more about – the various kinds of *response* amongst past and present audiences and readers (using Brewer, 1978 and Andrew 1991, for example).

3. Drawing on the notes in your edition, identify a passage where a narrator or character is using 'another's words in his own language'. What light does the use of that passage in the immediate context throw on the *dialogic* processes of adoption

and adaptation, citing and (re)siting? Go on to consider how you might adapt the same words so as to be said by someone else (another character or narrator, yourself, perhaps).

FURTHER READING: Burrow 1982: pp. 24–55; Rowland 1979: pp. 95–116; Rigby 1996: pp. 18–77; Ellis 1998: pp. 33–9; Ashton 1998: pp. 43–83; Davenport 1998: pp. 58–91; Brewer 1978; Bronson 1960; Donaldson 1970.

WOMEN AND MEN: SEX, LOVE AND MARRIAGE

KEY ISSUE

- How Chaucer represents the roles and relationships of women and men, inside and outside marriage, and how far he confirms or challenges current stereotypes.

Chaucer's writing has an abiding concern with women and men and the relations between them. This is a central and explicit – not marginal and incidental – aspect of his work. In fact, Chaucer constantly rehearses and intervenes in debates on sex, love and marriage that were very much alive in his own day. These include, but also exceed, what has been called 'the marriage discussion': the specific argument about who should wield 'soveraynetee' (sovereignty) and 'maistrye' (mastery) within marriage – the wife or the husband. This particular topic is treated later. However, it is important to first place it in a broader cultural and literary context. *The Prologue to the Legend of Good Women*, for instance, was part of an extended apology to ladies at court for offence apparently given by the author's representation of Criseyde. And yet, a century later the Scottish poet and translator Gavin Douglas could hail Chaucer as 'evir ... all womanis frend'. From the outset, then, there has been recognition that Chaucer openly and contentiously engaged with what by the late nineteenth century would be called 'the woman question' and what latterly, under the pressure of various feminist and gay movements, has been reformulated in terms of 'sexual politics' and 'gender identity'.

But whatever terms are invoked, we still cannot be sure which 'side' Chaucer took, or indeed whether 'taking sides' was – and is – altogether to the point. To be sure, Chaucer was a relatively privileged male in a predominantly male-controlled (patriarchal) society. The temptation to ask the crudely anachronistic question 'Was Chaucer a feminist?' is therefore strong. But before we can even think about addressing it we need to sort out some key terms. We also need to keep an eye on the differences as well as the continuities between the various times, contexts and cultures involved – his and ours, then and now. In the end, as you will see, this may well mean that we have to redefine and replace leading (and potentially misleading) questions about Chaucer's claimed 'feminism' or alleged 'anti-feminism'. Hence the alternative framing of the 'Questions and suggestions' at the close of this section. First, however, a crucial theoretical distinction needs to be made between 'sex' and 'gender', even though it oftens gets confused in practice:

Sex is biologically determined. It refers to the physiological make-up and instinctual drives of women and men. Sex is based upon differences in chromosomes, hormones, genitals and reproductive capacities. Sexually, we are all born either female or male. In Chaucer's day, with no contraception, sexual activity often had immediate and palpable consequences. Women's bodies were most obviously tied into the processes of procreation: being pregnant and having babies. For long periods they tended to function chiefly as mothers. Rape, inside and outside marriage, seems to have been comparatively common.

Gender is culturally constructed. It refers to the social conventions and norms whereby women and men are expected to dress, speak and behave; also to the social roles that women and men typically fill. In gender terms we all learn to be certain versions of 'masculine' or 'feminine'. In Chaucer's day, men could be knights, university students, priests, bishops and Popes – but women could not. Only widows could normally look to some degree of financial and legal independence. Wives were officially expected to be obedient, quiet and patient – husbands were not. Biblically, women were reckoned to derive from Adam's rib. Scientifically, they were reckoned to derive from weaker sperm.

The underlying issue then, is how far the women and men you encounter in Chaucer, whether as narrators or characters, are represented in terms of: (a) sexual activity (especially sexual desire, intercourse and childbearing); and (b) specifically gendered roles and modes of behaviour (especially dress, occupation, family position, speech/lessness, and in/action). The Wife of Bath may serve as an extended example. She is described in *The General Prologue* (ll. 445–75) as having 'hipes large' and being 'gat-tothed' (gap-teethed). The former denote her ample sexuality (though interestingly there is nowhere any mention of her having children); while the latter, according to medieval physiognomists, identified her as having a lecherous nature. She also has a 'boold ... reed' face and, in terms of medieval humours physiology, is evidently sanguine by nature. As for her dress, she wears fine-textured yet weighty cloth headgear topped by a hat as broad as a shield (advertising her cloth-maker's profession and emphasizing her martial side); on her feet are scarlet stockings (one of the original 'scarlet' women, perhaps?) and supple yet tightly laced leather shoes. Her manner of riding a horse – not side-saddle but astride it, and sporting spurs – is decidedly masculine.

Meanwhile, in her individual prologue, the Wife's sexual being carries a similar freight of complex gender traits, compounding the conventionally masculine and feminine. By her own account (ll. 609–13) she is a blend of Venus and Mars (love and war, sex and violence) and, astrologically speaking, was born with Mars in the ascending sign of Taurus (the Bull). Her prologue also amply demonstrates that she relishes speaking at length and without interruption. Her speech may therefore be variously characterized as nagging, garrulous, aggressive, assertive or assured – depending how you see it. Finally, it is palpably obvious from the Wife's vigorous fight with her fifth husband, culminating in her feigned, farcically knockabout 'death', that she is well able to wield her fists as well as her wits (esp. ll. 788ff.). The skilful combination of both means that she ultimately gains control not only of his property, but also 'of his tonge, and of his hond also'. Thus, in addition to persuading her clerical husband to burn his 'book of wikked wyves' himself, the Wife decisively takes over the 'maistrie, al the soveraynetee' (l. 818) in the marriage. She dominates her husband in every way: physically, financially and legally. She thereby literally as well as metaphorically ensures that the reins of their relationship are placed firmly in her hands ('He yaf me al the bridel in myn hond', l. 813).

In all these ways, we see how a figure that is sexually female can be constructed so as to express a wide and complex range of gender traits. The Wife of Bath is thus 'masculine' and/or 'feminine', simultaneously or by turns. She represents a distinctive blend of conventional yet potentially contradictory materials. Such a rich mix is the source both of her power to convince as a person and her contentious significance as an ideological construct. We may like her or loathe her, and reckon her convincing or contrived. But we are still bound to be exercised by how far we see her as 'man-made' (a puppet of patriarchy, if you like) or a genuinely formidable woman in her own right. The immediate judge of all this must, of course, be the reader her- or himself. Similar challenges meet us at every turn with Chaucer's women and men. We must therefore strive to recognize the shifting constructions of femininity and masculinity that Chaucer offers in his own time and terms, even as we renegotiate their significance for ourselves now.

One of the best ways of grasping the cultural conventions that inform the images of women and men in Chaucer is to approach them through the literary genres to which they belong:

- Women in the fabliaux (notably *The Miller's Tale*, *The Reeve's Tale* and *The Shipman's Tale*) are presented chiefly in terms of dress and outward appearance, and as objects of physical male desire. They are also represented as having a lusty female desire of their own. Characteristically, the men are introduced in terms of occupation (carpenter, miller, merchant, student, friar) whereas the women are introduced in terms of family role, as wives or daughters.

- Women in the court romances (notably Emelye in *The Knight's Tale* and Dorigen in *The Franklin's Tale*) are presented chiefly in terms of idealized virtues and beauty, and as inspirational idols which the male lover worships. They are relatively passive 'ladies' and have little individual agency; though it should be added that Criseyde in *Troilus and Criseyde* is very highly developed in terms of inner psychology (albeit, finally, to no avail), and May in *The Merchant's Tale* (though not interiorized at all, and virtually a Fabliau figure) is as quick with her words as her wits. The men, meanwhile, tend to fall into the categories of older knight or younger squire – the former dedicated more to chivalry and the latter to courtship. We can therefore trace figures such as Palamon, Arcite, Theseus, Arveragus and Troilus in so far as they are conquering heroes or lovelorn victims. Ideally, being the former underwrites their claim to be the latter. Hence the curiously 'split' (active/passive, aggressive/submissive) feel of many of these 'noble' men.

- Women in the genre of saint's or holy life are also curiously 'split' in terms of their qualities and capacities. In certain respects they are pious, patient and deeply submissive. In other respects they demonstrate remarkable strength and fortitude in the face of the harshest adversities — physical, emotional and spiritual. We shall consider this genre at length, for it includes several tales little studied and not treated elsewhere in the present book.

St Cecilia in *The Second Nun's Tale* and Griselda in *The Clerk's Tale* are the classic instances here. St Cecilia, for example, gently yet firmly draws her husband and his friend to be baptized as Christians. And though she is finally burned and hacked to death for refusing to sacrifice to pagan gods, she still miraculously manages to endure martyrdom for three days, preaching all the while. The situation of Griselda is similarly vexed and complex. A persistent problem in *The Clerk's Tale* is trying to focus Griselda as an icon of Job-like patience and compassion in the image of Mary Mother of God, while also accepting that Marquis Walter, the husband who tests or persecutes her, is on one level a Christian aristocrat and, on another level, a type of God the Father. Moreover, it is clear that Chaucer's male narrator, the Clerk, could not handle such stresses and strains easily either; hence his indignant outbursts (ll. 455–62, 621–3). Hence, too, the nagging aggravation of many a modern reader.

Other, perhaps simpler yet still challenging variants on the female holy life can be found in Chaucer. In *The Physician's Tale* the aptly named daughter Virginia is lusted after and threatened with legalized rape by a vicious judge. She is finally 'saved' by her father's decision to cut her head off and thus forestall the shame of defilement. Interestingly, the scene in which she freely consents to this and thereby complies with her father's demand for death before dishonour is 'pathetic' and 'pitiful' in both ancient and modern senses. The sheer pathos and pity of a distressed father reluctantly slaying his distressed daughter for honourable reasons are played to the utmost, both emotionally and ethically (see esp. ll. 205–53). Not surprisingly, most modern readers find the whole thing pathetic and pitiful in quite other, contemporary senses: 'How could he do that!' 'She's pathetic to agree!!' 'They're pitiful!!!'. One reason this happens is because *The Physician's Tale* has no developed narratorial voice like that of the dissenting Clerk in *The Clerk's Tale*. The Physician is a merely token presence as narrator (e.g., l. 117). There is therefore no-one to cast doubt on the wisdom of what is being represented or to gesture towards potentially resistant responses amongst Chaucer and his audience.

Similar but converse challenges arise in reading the holy life of 'Dame Custance' (Constance) in *The Man of Law's Tale*. This, too, has a narrator who does not obviously add anything to our view of the tale. And here, too, the heroine is aptly and symbolically named: she is a model of constancy in adversity – what we might now call a 'survivor'. The difference in this case is that we end with a family reunion (as in *The Clerk's Tale*) rather than with a martyrdom (as in *The Second Nun's Tale*). And yet, like the latter, the tale is still basically a pious kind of female romance; for women only tend to have adventures of their own in medieval stories when protected by their faith and, by heavy implication, the hand of God. Significantly, however, this is often a distinctly feminized helping hand. Divine aid is commonly invoked through the person of Mary, whether in her role as Blessed Virgin, Mother of God or both (hence the lengthy invocations to Mary in the prologues of *The Second Nun's Tale* and, a child-martyr miracle specifically attributed to Mary, *The Prioress's Tale*). Certainly, Constance's miraculous adventures in *The Man of Law's Tale* come thick and fast. The Christianized daughter of a Roman emperor, she is shipped and married to a sultan who embraces Christianity for her sake, but is murdered by his mother as a result. But Constance and their son escape to ancient Britain, where she again converts others to Christianity and marries a king. Eventually, following further adventures, she arrives back in Rome and is reunited with her father the emperor.

Interestingly, in all the above tales there is much about parents and children (especially mothers and children), as well as wives and husbands, lovers and rapists. There is also a common concern with oppositions between Christians and pagans, often couched in terms of various kinds and blends of sex and violence – threatened and enacted, legitimate and illegitimate. Each of these tales therefore deserves further study in its own right: not simply for its conformity to some holy life type, but also for its contribution to continuing debates on a range of pressingly actual, as well as exotically fantastical, constructions of families, faith and foreigners.

● The moral tract is the final genre to be featured. Especially relevant instances in Chaucer are *The Tale of Melibee*, *The Parson's*

Tale and *Boece*, his translation of Boethius. Again, these are rarely 'set' and studied nowadays, presumably precisely because they are so high on moralizing and relatively low in dramatic and narrative interest. They are largely in prose, too. None the less, both individually and together, these moral tracts throw a remarkably revealing – because commonly unremarked – light on yet other dimensions of the problems at issue: representations of women and men, their relations with one another, and the relations of both of them to such august abstractions as God, Justice, Mercy and Philosophy.

The Tale of Melibee deserves particular attention because it is one of the two tales Chaucer assigned to himself in his role as pilgrim-narrator (the other is *Sir Thopas*). It also celebrates a vision of marriage rooted in the growth of mutual trust between husband and wife. There is a particularly powerful realization of woman as counsellor and peacemaker, as well as companion and helpmeet. The story as such is very simple. The house of a rich young man called Melibee is broken into by his enemies while he is away, and his wife and daughter are badly beaten. On his return he vows violent revenge, but his wife, the aptly named Prudence, urges him against this. Instead of taking the law into his own hands, she counsels him to follow all due legal process and, meanwhile, to stay as calm and composed as possible. Most of the tale is devoted to a finely argued and copiously illustrated dialogue in which Melibee gradually learns to curb his naturally impulsive temper through the firm yet calming influence of his wife. By the end Prudence has even prevailed upon her partner to show mercy to the criminals who had beaten her and their daughter.

The Parson's Tale also promotes the view that 'womman sholde be felawe unto man', that 'Man sholde bere hym to his wyf in feith, in trouthe, and in love' and that, following St Paul, a man 'sholde loven his wyf as Crist loved hooly chirche' (*Riverside* edition, ll. 927–8). To be sure, this is in the context of an ultimately patriarchal view of marriage which also insists that 'a womman sholde be subget [subject] to hire housbonde' (l. 930). It therefore assumes, in the words of the then-current and remarkably persistent marriage service, that the wife should 'love, honour, cherish and *obey*' her husband; whereas he should simply 'love, honour and cherish' her – without the 'obedience'. That said, there is still much in *The Parson's Tale* which supports a sophisticated sense of common obligations and, to some extent, reciprocal relations amongst men and women in the eyes of God.

Chaucer's *Boece*, too, while in some ways simply an expanded translation of Boethius's *Consolation of Philosophy*, also attests to the translator's sustained engagement with and commitment to one of the most influential woman–man dialogues in medieval writing. For it should be observed that the ethical charge, as well as the dramatic structure, of this work derives precisely from the fact that it is a dialogue between an older, wiser and remarkably convincing woman ('Dame Philosophy') and a younger, confused man who has initially lost and must be eventually led back to a sense of conviction (i.e. the author in his roles as dreamer, prisoner and lapsed philosopher). Here, then, is another instance, like that of Prudence in *Melibee*, of woman as confidante, counsellor and mainstay of sanity and hope. And in this case she is at once more profoundly pragmatic and sublimely wise than any of the men she has dealings with.

What follow are some further materials to help frame discussion of women and men in your Chaucer text(s). These consist of two parallel lists. The first represents the *dominant* (stereotypical, orthodox, officially promoted) views of women and men current and widely circulated in Chaucer's time. The second represents the corresponding *muted* (atypical, obscured, officially discouraged – perhaps minority) views of women and men which were also current, but less widely acknowledged. Many of these oppositions, both dominant and muted, persist to the present day in one form or another.

Dominant (stereotypical) views of women and men

'FEMININE'	'MASCULINE'
inferior	superior
passive	active
emotional	rational
beautiful/ugly	strong/weak
body	intellect
domestic	public
family and child-centred	occupation and job-centred
mercy	justice
practical experience	book learning

Muted (minority) views of women and men

'FEMININE'	'MASCULINE'
equal before God	equal before God
sensitive	impulsive
nurturing	controlling
peace-maker	war-maker
counsellor	tyrant
communicator	dictator
mystical	theological
wise	knowledgeable
learned in life	learned in books

'Chaucer's discussion of marriage' has been a common critical topic ever since George Kittredge's highly influential article of that name was first published in 1912 (see Brewer 1978: vol. 2, pp. 305–28). In its own terms Kittredge's argument is neat, subtle and persuasive. It also affords a useful point of departure – if not of arrival – when considering the various views of marriage offered by Chaucer in certain key tales. The argument can be summarized as follows. The Wife of Bath presents a view of marriage in which women are in charge (have 'maistrye' and 'soverayntee'). At the same time, she attacks male clerics for perpetuating extreme views of women as either sinners or saints (esp. ll. 688–710). This prompts a rejoinder from the Clerk, who tells a tale about patient Griselda and the trials and tribulations she is subjected to by her husband Walter; though the Clerk insists that it be read not literally but as an allegory of humanity's obedient relation to God. The Merchant, meanwhile, responds with a distinctly cynical vision of marriage. This is based on his own two months of matrimonial misery to date and embodied in a tale of compromised complicity between a lecherous husband, a sly wife and a handy lover. The final 'act' of 'the Marriage Group of Tales' and its 'satisfactory conclusion' and 'solution', according to Kittredge, are all afforded by *The Franklin's Tale*. For there, he insists, we are presented with a relationship between husband and wife, the knight Arveragus and the lady Dorigen, which is based upon love within (not outside) marriage, and a kind of shared 'soverayntee' or mutual 'maistrye'.

There are a number of problems with Kittredge's argument, however, both in general and in detail. One is that the tales in the so-called 'Marriage Group' are, in fact, spread over three distinct fragments in the manuscripts and are interrupted by at least three other tales (those of the Friar, Summoner and Squire). They are therefore much less intimately interconnected than Kittredge suggests. Another problem is that much of Chaucer's other work is also concerned with explorations of love and power, within and outside marriage (among *The Canterbury Tales* those of the Knight, Miller, Shipman, Nun's Priest and *Melibee*, for instance; also *The Parliament of Fowls* and *Troilus and Criseyde*). In fact, almost half of Chaucer's work could lay claim to belong to an extended 'Marriage *and Relationship* Group'. But there is a particular danger in proposing *The Franklin's Tale* as an ideal 'solution'. For the fact is that the resolution of the plot and the 'solution' of the problem depend upon the decision of the knight alone and a kind of gentleman's agreement among the three men, each of whom tries to compete with the other in terms of 'gentillesse' and nobility. Where this leaves the wife's own powers of decision-making and the much-vaunted sharing of 'soveraynetee' by husband and wife is one of the main issues explored in the section devoted to this tale in Chapter 4 (pp. 114–20).

More recently, there has been increasing critical attention to models of sexuality other than those drawn on strictly heterosexual lines. There has also been an attempt to push the terms of the debate beyond those of raw sex, romantic love and pragmatic marriage. The final observations are made with this developing agenda in mind. The Pardoner in *The General Prologue* (ll. 669–91), for instance, has long been recognized as in some way 'sexually deviant': either as a eunuch (because he has a high voice, is hairless, and is referred to as a 'geldyng or a mare'); or as a homosexual (because of the foregoing coupled with his special relationship as 'freend and compeer' to the Summoner). Both these aspects of sexuality were readily confused in the popular medieval imagination, as they continue to be in modern views of homosexuals as deficient males, 'without balls'. In fact, it is precisely this aspect of the Pardoner's physiology that is so coarsely and cuttingly stigmatized by the indignant Host at the close of *The Pardoner's Tale* (ll. 948–55). The Host begins by complaining that the Pardoner is such a rogue that the latter would have him kiss his old stained underwear and try to pass it off as holy relics; and he ends by offering to carry the Pardoner's balls enshrined in a pig's turd! Such a crude mocking and, indeed, demonizing of the Pardoner's sexual nature is a strong reminder of just how strenuously, even stridently, the image of 'normal' heterosexual roles was maintained in the late Middle Ages. Legally, known male homosexuals could be maimed, branded or even burnt to death. Officially, female homosexuality did not exist at all.

The hairdresser, choirmaster and clerk Absolon in *The Miller's Tale* is another representation of complex and vexed sexuality. Though he is ostentatiously heterosexual in his courting of the carpenter's wife, Alisoun, he balks at kissing her 'naked ers' and revenges himself by ramming the rod of a red-hot ploughshare up Nicholas's (ll. 3730ff., 3798ff.). Absolon has already been carefully established in terms of fastidious dress-sense, high-fashion-consciousness, lavish attention to his artificially curled golden hair and the fact that he has a distinct squeamishness about farting ('he was somdeel squaymous / Of fartyng'; ll. 3312–38) It seems clear, therefore, that he is being set up as a kind of effeminate dandy or, at the least, in a state of sexual confusion. Put more positively, Absolon is a richly enigmatic, teasingly complex figure. Playfully ridiculed but certainly not demonized, he stands as one of the more sexually complicated of Chaucer's figures. For he too, like the Wife of Bath, is finally compounded of potentially contradictory gender traits. 'Squaymous of fartyng' he may be – but he's a dab hand with a red-hot iron!

Other complexities within, and complications between, the main 'masculine' and 'feminine' stereotypes can be grouped under three heads: virginity, rape and widowhood. For Chaucer and his contemporaries, a recurrent concern with virginity (of females) often goes hand in hand with rape (by males). The one is threatened; the other threatens. The one is to be kept; the other takes. There is no space here to detail the complex theological and legal arguments surrounding virginity, especially its crucial importance to a patrilineal inheritance system bound up with the assigning of male heirs (and therefore with proof of paternity). Nor is there room to explore the legal complexities of a system in which 'raptus' could cover not only sexual assault, but also semi-legalized abduction and kidnapping, chiefly for reasons of preventing or ensuring marriages (Chaucer himself was accused and, it seems, acquitted of a case of the latter).

What can be signalled here, however, is the fact that both virginity/ maidenhead and rape/violation figure prominently, and to some extent problematically, in several Chaucer tales. In *The Physician's Tale* the would-be rapist is a judge who abuses his office. However, the threatened maid, Virginia, can only avoid legalized rape by submitting to death before dishonour at the hands of her father, Virginius. The criminal may finally be punished, but the victim dies.

In *The Wife of Bath's Tale* (following a prologue in which virginity has been an explicit bone of contention) a knight rapes a maid and is required by a court of women to find out 'what thing it is that wommen most desiren' or be condemned to death. The answer is supplied by an old hag who eventually turns into a beautiful young and faithful wife and they both live happily ever after. The issue here is whether we see all this as punishment, reward or, in modern terms, 'counselling' for the rapist; also whether we call attention to the otherwise forgotten victim of the original rape. In *The Second Nun's Tale* St Cecilia miraculously manages to be both married and remain a virgin (recalling Mary as both Mother of God and Blessed Virgin). Meanwhile, *The Legend of Good Women* features several virtuous women who, again, only keep their virginity or honour at the cost of death.

Widows are yet another significant category of woman in medieval life and literature. In that they had been married they were no longer virgins; but they could decide to stay single or remarry. Widows were therefore relatively independent economically and potentially desirable prizes for men. The Wife of Bath and Criseyde are Chaucer's two most famous and fascinating widows. The former calculatingly exploits successive marriages and widowhoods as a means to wealth and power: only after marrying three rich old husbands does she opt for younger men more to her taste. Criseyde, however, ponders long and hard about whether she should give up her celibate widowhood and independence by getting involved with Troilus (esp. II, ll. 750–6). Poor but resilient widows figure in *The Nun's Priest's Tale* (ll. 3618–43) and *The Friar's Tale* (ll. 1581ff.).

QUESTIONS AND SUGGESTIONS TO RELATE TO YOUR CHAUCER TEXT(S)

1. How stereotypical do you find Chaucer's representations of women and men with respect to: (a) Feminine and Masculine roles (see above); and (b) genre expectations (kinds and combinations of Court Romance, Fabliau, Holy Life, etc.)?

2. How significant for your understanding of the text is the gender of each of the following: (a) the fictional narrator (whether pilgrim or dreamer); (b) the main character(s); (c) Geoffrey Chaucer as author; (d) yourself as reader? Go on to consider ways in which you might rewrite the text so as to explore other

FURTHER READING

EDITIONS

Geoffrey Chaucer: Canterbury Tales, ed. A. C. Cawley, 2nd edn Malcolm Andrew (London, 1996). Handy size with helpful glosses.
The Riverside Chaucer, ed. Larry Benson et al., 3rd edn (Oxford, 1988). Comprehensive standard edition with full apparatus.
Chaucer's Dream Poetry, ed. Helen Phillips and Nick Havely (London, 1997).
Troilus and Criseyde, ed. Barry Windeatt (London, 1984).

Other useful editions of individual texts are published by Cambridge University Press and Manchester University Press; also notice *The Tales of the Clerk and the Wife of Bath* ed. Marion Wynne-Davies (London, 1992).

TRANSLATIONS

These should be used as supports rather than substitutes. Chaucer in the original is always better.

Chaucer: The Canterbury Tales, trans. Nevill Coghill, Harmondsworth, 1951. A resourceful and charming but increasingly old-fashioned-sounding verse translation.
Chaucer: The Canterbury Tales, trans. David Wright, Oxford, 1964. A prose rendering in good modern English.
Geoffrey Chaucer: Love Visions, trans. Brian Stone, Harmondsworth, 1983. Verse translations of the 'Dream Poems'.

RECORDINGS AND OTHER RESOURCES

Chaucer's narrative verse was made for oral delivery. It is often more immediately enjoyable as well as more readily comprehensible when heard. Listening to some of the recordings produced by Caedmon/ Argo and Cambridge University Press is strongly recommended; also the 'Chaucer Studio Recordings', available from the Departments of English at Brigham Young University, Utah, USA, and University of Adelaide, South Australia. There is a CD-ROM and Video package on *The Canterbury Tales* – including searchable text, dramatized extracts and critical and visual support materials – produced by Cromwell Creative Educational Resources, Stratford-Upon-Avon, UK.

GENERAL STUDIES OF RECURRENT USEFULNESS

All these books cover a wide range of Chaucer texts and topics and are worth turning to time and again. Some of them, as their titles suggest, are devoted to particular approaches or bodies of text. Most offer further guidance on reading. Remember to consult the index as well as the contents to find what you need.

Aers, David, *Chaucer* (Brighton, 1986).

Allen, Valerie, and Axiotis, Ares (eds), *Chaucer: Contemporary Critical Essays*, New Casebooks (London, 1997).

Andrew, Malcolm (ed.), *Critical Essays on Chaucer's Canterbury Tales* (Buckingham, 1991).

Ashton, Gail, *Chaucer: The Canterbury Tales* (London, 1998).

Benson, C. David (ed.), *Critical Essays on Chaucer's 'Troilus and Criseyde'* (Buckingham, 1991).

Boitani, Piero, and Mann, Jill (eds), *The Cambridge Chaucer Companion* (Cambridge, 1986).

Brewer, Derek, *A New Introduction to Chaucer*, 2nd edn (London, 1998).

Bronson, Bertrand, *In Search of Chaucer* (Toronto, 1960).

Brown, Peter, *Chaucer at Work: The Making of the Canterbury Tales* (London, 1994).

Cooper, Helen, *Oxford Guides to Chaucer: The Canterbury Tales*, 2nd edn (Oxford, 1999).

Davenport, Tony, *Chaucer and his English Contemporaries: Prologue and Tale in the Canterbury Tales* (London, 1998).

Donaldson, E. Talbot, *Speaking of Chaucer* (London and New York, 1970).

Ellis, Steve, *Geoffrey Chaucer* (Plymouth, 1996).

Ellis, Steve (ed.), *Chaucer: The Canterbury Tales* (London, 1998).

Minnis, Alastair et al. *Oxford Guides to Chaucer: The Shorter Poems* (Oxford, 1995) – on the 'Dream Poems' and lyrics.

Pearsall, Derek, *The Canterbury Tales* (London, 1985).

Phillips, Helen, *An Introduction to 'The Canterbury Tales'* (London, 2000).

Rigby, S. H., *Chaucer in Context* (Manchester, 1996).

Rowland, Beryl (ed.), *Companion to Chaucer Studies*, 2nd edn (Oxford, 1979).

Windeatt, Barry, *Oxford Guides to Chaucer: Troilus and Criseyde* (Oxford, 1992).

MORE SPECIALIST STUDIES OF RECURRENT USEFULNESS

Beidler, P. (ed.), *Masculinities in Chaucer* (Cambridge, 1998).

Dinshaw, Carolyn, *Chaucer's Sexual Politics* (Madison, Wis., 1989).

Hansen, Elaine Tuttle, *Chaucer and the Fictions of Gender* (Berkeley, Calif., 1992).

Jordan, Robert, *Chaucer's Poetics and the Modern Reader* (Berkeley, Calif., 1987).

Kendrick, Laura, *Chaucerian Play: Comedy and Control in the Canterbury Tales* (Berkeley, Calif., 1988).

Kolve, V. A., *Chaucer and the Imagery of Narrative* (California, 1984).

Laskaya, Anne, *Chaucer's Approach to Gender in 'The Canterbury Tales'* (Cambridge, 1995).

Lester, H. Marshall, Jr, *The Disenchanted Self: Representing the Subject in 'The Canterbury Tales'* (Berkeley, Calif., 1990).

Mann, Jill, *Geoffrey Chaucer*, Feminist Readings Series (Brighton, 1991).

Martin, Priscilla, *Chaucer's Women: Nuns, Wives and Amazons* (London, 1990).

Patterson, Lee, *Chaucer and the Subject of History* (London, 1991).

Strohm, Paul, *Social Chaucer* (Cambridge, 1989).

SOURCES, CONTEXTS AND CRITICAL RECEPTION

Many of these books feature original documents. All in various ways help 'place' Chaucer in relation to his literary sources and intellectual influences, contemporary social and historical contexts, and the subsequent critical reception of his work.

Bakhtin, Mikhail, *Rabelais and his World*, trans. H. Iswolsky (Cambridge, Mass., 1968).

Blamires, Alcuin (ed.), *Woman Defamed and Woman Defended: An Anthology of Medieval Texts* (Oxford, 1992).

Brewer, Derek (ed.), *Chaucer: The Critical Heritage*, vol. I, 1385–1837, vol. II, 1837–1933, (London, 1978).

Bryan, W. R., and Dempster, Germaine (eds), *Sources and Analogues of Chaucer's 'Canterbury Tales'* (Chicago, Ill., 1941).

Burrow, John, *Medieval Writers and their Work: Middle English Literature and its Background* (Oxford, 1982).

Delany, Sheila, *Medieval Literary Politics: Shapes of Ideology* (Manchester, 1990).

Ford, Boris (ed.), *Chaucer and the Alliterative Tradition* (Harmondsworth, 1982).

Gordon, R. K. (ed.), *The Story of Troilus* (London, 1934, reprinted).

Gradon, Pamela, *Form and Style in Early English Literature* (London, 1971).

Mann, Jill, *Chaucer and Medieval Estates Satire* (Cambridge, 1973).

Miller, Robert (ed.), *Chaucer: Sources and Backgrounds* (Oxford, 1977).

Muscatine, Charles, *Chaucer and the French Tradition* (Berkeley, Calif., 1957).

Pearsall, Derek, *The Life of Geoffrey Chaucer* (Oxford, 1992).

Rickert, Edith, *Chaucer's World* (New York, 1948, reprinted).

Salter, Elizabeth, *Fourteenth-Century English Poetry: Contexts and Readings* (Oxford, 1983).

Windeatt, Barry (ed.), *Chaucer's Dream Poetry: Sources and Analogues* (Suffolk, 1982).

For annual up-dates and bibliographies, see *Chaucer Review* and *Studies in the Age of Chaucer*.

The 'top 100' most commonly misunderstood words in Chaucer

Look over this 'top 100' when you read a Chaucer poem and you will avoid the most common mistakes and misunderstandings (there are, in fact, slightly more than 100 words listed). Notice that in many cases there are variant spellings ('c' and 'k' or 'i' and 'y' are more or less interchangeable; many verb forms occur both with and without the final 'n'), and there is usually more than one meaning to choose from, depending on the context.

agayn, agaynes, ayein against, towards, in return
anoon straightaway, immediately
areden (*past* **aredde, aradde**) to advise, explain
arn are
auctoritee authority, authoritative text, judgement
avys advice; **avysen** to consider, reflect, understand
ay always, all the time

ben to be
bet better
bidden (*past* **bad**) to command, order, ask
biden, byden (*past* **bood**) to wait, delay
biheten, bihoten (*past* **bihighte**) to promise
bihoven (*past* **bihoof**) to be necessary
brouken to enjoy, profit by

can, connen, cunnen (*past* **coude**) to know how to
cas, caas affair, chance; **per cas, par cas** by chance
catel goods, property
clepen to call, name
crafty skilful, clever
curteisye generosity, nobility (stronger than 'courtesy')

daunger disdain, stand-offishness (not 'danger')
descryven to describe
disese discomfort, displeasure (rarely 'disease')
douten to fear, doubt

ech, ich, ych each (but **ich** can also mean 'I')
eek, eke also, furthermore
eft afterwards, again
ensample, ensaumple example,

219

warning, model, pattern, moral tale

entente intention, meaning, desire

er, or earlier, before

eschewen to escape, avoid

everich every

faren (past ferde) to travel, behave, happen

fayn, feyn glad(ly), eager(ly)

fer far; ferre(r) farther; ferreste farthest

for for, because of, in spite of

fre noble, generous (rarely 'free')

ful very; ful wel very much

gentil, gentillesse noble, nobility (of rank or character)

ginnen (past gan, gon) to begin; also a general auxiliary (e.g., she gan wepe she did weep)

glosen to comment, interpret, deceive

goon (past yede) to go

habit dress, mood (rarely 'habit')

hap chance occurrence; happy fortunate

hastow you have

haten, heten, hoten to promise, command, be called

heigh, hey, hy high, noble

henten to seize, obtain, attack

here, hire her, their (depending on context)

hit it

hool whole, perfect, healthy

ich I (but ich can also mean 'each')

ilik, yliche like, alike, similar(ly)

ilke, thilke same, the same, that very

iwis, ywis indeed, certainly

kerven (past karf) to cut, carve

leten, laten (past leet) to allow (do not confuse with the next word in this list, which looks similar but means the opposite)

letten (past lette) to prevent, desist

lever(e) rather; him was levere he would rather

lewed uneducated, coarse

listeth, lesteth, lusteth it is pleading, desirable to

looth displeasing, undesirable to

merye, murye, myrie merry, pleasant

mete (past mette) to meet; to dream

moot must, may

mowen to be able, to be allowed

nadde had not

neigh, ney near; nerre nearer; nexte nearest

nere was not (but can also mean 'near', 'nearer')

niste did not know

nyce ignorant, foolish, meticulous (not 'nice')

o, oo, on, oon one, the same one

or before

paraunter, paraventure perhaps, by chance

preef proof, test, experience; preven to prove, test, experience

privee, privy secret, private, intimate

queynte skilful, cunning, elaborate

quyten (past quitte) to reward, pay back, set free

reden (past redde, radde) to read, advise, explain (occasionally areden)

resoun argument, speech

reuthe, rewthe, routhe pity, a pitiful happening

reven (past rafte, refte) to take away, rob

seistow you say (singular)

sely happy, innocent (not 'silly')

siker(ly), seker(ly) sure(ly)

sin, syn, sithen since

sooth, soothly true, truth, truly

sote, swote, swete, sweet

soveraynetee, sovereyntee power,
   sovereignty
speden (*past* spedde) to carry out,
   succeed
swich such

thider thither
thilke the same, that very
tho those, then
treuthe, trouthe fidelity, a promise,
   truth

waxen, wexen (*past* wax, wex, wox) to
   grow
wenden (*past* wente) to go, depart (do
   not confuse it with the next word
in this list)
wenen (*past* wende) to suppose,
   imagine, expect
whider whither
whilom once upon a time, formerly
witen, weten (*present* woot; *past*
   wiste) to know, find out
wonen (*past* woned) to dwell, stay, be
   used to

yede went (past tense of **goon**)
yeven, yiven (*past* yaf) to give
yif if
yliche like, alike, similar(ly)
ynogh, ynowe enough, plenty
yvel(e) evil

INDEX